The Psalter

The Psalter

GALEN WATSON

THE PSALTER
Copyright 2012 © by Galen Watson

Cover design by InkSlinger Designs.
eBook design by the eBook Artisans.

To Susan, my wife, who was there at the beginning

For great is the value of deceit, provided it be not introduced with a mischievous intention. In fact action of this kind ought not to be called deceit, but rather a kind of good management, cleverness and skill, capable of finding out ways where resources fail, and making up for the defects of the mind.

—Saint John Chrysotom, Archbishop of Constantinople and
Doctor of the Church

Prologue

Mike Romano slipped into the confessional. The screen behind the lattice grill slid open. "Bless me, Father, for I have sinned."

"For the love of God, Romano, not again."

"Will you hear my confession, Father?"

"No."

"What do you mean?"

"I mean you haven't sinned. You didn't sin yesterday or the day before, last week or last month, and you haven't sinned today."

"How do you know?"

"I'm playing the odds."

"I need absolution."

"No, you don't. You need some fun. Go have a beer, see a movie, take in a comedy show. Do some damn thing that'll make you laugh."

"It's your job. You have to do it."

"Jesus, Mary, and Joseph! I absolve you from your imaginary sins in the name of the Father and of the Son and of the Holy Spirit, Amen. Get lost."

"That's not right. It's not the whole thing."

The priest slammed the sliding screen shut.

1
Father Mackey

Father James Mackey exorcised the *should* or *shouldn't* doubts from his mind. In their place, a simple Latin phrase whispered and made him shiver. *Alea iacta est.* Not from scripture or even pre-Vatican II mass. Just a few words uttered by Julius Caesar as he led his army across the Rubicon River, defying the Roman Senate and breaking the law. *The die has been cast.*

Clutching a floppy leather briefcase, he slipped from an apartment on the top floor of the Papal Palace and rushed down the long corridor. At the elevator, he inserted a key in the lock to call it up but decided to take the stairs instead. He exited next to the Post Office into the winter drizzle and pulled his overcoat together, leaning against the breeze-blown spray. Droplets stung his cheeks as he hurried past the Palace of Gregory XIII that housed the Secret Archives. He rounded the corner at the Hall of Bramante and trotted up wet stone steps to enter the Vatican Library.

A stooped, white-haired priest waited inside, hugging a rectangular bundle wrapped in wax paper. Father Mackey received the old priest's outstretched hand, kissing his cardinal's ring and the man's sunken cheek. The elderly cleric spoke in an unsteady voice. "You're taking a great risk. I beg you to reconsider."

Mackey gazed into the cardinal's eyes. "Surely, you of all people know why I must do this."

Tears seeped into the aged priest's rheumy gaze. "For once, I wish you could be less of a man, but then I wouldn't love you as I do."

Taking the bundle from the cardinal's hands, Mackey lifted the edges of the wax paper and opened the cracked leather cover. "I don't know how I missed this one."

"It hid from us all in the Secret Archives. I knew I had seen it many years ago when I worked there," the old man said with a smile, "but I couldn't remember where."

"How did you get it?"

"When you've reached my age, you have many friends; hopefully, more friends than enemies. I still have one or two in the Archives."

Father Mackey folded the paper around the ancient book and stuffed it in the satchel-like briefcase. He touched the cardinal's cheek with the palm of his hand and said softly, "Don't wait up. I won't be back tonight."

Mackey hurried along the lane behind Saint Peter's Basilica. A jogger approached, the hood of his sweatshirt pulled low. Father Mackey gripped the briefcase tighter and veered away. The runner followed. Mackey stopped dead in his tracks. "Christ, Romano. You scared me."

"I'm just jogging. Can you talk?"

"I've got an appointment."

"I'll walk with you," Romano said.

"No. Did you get that beer?"

"Not yet."

"Don't show your face again until you do." Mackey took a few steps, stopped, and turned back. "Listen, Romano. Chafing under a heavy yoke is no sin. We all bristle from time to time"

"I've read things I shouldn't have read. I feel like I should do something about it."

"You didn't write the words."

"But I can't forget them."

"No one's asking you to," Father Mackey said.

"Are you sure? Why are they hidden?"

"Stop blaming yourself. And for pity's sake, take the target off your back and people won't shoot at you. I've got to go. We'll talk tomorrow."

Father Mackey walked by the guard station manned by a lone officer of the Vatican State police. The officer nodded as he passed through the blue steel gate in the Leonine wall. Uniformed and plainclothes *Carabinieri* milled around the priests' and employees' entrance, chatting as they scanned the road. They paid no attention to the priest, although it was well after the hour when people entered or exited. Only a sergeant on duty gave the priest an odd look when he didn't turn toward the city. Mackey avoided his eyes as he headed up the hill. Hardly anyone went that way, and certainly not at night.

Father Mackey passed long stretches along the isolated western wall where he could spot a tail. He reached the summit, turned on the *viale Vaticano*, and started down the rain-soaked road on the other side.

A black Mercedes Benz S600 with Vatican City license plates sat idling next to the ninth-century buttress that separated the gardens from the street. The priest stepped into the middle of the narrow road to get around the car, uncertain in leather-soled shoes that slipped on the drenched asphalt. The window of the Mercedes lowered as he passed, and a half-smoked cigarette fell to the ground.

The priest tried to hurry on the slick surface. He thought about crossing the street since there was no sidewalk next to the wall and drivers drove too fast down the grade. But at this hour, he hadn't expected any cars, and his mind had blocked out everything except the package he carried. He edged closer to the massive barrier.

Mackey heard an engine rev and wheels spin. He turned to confront the car. The Mercedes fishtailed, gained traction and lurched forward. The side mirror slapped the sparse ivy that clung to the rock. The bumper scraped the stone blocks. Disbelief contorted the priest's face. He forced his back against the unyielding wall as the speeding Mercedes slammed into him.

The impact launched Father Mackey's body into the air. It hovered for a long moment, arms and legs contorted in unnatural shapes, then plummeted to the pavement with a sickening thump. The large sedan screeched to a stop. The wheels spun in reverse, and the car whined backwards. It stopped beside the crumpled body shrouded in a black overcoat. A dark-skinned man in blue jeans and an olive-colored jacket stepped out. He knelt over the broken priest whose dying hands clawed at the satchel.

A hundred meters up the road, a woman shrieked. The tall man holding her hand sprinted toward the accident. The killer glared at them for an instant, the corners of his lips curled in a sneer. He pried the leather satchel from the dying priest's hands, slid into the driver's seat, and stomped on the accelerator. He didn't see the man pull a cell phone from his raincoat pocket and dial one-one-three. The Mercedes careened right at the *viale Dei Bastoni de Michelangelo* and raced into the *Piazza del Risorgimento*. The plaza was lined with palm trees and colorful apartment facades, and was deserted at a little after midnight. The driver skidded to a stop. He unfastened the briefcase and pulled out the bundle, ripping away the wax paper. One hand fished a piece of stationery from his jacket pocket while the other lifted the cracked leather cover. He compared precise handwritten notes with the first few words of the book's ancient text. A gratified smile widened as he realized he had accomplished God's mission.

His self-satisfaction turned to alarm as a siren blared. His eyes darted to blue flashing lights atop a Police Alfa Romeo racing for the *piazza*. The killer tossed the heavy book onto the passenger seat. He yanked the shifter into gear and raced out of the square, toward the center of Rome, the low-slung Alfa right behind.

The Alfa would be no match for the powerful Mercedes on the highway. But the ninety-degree turns every few hundred meters gave the Alfa Romeo, with its sharp turning radius and rapid acceleration, a definite advantage. Then again, the killer knew the route and the police did not. He had practiced for a week, calculating possible outcomes and memorizing the side streets that led to escape.

The whining blue and white Alpha lost ground on the Mercedes down a half-mile stretch of *via Cola di Rienzo*. They shot across the

Tiber River on the *Regina Margherita* bridge. The assassin swerved left and the tail end slipped. He spun the wheel in the other direction, trying desperately to make the right on *Piazzale Flamino*. The Benz overshot and plowed into the opposite lane. It lost traction and hydroplaned sideways. The killer had scarcely an instant of horror to think, *oh God no*, as flashing yellow lights rocketed toward his face.

2
The Grand Inquisitor

A soft ringing chimed in the distance, then silence. Mike Romano tried to defend himself against the blows raining down on his small child's face. He was paralyzed, unable to lift his arms to block the flying fists. He needed to run, escape. The electronic tone grew nearer. He willed himself to move with all his puny strength, but a heaviness held him frozen. The artificial bell insisted, tugging him from the hideous crone whose form blurred around the edges then dissolved into murky vapor.

Romano jerked into consciousness steeped in sweat. The green glow on his clock read two forty-nine a.m. *Who would telephone at this hour*, he wondered? "Hello," he rasped.

"Father Romano?"

"Yes, this is Romano." His voice awakened although his mind struggled to cast off the drowsy haze.

"Cardinal Keller calling."

"You mean Keller's office," Romano said, rubbing an eye with his fist.

"No, Father. I am Cardinal Keller."

Romano snapped to attention. Why would the Defender of the Faith be calling him? The Defender of the Faith was the modern name for the historic Grand Inquisitor. Many still called him that privately and fearfully. Tonight, in the wee hours, the Grand Inquisitor, a man Romano had never met, was on the telephone. *What had he done now?* he wondered.

Romano had run afoul of the Inquisition before. Two years, earlier he had published an interesting little tract, not his own words but those of a controversial medieval theologian, papal biographer and anti-pope, Anastasius. He had not even provided a commentary, only a brief foreword explaining his translation and a short biography of the author.

Romano had followed the rules to the letter. He sent the tract to the censor and was given the official *Nihil Obstat* proclaiming the contents free of doctrinal error. Then he received the *Imprimatur* declaring the text acceptable reading for Roman Catholics. Finally, the church issued the thin booklet an authorization to be published.

A few weeks after publication, however, the Congregation for the Doctrine of Faith revoked the *Imprimatur*. Romano appealed, but received no response. A month later, an ultimatum arrived by mail: either he withdrew the booklet or he would lose his job at the Archives. In the end, Romano submitted to the Inquisition.

Then there were the requests from various outside groups, especially Jewish organizations, that the archives of controversial wartime Pope Pius XII be opened to the public after he had been beatified, the third of four steps to sainthood. Romano, along with many activist priests, supported the openness...publicly. The Inquisition fumed that an administrator in the Secret Archives would take such a stance in opposition to the Vatican's official one.

Anonymous Inquisitors had contacted Romano's cardinal demanding that he change his position. He refused. *After all*, he reasoned, *priests were allowed opinions even if they didn't agree with the authorized ones.* He heard nothing further.

"Father Romano, are you on the line?"

"Sorry, Eminence. How may I be of assistance?"

"This is urgent, so I'll get to the point. I understand you're a paleographer?"

"Actually, Eminence, I'm now a librarian in the Secret Archives, but I once taught paleography at the Pontifical Institute of Medieval Studies." Romano tried to be humble yet concise. If the Grand Inquisitor knew he had taught paleography, he had access to his personnel file. Romano felt sick.

"Of course. You're Vice-Prefect of the Archives and before that you were the Director of the school of paleography. I'm told you're the foremost paleographer in the church. Are you expert enough to date a first-century manuscript and confirm its authenticity?" The Grand Inquisitor sounded impatient.

"Provided the script is Latin, Greek, or Syriac." Romano heaved a sigh of relief. He was wanted for his expertise rather than some new transgression.

"My car will pick you up in ten minutes. Can you be ready?"

"Certainly Eminence. Do I need—" The line clicked dead.

Romano opened his tiny closet and slid hanging trousers aside. He eyed his soutane thinking he should put it on to meet the Grand Inquisitor. Many in the Vatican favored the soutane or cassock, especially the traditional or ambitious. Romano was neither. But after his first promotion, he had been advised to wear one. So he bought the thing, tried it on, and took it off. He hadn't worn it since. It seemed pretentious. He pulled down his *tenue de ville*, what Italians called the clergyman, an ordinary black suit, cleric's shirt, and collar. He started to reach for his navy hooded sweatshirt. After all, the clock glowed three a.m. Instead, he slid his arms into the suit jacket, a concession to propriety.

He stepped out of his apartment building into the chilly rain. An official Vatican Mercedes S600 sat idling at the curb. The driver hopped out and opened the rear door. Romano climbed inside, expecting to meet the Grand Inquisitor. The back seat was empty. The car sped off, exiting Vatican City, crossing the Tiber, and into the rain-soaked streets of Rome.

"Are you picking up Cardinal Keller?" Romano asked the driver.

"I'm sorry, Father. I have no instructions to pick up anyone else."

The priest felt his pulse quicken as the car dashed toward the city center. The opportunity to examine a first-century manuscript was extraordinary, and if this one turned out to be Christian, it was unheard of. No Christian text of any kind existed from the time of Jesus. In fact, no Christian scriptures existed from any part of the first century. A few papyrus fragments from the mid- to late-second century had survived, but that was all. The rest, both canon and non-canon, had been written in the third century or later. And one of the earliest fragments, Egerton 2, was disturbingly different from the Gospels.

Fantasies of discovery were playing in the priest's imagination when the driver stopped in front of *Carabinieri* headquarters. "Why are we stopping here?" Romano asked.

"This is where I was instructed to take you, Father."

Two uniformed *Carabinieri*, Rome's military police, chatted behind a plexiglass window in the entry. Romano spoke into a round, metal intercom, "Father Michael Romano."

"They're waiting for you, Father," one said. An electronic lock clicked and Romano pushed on the heavy door. One of the officers led him to an elevator and pressed the button for the second floor. They exited the lift and walked down the hall to a door labeled *Sala Conferenze*. The officer rapped twice, opened the door and waved the priest through with a gesture of his hand.

Romano hesitated a moment, gathering his thoughts as his mind flashed a warning. He was about to face the Grand Inquisitor. He rubbed his chin, feeling the coarse stubble on his angular jaw. He hadn't shaved. Not long ago, he had submitted multiple requests for an interview at the *Palazzo del Sant'Uffizio*, Inquisition headquarters, and was ignored. Then he had been forced to submit without a chance to defend his work. Yet tonight, his oppressor needed his help. Romano bristled. Sure, he feared the Grand Inquisitor. No, that wasn't quite true. He had never met the man, but he resented his absolute power, the power over his life. "Thank you, officer," he nodded to the *Carabiniere*. He gathered himself up to his six-foot height and stepped into the room.

"Ah, Father Romano, how gracious of you to come so quickly." A man in his mid sixties with gray hair topped by a scarlet zucchetto and wearing a black soutane with a red sash, rose from the table. Smiling, he stepped gracefully toward Romano and offered his hand. As Romano kissed the cardinal's ring, he couldn't help but notice the charm displayed by the man who had sounded so abrupt half an hour earlier.

"Your Eminence," the priest replied. "It's a pleasure to meet you, at last."

"Nonsense, Father. The honor is mine. Let me introduce you to *Generale* Giudici, *Comandante* of the *Carabinieri* in Rome."

"I apologize for summoning you at this ungodly hour, Father," said the General, an overweight man also in his sixties whose tailored uniform couldn't disguise his girth. A younger man in his mid forties with a powerful build rose at the same time.

"May I present *Colonelo* Del Carlo," the cardinal continued, "commander of the *Gruppo Intervento Speciale*." Romano knew all about the GIS as did everyone in Italy. The Italian press had mentioned them every day since the September 11 attack on New York's Twin Towers. They were the *Carabinieri's* elite counter-terrorism unit.

Colonelo Del Carlo pushed an old floppy briefcase in front of the priest. "This is why we need your expertise, Father. If you could identify the evidence in the briefcase, perhaps we'll discover something to help our case."

"Evidence of what?"

Del Carlo and *Generale* Giudici turned their questioning gazes on Cardinal Keller. "Father Romano has been given no details gentlemen," the Grand Inquisitor said. "I thought it prudent not to mention the accident."

Del Carlo took command of the conversation. "Do you know Father James Mackey?" The colonel's demeanor turned somber.

"Of course," Romano said. "The Pope's Secretary." They weren't merely close friends, but confessor and penitent as well, and Mackey was a compassionate counselor, if sometimes brusque. They also shared an interest in the writing style of a particular medieval scribe Father Romano had nicknamed Giovanni. He didn't know the scribe's actual name, of course, but he had seen enough of the monk's ninth-century texts to recognize his handwriting. Giovanni had been a most prolific scribe. Mackey had been a frequent visitor to the Secret Archives and often asked Romano's professional opinion about Giovanni's manuscripts.

"Father Mackey has been in an accident," the colonel continued.

"Is he all right?" Alarm shook Romano's voice.

"Father Mackey is dead."

Romano made the sign of the cross. "But I just—"

"He was killed by a hit and run driver. We haven't determined for sure whether it was intentional. You were going to say, Father?"

"Nothing, only...surely it had to be an accident."

"Even so, leaving the scene is a crime."

"He had this briefcase with him? Is the manuscript inside?" Romano's voice had an inflection of astonishment.

"Does that surprise you?"

"We never let scrolls out of the Secret Archives. Well, perhaps on rare occasions for an exhibition or special event, but only with the Library Prefect's permission and written consent from the Office of His Holiness."

"You received no such authorization?"

"Not from the Archives. One could have come from the Library, but I'm sure their rules are the same."

The cardinal interrupted. "Surely, Father Romano, the Pope's personal Secretary might have had permission."

"Of course Eminence." The priest acquiesced more than agreed. However, Romano thought that even had permission been granted, he would have been informed. He knew all six of the other librarians in the Archives, and as Assistant Archivist, he was in charge. Besides, Mackey himself would have said something.

Romano sensed Del Carlo's eyes on him. He met their gaze, then the colonel turned toward Cardinal Keller. "Perhaps your Eminence could provide us a copy of an authorization."

Keller smiled thinly. "I'll try to locate it."

Romano returned to the subject of the manuscript, impatient to examine the contents. "Did you recover the manuscript from the accident, *Colonelo?*"

"In a way. Perhaps I should tell you what we know."

The Grand Inquisitor added, "You understand, of course, that anything disclosed here must remain within these walls unless you receive instructions from me." The cardinal's charm was replaced by the same stern insistence Romano had detected earlier. Romano chafed but replied with the slightest nuance of a smile.

"A car with Vatican license plates struck and killed Father Mackey," Del Carlo said. "Then the driver stole the briefcase you see on the table. We have witnesses."

Romano was dumbfounded. "You can't believe one of the clergy committed the crime?"

"Of course not, Father." Del Carlo had reassurance in his voice. "The man wasn't even Catholic."

"You know who did this?"

"Yes. Regrettably, the suspect lost control of his car while being pursued and crashed into a garbage truck. He died instantly. That's where we recovered the manuscript." The colonel hesitated for a moment, gauging the priest, then said, "Father, have you heard of the Children of the Book?"

"Don't you mean the People of the Book," Romano said. "What Muslims call Jews and Christians?"

Del Carlo scanned an Interpol computer printout. "No, our intelligence says Children of the Book."

"Doesn't ring a bell."

"They're a sort of messianic sect on the Iran, Iraq border."

"Christians or Muslims?"

"I'm not sure. They're a mysterious group in an area with a number of small, unusual religions." Del Carlo looked down at the printout again. "The same general area as Mandeans and Manicheans."

"Of course. Very ancient religions. Saint Augustine was Manichean until he converted."

"The man who ran over the Pope's Secretary comes from the region and he's on the FBI's watch list."

"A terrorist?"

"Perhaps." Del Carlo said. "That's why I'm here."

"You think terrorists wanted Father Mackey dead? Why?"

"That's what I'm trying to determine. What we would like to know is the value of the manuscript and any other details you can provide, and I should like to find out why a foreigner was driving an official Vatican car." *Colonelo* Del Carlo flashed a look at Cardinal Keller. The Grand Inquisitor stared straight ahead.

"Do you need any special equipment to examine the manuscript?" the colonel asked.

Romano pulled a magnifying glass from his pocket. "I'm a paleographer. This is all I need."

"Excuse me, Father," Del Carlo said. "What is a paleographer?"

"A handwriting expert."

"Like personality assessments when you apply for a job?"

"Not at all. We analyze ancient scripts, handwriting if you will, to date manuscripts by the style used during a particular era." Romano pulled the heavy briefcase toward him and opened the flap. As he slid out the thick volume, his heart sank. He didn't need to look at the pages to see they weren't from the first century. The book was a codex, bound in a style common to the Middle Ages. He lifted the cracked leather cover. The text was Latin from the latter part of the ninth century.

"Well?" The Grand Inquisitor said, leaning forward, staring hard into Romano's eyes.

The priest couldn't hide his disappointment. He replied acerbically without thinking. "Eminence, this is a common prayer book."

"Are you certain? Look closer."

Romano scanned the front side of the first page known as the *recto*, studying the text below the *rubric*, or title. It read *Beatus*. Then something did catch his eye. The scribe who copied this book was without a doubt Giovanni, the same Giovanni he had discussed many times with Father Mackey. Something else caught his eye as well, faint and nearly invisible impressions. Romano turned the page, stopping to examine a few words with the magnifying glass.

"It's an early medieval prayer book called a Psalter." The priest explained to *Colonelo* Del Carlo and *Generale* Giudici that a Psalter was in essence a handwritten book of the Psalms, but often included canticles, a list of saints, prayers, and a calendar. "It's not from the first century, not even close. Psalters were medieval bestsellers. Every noble lady wanted one. We have hundreds, maybe thousands, in the Vatican Library in excellent condition. This is ninth-century Latin, very common. Did you look at it, Eminence?" Romano asked the Grand Inquisitor, a hint of condescension in his voice. He didn't mention Giovanni. That was his little secret, and secrets prompted questions. Romano didn't want any inquiries from the Grand Inquisitor, especially about Giovanni.

Cardinal Keller's face flushed as he marched around the table, pushing his way past Romano. He read out loud, seeming to ponder each word, "*beatus vir qui non abiit in consilio impiorum*...blessed is the man who hath not walked in the counsel of the ungodly." He flipped a page and then another, faster and faster. Romano wanted to stop him. He almost did. After all, it was still a twelve-hundred-year old-antique. Keller regained his composure, straightened himself, and muttered, "Killed for an ordinary prayer book."

Del Carlo broke the awkward moment. "How would you value this Psalter, Father Romano?"

"I'm no appraiser, but I've seen Psalters in this condition sell on the Internet for ten or fifteen thousand dollars, perhaps as much as twenty. Regrettably, rare document dealers buy them to remove the bindings so they can turn individual pages into framed artwork. They make more money that way. Printed pages sell for four or five hundred dollars. Illustrated pages go for three or four thousand, the finest as high as ten, but that's rare. Still, this is no priceless text."

"I was afraid of that," Del Carlo said. "Thank you for your expertise. May I call you if I need further assistance?"

Romano turned to the cardinal, and the dour Grand Inquisitor nodded. "I'm at your disposal, *Colonelo*." Romano hesitated for a moment, but couldn't help himself, "Can I return the Psalter to the Archives?"

"It's evidence, Father."

"You're right, of course, but we would take better care of it. It's our specialty, and if you need the book back, I'll deliver it personally. You have my word."

Generale Giudici spoke for the first time, "I don't see any reason not to release the book. It's not as though we'll be prosecuting anyone."

Del Carlo turned to face Romano, "Of course, Father, and you need not give me your word. You're a priest. I believe everything you say." The colonel glanced hard at the cardinal, who averted his eyes. Del Carlo showed Father Romano to the door, holding him by the arm. He added in a low voice, "Here's my card, Father. Should you think of anything else, please call me. My home telephone is on the back." Then he patted the briefcase. "Keep the book safe, even if it is just ordinary."

3
Secret Archives

Father Romano tucked the leather briefcase under his arm as he trotted toward the Secret Archives. He breathed hard—not from exertion, because his daily jogging kept him in superb physical condition. Rather, his suspicions left him exhilarated. *Why hadn't he mentioned those suspicions to the police*, he wondered? He knew why he didn't tell the Grand Inquisitor. *I've been down that road before*, Romano thought, *and almost lost my job*. He had no intention of leaving himself open to another anonymous denunciation with no defense against the arcane and capricious regulations of the Inquisition. *They might enforce grudging obedience, but they can't bully me into agreement.*

He could have voiced his speculation to *Colonelo* Del Carlo in private. The GIS colonel had extended a personal invitation. Perhaps he just needed to be sure or feared being wrong. That might be a piece, but not all. Romano had long suspected that Giovanni was hiding something significant. His pattern seemed too systemic, too perfect. Scribes filled parchment with elaborate and copious ink. Yet Giovanni wrote in small, slender strokes, as though he was taking great care to write around something hidden.

The paleographer side of Romano was disheartened this wasn't a first-century manuscript. Nevertheless, he had indeed noticed something unexpected and tantalizing at *Carabinieri* headquarters and kept it to himself. Nothing the cardinal would notice. Even had the police spotted the pinpoint dents in the vellum, they likely would have ignored them. Only a paleographer trained in ancient manuscripts could understand their significance.

He unlocked a side entrance to the Archives and rushed, not for the rooms housing thousands of books and church documents, but for the stairs to the underground level and the Conservation Laboratories. Inside one of the labs, Romano placed the leather-bound book on an examination table and pulled on white cotton gloves.

The dusty smell of antiquity filled his nostrils as he opened the Psalter to the first page. He swung around a powerful magnifying glass attached to a folding arm and positioned it over the verse he had already examined. His eyes skimmed the spaces between the letters and lines of Latin script. There were indeed indentations, so small they might have been made by a safety pin.

A neon light atop a pole, like the poles that dangled IV solutions, stood in the corner. Romano rolled it over and directed the lamp at the page. He turned off the overhead lights and flipped a switch on the stand. Ultraviolet light illuminated the text. Smudges appeared in the gaps between the lines and letters. Romano's heart pounded as he grabbed another lamp. He shut off the ultraviolet and pressed the switch on the other pole. An infrared bulb transformed the folio into a shade of dull scarlet and the smudges grew more distinct. They were clearly letters, but not Latin or even Greek.

The pinpricks in the vellum had been made by a stylus or a writing reed known as a *calamus*. High-quality reeds were common lettering tools in antiquity, used to write on papyrus and parchment. They left tiny impressions where the *calamus* began the pen stroke, or, in this case, the reed stroke, and where it ended if the scribe pressed hard enough. The stylus was also a sharp instrument made of bone or metal, used to prick and rule manuscripts without ink so scribes could write in straight lines with uniform margins. These small indentations, however, weren't underneath letters or at the beginning of sentences where they should have been, but in blank spaces between the lines.

Romano suspected the ordinary-looking Psalter hid a much older manuscript. Under ultraviolet and infrared lights, he confirmed it was a palimpsest, a book written over an earlier text. Writing materials in the Middle Ages were expensive. So scribes erased ancient scientific or philosophical literature, and especially heretical scriptures, to reuse the paper for acceptable theological works. They cut the cumbersome scrolls into pages and bound them together to make portable books.

Romano recalled a palimpsest discovered in Constantinople. Underneath a banal collection of Greek prayers, an erased copy of several of Archimedes' most famous mathematical writings lay hidden. One was believed lost forever: *The Method of Mechanical Theorems*, essentially proto-calculus. The librarian side of Romano wondered how many works of the highest scholarship and historical value had been obliterated for mundane sermons or stale prayer books.

He studied the script with his powerful magnifying glass. The letters looked familiar, but seemed out of context. He pushed the glass away and stood, rubbing tired eyes. Refocusing on the page from a few feet's distance, the solution popped into his head. "Of course," he said and turned the book ninety degrees. The erased text had been written at a right angle to the words copied over it.

The priest's heart jumped as he recognized what he saw. His paleographer's eye identified the Aramaic script, once the language of the Jews and the Lingua Franca of the Middle East. He swung the magnifying glass back over the book and skimmed the page, looking for an entire word, but spotted only fragments of letters. Then his eye fell on a complete character between the lines of Latin script, '〈ᄏ〉'. The letter was unmistakably Aramaic, the dialect of Jesus, and the writing style had been in use in Palestine during the time of Christ.

He searched for another letter and discovered a '𝐘' between two Latin words. Then he found '𝜽' near the bottom. They were the characters from an alphabet he had studied since his days in the seminary, letters he prayed he might find one day in a Christian text. The priest plopped onto his stool. Without a doubt, the page had been written sometime around fifty A.D., perhaps closer to forty, only a decade more or less after the Crucifixion.

Why did Father Mackey take the Psalter from the Library? Romano wondered. He certainly didn't have permission. Did he discover that ancient scriptures in Jesus' native tongue had resided for centuries in the recesses of the Vatican Library or the Secret Archives, concealed by Giovanni in an ordinary Psalter? And if they were hidden, would they be heresies? The church had a long history of suppressing non-canon scriptures and their devotees, through violence if necessary. And why did the Grand Inquisitor believe the Pope's personal secretary possessed a first-century scroll when it was simply a prayer book? Yet, the Psalter might actually be hiding a first-century text after all. Keller knew more than he had revealed, and why didn't *Colonelo* Del Carlo trust the cardinal? Most troubling was the possibility that Father Mackey had been killed for this book.

Questions and suspicions raced around hairpin turns in Romano's gray matter until one overriding thought crossed the finish line with crystal clarity: he had to translate the palimpsest. He would find no answers until he knew what the text said. But the Secret Archives didn't have the technology. It was far too expensive. Then a memory returned as a possible answer. Romano had attended a Library Science seminar at the French National Archives months earlier. One of the lectures had fascinated him: *digital imaging*, a sort of spectral analysis that had gone over his head. The lecturer had been a young archivist who had helped decipher the celebrated *Archimedes Palimpsest*.

The priest was searching the recesses of his brain for the lecturer's name when a lump swelled in his throat. He suddenly recalled that no complete work had ever been found in any single palimpsest because medieval scribes cut scrolls into dozens of pages and bound them into different books. Portions had to be recovered from several volumes to reassemble a whole document. This Psalter might have a large section of the original scroll or a fragment, perhaps only a single page.

Romano closed the Psalter and slid it inside the floppy leather briefcase. He turned off the lights and slipped out of the lab. *First things first*, he thought as he climbed the stairway to ground level and marched to the medieval section of the Archives, to the shelves holding Psalters. Most were in the Vatican Library where they belonged, but quite a few were here. He pulled the Psalter from the briefcase and replaced it with another from the shelf. Then he laid the briefcase back on the bookshelf, gathered up Giovanni's Psalter and started for the exit. He had to get to Paris. But if anyone came hunting for Giovanni's Psalter, they would find an almost identical one inside poor Father Mackey's briefcase.

4
Isabelle

The old woman was stronger than Mike. She sat on him, pinning his arms to the floor by his wrists while she ground her hips on his groin, making him hard. Tears squirted from his burning eyes and he tried to raise his body, but she was too heavy and the struggle left him breathless. He twisted his slight torso trying to roll over, but she bounced on his belly and he gasped, the wind knocked out.

Romano felt a soft tapping on his knee. His eyes fluttered open and he strained to focus on the blurry image of two teenage girls in tight jeans and pullover sweaters. They spoke words he didn't understand.

"I'm sorry," he said in English wiping his cheek with the back of his hand.

"Are you all right, Father?" one asked in a lilting French accent.

"Where am I?"

"We're at the terminus, Paris." The priest peered out the train window. A dark blue sign with white print read *Gare de Lyon*.

"*Merci, Mesdemoiselles,*" he managed, red faced. The girls lowered their gaze and scurried for the door, whispering. Romano stretched his aching joints. A sharp pain in his neck made him wince. Fifteen hours in a second-class seat and now he had a crick. Rubbing it with one hand, he slung the backpack over his shoulder, stepped out of the car, and headed for the exit. He looked for the *Metro* sign, the Parisian subway system.

Romano changed Metros at *Hôtel de Ville* then got off at the *Rambuteau* stop. Concrete stairs led to a pungent mélange of exhaust fumes and unfamiliar odors borne by the damp air; the clanging and banging of city traffic and the cacophony of another workday in Paris. Searching for a familiar landmark, he couldn't remember how to get to the National Archives and had forgotten to bring a map. He stopped a slender man in a gray business suit to ask for directions. The man listened to his elementary French, pointed and walked away without a word.

Romano made his way along on the *rue Rambuteau*, dodging pedestrians who came toward him at fast-forward speed. He crossed the *rue des Archives* and recognized the *Hôtel de Soubise*, one of the grandest mansions in the *Marais* district. Built around an older medieval castle, the newer one had been constructed in the early eighteenth century.

The mansion became the National Archives after the French Revolution and was a historian's fantasy world. It housed thousands of historical documents from the fifth century to the twentieth, such as the wills of Louis XIV and Napoleon, the *Declaration of Human Rights* and the *Edict of Nantes*. Romano walked down the long courtyard over uneven cobblestones and into the entrance. A young man sat behind a pedestal-type reception desk, his head lowered, studying something beyond the priest's view. Romano scanned the Rococo foyer waiting to be noticed. The room seemed light and airy despite the heavy stone construction, with tall windows and creamy walls.

"Excuse me, Father," the young man said finally looking up.

"I need to speak with Madame Héber."

"Do you have an appointment?"

"No."

"Well she's busy."

"It's important," Romano said.

The telephone chimed on Isabelle Héber's cluttered eighteenth-century desk. She ignored the call, letting it go into voice mail, but the caller kept redialing. Exasperated, she yanked the handset from the cradle, her right index finger pointing to her place on an open page. "*Oui*," she exhaled in a loud breath.

"Doctor Héber, this is the reception desk. A man is here to speak to you."

"I told you Eugène, no visitors."

"I know Madame, but he's not any man." Eugène lowered his voice to a whisper. "He's a priest."

Isabelle's interest was piqued. Why would a priest want to meet with her? She didn't know any priests except the local curé who kept insisting she return to the church. She had decided she was an atheist while still in high school. Religion never held the slightest interest for her. Science was her faith. Now, whenever she saw Father Demerest at weddings or First Communions, he began with the same reproach, calling her rebellious and proclaiming that God could forgive any transgression except abandoning the Holy Church. He always ended his assaults in tears, begging her to come to confession so she might partake of the Holy Communion. Horror invaded her reflection. *Someone has died.* "I'll be right down," she said into the phone and ran for the stairs.

Romano gazed at the dark-haired archivist as she dashed down limestone steps, a panicked expression on her face. "What's happened *mon Père*," she cried out as she rushed to his side, grasping his hand. "Is Father ill?"

Not being a pastoral priest, Romano had forgotten they often delivered tragic news so they could console their parishioners. "I'm terribly sorry," he said. The woman gasped, shrinking. He realized his words were ill-timed. "There's nothing wrong. This is a professional visit."

Isabelle glared at him, straightened herself, and pushed his hand away. "That was cruel, Father."

Romano felt foolish. "I can't tell you how sorry I am, but I have no experience as a parish priest. I should have…well, I'm truly sorry."

Isabelle eyed him. "Well, Father, your remorse appears genuine, but I'm still quite aggravated. How can I help you?"

Romano glanced at Eugène and back at Isabelle Héber. "Can we speak privately?"

"I'm very busy, Father. I'm in the middle of an important translation and already past my deadline. You can make an appointment with Eugène. I have a little time next week."

Father Romano took Isabelle's arm and guided her a few feet from the reception desk. "Please, Madame, this is urgent or I wouldn't ask. A priest was killed for this book," he held up his small backpack for emphasis, "and I need to know why."

Isabelle probed the priest's face and recognized his desperation and passion. "Alright, Father. I'll give you five minutes, but no more." She led him up the limestone steps to her office. Lifting a stack of books from a chair, she motioned for him to sit. Romano sank in the chair and set the backpack on his lap. He unzipped the top and produced a thick, leather-bound book. He offered it with both hands to Isabelle, who pushed aside a pile of papers on her desk. She opened the cover and appeared confused. "Father, this is Latin. You can translate it better than I."

The paleographer leaned over the desk and grabbed a pen. He pointed the tip at a space between two lines of Latin text. "Can you make out this minute indentation?"

"No," Isabelle said, lowering her face to the page.

"Use this." The priest offered his magnifying glass. "The impression was made by a *calamus*, but it's in the gap between these two letters, and look at this tiny crease. A stylus scored the paper to mark where a line of text should be, but there's no text. This ordinary page of Latin prayers was written over an older scroll. This is a palimpsest, Madame." The priest stared intently at the archivist, expecting his words to have an impact.

Isabelle Héber furrowed her brow. "Father, there are hundreds of known palimpsests. Scrolls were erased by the thousands for this type of book. It's not unusual at all."

"The palimpsest is not what's important, but the contents of the original scroll used to make the pages. I believe this was once a first-century document written in Aramaic." The priest still evoked no response. "The language of Jesus?"

"And millions of others. You're surely not suggesting that this is a New Testament scroll," Isabelle scoffed, "because the scriptures were written in Greek, by Greeks."

"We believe the Apostles wrote them in their own language and they were translated into Greek."

"What happened to the originals?"

"The theory is that they were destroyed."

"All of them," Isabelle said cynically, "and not a single survivor?"

"That's why this is so important. Scholars have been searching for original scriptures for almost two thousand years. I might have discovered some."

"On what do you base that?"

"I used an ultraviolet light to look beneath the Latin and found these three letters." Romano pulled a small notebook from his backpack. He showed the archivist a page where he had handwritten the Aramaic characters: ⅂, Ⴓ and ⊕.

Doctor Héber looked exasperated. "Father, with all due respect, Aramaic was the common language in every country of the Middle East, including parts of India, for over a millennium. So of the thousands upon thousands of documents written during that era, you found a single page with three Aramaic letters and you conclude it must be a New Testament scroll?"

The paleographer realized how ridiculous he sounded after hearing his suspicions criticized out loud by a PhD who was noted for her expertise in analyzing manuscripts. He grew defensive and pressed his argument. "Listen Doctor," Romano's pitch raised a notch. "The Pope's personal Secretary had an uncommon interest in a certain scribe who made habit of writing over heretical texts. He took this book," Romano rose from his seat and pointed at the Psalter, "from of the shelves of the Vatican's Secret Archives. He had no right. If he weren't a priest, I'd say he stole it. Then he was run down and killed by a man on the FBI's watch list, and the only object the killer took from his body was this. The Psalter may or may not hide scriptures, but beneath the Medieval Latin is a first-century text that someone wants badly enough to kill for." The priest glared at the raven-haired archivist breathing hard. Doctor Héber stared back impassively.

The paleographer, who had been so confident he fled with a valuable relic belonging to the church, had his theory discredited in a single concise sentence. All that he had discovered were three Aramaic letters and nothing to indicate they were part of any Biblical text. And his counter-argument made him sound more like a conspiracy nut than a reputable scholar. "I'm sorry to have bothered you." Father Romano held his hand out for the Psalter.

"Hold on a minute. I recognize you." She kept her hands over the prayer book. "You attended one of my seminars, no?"

"Yes," Romano said sourly. "Last winter."

"Aren't you the paleographer who had a special interest in a certain scribe you called...?"

"Giovanni."

"*Oui*, very interesting and remarkable that you can recognize a particular scribe's handwriting when thousands tried to write exactly alike."

"Well, not truly alike. Every region and even each monastery had their own style."

"Fascinating and I'm intrigued that you're able to date a document by the type of calligraphy used during a specific era. I should have thought something technological would be far more precise, like carbon14 dating?"

"Carbon14 isn't accurate at all," Romano said. "It can tell when the animal died, but not when the words were written. These pages were erased and reused. There could be a thousand-year difference between the expunged text and the one copied over it. Analyzing the style of the script can give an exact date. But I know how busy you are, and you were kind to meet with me." Father Romano held out his hand again.

"Father, please sit for a moment." The priest stood immobile for a few seconds, then sank back into the chair. "Listen," Isabelle said. "I use infrared, x-ray, digital photography, and computers to rediscover damaged or erased texts. I need dictionaries and my knowledge of dead languages to translate manuscripts. I have a mechanical skill. You, on the other hand, examine stylistic nuance and minute differences in handwriting. And from that, you can tell not only when words were written, but by whom. Please forgive me Father…?"

"Romano, Michael Romano."

"I didn't intend to demean your professional skill. I remember being quite impressed with your credentials. You said someone killed a priest for this book?"

"Not any priest, the Pope's Secretary."

Isabelle involuntarily made the sign of a cross, even though she no longer believed in God. "Was he a friend?"

"Yes. Still, I wish I'd known him better, but we shared the same interest in Giovanni, the medieval scribe I told you about. He asked me to find every prayer book in our Archives copied by this scribe. I thought it odd in the beginning, but it became sort of a hobby. We enjoyed long discussions trying to imagine this monk. A few of the parchments weren't erased well, and some of the original words were visible under ultraviolet or infrared. This one, on the other hand, had been erased exceptionally well."

"And you want to read what's written underneath?" Isabelle Héber spoke more sympathetically.

"Yes. I'm convinced the Pope's Secretary was looking for a particular scroll."

"You realize, of course, that all New Testament manuscripts were composed in Koine, a dialect of Greek."

"But Jesus spoke Aramaic."

"You should know that this palimpsest might be anything, so don't get your hopes up."

"You'll help?" Romano asked hopefully.

"After the Archive closes. Can you come back at six?"

"I'll be here."

5
IsyReADeT

Father Romano walked down the *rue des Francs-Bourgeois* through a canyon of chic apartments and private mansions from centuries past in one of Paris' oldest quarters. He often felt out of place outside the Vatican. But passing trendy boutiques where his reflection gaped back from the windows, an unshaven, heavy-eyed cleric toting a knapsack, he looked more like a hobo than a man of the cloth. Romano noticed pedestrians staring. "Humility," he muttered to himself.

His stomach growled. He hadn't eaten since he'd left Rome. He searched for a bistro, café, or even a local bar where he could order a quick sandwich, but saw only shops and historic buildings. Wandering out of the chasm of apartments into an open space, he found himself in the seventeenth-century *Place des Vosges*, Paris' oldest square. A rectangular brick arcade surrounded the plaza, with pale stone residences above. The *Place* was the French capital's first attempt at community housing. Richelieu had lived in number 21, and number 6 housed the Victor Hugo museum. Now, the interior of the square was a green space lined with trees and paths, with a play area in the center. Children ran and squealed as they kicked soccer balls, rode on teeter-totters, and climbed up the slide.

The aroma of dark coffee floated to Romano's nose and lured him to bistro tables filling the sidewalk. A few couples sat, chatting while they sipped from demitasses and savored tarts and pastries. Romano found an empty table furthest from the snackers. A graying waiter in dark trousers, white shirt, and a black vest, balancing a small round tray approached. "Good afternoon, Father. May I bring you something to drink?"

"A Coke and a large glass of water."

"Would you like a menu, Father?"

"What's the *plat du jour*?"

"*Poulet rôti* or Andouille sausage."

"I'll take the chicken. Could I get fries?"

"Of course."

Romano set his knapsack on a chair and pulled out a note pad and pen. Glancing up, his eyes met the waiter's, who had not budged. "Yes?"

"Excuse me, Father, if I'm impolite, but you look terrible. Are you all right?"

He rubbed the two-day stubble with his hand. "I've been traveling. I'm just tired."

"We have a bathroom inside if you'd like to wash up. Turn left at the door and down the stairs."

The considerate word from the sympathetic waiter cheered Romano a bit. "You're very kind." He snatched up the backpack and headed inside, descending narrow, winding steps to the bathroom. Splashing cold water on his face, he rubbed liquid soap from the dispenser on thick, black whiskers. He pulled a disposable razor from an old leather case and began to scrape away two days' growth. Patting his cheeks dry with the continuous towel in the white holder, a loud ring startled Romano. His hand groped along the bottom of his pack until he grasped his vibrating phone. "Hello?"

"Father Romano?" The priest recognized the voice, but couldn't put it with a face.

"This is Romano." He tried not to sound guilty, but the call reminded him he had left the Vatican without permission.

"*Colonelo* Del Carlo of the GIS," the authoritative voice said.

The priest stuffed his toiletries into the backpack.

"Father, are you there?"

Romano trotted up the stairs. "Sorry, *Colonelo*, the reception is bad. Give me a moment." Back at his small table, the waiter had already served the cola and water. The priest finished half the tall glass of water in two hurried gulps. "Yes, *Colonelo*, I'm here."

"Father, I need to meet with you right away."

"I'm sorry, *Colonelo*. It's not possible. I'm," the priest hesitated, "out of town."

"I hate to insist, but I have evidence Father Mackey was killed deliberately."

Romano didn't reply.

"Did you hear me, Father?"

"I'm listening."

"Crime scene investigators found a handwritten note in the assassin's car, in Latin." This was the first time Del Carlo used *assassin* and the word made the priest shudder. "I'm not an expert, Father, but when I was a boy, Mass was celebrated in Latin and I took a few years in high school. I remembered enough to recognize one of the words in the note, *Beatus*, the same as the title in the Psalter, no?"

"It's the same, *Colonelo*."

"I must examine the book immediately. Can you bring it to headquarters?"

"Impossible. As I said, I'm out of town. I left a Psalter in the antiquities section of the Library in Father Mackey's brown briefcase." Father Romano closed his eyes at the quasi-lie. "I'm sure one of the archivists can help you."

"Father, I need to see you. Where are you?"

"I'll be back soon and we can meet." Father Romano had no idea when he would return, but was certain he couldn't go home without learning the secret Giovanni's Psalter hid.

"I should tell you that I've spoken with Cardinal Keller, and he's anxious to meet with you as well."

Romano bristled.

Del Carlo continued to probe. "When I spoke with the cardinal, I sensed he didn't know where you were, either."

"I'll telephone when I get back to the Vatican," Romano said. He pressed the *end call* button and switched the cell phone to *off.* Now there was no doubt that Del Carlo suspected him of knowing more than he had revealed and the Grand Inquisitor was searching for him too. He was well and truly in the soup.

The waiter set a small basket of sliced baguette on the table with the plate of roast chicken and fries. "Drink some Coke, Father. Cola is good for an upset stomach, although I hate the stuff. It reminds me of the syrup doctors mixed with medicine when I was a boy. Makes me shudder, but my children love it." The waiter tried to be friendly, but got no response and retreated.

Romano shut his eyes, trying to close his mind to the last two days. His hasty and unauthorized departure would bring consequences. He had stolen a book, one he was charged to protect. Of course, many books in the Archives hadn't even been catalogued. No one would be the wiser if he chose to keep his indiscretion a secret. But his vows of obedience required him to admit what he had done, and not only in the confessional. Perhaps if he returned to Rome and made a clean breast of it?

Then Romano had Del Carlo to consider. The Curia in Rome might protect him from the colonel, but neither Del Carlo nor Keller would get the Psalter back until he discovered what Giovanni had hidden. He might be denounced yet again, and the Inquisitor could fire him from his job and end his career. They would not, however, take the knowledge that lay beneath the lines of the *Beatus Psalm*, not this time. No one would grind him into submission until he finished the task he had come to Paris to do. He opened his eyes and took a sip of Cola. His appetite returned in a wave, and he poked his fork into a bunch of fries, stuffing them in his mouth.

Romano motioned to the waiter for the check. "You look much better now, Father." The middle-aged man smiled as he handed the priest the *addition.* "A meal is just what you needed." Romano offered his credit card, and the waiter swiped the magnetic strip on a hand-held bank card processor.

𝔄 **Carabinieri lieutenant** burst into Del Carlo's office waving a computer printout and shouted, "We have him!"

"Where is he?"

"In Paris. He used his credit card in the *Place des Vosges*, a bistro in the square."

The GIS colonel clenched his jaw. "Find out everywhere this priest has been for the last two years: every plane, train, hotel, and restaurant. Who does he know in Paris? And I want it all in an hour."

"*Si, Colonelo,*" the lieutenant saluted and rushed back out the door.

Del Carlo pressed the intercom on his desk. "*Prego?*" a female voice from the speaker said.

"Call Alitalia. Get me on the next flight to Paris!"

Cardinal Keller was engrossed in a treatise published by a rogue French priest who continued to hold the Tridentine Mass in Latin without permission. Something had to be done, yet the cleric was popular among his parishioners, especially conservatives. The Grand Inquisitor was on the verge of choosing the appropriate rebuke and threat when a rap came from the thick door of his office in the *Palazzo del Sant'Uffizio.* "Yes," he said, frustrated by the interruption.

A Swiss Guard officer garbed in a blue work uniform with a black beret entered the room. The cardinal didn't look up. "Captain?"

"We've found Father Romano, Eminence."

The Grand Inquisitor bolted out of his chair. "Where?"

"Paris. We located him through his credit card. Shall I send the Swiss Guard to find him?"

"No. Notify the Archbishop there. Find out where Father Romano goes and who he meets. Most of all, I want to know if he's coming back."

"Are you sure, Eminence? He may not wish to return, in which case..."

"Captain, Father Romano is a priest!"

"Forgive me, Eminence. My place is not to question or provoke, only advise. I simply wish to point out that as Vice-Prefect of the Secret Archives, Father Romano has access to the church's oldest and deepest secrets. Do you want him roaming the streets…unattended?"

The Grand Inquisitor pondered the captain's observation and replied more deftly. "As I said, Romano's a priest and feels the full weight of his vows. Nevertheless, find out everyone he has spoken with in Paris and what he has said verbatim, understood?"

"Of course, Eminence."

Doctor Isabelle Héber waited for the unkempt priest at the entrance to the French National Archives. As he walked with long easy strides through the courtyard, she pictured the American cleric more on a ranch in Montana than hovering over musty manuscripts. That was her province. The priest wasn't classically handsome. Life had lined and scraped his face into battered good looks.

She unlocked the glass double doors and opened one side so Romano could slip in. "The equipment is ready. Follow me," she said, leading him up the stairs. "I hope you're not in a hurry," she spoke over her shoulder, "because this is a slow process, although a great deal faster than what's used in the States. We call it *IsyReADeT*."

"Come again?"

"It's an acronym for Integrated System for Recovering and Archiving Degraded Texts—*IsyReADeT*. The program isn't perfected yet. We're still testing, but I have one of the prototypes." Isabelle unlocked one of the doors in the corridor and led the priest into a photography studio. A bulky camera that resembled a 1950s Bell & Howell movie projector stood on a tripod. Doctor Héber removed the side cover, exposing a wheel behind the lens that spun different-colored filters into place. "What do you remember from the Archimedes Palimpsest seminar?"

"I am ashamed to say that a lot went over my head. We have a Computer Lab in the Secret Archives, but that's not my department."

"Then let me explain how we use digital imaging to uncover the past. Archimedes' treatises were copied in a codex sometime in the tenth century. Two hundred years later, the pages were erased and reused to write a Byzantine prayer book called the Euchologion. We needed a nondestructive technology to make the prayers disappear so we could read what was underneath. So we take multiple photographs of the same page using different colored filters. With computer software, the color representing the Euchologion is deleted and what's left is the original text. Even then, not all of it is visible."

"You said that's how you used to do it. What do you do now?"

"European libraries and archives are dealing with an overwhelming problem of deteriorating texts. Aside from the damage caused by floods and fire, the iron ink used in the sixteenth and seventeenth centuries is faded and has often disappeared. And the poor quality paper from the nineteenth century is disintegrating because of high acid content. We had to develop a low-cost method to recover the contents, even if the actual documents couldn't be saved."

Isabelle walked to the tripod in the middle of the room. "This type of digital camera is used by American spy satellites and forensic scientists, as well as art museums, to authenticate rare paintings. The camera takes multiple photographs using these different colored filters." She pointed behind the lens to the wheel holding round disks. It's linked to our own computer program, so the analysis is done automatically. The system is small, cheap, and simple to use. Put the Psalter on the easel and open it to the page you want deciphered while I set up the computer." She walked to the monitor. "Are you ready, Father?"

"I suppose."

Isabelle typed a command on the keyboard, and the camera lit up. The wheel spun until the correct colored filter moved behind the lens. An internal fan began to whir.

"What do we do now?" Father Romano said.

"We wait."

Romano slid down in his chair, stretching his long legs and crossing them at the ankles.

"Tell me about this Giovanni," Isabelle was intrigued. "What can you learn about a scribe from his handwriting?"

"Believe it or not, ninth-century scribes were mostly uneducated. Writing was more like painting a small image that happened to be a letter. But this one was different, not just lettered or clever. He had uncommon intelligence even by today's standards.

6
Johannes Anglicus

Iunius in the Year of Our Lord 843
June

The reek from the wooden bucket gagged the frail youth as he dipped a coarse rag into foul, diluted lye. Its rank odor made him want to retch his meager breakfast. Later in the day, he would notice less. Nevertheless, each new morning found the power of the vapors renewed and filled his head with nauseating stink.

He seemed at an age between a boy and a man, slender with delicate features accentuated by a straight, narrow nose and red curls, yet looked even thinner in a brown robe that was too large. A braided cincture made the cloth billow above and below his waist.

He rolled out a long scroll on rough-hewn planks in the courtyard of the *patriarchum*, the Papal Palace of Pope Gregory IV. Holding the soaked rag over the parchment, he dripped fetid liquid onto the writing. Once a section was sufficiently wet, the novice grabbed a pumice stone and scrubbed. The words blurred, then dissolved into rivulets of black ink.

The boy was disgusted by the destruction and turned away. He gazed instead at the ancient Apostolic Palace and adjoining basilica of Saint John. The palace had originally belonged to a noble family of Roman emperors, the Laterani. Constantine's wife, Fausta, had given the property to the Emperor as part of her dowry. As a rebuke to the Laterans, who were virulent anti-Christians, Constantine had donated it to Pope Melchiade for his official residence. Now the Laterani legacy was the *patriarchum*, the Papal Palace, capital of all Christendom.

Who invented such a miserable concoction, the novice mused, shaking his head as he scrubbed. *Surely someone could concoct a less disgusting formula to erase parchment than this unholy stew of urine, limestone, and chicken droppings.* The ink on one portion of the scroll refused to budge. He dabbed more vile juice and rubbed faster with the pumice.

Stubborn, unfaded words mocked his labor. His mind began to translate the text. *And when the tempter came to him, he said, if thou be the Son of God, command that these stones be made bread.* The realization of what he erased struck like lightning, and he gasped. Just then, a loud bang at the end of the worktable jolted him out of his shock and he jumped, startled.

A stout, dour priest with a sparse beard covering a round face had dropped three large scrolls. In a snarl, he said, "All of these must be finished by Vespers or there'll be hell to pay."

The novice rushed to the other end of the table and shoved the portly priest aside. He rolled open one of the scrolls. His eyebrows arched in horror. He opened another and slammed his fist. "You ignorant dolt." The boy spit the words in the priest's fat face. "Do you realize what you've done?"

Outrage turned the overseer's puffy cheeks and tiny ears bright red. Eyes bulging, he struck like a cobra, cuffing the youth's head and knocking him flat. He grabbed the cowl of the boy's frock and jerked him up. Other priests looked on, some shocked and others amused, as the fat priest hoisted the novice like a marionette whose legs churned but scarcely touched the ground.

Up the stone steps and into the Lateran, he hauled the youth, parading him down a cool corridor toward the chapel of Saint Sylvester. He dragged him down the *scala pilati*, the Holy Stairs, brought to Rome from Pontius Pilate's own palace. Jesus himself had sanctified these marble steps when he climbed them to be condemned to the cross by Judea's Procurator.

Baraldus burst into the *scrinium*, the church archives, with the novice in tow. He cast the boy onto the floor in front of a heavy desk. A tonsured priest peered up from a scroll as he deliberated on the scene. "Well, Father Baraldus, do you have something to tell me?"

Baraldus tried to speak, but only unintelligible grunts came from his mouth as he jabbed his thick finger at the prostrate figure. The stick of a youth swathed in a tent of brown cloth raised himself on one arm, dazed and humiliated. The seated priest rose from his chair and while he seemed rather average when sitting, he was uncommonly tall. He stepped around his desk and lifted the novice from the stone floor, straightening his frock. "Perhaps you can enlighten me, son?"

Father Baraldus, who had recovered his voice, blurted out, "He... he called me a dolt, an ignorant dolt." The tall priest stared hard at Baraldus who added, "I mean, *primicerius* Anastasius."

"You need not call me Prefect, Brother. Father Anastasius will suffice." He turned to the novice, a faint smile on his face. "Is this true? Did you call Father Baraldus an ignorant dolt?" He tried to sound like the arbiter his position as prefect in charge of the archives required, but had difficulty repressing the laugh that struggled to get out.

The boy lowered his head in shame. "What the good father said is true." Baraldus' fleshy lips smirked in vindication until the novice added, "and I'm ashamed of my words." The fat priest's smile sank into a scowl at the sudden contrition. The youth continued, passion in his voice, "But erasing these scrolls is wrong."

Baraldus' scowl reshaped itself into a vengeful sneer. "You see, *primicerius*...I mean Father Anastasius, he's not repentant. He's a scoundrel."

"Patience, Brother. I'm sure you're right, but let's investigate our young brother's zealous impudence." Anastasius turned his gaze on the novice.

"I didn't mean to insult Father Baraldus and what I said was sinful, but I was shocked when I read the text I was erasing, and the words just slipped out."

"You understood the writing?" The prefect gaped at the boy, and Baraldus' double chin dropped. "Do you realize that the language is a dialect of Ancient Greek?"

"Yes, and I realized too late that I was erasing the Gospel of Matthew."

Baraldus fell to his knees. "I didn't know, *primicerius*. I would never...I was following orders."

"Of course, Brother, my orders."

Tears began to drip down the corpulent priest's cheeks. "The boy was right to call me ignorant," he sobbed. "I've destroyed the Word of God."

"If blame is to be assigned, it's mine and mine alone." Anastasius paused for a moment. "Perhaps in the future, you'd do well to question the boy before you deliver one of your famous blows. You're right to command obedience, but you don't know your Lombard strength."

"Forgive me, *primicerius*." Baraldus hung his head, which made his double chin bulge.

"I won't say you were wrong, but I cannot say you were correct, either. I simply beseech you to meditate on your violence."

Baraldus covered his face with his hands in shame. "Give me a heavy penance."

"You need not atone for my carelessness. Go in peace that I may speak with our insubordinate young brother who evidently reads ancient Greek."

"I should retrieve the other scrolls before they're destroyed, shouldn't I?"

Anastasius pondered the question. "Of course. Leave them in the antechamber and I'll be more vigilant."

Baraldus pushed his bulk off the floor and backed out of the *scrinium*, bowing up and down like a child's toy.

The *primicerius* returned to his seat behind the lectern. "Sit down," he said to the novice. The boy pulled up a cross frame chair and slouched sullenly before the master of the archives. "What's your name?"

"Johannes."

"Indeed. Well, learned novice, I think you have a story to tell."

"Sir?"

"How can one so young read Koine Greek, the dialect of the Holy Scriptures?"

"Shouldn't we speak about the scroll of Matthew?" The boy's sullenness changed to fervor in a flash.

"So we shall, my impetuous friend, for it holds great import and perhaps greater consequence for you. First, please try to reply to at least one question." The *primicerius* smiled, and his words held no threat.

"Of course, Father. I learned Greek in Athens, where I studied before coming to Rome. Athens isn't the seat of learning it was a thousand years ago, but the city still has brilliant philosophers and mathematicians from the world over."

"You're full of surprises," the librarian beamed. "We don't often receive a novice into the church with such an education. What else have you learned?"

"I speak Latin, of course, and German since I was raised in Mainz. I spoke English at home because my parents are from Engla-lond and only traveled to Germany to convert pagans."

"That would account for your fiery hair, my young Englishman." Johannes blushed at the reference and smoothed the back of his red tangle. "Is that all?"

"I can also read Aramaic," Johannes said.

"The language of our Lord! How came you by this knowledge?"

"It was commonly taught in Athens since it was needed to translate many Old Testament scriptures."

The *primicerius* leaned back in his chair, touching his fingertips together in an arch. "To my recollection, I've never met a novice with an education such as yours. Yet we have you laboring all day, up to your elbows in lye."

"I don't mind. I'm a hard worker."

"You're an opinionated laborer."

"I believe it's wrong to destroy any work of knowledge."

Anastasius nodded, understanding. "I used to feel as you, Johannes. I spent many days of my youth rubbing out works of antiquity. The worst is recognizing the genius required to create such books. My passion is Greek history, and when I think of the countless chronicles destroyed because it's cheaper than making new parchment, well, I, too, had many dark days. Nevertheless, we put the pages to good use in the writing of prayer books, our Psalters. Noble ladies have developed a passion for the Psalms, and we can hardly make enough to keep Rome supplied. The commerce earns the church a tidy income."

"Would you destroy priceless histories for mere money?" Johannes raised his voice.

"The church has just and good reasons to expunge some writings. Come here. I want you to translate a passage." Anastasius pointed to the scroll on the slanted lectern from which he had been reading. "The first verse."

Johannes started slowly so his translation would be precise. "*In those days came John the Baptist, preaching in the wilderness of Judaea, and saying, repent ye: for the kingdom of heaven is at hand.* The words are from Matthew, the same as the one I erased."

"Correct, and your translation is precise, but didn't you notice something out of place?"

The novice furrowed his brow. He re-translated the verse in his head, positive he hadn't erred.

"Focus on the chapter," Anastasius said.

Johannes didn't understand at first, then his eyes widened as he spotted the omission. "They're missing."

"They?"

Johannes studied a few moments more. "The first two chapters."

"Quite right. You're not only a linguist, but you know the scriptures."

The novice puffed out his chest with pride. He had always been the best student in his classes in Athens. Now, he had received his first words of praise in Rome from the man who was renowned as the Western World's greatest expert in ancient Greek. Then Johannes appeared confused. "Why would scribes copy Matthew and leave out chapters?" Before the prefect could answer he added, "Are all the scrolls brought to me to erase the same?"

"Yes."

Johannes smirked as he said, "What a colossal blunder."

"It was assuredly no mistake. The chapters were left out by design. Do you recall which story they told?"

Johannes put one hand on his chin, mumbling barely audible words, "The lineage of our Lord and his birth, and Joseph and Mary fleeing to Egypt."

"Correct again! But did I hear you recite Matthew from memory?"

"In a way."

"How can one so young quote the scriptures by heart? Is your recollection that prodigious?"

"It's not remembering really, more like seeing."

"I don't take your meaning," Anastasius said.

"Well, I can't remember everything. For instance, I couldn't tell you who sat next to me at Vespers last night or what we ate at the noon meal on Tuesday. But if I've read something and need to recall the words, I simply look at the page in my mind."

"Indeed, I've heard of this thing. A century ago, a monk in the monastery at Monte Cassino was said to possess such a memory, but in truth, I believed the story an exaggeration."

"It seems normal to me, yet I realize it's not. But pray tell, why would anyone care about our Savior's ancestors?"

"Some things they didn't teach you in Athens. The story of the virgin birth shows the divinity of Jesus since God was his father."

Johannes looked disappointed. "Everyone knows that."

"Perhaps in our world they do, yet it was not always so. These scrolls were no *blunder* as you presumed, nor were they an accident of overworked scribes. They were created by a group of ancient heretics we call Ebionites, from the Hebrew word *ebionim* meaning the poor ones. We like to think of them as poor in spirit."

"Such a translation is a stretch," Johannes said. "Even our Lord could be called *ebionim*, since he was poor as well."

Anastasius smiled. "Like you, I think our rendition includes some editorializing and reflects our abhorrence of their heresies."

"But look at the writing." Johannes pointed at the Greek letters. "It's very old, and if the words were written by Jews, were they not the first Christians, even before gentiles? Could these scrolls be older than our Gospels?"

"Are you here to convert the *primicerius* of the archives to this heresy, or do you follow the teachings of the church?"

The young novice hung his head. "Forgive me, Father. It's a bad habit I learned in Greece, to argue every point. I swear I'm a faithful follower of the universal church, and I submit to her teachings."

"There's nothing to forgive. I merely wish to make a point. You may discuss with me what you will in the privacy of my cell, but if you would become a priest in the order of Saint Benedict, I beseech you to suppress your arguments. I assure you that because of your learning and young age, you'll incur the jealousy of many brothers. Give them no reason to condemn you."

Chastened, the novice said, "Of course, Father. Thank you for your counsel."

Anastasius waved his arm, motioning to the scrolls and heavy volumes stacked on shelves in the room. "This is the accumulation of the world's knowledge about our Lord. I have the advantage of access to everything here. Believe me when I say there are few texts, gospel or heresy, that I haven't read. I know the story of the Ebionites and I, too, wrestle with it. They deny the divinity of Christ yet still claim Him as the Messiah. They reject the virgin birth and avow that Jesus was adopted by God. And there are many other heresies in the *scrinium*. All of this I keep to myself and I counsel you, Johannes Anglicus, to do the same."

"These scrolls of Matthew that we destroy, are they the scriptures of the Ebionites?"

"Indeed. Now you understand why the account of the virgin birth is missing," Anastasius said.

"So that I may know for myself since we're alone in your cell, did the Ebionites remove the chapters, or did the church add them later?"

"You must decide for yourself and not even I can tell you, for I don't know. Perhaps one day, you will be the one who finds the truth."

"I?" Johannes arched his eyebrows.

"Yes, you. I now grasp the depth of your knowledge and I believe you would use such wisdom prudently."

"Thank you, Father."

"You may or may not thank me once you hear my request. I want you to assist me in the *scrinium*, the Holy Archives. You already speak more languages than anyone in Rome. You have a remarkable understanding of the scriptures, and I think you have the good sense to keep your scholarship to yourself. Do I read you rightly?"

The boy could scarcely believe what he was hearing. The newest of novitiates, he had hoped he might be allowed to study after a few years of menial labor. Yet it had only been a month and he was asked to assist the *primicerius* of the *scrinium* in the capital of Christendom. Tears welled up in his eyes, "Of...of course I'll work for you."

"Dear Johannes, I'm not asking you to work for me. I want you to assist me as my *secundarius,* the vice-prefect." The boy's jaw dropped. "You shall take over the task that I now perform. It will be you who decides which texts to expunge, leaving no trace of them, and which to archive for posterity. So consider well, because the responsibility for the destruction of these scrolls shall be yours and yours alone. Is this a commission you can accept?"

Johannes only now realized what Father Anastasius asked of him. The words would still be erased, but he would be the one to silence their authors, forever. The boy hung his head. "Yes, Father, I'll do it."

7
Parchment
October in the Year of Our Lord 843

Father Baraldus stood at Johannes' desk tapping his heavy, sandaled foot, occasionally blowing out a breath of exasperation from his round cheeks. "Please, *secundarius*, the novices have no work. The scribes in the *scriptorium* will soon be out of parchment and they'll blame me. You must come to a decision."

"Yes, I know." A stout worktable in the *scrinium* held two piles of scrolls, a large pyramid-shaped stack and a much smaller one. "But please don't call me *secundarius*."

"What shall I call you? You're so young that I'd be embarrassed to call you Father."

"Johannes will suffice."

"I cannot. You're a superior and I must show respect for your position, although you're just a young man, if that. I dub you Brother, for I can think of you as my younger, most learned brother, but only in private. In public, you're the *secundarius*."

Johannes rolled his eyes.

"But please, Brother," Baraldus said, "we need parchment. We can wait no longer."

The red-haired youth resigned himself to the fate of the scrolls. "Very well. Take the large pile." Baraldus began to scoop up rolls. "Not the small pile." Johannes cautioned his assistant. The hulking priest let a scroll fall and trotted to the door. He stopped, trying to figure out a way to close it with his arms full.

"I'll get it," Johannes said and rose to shut it himself. He returned to the scrolls still lying on the table. Unrolling one, he scanned the first few lines of a Greek copy of the Gospel of Luke. The author's name was emblazoned at the top. The earliest scriptures did not include authors' names, which were only added centuries after the books were written.

This Greek scroll, like many Bibles before Saint Jerome's translation into Vulgate Latin, was replete with errors, accidental and intentional. Johannes felt overwhelmed that one of his tasks was to correct the unintended mistakes, but not the ones sanctioned by the church since they represented official doctrine. Now, because of his new position, he needed to know the difference.

Some inaccuracies were careless mistakes caused by scribes toiling tedious hours more asleep than awake in dim *scriptoriums*. However, the proclivity of certain priests to alter words intentionally was most disturbing.

Johannes examined the Greek text, passing his finger underneath the lines until he came to the verse recounting the story of the child Jesus in the Temple. It read, *Joseph and his mother marveled at what was said about Him.* Something wasn't quite right. He opened a second scroll written at least a hundred years earlier. It was almost identical, but had no title. He skimmed the chapter until he found the same line, yet it was slightly different. This version began with the words *his father* instead of *Joseph.* Obviously, a scribe had removed the words *his father* in the later edition and replaced them with *Joseph.* It was a small change, only a few words. Yet like magic, Joseph was no longer Jesus' father.

Staring at the stack of scrolls, Johannes didn't understand the church's compulsion to alter or forge any part of the scriptures. *These earliest versions must be saved,* he thought, *even if the church wants them destroyed. Otherwise, future generations will have no true record of the Bible. Perhaps one day,* he mused, *scholars will possess enough knowledge to discern which were truly original scriptures.*

The heavy door squeaked and Baraldus' face reappeared. "*Secund* …I mean, Brother Johannes, the tanner is here to speak with you."

The young archivist knitted his brows. "I have no appointments today."

"I'm sorry, Brother. I sent for him. I wasn't sure if we'd have enough parchment for the scribes. I don't blame you. You're new to the job and it'll take time to make quicker decisions."

"Well, now we have plenty, so send him away." Johannes' voice dripped with irritation.

"Yes, Brother." Baraldus' face flushed as he pulled the door closed.

"No, wait," Johannes called out. The round Lombard peered through the half-closed entry. "I apologize, Father. You're quite right. Send the man to me."

"But Brother, the skins are on his cart in the courtyard. They're heavy and they stink."

"Of course. Tell him I'm coming." Johannes realized that Baraldus had found an answer for his latest problem. If he were to hoard scrolls to create a secret archive, there'd be a shortage. The solution was new skins.

The Jew stood next to his cart pulled by a team of oxen. He wore a maroon knee-length caftan over a brown chemise, and hose covered his legs. Church rules compelled Jews to wear distinctive clothing so they could be easily identified, and often ordered styles to humiliate them. But with his curly black beard draping to his chest and four-pointed cap, the tanner seemed more like a teacher or sage.

"I'm Johannes," the *secundarius* said, still uncomfortable with his priestly appellation. He held out his hand, but the Jew simply bowed.

"I'm Elchanan HaKodesh."

"Pleased to meet you. Now, let's look at your hides."

The Jew eyed the stout Lombard suspiciously. "I was told I would deal with the Vice-Prefect of the *scrinium*."

The boy straightened his new robe and tightened the cincture. "I am the *secundarius*." Although he knew he resembled no personage of authority.

Elchanan turned his suspicious eye to Baraldus who said, "He truly is." The tanner bowed even lower. "Forgive me, master Vice-Prefect, a natural mistake."

"There's nothing to forgive. I can hardly believe it myself. Well, then, let's inspect your stock."

The Jew pulled back the corners of hides to reveal the reverse side. "These are lamb skins for the manufacture of vellum, the best quality to make the thinnest, finest paper for the highest works of scholarship." Johannes nodded his head. The tanner then hefted calfskins, folding the hair side over to expose the hide. "Superior, but not as good as sheepskin, they're for more common books. I own the largest tanning yard in all of Rome and can provide as much as you desire. If you need even finer skins, I also import from the shores of the Black Sea and Cyrene in North Africa."

Johannes smiled. "I'll take everything you have."

Baraldus' jaw slacked, but the tanner simply shrugged his shoulders. "Young master, this is only a sample of my stock. I could deliver enough hides this very day to fill the *scrinium* to overflowing. You must tell me what you require and when you'll need them. We'll settle on a price, and our contract will be concluded."

Baraldus stepped between the tanner and Johannes and said under his breath, "Brother, this is beneath you. Tanning is the lowliest of professions. It's unseemly for a priest of your rank to bargain like a coarse housewife, and with a Jew, no less. Leave the dealings to me. I might be a dolt in areas of scholarship, but when it comes to animal hides, I'm an expert and can get a respectable price."

Johannes placed his hand on Baraldus' massive shoulder, "Good Brother, did not our Lord wash the feet of his Jewish disciples? You're right about one thing, though. I may know the scriptures, but I'm the dolt when it comes to bargaining."

"Very wise, Brother," Baraldus said, proud he had made his superior see reason. "How many hides shall I buy?"

"Begin with a cartload like this each week."

"Each week?" The fat priest howled. He lowered his voice to a throaty whisper, "But *secundarius*, we store ample parchment in the archives, which can be reused. Labor is free and hides cost money. I intended to purchase only enough to fill the temporary shortage, perhaps eight or nine score."

"Things change, Father, and I now have need of new parchment. So please conclude our negotiation, then send the tanner to me in my cell."

"The Jew…in your cell…in the *scrinium*? *Secundarius*, you should not…"

Johannes said sternly, "Father Baraldus, I want a word with the man in private."

Baraldus pointed the way to the vice-prefect's door as scribes in the *scriptorium* looked on horrified, some muttering under their breath. Baraldus heard the sound of someone spitting. A glower from the huge priest silenced them and sent their ink-stained hands back to copying. The tanner held his four-sided hat as he peered into the archivist's cell, ill at ease.

"Come in." Johannes stood up from his seat and pointed to the carved backless chair in front of his desk. "Please sit."

"I thank the young master," the tanner said, head bowed but eyes raised suspiciously. "I prefer to stand."

"I'll stand as well, then. I've been sitting all day and need a stretch."

"I've concluded our agreement with Father Baraldus. He's an expert in the art of the trade and I fear I've sliced my profit miserably thin in exchange for exceptional hides. I shall hardly make a denier in the bargain."

"I had no idea my assistant was so shrewd. Perhaps you can compensate for your meager margin with volume."

The tanner chuckled politely, then cleared his throat. "Do you wish to enter into some other business arrangement?"

"No, master tanner, I want to ask a question." Johannes searched for the most diplomatic words, but found none that would blunt his intent. "You don't believe Jesus is the Messiah, is that not so?"

Elchanan HaKodesh passed his cap from hand to hand. Beads of perspiration formed on his brow. "Our Hebrew religion is an ancient one, *secundarius*." He bowed his head again, not daring to look up. "Only He Who Cannot Be Named can know if your Lord was the Messiah."

"Fear not, Elchanan. I'm aware of your beliefs. Many of my teachers in Athens were of the Jewish faith and men of great wisdom. Your business is safe no matter what you say."

"Then you already know we don't believe Jesus was the Messiah."

"Of course. What I wish to understand is why."

"*Secundarius*, I'm not learned in these matters. I keep the law, the High Holy days, and I attend the synagogue on the Sabbath. For a subject such as this, you should consult someone who studies such things." Elchanan bowed, trying to back away.

"Wait. Who can I speak to that does study such things?"

The tanner stopped. He realized he couldn't politely retreat. "Would it not be unwise for you to be seen consorting with Jews that many Christians believe are the killers of your Christos? And such holy men of my faith consider Christians to be…"

"Unclean?" Johannes grinned. "Still, I want an answer. It would be better if you could direct me, rather than my having to search for these men by walking the streets of your ghetto."

"The man you seek is the Rosh Yeshiva, a rabbi who's the wisest in our community. He's the leader of our Talmudic schools, much like your library. He can answer your questions."

"Would you lead me to this man?"

Elchanon stared long at Johannes "If he agrees to meet with you, and only if he wills it, then I shall send for you."

"Who is the man?"

"He's my father."

Baraldus escorted the Jew to the steps of the palace. He shook his head as he watched him lead his ox cart through the *piazza* toward the *via Papale*. "What have I done?"

A priest in the far corner of the *scriptorium* wiped spittle from his mouth with the sleeve of his robe. He opened a small square of parchment, dipped his sharpened reed into black ink, and wrote,

𝔍𝔬𝔥𝔞𝔫𝔫𝔢𝔰 𝔟𝔲𝔶𝔰 𝔥𝔦𝔡𝔢𝔰 𝔣𝔯𝔬𝔪 𝔱𝔥𝔢 𝔍𝔢𝔴𝔰!

He folded the sheet in half, then quarters, and slid it inside his wide sleeve, into a pocket.

8
Hogsmouth

Pietro di Porca muttered to himself, "I would never come this way at night," as he endured whistles and jeers from the perpetual rabble posted outside the Colosseum. He pretended to ignore them as he shuffled past, making for the fashionable row of towers and mansions in the Monti quarter. His young nephew, the Count of Tusculum, had commanded his presence. "How dare he? I'm an Archpriest after all, and the Cardinal Priest of Saint Martins. One doesn't summon an Archpriest. I do the summoning. The least he could have done was send a litter. These cursed hills are too much."

Panting and sweating from his morning exertion, he made the sign of the cross as he passed the church of Saint Peter in Chains. Its beauty was glorious since it had been restored some forty years earlier. Inside its walls, the relic of the chains that had bound Saint Peter when he was a prisoner in Rome was prominently displayed. Today, Pietro felt their weight as he lumbered toward his obligation to his impudent nephew.

Pietro was, however, more fearful than angry. His arrogant nephew, with his violent temper, commanded the respect of all Roman nobles, especially his many enemies. He was no man to defy and he certainly couldn't be ignored. Even priests took pause at the mention of his name, Theophylact.

At least he hadn't missed Lauds, what some were beginning to call Matins in the vernacular, morning prayers sung at the cockcrow. Lauds was his second favorite ritual after Vespers, but only because he'd never become accustomed to waking barbarically early, even after all his years in the service of the Lord.

Singing was his passion, and his voice was a miracle from God. By the age of eight, his reputation had reached the ears of Pope Leo, and he sang for him by special request at Saint Peter's. Alas, others were jealous of his melodious gift and made fun of him, calling him *Hogsmouth*, an odious nickname that had stuck.

"This heat and dust is corrosive for the throat," he said to himself between gasps. "I'll sound dreadful at Vespers this evening. The only bright note to visiting my nephew is that he employs the finest cook in Rome." Just thinking about the sweetened meats and pastries he would likely taste at Theophylact's table made his mouth water.

Archpriest Pietro trudged up the ancient *vicus patricius* near top of the Esquiline Hill. He was relieved to be away from the pitiable but treacherous poor and more at ease here where the nobility congregated. The *vicus patricius* had been an exclusive street even in the time of Nero and now, with the aqueducts broken, the rabble never came around. There was no water. Only patricians had money to cart water up the hill, so the neighborhood had become even more private.

Nobles kept towers in Rome; the greater the noble, the taller the tower. The Count of Tusculum, being the most powerful of the Roman nobility, although the Crescentii clan vied for the position of preeminence, had the tallest and grandest. The Archpriest rapped on the heavy door.

The steward of the house swung the door open and beamed at the sweaty, breathless cleric. "Dear Cardinal di Porca, enter and rest your weary bones."

Pietro staggered in and was instantly relieved as the chill from the travertine floor radiated up his black robe. "It's so peaceful here, like our own cathedrals."

The steward poked the chubby priest's middle. "I heard you were coming from the *seigneur*. The cook is baking the sweetest cakes and most savory pasties. I hope you're in good appetite."

Pietro's spirits soared. His fatigue disappeared as though he had taken but a few minutes of exercise. "I'm that parched," he said. "Could I have a goblet of wine?"

"I'll bring it to you in the great hall," the steward chuckled. It'll soothe your soul. None of the ordinary Tuscan juice, mind. I just received a heady vintage from Aquitania's King, a gift to the count." His demeanor turned serious. "Today, you'll need more than a goblet. I'll bring an ewer. My lord is wroth, so steel yourself."

Pietro's eyes bulged in anxiety. "Why is he angry?"

"I know not, but he raves like a madman and throws the furniture. I'm hiding in the kitchen. I hear the bellowing, but not the words."

The panicked priest hung his head in gloom until the steward brought the wine and a platter covered with golden-brown tartlets. Pietro filled the goblet from the pitcher and emptied it in two long swallows. He poured again and took another draft. Breathing a deep sigh, his anxiety waned a little. He remembered the tartlets and stuffed one in his mouth. *Truly*, he thought, *Theophylact with his unrefined palate doesn't deserve such a cook as this Frankish one. There's not the like in all of Rome. Pope Gregory is far more deserving, although he's too austere of manner to consider the culinary delights.* He bit into another pastry. The intermingling of its sweetness with the tart earthiness of the wine created a sublime mix on his sensitive tongue.

Just as he began to feel a warm glow, the door burst open and the Count of Tusculum, a youthful giant, roared into the room. "Ah uncle, you're here. The man I wanted to see."

"Yes, nephew. You sent for me, remember?"

"Of course I do. Do you take me for an idiot?" Theophylact stood next to the Archpriest, waiting for a proper greeting, but Pietro sat frightened, cup in one hand and a tartlet in the other. "Well…?" The count lengthened the word expecting a response. He got none and barked, "Get up you fool and let me kiss you."

The priest bolted upright, knocking his chair backward and Theophylact kissed him gruffly on both cheeks. The steward rushed forward, righted Pietro's chair, and placed a chalice in front of the young patriarch of the Tusculani clan. He started to pour from the pitcher of wine, but Theophylact stopped him with his hand. "Bring me some water." Appraising the portly priest, he grinned—although no mirth showed on his face otherwise. He patted the Archpriest's belly. "You don't put much stock in fasting."

"Alas, nephew, I pray often yet receive little inspiration."

"Your profession was well chosen then and you've gone far, thanks to the patrons who paved the way for your remarkable advancement."

Pietro di Porca was not so drunk or panicked that he didn't notice the count was about to demand something of him. "I hope you're not implying that my promotions were arranged by the family and not God's will."

Theophylact pierced the priest with a glare of malice. "Don't feign piety with me, and don't deceive yourself, either. I receive word of your little vices. You're an archpriest and cardinal because we nobles wish it so. Give to God what you must, but never forget that your allegiance is to the family and, above all, to me. Gregory forgot his obligation, despite our having made him Pope. Our dealings with him are not finished, however. He'll pay for his betrayal."

The priest was broken. He couldn't resist. Whatever boon his nephew might ask, he must obey. Nonetheless, he made one last feeble attempt. "Are not the dealings with the Holy Father within the province of Emperor Louis or at least his son, Lothair?"

"That nest of scorpions? They spend too much time fighting one another to take note of what happens in Rome. When Louis divided the empire among his sons, he should have realized he would lose power. Now his eldest, Lothair, fights to get back his own lands. To make matters worse, our Pope ignores us, spending all of his time away from the city, trying to patch up the Imperial mess. No, Uncle. We Romans shall enforce the law, and you'll help."

"I'm not the Pope. What can I do?"

"When the time comes, you'll do my bidding, then you will be Rome's Pontiff. Now, what's this news about a librarian buying hides from the Jews?"

"You called me here to talk about animal skins?" The Archpriest's shoulders slacked and he exhaled a breath of relief. "Nephew, I assure you I know nothing of hides. That's the province of the Archives."

The count glowered. "Well, I suggest you learn." He pulled a square of parchment from an inside pocket and slapped it on the table.

Pietro examined the uneven scrawl. Grinning, he said in a wry singsong voice, "You have a spy."

"Don't be naïve. Not a sparrow falls that I don't know it. However, knowing a thing doesn't mean controlling it. Why does the library buy from Jews? They're not members of the tanner's guild. They're not even Christians." Blood percolated into Theophylact's head and his voice boomed. "They're the killers of Christ, yet the church puts money in their pockets. I'm the biggest landholder in Rome, all of Italy, and I tithe mightily⊠as Gregory well knows."

And to impress the other nobles, Pietro thought to himself.

The Count of Tusculum added with spite in his tone, "I own the largest herds of cattle and sheep, yet I've not sold a single hide or sheepskin or even meat to the *patriarchum*."

"Be reasonable, nephew," the Archpriest said. "The Jews make the best parchment. They import the finest skins from North Africa, and they raise their own beasts in the same manner. I've seen music written on local skins. It's coarse and stiff, quite unsuitable, and the guild won't match the Jews' prices."

Theophylact exploded, slamming his fist on the table. "Quality be damned! If buying's to be done, it will be from me. Do you understand? I've invested a great deal in you and I expect a return."

The priest cowered. "I…I hardly know where to begin." Pietro tried desperately to keep from bursting into tears. "I have no authority in the *patriarchum*."

"Those are the soundest words you've spoken this day. Nevertheless, I'll guide you, uncle, as my father did before me. You need help for this task, and I shall provide it. You have not the skills of wile and cunning that I require, but you're well placed and can promote someone who does."

"Who do you have in mind?" The Archpriest knew Theophylact had many who did his bidding within the walls of the church.

The count rose to his giant stature and motioned with his hand. The steward who had witnessed all opened a door. Pietro twisted his fat neck and craned to see who his nephew had chosen to do his dirty work. A handsome man with muscular legs in tight hose, wearing a luxuriant caftan robe, pranced in with haughty confidence. Pietro seemed to recognize the smiling dandy as he watched him embrace Theophylact. Then the recognition slapped him. "Benedict," he choked on the name.

"Your beloved brother," Theophylact sniggered.

"But…but he's not even a priest."

"That's easily remedied," Theophylact said, "and you'll find the way, dear Pietro."

Benedict clasped Pietro's shoulders with his two large hands and kissed him on his cheek. "Dear brother," he said in a honeyed voice dripping with derision. "Reunited at long last."

Although Pietro had not seen his brother in nearly a decade, he had received word of his many scandals. His whoring was renowned throughout Rome, and he was reputed to perform prodigiously in the bedchamber with skillful arts of amour. Even more infamous was his insatiable need for money to finance his philandering life. To satisfy his vast budget, he had plucked several nobles' wives and daughters, all of whom vied like giddy suitors to shower their families' wealth on him.

His despoiling of Roman women, however, had come to an end when he was caught *in flagrante delicto* with the wife of a Crescentii noble. Set upon by her enraged husband who was armed with an antique glaudius, the short sword of the Roman Legions, he had nearly been skewered. But in his blind fury, the husband missed his thrust and pierced only blankets. Benedict clasped his own dagger, which he had placed under a pillow, as was his custom while in a woman's bed, and plunged it between the nobleman's ribs. He had stolen not just the wife's virtue, but her husband's life as well.

Benedict had sought asylum with Theophylact's father, who

thought he might have to turn over his troublesome relative to avoid a blood feud. Instead, he spirited him out of Rome, and Benedict continued his lechery unabated in the Emperor's Frankish lands. But the humiliation of his rivals now pleased young Theophylact's sensibilities, and having a vassal who was unprincipled could be put to considerable use in the *patriarchum*. The time had come to call in Benedict's debt.

"Nephew, this is impossible," Pietro said. "Benedict's reputation hasn't been forgotten. The Pope would never let him enter a church, let alone be ordained as a priest. It can't be done."

"It can and will and you'll do as you're told. Besides, nothing is so irresistible as the return of a prodigal son. It's the reassurance of God's grace. Of course, Benedict must perform an appropriate penance." The Count of Tusculum laid his hand on Benedict's shoulder, and Benedict bowed his head deferentially. Theophylact could not help but smirk. Not only would he have a crafty and ruthless vassal strategically placed in the *patriarchum*, but as a priest, he would be untouchable to the Crescentii clan. Yet his presence in Rome would be an enduring proclamation of their shame. Theophylact laughed aloud, "What a propitious homecoming."

9
The Rosh Yeshiva

Father Baraldus spread the bundle of clothes on the sleeping pallet in Johannes's cell. "This is a terrible idea you've contrived, and I'm ashamed to be helping you." A runner had arrived in the afternoon with a message that the Rosh Yeshiva would indeed meet with the *secundarius*, but their meeting had to be in the Trastavere after dark. The Rosh Yeshiva suggested that Johannes might be wise to dress like a common Roman since a priest in the Jewish ghetto would attract the attention of the entire quarter.

Johannes rifled through the peasant clothing, which was more tattered rags than an actual costume but nevertheless delighted the youth, who scarcely contained an excited giggle. "These are perfect, Brother, but how did you find them?"

"I do a bit of trading at the bazaar now and again," Baraldus admitted. "They're only rags, but they must do." Johannes eyed him playfully as though he had committed some minor sin and the fat priest grew defensive. "You had need of them, and trading is in my miserable Lombard blood."

Johannes couldn't hide his pleasure. "And just what did you trade? No, don't tell me. I asked if you could find some clothes, and I'll not criticize your methods." He held up a short tunic with a low collar, which had been dyed blue at one time, but wear and countless launderings had turned the fabric an uneven shade of gray. Then he held short brown trousers to his waist. The legs came to the knee.

"I hope the boots fit," Baraldus said. "Your feet are uncommon small and I couldn't find a cap, so this turban must suffice." He raised a length of white linen.

"It's perfect. I feel like an actor in a play," Johannes said, enchanted by the outfits.

Baraldus wrinkled his nose. "A lowly profession indeed. All I found to cover your face was this woolen cloak. It'll be too warm, but it has a hood. Dress yourself, for the sun sets and a long walk to the ghetto awaits us."

"Us? I said nothing about you coming with me."

"Brother, you possess powerful knowledge in your young head, but it's book learning. I'll wager you know little of the streets after dark. I'll obey you in all things of the church, but this is not that." The stout priest pulled off his brown robe. He was already dressed in peasant clothing. He produced a short sword in a leather scabbard and slid it through his belt.

"That's a sword!" Johannes was shocked at the sight of a priest with a weapon.

"Change your clothes if we're going," Baraldus said.

They would be missed at Vespers and the evening meal, but there was no other option since the walk to the Jewish quarter would take an hour. It was just a league and a half, but the road was straight and paved with flat stones only as far as the Colosseum. Further on, the serpentine streets were broken, rutted, and often muddy, especially near the marshy banks of the Tiber.

Johannes set forth with Baraldus after the setting of the sun. The walk was easygoing on the *via Papale* toward the Flavian Amphitheater, now known as the Colosseum. Baraldus set a quick pace despite his girth. They passed the basilicas of Santi Quattro Coronati and San Clemente in no time. "You're more athletic than I would have thought," the youth jabbed at his assistant, still piqued the Lombard insisted on coming.

As they arrived at the sunken *Ludus Magnum* that once housed Rome's largest gladiatorial training school, the new *secundarius* could not help but glance at the sword Baraldus had slid through the leather strap he used as a belt. He was troubled that the priest displayed the weapon openly, even if he was in disguise. Yet as they reached the Colosseum, Johannes understood.

The grandiose Colosseum, which was once home to the Empire's bloody entertainment, had become a virtual city within the city. Rome's poor had converted many of the vaults under the seating to apartments. Shopkeepers and artisans set up businesses to serve the newest denizens. A small brick church had even been built inside the walls, into the very structure, to provide the village's spiritual needs. The cursed arena was transformed into the local cemetery.

Outside the walls of the makeshift commune, the resident's toughs, delinquents, and their admiring adolescent toadies stood near small fires swilling cheap wine from clay cups, laughing and taunting passersby in vulgar argot. Baraldus slid his sword around his middle for the reprobates to behold. Their taunts softened to unintelligible grunts. Johannes was now glad of his company and protection despite earlier protestations. Eyeing his escort with a new appreciation, he couldn't help himself. "Tell me where you got the sword."

"The sword is mine. It has always been mine. I realize we're required to give up our possessions when we enter the order, but I couldn't part with it."

"How came you to possess it?" Father Baraldus' simple exterior seemed to disguise a hidden past, perhaps as a rogue.

"I wasn't always a priest and, believe it or not, I wasn't always fat. My father was a farmer who tilled the land for a manor lord, but I'm the youngest of three brothers. We're not like the Franks who divide their property amongst sons. The eldest alone inherits. My brother likely tills the fields, though I've received no word from him for many years. However, my liege lord looked kindly on me and secured a position in the army, curse him for his generosity. I fought the Norse and Saracens as well, but I've had enough of death and killing for ten lifetimes. I left my closest friends on the plains the lords call fields of honor, although there was never any honor in it."

Baraldus had no end to his surprises. Like a sweet onion, peel a layer and an even more succulent one waits to be explored. "So how did you become a priest?"

"One day I collected my pay, resigned my commission and walked away. I'd thought about quitting after many a bloody battle, but never did. Time overtakes us all, however, and looking around one autumn morn at our drear encampment, I saw only youths like yourself. Those who had joined up with me were dead or retired to a safer profession. So I resolved to seek the path of peace and pray for my comrades, as well as those I sent to their reward. Even so, I cannot part with the sword. It was given to me by my liege lord the day I joined up and reminds me of the man I wish never to be again."

They walked in silence the rest of the way. Johannes realized he might have the benefit of knowledge from the volumes he had read, but no real comprehension of the pain of losing lifelong friends or the guilt of senseless murder. As he cast a glance at his assistant, he saw him with different eyes. The great hulk of a priest had perhaps little education, but had earned a lifetime of wisdom.

Baraldus knew every narrow lane, alley, and pathway through the ruins. They picked their way around the remnants of the terraced *Elagabalium*, a temple dedicated to Sol Invictus on the Palatine hill, then followed an uneven dirt road between the derelict and crumbling Imperial Palace to the left and the palace of Tiberius perched on a crest to the right. Their roofs had long since caved in, victims of the Goths, Visigoths, and centuries of earthquakes and gravity. Yet the greatest despoilers of the city were the citizens who pilfered valuable veneers of marble and the best quality stone for churches and towers and country villas.

They arrived at the crumbling *Aemilius* Bridge, which needed serious repair although engineers with such skills were no longer left in the shrinking city, and crossed the Tiber into the Trastevere. Johannes pulled a small shred of parchment from his cloak to reread the directions. Passing the stone synagogue, which was much larger than he had imagined, they arrived at a house with a low roof and walls of long, narrow Roman brick. Baraldus knocked on the heavy door. No one called out from inside to inquire about the identity of the visitors before a bolt slid and iron hinges creaked.

"Do you admit any stranger to your home, old man?" Baraldus was trying to be kind in his brusque way by warning the wizened, bent man who opened the door.

A smile beamed from beneath a tousle of long, frizzy white beard. "Greetings to you also Baraldus." The fat priest's mouth gaped as the man added, "You're no stranger to me since my son, Elchanan, gave good account of you." Then turning to Johannes he said, "And you must be the young scholar."

"We might be anyone, a thief or, worse, an assassin," Baraldus scolded.

"And yet you're not. You are who you are." The Rosh Yeshiva's smile infected Johannes, who returned a sincere grin. "I'm just about to enjoy tea and cakes. I'd be honored if you'd join me." Wrapped in a tasseled black shawl, his head covered with a white linen cloth, he led them from the foyer into a dining area adjoining the kitchen. The smell of pastry filled the warm, cozy room. The young priest heard a growl from Baraldus' belly, and his own stomach answered sympathetically. "Have I not prophesied hungry travelers, although Pope Gregory's *patriarchum* is not that far?"

"We forgot to eat, in our haste," Johannes said.

"Many hunger for knowledge, but learning doesn't satisfy the needs of the flesh," the old man quipped. "Come, sit and have a bite. I made these myself." A platter with brown flat cakes lay on a long table, and wisps of steam rose from a crockery pot. Johannes sat at the end of a bench, but Baraldus remained standing. "Sit, good Father," the Rosh Yeshiva said. "You've earned your rest and restoration."

"Thank you, sir, but maybe I'll stand watch outside."

"Fear not. Our quarter, while poor, is quite safe."

"Sit, Brother, and be at ease," Johannes said.

Baraldus looked sheepish. "Theological discussions make my head spin. I get enough at the *patriarchum*. Now, if you were going to talk about farms or hides or even soldiering, I might have something to say. So I think I'll poke around outside, just to make sure."

"You cannot leave without accepting some small hospitality." The Rosh Yeshiva pleaded with the stout priest. "Take a few cakes. I would be shamed if you did not." Baraldus scooped up two handfuls and fled outside.

"I'm sorry for my brother. He's not discourteous, it's just—"

"You need not apologize. Each man does what he thinks is for the greatest good. There are blessings in all of our deeds. My deed for today is my cakes. Some might regard them as small and insignificant, but they nourish you and your colleague, and that gives me pleasure. However, I'm the one who should beg forgiveness since I know your names, yet you don't know mine. I am Rabbi Avraham HaKodesh, the Rosh Yeshiva for all of Rome."

Together they ate cakes and sipped chamomile tea while the rabbi explained he was not unlike the Librarian of the Catholic Church. "As Rosh Yeshiva, I'm the academic leader of the school of Talmudic study, an ancient tradition whose origins come from the council of seventy-one Jewish sages who once ruled the Jewish people. It's my task to try to understand the will of He Who Cannot Be Named through His Law so we may lead righteous lives."

Johannes listened to Avraham's patient explanation. "Christians believe we're no longer subject to the law."

"Can something God gave us be so insignificant? Did not your own Messiah say, *Until heaven and earth pass away, not the smallest letter or the smallest part of a letter will pass from the law?*" Rabbi Avraham stared long at the young priest, then beamed again, brightening the room. "Yet heaven and earth are still here. Trying to understand the mind of the almighty is the holiest thing we can endeavor, and the law is our direct link to Him. If we could only fathom the tiniest sliver of the mind of God…but then, who can comprehend the mind of God?" The rabbi shrugged. "Nevertheless, I've dedicated my life to trying, but you didn't come here to discuss the law. You want to talk about the Messiah."

Johannes explained his job at the *patriarchum*; that he had been charged with erasing writings considered heretical as well as works of scholarship, so the church might save money by reusing the parchment.

"A heavy load indeed for such a young mind," the rabbi said.

"I don't agree with everything I'm required to do."

"To judge whether one's decisions are God's will or men's is one of the most difficult. I'm always suspicious of those who believe they have the answer."

"Our holy councils decided which scriptures are canon and which are heretical. Yet each one of these writings was authored by men who believed they were doing God's will. I also wish to do God's will. I realize that Jews don't believe in Jesus and I need to understand why."

Avraham whistled a long sigh. "Jews and Christians come from the same belief in He Who Cannot Be Named, yet the chasm between us is the Messiah. But of which Messiah do you speak?"

The question took Johannes by surprise. "Why, Jesus of Nazareth, of course. I've heard of none other."

"Truly, because dozens of Messiahs materialized before Jesus and after. There was Judas son of Ezekias, and the illustrious Shim'on bar Kochba, and Simon of Peraea just four years before Jesus. I can think of at least fifty Messiahs, and I'm quite sure many more names have been lost to history. Every time we Jews are sore oppressed, a new Messiah appears."

"So tell me, why do Christians believe Jesus was the Messiah, yet Jews do not?"

"Is that truly your question?"

Johannes looked perplexed.

"I think you're really asking how one makes a judgment, which are true scriptures and which are not, for that's the basis of our beliefs. And for that, I cannot counsel you. Our Torah has never changed. Books have never been added or deleted, nor have our scriptures ever been altered. Yet you're required to make such a choice. I've never been asked to render this kind of judgment and, truth be told, I could not. How does one presume to play God?

Johannes thought to reply, but, staring at the learned Rosh Yeshiva, he realized he would not receive that which he sought. The profound burden must be his alone. Avraham uncharacteristically held out his hands, taking the priest's between his own. "I'm sure we shall meet again. I will watch for you." He paused, probing the depths of Johannes' eyes. "Your church doesn't know everything about you, do they?" The young priest pulled his hands back, but Avraham consoled him in a soothing voice. "You need not fear me. Little escapes old men's eyes, especially for those of us who can see beyond our differences."

Johannes Anglicus stepped into the night, his head filled with the rabbi's words. Passing from the light of the cozy home into the moonless darkness, he stumbled around, arms outstretched, calling Baraldus' name. The toe of his soft leather boot struck an upended cobble and he fell to his knees, wincing in pain. A hand grabbed his shoulder and he jerked away in fear. "Peace, Brother. It is I, Baraldus."

"Where were you?"

"It's a good thing I decided to guard the door. We've been followed. By who, I know not."

Rabbi Avraham had not meant to scare the young priest. He had only wanted to convey that he would be a refuge if the youth ever had need. *I bungled that*, he thought to himself. *Ah well, Johannes has bigger challenges facing him than my ill-timed words*. He mouthed a soft prayer, "May He Who Cannot Be Named protect and guide this young seeker. His need will be great."

He fetched a small tripod and copper bowl from a cupboard and placed them on the kitchen table. He filled the vessel with water from the crockery teapot and watched as the ripples smoothed. Reflections from the flame of an oil lamp danced on the water's surface. Avraham took a deep breath and exhaled. He relaxed his bent frame and calmed his mind. He formed the images of three Hebraic letters in his mind, ו ה י. Their edges grew more and more distinct. Seeing them clearly, he transferred their image into the bowl and stared as he spoke their names silently. Over and over he chanted, just one of the seventy-two names of God.

10
Pascal

Doctor Isabelle Héber laid the page-size photograph on a rectangular table in the Archive laboratory. Father Romano leaned over the image and traced the line of text with his finger from right to left. He felt a sense of awe as he always did when reading words not read for hundreds or even a thousand years. The author, though dead for centuries, seemed to be able to reach across time to speak to him personally.

"Translate it for me." Isabelle said.

Romano shrugged his shoulders. "I can't read Aramaic. The script is my specialty for dating purposes, and I can tell you that this handwriting style was in use in Palestine around fifty A.D., but it's Greek to me." Romano smiled apologetically, hoping his play on words would amuse the archivist. "We learn Latin because it's the language of the church. Some of us study Greek since it's the language of the New Testament, but never Aramaic. Semitic tongues are a stretch for those of us with European linguistic backgrounds."

Isabelle snatched up the photograph and walked to her desk. She slid it inside a manila envelope. "Grab your backpack, Father."

"Where are we going?"

"I can't translate the text and neither can you, but I know someone who can."

Isabelle led the priest out of her office and switched the light off. The low heels of her black pumps clicked as she glided down the staircase. Romano struggled to keep up. She paused at the glass doors to enter the alarm code. Pushing Romano out, she slid the key in the lock and turned counterclockwise. She laced her arm through the priest's and dragged him into the damp night air. Romano felt uncomfortable at first, walking arm-in-arm in public, then he relaxed.

Even though it was close to eight o'clock, pedestrians filled the streets, window shopping, pushing strollers, or carrying plastic sacks of groceries. Isabelle passed a Metro station, but continued on. "Couldn't we take the subway," Romano said.

"It's not far. Just a few more blocks." The archivist turned down a narrow side street. She tapped on metal buttons attached to a stone façade, and the heavy oak door clicked. The long entry led to a winding, wooden staircase, and Isabelle began to climb.

"Hasn't anyone in Paris heard of elevators?" The priest sounded exasperated. Isabelle laughed, and her intelligent face brightened. *She's quite pretty*, Romano thought.

"The Marais is one of the oldest neighborhoods in Paris, the old Jewish quarter. Buildings had no elevators in the seventeenth century and the stairwells are so narrow, there's no space to retrofit them. I'm sure you can manage a few steps." The *few steps* turned into four flights. Breathing hard behind the slight and nimble archivist, Romano watched her insert a key in the door. "Is this your apartment?"

"Yes and no. I just live here."

"Is that you, *chérie?*" a male voice called from inside.

"Your husband?" Romano arched an eyebrow.

"I'm not married."

Wafting savory aromas engulfed the priest and his stomach growled. He hadn't quite recovered from his extended fast, even though he had eaten a late lunch.

Isabelle hung her coat in the entry closet. "*Oui*, Papa and I've brought a guest. I hope you made enough for three." She turned to Romano, "He always makes enough for six."

An elderly man with a lean face and longish gray curls peered from around a corner at the end of the hall. He wore an apron over a tan cardigan and sported a yarmulke. "Ah, *mon Père*." His face lightened. "Welcome." The man stepped forward and offered his hand. Romano grasped a handful of potholder. The man laughed as he pulled off the padded glove. "I'm Pascal, Isabelle's father. Finally," he said, "my daughter has brought home someone interesting. You're an American, no?"

"How did you know?"

"I'm not sure. We Parisians can always tell, but come in. Let's not talk in the entry."

The narrow hall led to a large living room. Bookcases crammed with volumes covered the walls. "Dinner is ready if you're hungry. We should eat while it's hot. You can wash in the bathroom down the hall."

As the priest scrubbed his hands, he reflected that Pascal Héber was Jewish, yet called him by the common Catholic term *mon Père*. Remembering his first conversation with Isabelle, who must be Jewish as well, she had also called him *mon Père*, and thought he was the parish priest.

Back in the living room, Pascal led Romano by the arm to a small dining room as though they were old friends. "Please sit at the head of the table, Father."

The priest tried to decline. "No, *Monsieur*, this is your home," but Pascal had pulled out the chair and motioned for him to be seated.

"This way, Isabelle and I can share you. Besides, I sit nearest the kitchen. It's easier to serve." He disappeared then returned with a casserole emitting puffs of steam. "I'm glad Isabelle invited you because I poached a lovely turbot. This is Friday, after all." He turned to Isabelle. "Could you pour the wine while I serve, *ma chère*? I assume you're a colleague of my daughter's since you can't be a boyfriend." Monsieur Héber slid a portion on the priest's plate.

"We're not really colleagues," Romano said. "I needed to talk to Mademoiselle Héber regarding—"

"Father, please," Isabelle interrupted, holding a green translucent bottle. "Can't you wait a minute before the interrogations begin?"

Pascal shrugged his shoulders. "Just a little conversation darling. We invite so few guests, only my old friends, and I know every one of their boring stories by heart."

"At least let him eat a bit first. I'm sure he's starving."

Their banter amused Romano, but also made him uncomfortable. He hoped Isabelle would keep the secret of the Psalter. She appeared to his right, pouring a golden liquid into his glass as Pascal offered, "*Bon appétit.*"

"Thank you, sir," Romano replied and bowed his head to pray. Opening his eyes, he glimpsed Pascal crossing himself. "I don't mean to pry, sir…?"

"Sir? Sir?" Pascal raised his inflection in mock offense. "I called my father *sir*. Call me Pascal."

"Alright Pascal, I couldn't help but notice you making the sign of the cross. I had the impression you're Jewish."

Isabelle shook her head, but her father said, "he asked." Pascal turned to the priest, his eyes gleaming. "Are you asking if I'm a Jew or a Christian?"

"Well…yes."

"Then the answer is both and neither." The elder Héber smiled, satisfied with his little joke, but Isabelle didn't seem to share his amusement. She arched her eyebrows as if to say *please don't start.*

"I don't understand," Romano said.

"I suppose I'm saying that I'm a Jew and a Christian as well, but not in forms you recognize."

"I don't pretend to be an expert on theology, but I feel certain Judaism and Christianity are two different things. Unless you're saying you're Jewish by heritage and converted."

"Not at all, I'm Jewish by accident of birth, as is Isabelle, and I'm also a follower of Judaism, but not very orthodox. Still, I'm a disciple of Jesus, but not the Jesus you know."

Romano didn't wish to sound impolite so he said as delicately as possible, "I just don't believe one can be both."

Pascal leaned forward in his chair, hands on the table clasping his knife and fork, "*Mon Père*, I assure you one can."

"I don't understand how."

"I'm a Jew who believes Jesus was the Messiah and could have become the rightful King of Israel, but not in the way Christians view him. I consider myself a Nazorean. Your church stuck us with the name Ebionite."

"The heretical group?"

Pascal hunched his shoulders. "The church thinks Ebionites were heretics, but many scholars believe the Ebionites, who were led by Jesus' relatives, were more faithful to his teachings than Paul."

"You're not trying to convert me, are you?"

"Certainly not, Father. I'm not a proselytizer, only an arguer. I think every man comes to his own philosophies through personal experience and study. It's rare when one man changes another's mind. I'm simply telling you my beliefs."

Isabelle gave Pascal a sidelong glance. "Father never says anything simply."

"That's not fair, *chérie*. Perhaps I'm a bit provocative, but you make me sound sinister." Pascal feigned hurt feelings.

"Maybe I'm not fair Papa, but you must admit it's true."

Romano was confused by Pascal's claim. "The Ebionites haven't existed for over a thousand years. How can you claim to follow a group that doesn't exist?"

"I wouldn't say I was a follower." Pascal spoke more reflectively. "I don't follow anything. My belief in Ebionite doctrine grew out of my loyalties. Or more accurately, I knew who I had become when I discovered their ancient beliefs and they fit me well, like an old sweater. But here I am assaulting you with provocations you certainly find objectionable. In truth, I owe my life to the church."

"I don't understand," Romano said.

"Of course you don't." Pascal Héber shoveled the last morsel of fish into his mouth and pushed his plate forward. Isabelle, as if on cue, refilled his glass with wine. "It's obvious that I'm Jewish since I wear my yarmulke and perhaps you recognize that my name is Jewish. In fact, my parents raised me as an Orthodox Jew. The war changed everything. I remember the day so well because my friends and I couldn't concentrate on our lessons and we whispered back and forth. Not because of the heat, although that summer was certainly hot, but because the next day was Bastille Day and we could only think about fireworks. Our poor teacher was quite relieved when class was over. As usual, I dawdled to avoid coming home to Torah studies and homework. Marseilles was awash with Jews, in those days, who had fled the Nazi invasion of Paris. The Germans began rounding us up by summer. I listened to my father and mother whisper about it when they didn't think I could hear, but a ten-year-old can scarcely grasp terror. I had just rounded the corner to our building and a hand grabbed my arm. It was my teacher, red-faced and out of breath. I tried to jerk away and turned to yell as I watched the Gestapo pushing Mother and Father into a black car. I never saw them again."

"I'm so sorry," Father Romano said sincerely.

"Thank you Father. You're very kind."

"But how did the church save you?"

"Ah, yes. I remember clearly that I wanted to scream at the Nazis to let my parents go. The teacher must have anticipated it. He slapped his hand across my mouth and pulled me away. I don't recall how we got to the monastery since my eyes were filled with tears as we wandered through the streets. I didn't understand at the time, but he was taking me to my next home and to the only other father I've ever known. You certainly heard of Father Pierre Marie-Benoit?"

"I recognize the name."

"Father Benoit was a Capuchin monk. Mother and Father worked with him to get Jews out of France and place hundreds of children, whose parents had been arrested, with Catholic families. He had organized a printing operation in the basement of the Monastery to produce thousands of travel documents, Baptismal Certificates, and the like. He told me he had begged Mother and Father to leave France, but they refused." Pascal leaned back in his chair, reflecting. "I think he must have wished he had insisted more forcefully because instead of putting me in a family like the others, he kept me with him. I helped him forge papers and studied Catechism so the Germans would believe I was Catholic. So while I owe my birth to my Jewish parents, a monk saved my life. Now, I belong to both and thanks to Father Benoit, I'm an expert forger." A sly smile accented Pascal's face.

"But if you're a Christian, why aren't you Catholic?"

"Certainly, my parents influenced my study of the Torah. However, I also learned to understand Christianity because of my gratitude to Father Benoit. Still, I have a third loyalty, fidelity to history. My studies of Judaism and Christianity led me to believe they're the same religion, extensions of each other. I'm convinced the original followers of Jesus held the same belief. When I think about the person I became, I sometimes reflect on my name. Did you know that Pascal comes from the Latin *pascha* for Easter, which in turn comes from the Hebrew *pesach* for Passover. I seemed to be destined somehow become both Jewish and Christian."

"Your story is touching, Pascal, and I'm sorry for what you've been through. I hope you won't think ill of me if I say that I don't share your belief."

"Not at all, Father." Pascal reflected for a moment as though he was trying to read something on the priest's face. "Your name is also quite interesting."

"Romano? Pretty common in the States, at least in Italian neighborhoods."

"Of course, you must know Romano means the Roman."

"I suppose so. I never thought about it."

"If your name were Peter, then you would be Peter the Roman."

"You mean like the Apostle Peter?"

"Peter was in Rome, but he wasn't Roman. No, I'm thinking about a medieval prophet."

"Like Nostradamus?" Romano raised his eyebrows.

"Much earlier—twelfth century—and this prophet was an Irish priest, Saint Malachy. He had visions of the future popes and wrote down their names. The last was *Petrus Romanus*, Peter Romano."

"Did he mention any Michael Romanos?" The priest smiled, making light of Pascal's interest in Catholic esotericism.

Pascal giggled, "Not that I recall. I'm surprised that being raised Catholic, you didn't learn about Malachy."

"I wasn't raised Catholic."

"Protestant?" Isabelle said.

"I wasn't anything."

"That's difficult to believe," Pascal said. "A man such as yourself? How were you raised?"

"On the streets mostly."

"An orphan?"

Romano squirmed in his chair.

"I'm sorry, Father," Pascal apologized. "We're being impolite."

"It's an unoriginal story. My father left when I was so young, I don't remember him. Mother was…well, intolerant. Maybe she saw Dad in me. So I ran away and ended up in foster homes until I was tough enough to run from there. January is cold in New York, so I hid in a church to sleep. Like you, Pascal, a priest saved me. He sent me to a Catholic high school on the Upper East Side, which is where my life and education began."

"Now I'm the one who's sorry. It's one thing to have your parents taken from you, but quite another to have to run from them."

"It was for the best. I found my home."

"So we both ended up alone."

Isabelle stood up from the table. "It's getting late, Father, and we still have a document to translate."

Romano rose as well and offered his hand to Monsieur Héber, who rose and shook it affectionately. As the priest turned away toward the entry, Pascal called to him, "Where're you going?"

"Like your daughter said, we have some work to do."

"Of course you do. You have a first-century Aramaic text to translate."

Romano was flummoxed. His eyes bolted toward Isabelle, who cleared dishes.

"Father," Pascal said with a grin, "I'm the translator."

11
Gospel of Thomas

Romano sank into a green, overstuffed chair. His heavy eyes surveyed the walls. Old paint covered uneven plaster. Dark beams jutted from above. The junction of the wall and ceiling had been deformed by centuries of settling. Isabelle handed Romano a demitasse, then held out a silver bowl. He took two sugar cubes from the bowl and plopped them into the cup.

Pascal Héber sat opposite the priest on the other side of the coffee table. The photograph of the ancient page lay in front of him. He peered at the image through half-moon reading glasses while scratching notes on a tablet. Isabelle had neglected to explain that her father was a retired professor of linguistics at the Sorbonne, where he had been the department head of Arab and Hebrew studies. Most importantly, he had a perfect working knowledge of Aramaic.

The coffee helped revive the priest, who had become drowsy after dinner. As he savored its aromatic richness, the caffeine awakened his brain. Only then did he realize Pascal was speaking to him as he read and scribbled notes. "This apartment has been in my family for two hundred years." He didn't look up as he spoke. "It belonged to my aunt and uncle. After the war, I was the only one left, so I inherited it. Someday, it will belong to Isabelle. She's a lovely old building, don't you think? Age adds lines and texture like grooves gouged in vinyl records. I've always thought that buildings record the essence of the lives lived in them. It gives them character, like me."

Romano gazed over at Isabelle, who appeared and disappeared, carrying dishes from the dining room to the kitchen, casting looks at her father as she passed. Finally, she walked to the sofa and sat next to him, staring at his notes. Romano tried to divine what she read by the expression on her face, but her widened eyes could mean anything.

Pascal rose and stepped to the bookshelves that covered an entire wall. He pulled down a thick volume and flipped the pages. He scribbled on his notepad and read a little further. Finally, he took off his glasses and folded them slowly. Romano and Isabelle edged forward in their seats.

"Well, Papa?" Isabelle asked.

Pascal turned to the priest. "Are you certain this is a first-century manuscript and not a few hundred years later, perhaps?"

"Positive. Around fifty A.D., plus or minus."

Pascal blew out a breath of astonishment. "Then, my boy, let me be the first to congratulate you. You've discovered what scholars have sought for almost two thousand years."

The paleographer was now wide awake. "Is it a New Testament manuscript?"

Pascal half smiled. "You found the only first-century Christian *scriptures* written in Jesus' language."

Romano noticed the emphasis Pascal placed on the word *scriptures.* "What do you mean? Is the passage from a Bible book?"

"Papa, don't play games," Isabelle said. "This is too important."

"My child," Pascal touched his daughter's cheek, "I never play games with God." He scanned the first line once again. "It appears to have been written by a certain *Mathaias* who is recalling a conversation between Jesus and his Apostle Thomas."

"I don't recall those scriptures," Romano said.

"Why don't I read the important part." Pascal translated the text into English. "*The Savior said, 'Brother Thomas,'*" Pascal mumbled some unintelligible words, then, "Oh yes, here it is, '*it has been said that you are my twin and true companion.*'"

Romano leaned back in his chair, dazed.

"What do you mean *twin*?" Isabelle looked dumbfounded. Are you saying Thomas and Jesus were twin brothers?"

"You see darling, rumors circulated from the earliest Christian days that the Apostle was in fact Jesus' twin, but this was more than a rumor. There are certain—" Pascal paused as though searching for precise yet diplomatic words, "problematic books that weren't allowed into the Bible. Historians had only heard rumors about them because they were destroyed by the church. We would never have known what they said had they had not been discovered by an Egyptian peasant digging for fertilizer."

"You mean the Dead Sea Scrolls?"

"No, *chérie*. It's a misconception that the Dead Sea Scrolls are Christian. They're all Jewish. The discovery at Nag Hammadi, on the other hand, was completely Christian. The books were buried near the Egyptian monastery of Saint Pachomius after the church declared possession of these types of writings heresy." Pascal scratched his head, stood, and padded to the bookshelf. He slid his finger down a row of tomes until he came to a thin booklet. He pulled it out and opened the cover to the first page. *"These are the secret sayings that the living Jesus spoke and Didymos Judas Thomas recorded."*

"So?" Isabelle shrugged.

"You're an expert in ancient Greek. How do you translate *Didymos*?"

Isabelle thought for a moment. "It means twin."

"Very good, darling, but what you couldn't know is that Thomas is the Greek spelling of the Aramaic word *Te'oma*, which also means twin. So Thomas' name is really Judas the twin, twice over. Whenever they call him Thomas in the New Testament, the author is calling him the twin."

"What book are you reading from?"

"The *Gospel of Thomas*, a Nag Hammadi find."

"Does the Bible refer to the Apostle as a twin?"

"The Gospel of John uses the name Thomas Didymos or twin, twin on three separate occasions."

Father Romano's face was glum. "What else does it say?"

Pascal rose and put his hand on the priest's shoulder. "Will you be all right?"

"Sure. I'm just shocked to learn Jesus may have had a brother—and a twin no less. So if he had a twin who was not God's son, then..."

"Mary had another son and Joseph fathered at least one of them. I think I know which book this is. One text discovered at Nag Hammadi is called *Thomas the Contender*. Many scholars believe the book is actually the lost *Gospel of Mathaias*. This is certainly written by a *Mathaias*."

"Read the rest." The priest's face bore a mix of weariness and distress.

Pascal scanned the rest of the page. "I'm happy to report nothing earthshaking in what's left, Father, so you can breathe easy; only something about Thomas getting in touch with his inner self. Very 1960s. I'll draft a translation for you."

Romano pushed himself out of the overstuffed chair. He offered his hand to the seated professor. "Thank you for your help, Monsieur Héber. It's late and I need to find a hotel."

Pascal rose and took the priest's hand between both of his, "Nonsense, Father. You can stay here. Isabelle, please show Father Romano to the guest room."

"I've already imposed too much."

"Don't be silly. You've had an exhausting day and I won't accept no for an answer."

Isabelle placed clean towels on the nightstand and turned back the bedspread, fluffing the pillows. "You'll be more comfortable here than a hotel."

"You and your father are too kind."

"Get some sleep, and we can talk tomorrow." Isabelle kissed him on the cheek and Romano jerked away.

"Oh, I apologize, Father. We French kiss everyone. I should've thought."

"No, I'm the one who's sorry. It's not being a priest...but... something else."

"Well, let's forget it." Isabelle squeezed his hand and closed the door.

As the priest pulled the blankets on the iron-frame bed to his chin, the implications of the *Thomas* fragment spun in his head. He hoped he would sleep; he had to sleep. His overtired brain wasn't processing clearly and he needed clarity, but the coffee or the shock of the discovery made him feel as though he could jump out of his skin.

He had ended up in the Secret Archives by sheer circumstance. He only wanted to study ancient books and manuscripts to learn their mysteries. He seemed to have spent his life looking for answers to secrets. Why was his mother violent, his father gone? Why did people hurt others for their own gratification? If he could but read the thoughts and disputations of the earliest Christians, those closer to the era of the Lord, he might understand more, get closer to the truth. But the School of Paleography fell under the auspices of the Secret Archives. He was educated there and was now the vice-prefect.

However, much more resided in the Secret Archives than just the School of Paleography, hidden things not intended to be seen by outsiders, even priests. Romano had access to everything and had read many texts branded as heresies. Yet these long-lost accounts were not written by pagans or unbelievers, but by Christians who wrote what they believed. Priests like the author of the little tract he had translated, Anastasius Bibliothecarius, and Disciples of Christ like the author who claimed he was Jesus' twin brother.

Who had the right to say what should be part of the canon or what would be forever branded as heretical, suppressed, and destroyed? Romano asked himself the question over and over. Now, however, he had begun to grasp that what the church allowed to be read, published or even uttered was scrutinized, dissected, and censored. How had he not seen this before? Perhaps he had chosen to turn a blind eye.

Romano had translated a simple pamphlet and almost lost his job at the hands of the Grand Inquisitor. But what he had uncovered tonight would shake the very foundation of the church. Jesus had a twin brother; Joseph was his father, Mary their mother. Such a thing was unthinkable and definitely punishable by the anonymous enforcers within the thick, impenetrable walls of the *Pallazo del Sant'Uffizio.*

Romano took a deep breath and another. An arc of inky blackness devoured the pinpoints and jagged waves of light underneath his eyelids. His breathing grew slower, more regular. His last thought was of Isabelle's kiss as he sank into a turbulent oblivion.

The creak of an antique door disturbed Pascal's sleep. *I'm sure Isabelle showed our guest the bathroom*, he thought. *Did she remember to leave the hall light on for the priest?* He looked though the darkness to where the crack under his door should be, but there was no light. Throwing back the blankets, he sat on the edge of the bed and stepped into his slippers.

He turned the doorknob and pulled on the door. It slammed against him with a force that launched him to the floor. Stunned and uncomprehending, Pascal shook his head. He recoiled from a muffled wallop and gasped from the sting on his face. A broad gloved hand swung to strike the other cheek just as a slender figure in flannel pajamas wrapped herself around the dark form.

Isabelle clutched the man's throat while the Pascal grabbed a wrist with both hands, trying to hang on. The assailant flung his free elbow back and caught Isabelle on the jaw, knocking her to the floor. He raised his fist to punch down, but the hand hung in the air suspended.

Romano grabbed the fist in mid strike and unleashed a crushing blow to the intruder's chin, knocking him off the old man. The attacker rolled and jumped to his feet facing the priest, his hands raised in a fighting pose. The priest stood upright and cocked his fists in the boxing stance he had learned first on the streets and then in Catholic school. The assailant launched a sweeping hook. Romano rotated his right foot, pivoting toward the blow, and ducked his head. The swing went wild. He shifted his left foot in the opposite direction and snapped his hips, delivering a shot to the ribs that doubled the man over. He followed with a combination right jab to the face and left hook that struck the man in the mouth. The attacker reeled into the wall, his arms splayed.

"I've got them!" The shout came from another room. The attacker stumbled to the open door and Romano lunged after him. The man balanced on one leg, turned his body horizontal, and delivered a thrusting kick to the priest's groin. Romano grunted and crumpled in a heap. The assailant stood over him, poised to finish the job. Pascal flung his body over the groaning priest.

The voice in the other room shouted again. "Let's get the hell out of here." The attacker spat bloody spittle at the two men and fled the apartment.

Romano and Pascal knelt over Isabelle. Pascal wiped blood from the corner of her mouth with a kerchief while the priest cradled her head in his hands. Romano felt a growing goose egg. A tiny groan came from deep within her chest as she tried to lift her hand to the lump. "Lay still, *chérie*," Pascal said.

"Oh, my head," Isabelle groaned. Her eyes shot wide open and she tried to raise herself.

"Please lie down, darling. You've suffered a nasty blow."

Isabelle would not be consoled. "Father, the prayer book!"

"I'm afraid they've taken it," the priest said.

And the photograph?"

"Yes." Her father added, "but at least we're alive, thanks to Father Romano."

"I didn't do so well. They got away with everything."

"I saw the look in the man's eyes, Father. If you hadn't battered him soundly, he would have taken your life—and ours, too. He wanted more than the Psalter. He wanted our silence."

Isabelle pushed her father's hand away and forced herself to her knees.

"*Chérie*, you must lie down."

"Let me go Papa. Don't you understand? They followed us to the apartment. They know about the Psalter and the photograph. We must get to the Archives before they do. Stay here," Isabelle said to her father as she reached for her overcoat. "I'll call you from the office."

"Not on your life. I'm not letting you out of my sight."

The battered trio rushed down steep wooden steps in the building stairwell and into the fog-soaked street. The realization came to Romano that even through her addled brain, Isabelle had seen the logic. These men were professionals. If they knew enough to target the prayer book and photograph as well, they would head for the lab where the photo had been made. *But how could they know?* The priest wondered. *Only he knew about the palimpsest and it was just a hunch after spotting telltale signs of Giovanni's handiwork. The only other person who knew about the ninth-century monk was the Pope's Secretary, and he was dead.* Romano searched his recollection, wondering what he might have said to Father Mackey.

They rushed under the Roman arch into the National Archive courtyard to the flashing of blue lights against the pale stone walls of the ancient Hôtel de Soubise. Half a dozen police cars formed a barrier around the entrance doors. *Please God*, the priest said a silent prayer, *help the cops arrest these criminals.*

12
Shochetim

Two uniformed gendarmes blocked the trio outside the French National Archives door. "I'm Doctor Isabelle Héber, Director of the New Technologies department." The officers opened the front entrance to let her pass, but barred the way to Pascal and Romano. "They're with me," Isabelle said.

"Sorry Madame, orders," one of the *gendarmes* replied and pushed Pascal and the priest off the steps.

Isabelle hurried through the door. "I'll see what I can do."

"Thank God you're here, Isabelle." The words came from a short, distinguished man in a navy pinstriped suit whose gray hair fell below the collar. "What happened to your face?" He pointed to her swollen, split lip.

"I'll tell you later, Philippe. Did someone break in?"

"Worse, much worse," the Director General of the Archives, Philippe de Montfaucon, said as he wiped perspiration from his forehead with a monogrammed kerchief.

His explanation was interrupted in mid-sentence by a plain-clothes officer who confronted Isabelle. "We've been trying to tele-phone you. What a coincidence you should show up at precisely this time."

"Whoever you are, you may address me as Doctor Héber or Director Héber or Madame." Isabelle bristled that the detective would address her impolitely.

"Of course Ma-dame," the detective said. "I'm *Cap-i-taine* Gérard Desmoulins of the GIGN, the *Groupe d'Intervention de la Gendarmerie Nationale*. However, you can call me *Capitaine* Desmoulins or simply *Cap-i-taine*, if you wish. Now please, why are you here in the middle of the night?" Before she could reply, a uniformed gendarme with chevrons on his shoulder whispered something in the captain's ear. "Escort them in," he replied. Turning back to the archivist he said, "You've brought guests. Now, I'm waiting, Madame."

Isabelle glared at the detective, contemplating how much she should reveal. "Someone broke into my apartment and I thought it might have something to do with the Archives."

"Why would you think so?"

"Well…"

"Come, come, Madame Héber," the captain said. "It's obvious you've been attacked and you must believe the motive is related to your work or you wouldn't be here. Ergo, it's a matter of National Security. So don't be coy."

Romano and Pascal were escorted to the group by a sergeant, and the priest said, "She's not being coy, captain. She's trying to protect me."

"Who are you?"

"Father Michael Romano from the Vatican."

The detective seemed to understand. "Go on."

"Doctor Héber is a professional colleague and was kind enough to use her equipment to translate an old book."

"Doctor Héber!" Isabelle wasn't sure whether Philippe was simply trying to impress the detective, but he appeared in genuine distress. "You're well aware the Archives are for the work of the State." He peered solicitously at *Capitaine* Desmoulins.

The captain ignored him. He turned instead to Pascal. "And you are…?"

"I'm Pascal Héber, her father."

The Director General extended his hand to Pascal with a nervous, polite smile. "Ah Doctor Héber, a pleasure to meet you. I've tried for years to get Isabelle to introduce me to—"

"Please Director," the captain interrupted, "this is an investigation, not a reception. "Why are you here, *Monsieur*?"

The retired professor responded matter-of-factly, "They attacked me, too. I would never let my daughter investigate alone. These are serious men."

"It appears they were very serious," Desmoulins replied cryptically. "Why don't you all follow me to Doctor Héber's office. I wish to show you something. Madame, would you lead the way?"

Isabelle led them up the stairs toward her lab. Turning back as she climbed, the expression on the Director General's face scared her. He walked with halting steps, a kerchief over his mouth as though he was about to be ill. *How serious had the burglary been?* she wondered as she approached her first floor office. The door was ajar. Light from inside shone into the hallway. As she reached the handle, she stopped short, alerted by the shrill voice of the Archive Director, "Stop, Isabelle! Don't go in." Captain Desmoulins glared at the Director General to which Philippe said, "*Monsieur Capitaine*, you go too far. Interrogation is one thing, but cruelty quite another."

"What's inside, Philippe?" Isabelle asked her boss.

"I'm afraid…"

"Silence!" the detective captain barked. "I'm in charge of this investigation."

Isabelle Héber turned back toward the light and startled as a man appeared in her office doorway, inches from her.

𝕽𝖔𝖒𝖆𝖓𝖔'𝖘 𝖍𝖊𝖆𝖗𝖙 𝖌𝖆𝖛𝖊 a heavy thump as he came face to face with the last person in the world he wanted to meet. "Well, well, Father Romano," the man said to the priest. "What an expected surprise."

"*Colonelo*," the priest replied.

The French captain addressed the group. "May I present *Colonelo*

Del Carlo of the Carabinieri's GIS. I believe, Father, you two know one another."

The priest tried his best not to look guilty. "Yes, Captain, I've had the pleasure."

Del Carlo confronted the priest. "You didn't return my telephone call, Father."

"I apologize, *Colonelo*, but I had critical work to do here."

"Does your work have anything to do with the evidence I foolishly let you return to the Vatican?"

Romano saw no further reason to lie. "Yes."

"I thought so. Am I correct in assuming that Madame Héber and Monsieur...?"

"Héber, also," Pascal held out his hand smiling. "I'm her father."

Del Carlo didn't take the hand. "Do they know about the prayer book?"

"Oh, yes," Pascal said. "Magnificent, Colonel, the greatest discovery of the century, maybe the last two thousand years."

Del Carlo threw up his hands in exasperation. "It appears everyone knows more about this book than I, for which, I might add, a priest was murdered."

"I'm sorry, Colonel," the Director General of the Archives said, "but Pascal Héber isn't just anybody. He was a most illustrious professor, head of the department of..."

"Arab and Hebrew studies," Pascal helped the Director's memory.

"Thank you, professor."

"You're welcome, *Monsieur* Director," Pascal nodded.

Romano interrupted their solicitous exchange. "Listen, Colonel. I admit I suspected something when you showed me the Psalter. But I had to be certain and I didn't want to make a mistake in front of Cardinal Keller. The Vatican's technology is limited, so..."

"So you brought it here?"

"I'm afraid so."

"Father, The Psalter is evidence in a capital crime. You'd better hand it over"

"I can't."

"You gave me your word," Del Carlo said.

"It's just—"

"I am not asking, Father. I'm ordering."

Pascal cut in again. "He can't, Colonel, because he doesn't have it. He brought it to my apartment to translate, and two men broke in and attacked us while we slept. I was certain they were going to kill us, and they stole the—"

"They stole the prayer book?" Del Carlo shook his head.

"Not only that, Isabelle discovered what was written underneath the Latin and made a photograph, and they pinched that as well. We came here to make sure they hadn't taken her computer."

Pascal wanted to continue, but Del Carlo held up his hand to stop his rapid-fire soliloquy. "You're quite informative, Professor. I pray we can write fast enough to take your deposition. Now, however, I'd like all of you to join me in Doctor Héber's office. I would value your opinions of the crime scene. Madame, I should warn you that there's a dead body on the floor, so prepare yourself."

The Director General grasped the colonel's arm, "Is it necessary for Doctor Héber to witness this? After all, Eugène was a colleague."

"Eugène?" Isabelle gasped. "Is he…?"

The GIS Colonel put his hand on the raven-haired woman's shoulder. "I fear he's dead, Madame." Isabelle plunged her face into her hands to hide the tears flooding her eyes. "We must ascertain what they've taken. Are you willing?"

"I'll help however I can."

Del Carlo looked squarely into Isabelle's dark eyes. "We've covered the corpse, but the scene is macabre. Nevertheless, I would like for you to identify anything that has been taken or moved. Can you do that?"

"I think so."

"Try not to look at the body," he counseled, "just the surroundings."

Isabelle took a deep breath, steeling herself as she walked into her laboratory. She had been to funerals before and seen dead bodies, but they

had been coiffed and dressed in their best clothes to appear at peace. She
was unprepared for the indistinct outline of a body on its back, covered
by a white plastic sheet, or the viscous red that spread across the floor,
as well as fiery spots splattered on the walls. Isabelle felt as though she
was rising off the ground, weightless. Shadows crept into her peripheral
vision and closed in from all sides. Pascal tightened his arm around her
narrow shoulders, too late. Her legs gave way before her father could
react. Romano caught her just as she slumped to her knees.

Del Carlo pulled up a chair, and Romano eased her slight frame
into it. Her eyes fluttered. She tried not to look at the contorted
outline under the white sheet or the scarlet pool seeping from underneath. "Isabelle?" Father Romano said to her. "Isabelle," he called
louder and broke the trance.

"Yes."

"You don't need to do this." The priest held her hand. "I can take
you out of here."

Isabelle squeezed his palm. "I'll be alright."

"How well did you know him?" *Colonelo* Del Carlo asked.

She answered from a far away place, "Not personally. He was
a graduate student who wanted to work at the Archives when he
completed his studies. He visited the lab often and asked technical
questions about restoring old documents."

"What's out of place?"

The archivist's eyes went first to a rack of shelves. The steel cover
had been detached from her computer processor. She forced herself
out of the chair and edged gingerly around the body for a closer
inspection. "They've removed the hard drive. Nothing's left."

"I thought as much," the colonel accepted with resignation. "Has
anything else been taken?"

Isabelle walked the perimeter of the room, passing her hand
over books and equipment, but avoiding the bloody spots. Finally
she turned to Del Carlo. "Nothing. They got what they came for."

"Thank you for your courage, Doctor Héber. I'm sorry for subject-
ing you to this grisly scene, but I needed to confirm what I believed
to be true. Why don't we talk outside?"

The Director General led them to the conference room at the end of the hall.

Isabelle addressed no one in particular. "Why was there so much blood?"

"He was tortured," Del Carlo said.

"My God."

"They cut his jugular veins."

"His throat?" She shuddered.

"Not the throat, just the veins. They probably forced him to tell what he knew."

"He must have surprised them and tried to stop them." Isabelle noticed the Director General hang his head.

"They didn't break in, Doctor." Del Carlo said.

"You can't believe Eugène opened the door?"

"That's precisely what I think."

Pascal listened with a professor's objective interest, weighing what had been explained. Then with conviction, he spoke a single word, "*Shochetim*."

"Excuse me?" The colonel answered while the entire room looked, uncomprehending, at the retired professor.

"I'm sorry, *Monsieur Colonel*, but you're wrong."

"About what?"

"It's quite logical," Pascal said. "If these men wanted information, they would have inflicted a great deal of pain on the poor boy. They did no such thing. The only discomfort Eugène endured was the slash on his neck. I'm guessing they used a razor, possibly a straight razor."

"That's what we suspect."

"Did you ever witness someone having their throat slashed?"

"No," Del Carlo admitted.

"Had they cut just one jugular, blood would spurt out rapidly. The heart is a remarkable pump, as you can see by the spots on the walls. Within several seconds, he would lose so much oxygen to the brain that he'd be groggy. They cut both, so the loss of pressure rendered him unconscious almost immediately. He didn't say anything."

"How do you know this?"

Pascal shrugged. "Nothing suspicious, I assure you. This is how Jews slaughter animals for kosher meat. The *Shochetim* are the slaughterers."

"Are you suggesting Jewish butchers killed him?"

"Don't be ridiculous, but look at the facts. Eugène was bound and placed on his back, the prescribed position for slaughtering animals, according to Jewish law. Then they cut his jugulars and he bled to death—or rather, he was bled. What I suggest is that the men who murdered him were familiar with traditional methods of sacrificial slaughter. They didn't do it quite right, however. They were supposed to sever his trachea and esophagus, leaving the spinal cord intact. Maybe they were squeamish?"

"What do you mean, sacrifice?"

"If I understand correctly, a priest was murdered for a religious book, and now it's been stolen. The killers bled Eugène to death like a lamb on an altar. This might be a religious killing."

Pascal now had the GIS Colonel's attention. "I want to speak more about this, this..."

"Sacrifice."

"Yes. But first, can I talk with you in private, Father?" Del Carlo nodded to *Capitaine* Desmoulins, who opened the door and ushered everyone out. Pascal cast an encouraging glance at the priest as he helped his daughter. Romano acknowledged him with a nod and half-smile.

The librarian knew Colonel Del Carlo was about to chew him out. Sure, he felt culpable, but also defensive, and he bridled as he anticipated the reproach. He had the same feeling as a child waiting for a beating, guilty but still prepared to defend himself. Nevertheless, it was a rebuke that didn't come.

"Listen, Father..."

"Call me Mike."

"Okay, Mike. I told you in Rome I trusted you. God help me, I still do, although I don't know why. It should be obvious now that this is an organized group that will stop at nothing. Another man is dead, and they've taken what they were after."

"Do you still believe these people, the Children of the Book, are behind it?" Romano asked the colonel.

"They're my only lead. I've sent inquiries to Washington. Unfortunately, we've lost the one piece of evidence we had, and I discover the book is more valuable than we thought. How would you value the Psalter now?"

The priest didn't hesitate. "Priceless."

"Theft might be a motive. The black market for rare documents is voracious."

"No one else understood what the Psalter actually was. I only discovered the truth tonight."

"Maybe the Pope's Secretary guessed, and perhaps he took it from the Vatican to verify what he suspected, just as you did."

"He certainly had the same interest in certain prayer books produced by one scribe in particular."

"Since we no longer have the evidence, perhaps you can tell me what the professor meant by what you discovered underneath, and why the book is priceless." Del Carlo retrieved a notepad from his suit jacket pocket.

Romano explained the theory that the Gospels had been originally composed in Aramaic, the dialect of Jesus and the Apostles, and translated later into Greek, and that none of the Aramaic scriptures had ever been discovered. However, the Psalter had been copied over an erased page of parchment, and the original text was the only first-century scripture in existence written in the language of the Son of God. Thus, the document was likely the most valuable in the world, and no price could be placed on it.

Colonelo Del Carlo listened intently while he scratched notes. He stopped the priest at a pause in his explanation. "What did the page say, Father?"

Romano thought for a moment. "It said the Apostle Thomas was Jesus' twin brother."

"I've never heard of such a thing."

"I work in the Secret Archives, *Colonelo*. I've heard that and much more. To think those words were written by Christians; moreover, to suspect they might be true."

Del Carlo thought for a long moment. "Father, have you considered that perhaps these men were hired to steal the book, not for the monetary value, but because of what the text reveals—or more to the point, to keep it from being revealed?"

The vice-prefect of the Secret Archives had tried not to think about it, but the very suspicion had crept into his mind. "As I told you, the only other person who might have guessed the book contained a concealed text was the Pope's own Secretary."

"Who paid with his life. How would Father Mackey have known this prayer book held hidden scriptures?"

The librarian explained about the ninth-century monk who worked in the *scriptorium* as a scribe, whose prayer books always seemed to be written over erased heretical scrolls; the monk whose unique calligraphy was out of place among the scribes in Rome; the monk he had nicknamed Giovanni.

"You're an American, Father. What's the English translation for Giovanni?"

"John, or in Latin, we say Johannes."

"What can you tell me about this monk?"

"Not much, but some things I can guess at. He lived during a turbulent, violent era in Rome's history, the church's history."

13
Hall of Blasphemy

November in the Year of Our Lord 843

What can you be thinking, Johannes, to go out in the middle of the night to the Jewish quarter?" Anastasius was red-faced despite the chill in his cell that the brazier could not drive out. "Not only is it dangerous, you were seen."

"Baraldus was right. We were being watched," Johannes said more to himself, but loud enough for the Archive *primicerius* to hear.

"Of course you're watched. This is not some monastery in the countryside. We're in the *patriarchum*, the capitol of Christendom, where Pope Gregory rules and many are impatient to unseat him. You were missed at Vespers, and I listened to more than one whisper that you were half asleep at Lauds. Everyone spies on everyone."

Johannes grew defensive. "I've done nothing wrong. I simply wished to speak to the head of the Jewish school. You sound as though I've committed some iniquity."

Anastasius softened his voice, trying to maintain composure. "War is about to erupt, and we have few allies. I chose you to be my *secundarius* not just because of your intellect but your independence, as well. You're a foreigner and owe no allegiance to any family, but you've displayed a famine of intelligence and copious independence."

Johannes tried to defend himself to the man he had come to admire more than anyone on earth. "I know the Emperor fights his brothers in a civil war, but I've heard it's over. And everyone knows the Norse attack Normandy, Francia, and Germania, while the Saracens occupy Sicily and Brindisi in the south. They've taken Messina, but the battles are far from here."

"Can you be so thickheaded?" Anastasius said, exasperated. "It's not Vikings or Arabs we must fear."

Johannes realized he didn't understand what his master was trying to tell him and bowed his head at his ignorance. The librarian rose and placed a comforting hand on the young priest's tonsured red hair, then walked to the warmth of the brazier and pulled his shawl around. "Forgive me, brother," Anastasius said with his back turned.

"Help me to understand."

The Librarian returned to his desk. "War is being waged right under your nose, my friend."

A theological battle?"

"It's the theology of power. Alas, Pope Gregory is not long for the throne of Saint Peter. He's getting older, and the vultures gather. I believe the masters of Rome will not let him rule much longer. The pendulum of sovereignty swings in another direction."

The young priest was shocked at the implication. "You can't be saying someone would dare lift a hand against the Holy Father?"

"It has happened before. Nevertheless, whether some pretender to the Apostle's throne takes Gregory's life or he passes naturally, many wish to seize the papal crown. Listen to me for I shall need of your brain if we're to survive the firestorm that's sure to come."

Johannes dragged his chair across the cold tiles, close to his master's desk, and gazed into the librarian's tired eyes. He couldn't help but admire the chiseled, handsome face that might have adorned any grand palace, but chose to shine for the church.

"The princes of the city are angry with Gregory, believing he spends too much time pandering to Emperor Lothair. Gregory named many Franks as bishops instead of Romans, and they try to impose the Emperor's will in the Papal Palace. Rome's aristocracy may fight each other to the death on most issues, but they're unified in their resolve to take back the Papacy, by force if necessary."

Johannes was aghast. "How is this possible? The *Constitutio Romana* of 824 gives all Romans, ordinary citizens as well as nobles, equal voice in the election of the pope. Then the pope-elect must swear an oath of allegiance to the Emperor before he can ascend the throne of Saint Peter."

"You studied law as well as the scriptures. The constitution was meant to end the domination of the Roman gentry over the papacy, but Lothair has not kept his eye on the Holy See. He spends all his time trying to save his own empire from his greedy brothers who covet his lands and would put him in his grave if they could. And Roman aristocrats grow bold in the Emperor's absence."

"You, too, are from a noble house, are you not?"

"True, and my clan traces our ancestors further than most of these rascals who invent absurd genealogies all the way to Romulus and Remus. We're an international family, having relations through-out the empire. I, too, could have been a prince of the city, more powerful even than Theophylact. But because of my family's foreign influence, we're mistrusted. The Roman nobles suspect we support Emperor Lothair."

"Do you?"

A shadow flitted at the door, which was ajar. Anastasius crept across the room and jerked it open. No one was outside, so he pushed it shut and slid the bolt. "What words are spoken here are for your ears alone. You realize we're forbidden to discuss the successor to the Pope while he still lives, on pain of excommunication?"

"Of course. Pope Boniface's decree."

"Well, that's what I'm about to do. If you feel compelled to leave, I'll understand and harbor no ill feelings. Should you choose to stay, I require your oath that you'll repeat what you hear to no living soul."

"You need not my vow. Nevertheless I swear."

"I knew I could count on you, so listen well. Three powers desire the papacy, and two will usurp it for their own ends. Emperor Lothair holds the lawful authority, but the reality of his power is far less than he would wish. Nonetheless, his is the only army large enough to protect us from foreign invaders, especially the Saracens. Alas, he's been too busy fighting his own brothers to give the heathens much thought."

"A family feud." Johannes said.

"Siblings waging war to fight for their birthright. When Lothair's father died, he claimed the whole Empire, even though his father had divided the land amongst all of the brothers. So Lothair's brothers combined forces and defeated him. Lothair was left with only the Kingdom of Italy and the title of Holy Roman Emperor. He has authority over Rome, but his power has been greatly weakened."

"Then, legally, Lothair rules the church and the Roman nobles as well. No one can question his sovereignty."

"The right to rule comes with an obligation to defend. While Lothair and his brothers are squabbling over their inheritance, the Saracens have met little resistance and conquered not only Sicily, but also have a foothold on the mainland. Many feel the Emperor cannot be counted on to defend Rome. The most radical families believe he relinquished his right to rule us."

Johannes began to view the conflict clearly. "Of course the nobles would love nothing more than to rule the church and Rome. Do they think they can do a better job protecting the city? They've lost every campaign against the Arabs."

"The fight is not about who is better able to defend. That's an excuse offered by both sides. It's about who rules the land and the church and the wealth they yield."

"You said three factions. Who's the third?"

"Why, the people themselves."

"The people?" Johannes was incredulous. "How can commoners organize to back a single candidate, one who could win? Romans argue about everything, even the time of day. Neither do they have the slightest influence in the *patriarchum*."

"We must help them. The papacy was not meant to be a mere pawn of influential families, no matter how royal. The church is for all, not just the gentry."

Johannes saw by his sternly set jaw that the librarian had conceived more than just a philosophy; he had a mission. "Do the people support a candidate for the next pope?"

"They do. A man low of birth yet noble of intellect, much like you. Godly in spirit, he's a deacon of the church, Deacon John Hymonides."

Johannes knew the deacon from his days as an acolyte scrubbing parchment. He appeared every morning in front of the Lateran Palace in a plain brown frock, distributing bread and meat to the poor. The church's policy was to distribute a loaf, a cup of meat and two cups of wine to but one hundred of the city's unfortunates, a fraction of those in need.

Johannes marveled how the good Deacon devised ways to divide food to serve many more than the pittance of one hundred. He was reminded of Jesus feeding five thousand from five loaves of bread and two fish. Some of Rome's destitute were given meat and others bread, depending upon their need. The loaves were torn in half and little wine was dispensed. Many a morning Johannes had spied Baraldus leaving after Matins, pushing a wheelbarrow loaded with small casks only to return with bread and vegetables which were added to the provisions. Johannes suspected that at the bidding of Deacon John, Baraldus traded wine in the village for food, of which the piteous unfortunates had greater need. "Of course," Johannes said realizing the obvious choice, "such a man would make the perfect pope; a Holy Father from the people and for the people."

"But like the people, John will need all the help we can give."

"So who will be the Nobles' candidate?"

Anastasius sighed heavily, "Alas, Archpriest Pietro di Porca."

"Hogsmouth? You can't be serious. He cares for nothing except singing and his stomach. Who would cast their lot behind such a man?"

"Don't underestimate Pietro. He's shrewd and conniving. He was not promoted to Archpriest for his voice alone. More importantly, he's Theophylact's man and commoners recognize him. Why do you think he performs in the *piazzas* and churches all over Rome? The man is vain of course, but he publicizes his name since he knows well

that the next pope needs at least some support from the commoners."
Anastasius rubbed his eyes. "Now my young friend, I must attend
to many things, so tell me why you're buying skins from the Jews
when we keep ample parchment in the *scrinium*."

"But who will be the Emperor's candidate?" Johannes edged forward in his chair.

"The Emperor chose me."

"You? What was all this talk about a pope for the people? Weren't
you serious?"

"Of course I was. I am! I just don't think they can win, not yet.
We will try, but we cannot win."

"Are you saying you would hand over the papacy to the Emperor
to wrest it from the Roman nobles?" Johannes grinned.

"It's not my idea, but my uncle's, Bishop Arsenius. If we can't
deliver Christ's church to the citizens in a single decisive blow, then
we must wage a war of attrition and weaken these greedy families."

"Your uncle's a wise man," Johannes said. "When faced with two
devils, let them fight each other. Perhaps once they're both weakened,
we can win."

"Exactly what my uncle said, but I pray his plan won't be necessary, for I don't desire to sit on Saint Peter's throne. I weary of the
politics of the *obedientiary* officers who attend his Holiness and
administer the will of the church. Leave me to my books. Now, what
about the parchment?"

Johannes stammered. "I…well…"

"Out with it, Brother."

"I want to build an archive."

"An archive?" Anastasius laughed. "Is that all? This is an archive.
Why would you rebuild what already exists?"

"That's not what I meant. I wish to make…a secret archive."

Anastasius frowned and eyed his assistant with suspicion. "What
do you mean *secret*?"

"Writings of history, philosophy, mathematics, and other works
must not be destroyed. We're obliterating thousands of years
of knowledge."

"Such literature is of great value, I grant you. I myself kept scrolls from being turned into prayer books for scarcely literate priests and nobles who play at piety. But there's no need to keep them secret, and what do you mean by *other works*?"

"Alright, I think it's wrong to destroy scriptures just because they're judged heresies."

"You don't agree with the Holy Father, who said such works are sacrilege and words of the Devil who would plant tares to deceive the faithful?"

"I don't know, but that's not the point."

"So tell me, Johannes Anglicus, what is the point?"

He reflected for a moment, not because he was uncertain in his conviction but rather, he wanted to say what he meant. "I was studying a text, scriptures on the finest vellum written by an unknown author. Half the pages had been ripped out. I had almost resigned to give the damaged book to my assistant to erase when my eyes chanced on a passage. Mary was speaking to the disciples. At first I believed it must be Jesus' mother. Then I read that the Apostle Peter called her sister and I realized he was referring to Mary Magdalene." Anastasius nodded his head. "Well who cares which Mary, but I thought, what if I destroyed the true words of Mary Magdalene or worse, the Holy Virgin? Would that not be a bigger sin than disobeying the church? I couldn't bring myself to destroy the text." Johannes bowed his head as he admitted his disobedience. "I'm afraid I possess quite a large pile of similar scrolls and codices."

Anastasius leaned on his forearms halfway across his desk. "So you wish to save them."

"The church believes they're heresy since many of the books contradict our doctrines of faith, but we must consider the historical value. And God forgive me, what if some are faithful records of Our Lord and his Apostles. So I thought…"

"You thought of making a, how did you put it, *secret archive* to house these banned books…only for an historical record, of course." Anastasius spoke with feigned scorn. "Hence, you need to buy animal skins to replace the scrolls you would put into a *secret archive*."

"Yes."

Anastasius appeared to ponder the notion. "You're not the first to contemplate such an idea. At your age, I told my old mentor, Father Paulus, I wanted to create a hall of blasphemy. He told me that in his youth he had made the same request of his *primicerius*. He didn't allow it of me, so I submitted to what he believed was for the good of the church, although I always regretted it. In truth, Johannes Anglicus, I believe through you, I might be able to right a wrong."

"You mean to say..."

"Yes, I give my permission."

Johannes leapt out of his chair in jubilation.

"Sit down and listen well." Anastasius was stern. Johannes took his seat, leaning on the edge of the desk, focused on his master's face. "It's a dangerous game you play. We're already mistrusted by most, and I was serious when I told you we are watched and now you know why. Find somewhere hidden where you can store the scrolls. I would search for a place outside the city. The building must be dry and well protected. Most of all, tell no one."

"I won't say a thing except to my assistant, and he can scarcely read." Johannes giggled in glee at their academic conspiracy.

"You mean Baraldus?"

"Yes."

"Umm, he's a good man. Keep him close. He was a soldier once, a captain, quite heroic if a little overbearing. A rather unlikely person to become a priest, but just the one to have at your side in a pinch." The Library *primicerius* added, "The scripture you were reading...?"

"Yes?"

"I call it the *Gospel of Mary Magdalene*. The pages were missing when I studied the book years ago. I'm glad you found it. I couldn't destroy it either."

14
Silver Hammer

Johannes stared in disbelief at mountains of scrolls, books, and codices piled around *the Altar of the Confession*, erected over Saint Peter's holy tomb. Mounds of documents surrounded the altar, divided by pathways like pie cuts to allow access to pilgrims and priests. "Thank the Lord, Anastasius sent you," the old priest said. "We have nowhere to put anything else."

The archive *secundarius* lifted a codex from one of the mounds and opened the leather cover. The dusty pages recounted Pope Stephen's Synod of 764 that ended traditional papal elections by Rome's citizens, giving the church a monopoly in naming the Pope. Then Johannes opened a small scroll and read a newly appointed bishop's oath, promising to follow the rules of his diocese—at least, he was newly appointed in the year 609. He skimmed fragments of various documents pulled from the pile: confessions, professions of faith, vows that promised loyalty to a certain pope, as well as vile oaths cursing another. Unfolding a large parchment page, he found a deed to the property of a Duke that had been donated as payment for an *indulgence*, the price paid for forgiveness of an unnamed sin. Johannes thought such a sin must have been great indeed. "Is there a catalog of what's here?" he asked the old priest who stood by.

The frail stick of a priest, Linus, shrugged his shoulders. "No. I'm one of the *mansionarii*, sextons of the basilica. We guard Saint Peter's treasures and vestments, but we have no time nor can we fathom what to do with this…stockpile of parchment. They arrive daily, clerics, penitents, kings, and even His Holiness, adding more writings to the mound. These souls have their own reasons that God should bear witness to their words, so they place them at the Altar. Perhaps they feel closest to Him on this sacred spot, but what do we do with all this? And there's more."

"More?"

The old cleric, wobbly on spindly legs, led Johannes down narrow, stone steps into the grotto beneath the altar. The *secundarius* made the sign of the cross as he spied the tombs of popes past who, though now in eternal repose, had once reigned over the Holy Church. Papers lay scattered across the cold stone floor, and several sarcophagi overflowed with the unmanageable sea of historical records. Johannes' mouth gaped.

"Fear not, Brother," Linus said. "The tombs were empty before I made use of them. Some of the remains were moved to the basilica atrium and others to churches or the catacombs of Saint Callixtus."

Stout Baraldus slid the heavy oak desk against the chilly grotto wall. The thick legs scraped the pavement stone, upsetting the sanctified silence. The acolyte who helped him made the sign of the cross, goosebumps dotting his pasty arms, and sprinted back up the steps. Johannes set his oil lamp on the desk and pulled up a backless chair. "I shall need a brazier to keep the chill off."

"It's not a fit place for you to work, Brother. There's no window, and your poor lamp provides scarcely enough light to read. Besides, the cavern makes my flesh crawl." Baraldus shivered.

"After all the stories you told me of fierce battles against merciless Vikings and outnumbered by dark-skinned Saracens, don't tell me you're afraid?"

"Those were mere mortals and the worst I would have suffered was my miserable death, which I likely deserved. Yet here among the dead, demons and all manner of spirits might be lurking. I fear for my immortal soul."

"My friend," Johannes was sympathetic to his superstitious nature, "if spirits are indeed with us in this chamber, they're the souls of saints and martyrs and popes who followed in the shoes of the fisherman. No evil can enter this holy place."

"Well, maybe that's worse," the hefty priest said. "It makes me feel transparent, as if they're looking right through me."

"Does your soul have anything to fear?"

Baraldus hesitated, then stammered, "I...I've committed many sins for which I'm aggrieved. It's as though someone watches and can see my past crimes."

"Someday, we shall each of us stand before our Lord, reminded of our transgressions, and they will be forgiven."

"I just don't want to be reminded today, thank you very much. Besides, in your young life, I'll wager you have little to confess."

The *secundarius* picked up a document and examined the words. The abbess of a nearby convent had written a curse condemning Pope Stephen II after his election. Johannes shivered. He remembered tales whispered around the *patriarchum* that after his ascension to the papacy, Stephen suffered a fit of apoplexy. There were rumors of poison delivered by an assassin, sent at the behest of one of the noble families who had opposed him. He died a few days later. His was the shortest papacy in history. Perhaps Baraldus' fear of ghosts and demons wasn't so farfetched, after all. Without raising his head Johannes answered the Lombard, "I, too, have my fair share to confess, Brother. Now, go back to the *scrinium*. I need a large book of blank pages, the largest you can find. We must record every scroll, book, and document before they're moved." Johannes studied the texts with care to summarize their contents and list them in his *register.* He saved a column at the end to note where each one had been stored, but where to put everything? Johannes needed a building, or at the least some sizeable rooms—and lots of them.

Rome was littered with thousands of empty mansions, temples, and villas, but these had been abandoned for centuries and lay in ruins. In the second century, Rome had been the largest city in the world, with a population of a million and a half. But with barbarian invasions and the plague, only about twenty thousand souls remained. Most of the noble families and skilled workers had moved to the new capital of the empire, Constantinople, or the ruling capital of the Italian kingdom, Ravenna. Peasants fled to the country to farm a subsistence living, leaving most of the city deserted. Rome had become a delinquent backwater.

To make matters worse, the government sanctioned spoliation: the plundering of buildings, particularly pagan temples, for new construction. Much of Rome was derelict and dangerous. Johannes needed a building in good repair near commerce or a large church. The Vatican was on the far side of the Tiber, outside the city, far from the populace and away from the wreckage.

Johannes finished his daily work cataloguing documents. His eyes were red and bleary from the strain of reading and smoke from the lamp. He climbed out of the grotto and plodded past the *ostiarius*, the basilica's doorkeeper. A light shower blown by a winter wind struck his face, waking him from his work-induced stupor. He pulled the hood down over his brow and wrapped his frayed brown shawl around as he started down the muddy road to the Papal Palace on the other side of Rome. He had scarcely gone two hundred paces when lofty notes from a hymn reached his ears on rain-soaked gusts. Light from an open door leaked onto the road ahead.

He peered into a finely plastered room adorned with intricate mosaics and radiant frescoes. A middle-aged, round priest extended his arms wide and pointed his gaping mouth at the ceiling. A bronze-skinned slave boy held a sheet of music in his two small hands raised over his head. Johannes recognized the Archpriest, Pietro di Porca. He had no desire to speak with him and spun on his heels, but before he managed to flee unnoticed, his name echoed off cavernous walls.

"Oh Brother Johannes."

He turned toward the lump of a priest with gray tonsured hair, waving from the other side of the room. There would be no escape. "Why, Cardinal di Porca," he greeted the richly dressed priest and trotted across the chill stone floor. "I didn't wish to interrupt your beautiful singing."

"I'm practicing a new hymn. What do you think? I wrote it myself."

Johannes was taken aback. He had no idea the Archpriest knew who he was. "I don't know music well." That was a lie. He loved music, especially theory, which he had studied as a student in Athens. He found Greek harmonies more melodious and their rhythms livelier than the somber, single-voice hymns sung in Gregorian chants. "Your singing is magnificent, Cardinal di Porca."

"What do you think of the composition?"

"Well...I only listened to a few lines. I'm not sure..."

"Here, let me perform the whole piece for you. Take a meat pastie and sit, sit."

The archive *secundarius* sat on a cushioned stool beside a table. A plate of small pies lay next to an ewer of aromatic wine. Thinking of Pietro's nickname, Hogsmouth, the young priest willed his lips not to smile.

The Archpriest began the hymn in a soft voice that wept with emotion. As the song progressed, so, too, did his volume, and Pietro's face appeared gripped in rapture. The slave boy stole a glance at Johannes. As he did, one arm drooped, tilting the sheet of music. Hogsmouth cuffed him on the side of the head without missing a note or altering his expression. The lad snapped back to attention.

Johannes recognized the refrain as the first line from one of the Psalms, the *Beatus*. Pietro had paraphrased the verse, inserting every word for beauty he could think of. Some were a stretch of the imagination and others superlatives beyond belief. The metaphors were but old clichés. In short, the composition was worse than ordinary; it was a caricature.

"Well?" Pietro bounced up and down, more like a twittering child than a man of fifty.

"Eminence, you have the voice of an angel."

"But the song, what do you think?"

"It is…." Johannes put his hand
 on his chin as he searched for a diplomatic answer.

"Oh come on, out with it."

"Um, quite poignant."

"I just knew it. My nephew hates my songs, but he's a cretin. Even the priests in the *schola cantorum* don't like them. But with praise from a scholar with your reputation, I shall ask if I can sing the new hymn at Vespers."

Johannes had stuck his foot in it. "Perhaps I shouldn't mention this…?"

"Yes, yes?"

"Well, do you think the governing priests are ready for a work of such…sophistication?" Johannes glimpsed a derisive smirk on the slave boy's lips.

Pietro di Porca seemed to reflect.

"I hate to sound snobbish, but a gifted ear cannot be found in the bunch."

"Right you are, Brother," Pietro said. "I offer many of my own hymns, but they seldom deign to let me perform them. Everyone loves to hear me sing, but, alas, not my songs."

"Why don't I accompany you?"

Pietro's eyes narrowed. "Can you sing?"

"Of course, Eminence."

The portly cardinal began to vocalize in his high voice. Johannes joined in, but sang his own notes a third higher than the melody, forming a harmony.

After the first line, Pietro stopped abruptly. "What are you doing?"

"I'm singing."

"Don't take me for a simpleton. It's obvious you're singing, but I've never heard such sounds."

Johannes smiled knowingly. "It's called harmony. I learned the technique in Athens. It's quite a different sound than chanting in one voice."

Sergius was atwitter with excitement, hopping up and down, his belly rolling underneath his robes. "Can you teach me?"

"Of course. The church is slow to change and their ears are dull, but with harmony, you would show our brethren something new. I only added a second tone, but a third might be added as well."

The corpulent cardinal was beside himself. "Rome has never heard such music. My songs will be the talk of all society, even in the *patriarchum*!"

"Surely music masters will recognize your work for its...innovation. I can also show you which notes make harmonies and how to create them. You could even archive your compositions."

"Of course, a music archive featuring my own hymns; why didn't I think of it? I could compose my own manuscripts and the finest illuminators would illustrate them." Hogsmouth pursed his lips in a pout. "Would I have to put my music in that dreary library beneath the Lateran Palace?"

"In truth, Cardinal, that's why I've come: to inquire whether you might have any rooms available for an archive."

Hogsmouth beamed. "You wish to make a music archive for me, here in the *scola cantorum*?"

"Not exactly, I mean, yes. I need space for the documents stored in Saint Peter's. Now that you mention it, I could design a place for your music collection at the same time. In fact, a music archive added to the other works would be the beginning of a real library."

Pietro di Porca clapped his hands with glee. "We'd hold poetry readings and concerts, and scholars from around the world could study music like in Athens or even Constantinople." The fat Archpriest arched his sparse eyebrows, "Oh, I love this old place. I was raised here, you know?"

"No."

"Oh, yes. Pope Leo chose me to be an acolyte in this very mansion when I was a boy. I have so many fond memories of the place and to think that this beautiful old building might be a library. Oh, Johannes, you've made me so happy. You're the only one in Rome who understands what I want to create." Pietro grabbed the boy and held him close. Rolls of soft, flabby flesh pressed against Johannes' small frame and made his skin crawl. He wondered how to push away from the groping Archpriest without offending him when the peal of a single bell split the evening silence. Pietro recoiled as though God had shaken him with divine hands. Johannes recognized the bell from the basilica of Saint John's Lateran. Another bell from a nearby church tolled, and yet another replied. Clanging resounded all over the city.

"Why would they ring the bells at this hour?" Johannes asked. "Something must be wrong."

Cardinal di Porca buried his round face in pudgy hands. "I know not!"

Johannes ran from the *schola cantorum* into the gloomy darkness, leaping across pools of water in the Vatican countryside, the hem of his robe clutched in his fists. Past the ruined Hadrian's tomb sacked four hundred years earlier by the Visigoth Alaric, he fled over the Sant'Angelo bridge and crossed into Rome.

The defenseless wisp of a priest should have picked a safer path to the *patriarchum* as Baraldus had shown him, farther from the river, but the bells urged him to make haste. Instead, he followed the muddy *via Maior Arenule* that paralleled the Tiber. It was a dangerous, low-lying street that led straight through the *Campus Martius*, the field of Mars, where Rome's proud heroes once walked. Centuries later, only the poorest souls lived their meager lives near the riverbank in the unhealthy air. Fortunately, Johannes reached the corridor between the crumbling Imperial Palace and Tiberian's palace without incident. He lengthened his stride along the paved *via Papale* from the Colosseum to the *patriarchum*.

Mud stained and heaving, he dashed into the *scrinium*. The door to Anastasius' cell was closed. The *secundarius* burst into the room without knocking. Anastasius sat at his desk opposite a deacon, their heads pushed together.

The archive *primicerius* bolted from his chair, but relaxed as he recognized his assistant. "Shut the door Johannes," he said.

"What news? Is it an attack, the Saracens?"

"Worse, it's the Holy Father."

"Gregory? Is he..."

"*Vicedominus* Adrian tapped on Gregory's head three times with the silver hammer, calling his name. His Holiness did not reply. He's gone to his brethren."

Johannes' lip quivered. He had never met the Pope, but Gregory had been God's emissary on earth and represented everything holy.

The man sitting across from Anastasius stood, and the *primicerius* introduced him. "Have you met Deacon John Hymonides?"

The *secundarius* dabbed his eyes with his shawl. "No, but I'm aware of your work with the poor and I read your writings." Turning back to Anatasius, he asked, "His Holiness was old, but seemed in good health. I had no idea he was ill."

"He wasn't ill."

"How did he die?"

"The *vicedominus* said he suffered an attack of apoplexy."

"I saw his holiness last night at the evening meal," Deacon John said. "He became dizzy and slurred his words until he was no longer able to speak, as though he had been struck dumb. His hands and arms went limp, and he sweated freely as if he worked in the hot sun. His breathing was labored."

"Hemlock," Johannes said.

"You know your poisons," Deacon John replied. "I scoured my brain to think what would cause such a seizure. It didn't occur to me that His Holiness might have been poisoned until Cardinal di Porca announced that Gregory had succumbed to apoplexy. Then I knew. Of course, the symptoms are similar, paralysis and dizziness, but not the sweating nor difficulty breathing. I asked to view the body but was refused."

"Hogsmouth told you this? When?"

"This morning after the prayers of *Terse* in the palace dining hall. He said His Holiness died at dawn. Why?"

"I was just with him in the *schola cantorum*. When the first bell rang, he seemed as shocked as I. I thought it was because...well, I asked if he knew why the bells tolled and he said he did not."

Anastasius turned to Deacon John. "They begin even now to weave their web."

"What do you mean?" Johannes felt alarmed.

"Don't you grasp what's happening? The poison would take but a few hours to do its work, so Gregory passed away last night. Yet they tell the senior clerics he died at dawn and the bell announcing his death rings a full day later. Then Hogsmouth denies he knows anything. They're buying time to move their pieces into place. We cannot waste a minute."

Deacon John Hymonides took Anastasius' hand in his own. "I beg you to listen, Brother. I hold no lofty ambitions, and you'll put your life in danger."

"My friend, it must be done for the church. I would do it myself, but the people don't know me, and they love you. Alas, time is not on our side. Your name must be put forward at once so the citizens can be alerted and organize. Then you need to go into hiding and stay alive until the people choose you as pope. The nobles wouldn't dare touch you once you're elected, at least not openly."

"Perhaps, but once you put my name forward, your life in Rome will be over. Worse, when the Emperor discovers that you nominated me instead of standing yourself, you'll lose his favor and his protection. Then Theophylact and the other lords won't hesitate to harm you. This I cannot allow."

"There might be another way." Johannes spoke in a soft, uncertain voice.

Anastasius and the Deacon stared at the young *secundarius*.

"What if Deacon John's name was shouted from the crowd? I mean from the entire crowd at once, a sort of spontaneous proclamation?"

Anastasius looked skeptical. "How could it be done? First, the public must be told that Deacon John is a candidate, and secretly. Then the assembly would have to be prompted to proclaim his name at the right time and loud enough to drown out the nobles. This is a complicated undertaking and John and I are watched. Spies are everywhere."

"I travel unmolested through the city every day."

"Who do you believe might accomplish such a thing?"

Johannes Anglicus smiled slyly. "The most unlikely of Romans."

15
Interregnum

Children wrapped in homespun rags, chosen from penniless families, led Gregory's funeral procession. One of the older boys held a large wooden cross aloft with both hands. Archdeacon Nicholas and the Lateran's *vicedominus*, Cardinal Adrian, trailed side by side, festooned in sumptuous robes covered by sleeveless chasubles. The cardinal priests followed, surrounding a horse-drawn cart. Upon the cart lay Gregory's remains, robed in Papal white, resting on a bier.

Archpriest Pietro di Porca should have led the cardinals, but chose instead to lead the singers of the *schola cantorum* as they chanted mournful *te deums*. His lofty tenor voice rose above the others, angelic yet somehow out of place. The proud aristocracy in their finest fashions marched after the choir, led by Count Theophylact, who measured his pace, leaving an ample gap between the nobility and senior clergy. Rome's commoners followed in a quasi-organized column: common priests, then merchants and artisans, with farmers and the poorest straggling at the end.

The procession stretched more than a mile as it inched from the *patriarchum* to the basilica of *Santi Quattro Coronati*. Johannes walked among the weeping clergy. He spied tall and stately Anastasius ahead, walking next to Deacon John Hymonides. Their heads were bowed and hands tucked inside wide sleeves. As they passed the needy inhabitants of the Colosseum, no whistles or taunts were hurled. Ragged souls crowded outside the arcade and simply fell into step behind the long, creeping line.

All morning, the funeral march trod the streets and broken roads. Citizens filled the ranks, swelling the pageant of mourners. People at the edges were forced further down the parade. The column bulged in the middle like a just-fed snake as it wound through the remains of the Roman forum, once the center of commerce and politics. Now, however, the dilapidated Forum was covered with earth, and oxen grazed on the grasses.

Johannes felt a wave of revulsion as they turned northwest at the basilica of Santa Maria in Aracoeli. Criminals had been executed on the steps, and blood stains tinted the stone a gruesome pink. He was relieved when they had passed it for the blemishless basilica of Saint Mark. Finally reaching the Sant'Angelo bridge, they crossed the Tiber.

The throng filled Saint Peter's to overflowing, and thousands were relegated to the winter chill outdoors. Menacing black clouds threatened to drench the bereaved. Gregory's bier was placed in front of the Altar of the Confession. The mounds of parchment had been nearly emptied, thanks to Johannes' labor. Only a few small piles remained.

Requiem mass lasted the entire day, with the required prayers of the *office of the dead* recited. Five different bishops gave five absolutions, beseeching God's mercy on Gregory. The last was delivered by Anastasius' uncle, Bishop Arsenius. At the appointed hour, Archdeacon Nicholas arose. His subordinate deacons followed, including John Hymonides. They lifted the bier and carried Gregory through the *Door of Death* which led to the grotto, the popes' cemetery beneath the basilica. The bell in the tower tolled and the ring vibrated off stone walls, then softened as the echo faded to stillness.

The clergy followed, descending rough-hewn steps as they chanted hymns with antiphons and responsories. Johannes noted the look of surprise on their faces as they passed the shelves crammed with documents. *Where did they think the mountain of paper had gone,* he thought to himself.

Deacon John scattered salt to exorcise the tomb, and the cardinal priests lowered Gregory's body into a casket of cypress covered with a lead-and-fir exterior. The coffin was closed and carried into the empty crypt. The hovering sextons began to seal the stone even before the assembly climbed out of the grotto.

A crowd of thousands milled in the basilica's *piazza*. At the edges of the throng, they started to disperse. Rivulets of people turned into streams flowing back to the city. Johannes thought he might stop at the *schola cantorum* to consider which rooms would be most accommodating for a library. But in his pensiveness, he had no desire to be confronted by Hogsmouth. So he walked on, carried by the gentle current of common Romans.

It was somehow comforting to share his grief with the rabble who wore no official masks. Tears flowed and snippets of conversations reached Johannes' ear as people related anecdotes about a charity the Pope had shown or a forgiveness bestowed. Some spoke of his untiring efforts to reconcile the Emperor with his greedy sons.

Johannes eavesdropped on a poignant conversation. A mourner held his audience rapt with a tale that the pope's mere blessing had cured his beloved child of an evil malady. The *secundarius* was dabbing at a tear with his sleeve when a hand grabbed his frock and steered him into an unsavory inn, pushing him onto a stool in the darkest corner. Anastasius was out of breath and blew hard. "I saw you leave, but couldn't reach you through the crowd."

"What's happened?"

"I overheard Theophylact speaking to Hogsmouth. The papal election is set for tomorrow."

"Impossible. There must be an *interregnum*, a delay of at least three days."

"Do you think Theophylact or Pietro di Porca care a whit for the law? They need a new pope before Emperor Lothair can react to Gregory's death."

"Perhaps they feel safer asking for forgiveness rather than his permission. The outcome would be more certain."

The innkeeper returned with wine, and Anastasius took an

uncharacteristically long draft. "We must thwart their strategy. What have you done to get Deacon John nominated?"

"Done? There's been no time."

"There's less now. Can you do it or not?"

"By tomorrow? Organize the entire city? It would take a miracle."

"That's what we need, for I fear we've been outwitted." The archivist hung his head. "I'm left with no choice."

"What do you mean?"

"Only one chance is left under the circumstance. I must put my name forward as the Emperor's candidate. Many foreign priests would raise their voices for me."

"Perhaps, but they're not here and can't arrive in time. That's what Theophylact has counted on. The nobles will carry the day. Our only hope is for Lothair to nullify the election. You must get word to him."

"Uncle Arsenius has already sent riders, but Lothair is capricious and shrewd. Should he sense that Hogsmouth has the support of the nobles, he might waver. It rests with me to stop Theophylact."

"If you do this thing, disaster will rain upon your head," Johannes said.

"The count's grip on Christ's Church must end."

Johannes recognized desperation in Anastasius' dark eyes. "I have a day. Let me try."

"My dear friend, thank you for your help, but the game's over."

Johannes Anglicus finished his wine in one long swallow. "I have a day. Promise me you'll do nothing 'til the morrow."

Anastasius shook his head.

"Do you swear?"

"I will wait until tomorrow, but only until the nominations."

Johannes fled the inn, heading toward the Tiber. The going was slow, weaving in and out of mourners shuffling in the opposite direction. He crossed the Jews' Bridge onto Tiber Island, then the *Cestius* Bridge into the Trastevere. The streets were empty even though the sun had not yet set. Shops were closed, their shutters shut. The bustling multi-storied apartment blocks were silent. An eerie calm had settled on the Jewish ghetto.

Johannes easily found the Temple of the Hebrews. Everything, however, looked different in the daytime, less forbidding. In the light, he saw that the synagogue had been fashioned with simple, straight lines in a massive rectangle with a triangular gabled entry, like the elegant classical buildings of ancient Greece. It was larger than he remembered. He reckoned that a thousand would fit inside the stone walls.

He rapped on the door of the Rosh Yeshiva's low, brick house next to the temple until it opened narrowly. A dark-bearded face peered from the opening. "Ah, Father Johannes," the voice said in a hushed tone. The hide merchant, Elchanan HaKodesh, widened the opening a bit more.

"I must talk to your father."

"The Rosh Yeshiva confers with rabbis of the city. These meetings often last long into the night. I mean no disrespect, but tomorrow would be better."

"Can he not spare a few—"

"Do I hear the young priest's voice?" Avraham's welcoming face greeted Johannes from the foyer. "Enter, enter. Such a coincidence; I was just speaking to my colleagues about the learned priest from the *patriarchum*." He placed aged hands on Johannes' slight shoulders. "I'm sorry to learn of Gregory's passing. I have called for seven days of mourning and reflection out of respect for His Holiness."

Johannes' mouth gaped.

"Don't look so surprised. Is a holy man not deserving?" Come in and meet the rabbis. They sit with me for what we call *Shivah*, a deep mourning. I'm sure they would like to express their sympathy, and I made far too many cakes as usual. You can help us eat them while we mourn together."

Johannes held the Rosh Yeshiva's sleeve, "If I might speak to you privately, a matter of great urgency."

"Of course, my son. My old colleagues and I have all night, but youth is impatient."

Johannes scarcely knew where to begin. He started with an abbreviated description of the political powers in the Lateran Palace that jockeyed for supremacy, then bumbled through a recital of the nobles calling for an unlawful election. Finally, the *secundarius* launched into a disjointed explanation that the clergy needed to take back the church from the rapacious aristocracy. Johannes was flustered at his inability to condense a volume into a few logical points.

The Rosh Yeshiva held up his hand. "What do you require?"

The priest could tell from the rabbi's face that, despite his rambling, Avraham had grasped all. "I need a miracle," Johannes said. "I know the people would elect Deacon John Hymonides if given half a chance, for he's their champion. But Count Theophylact plans to elect a puppet before the citizens get wind of an election."

"And before Lothair arrives, of course."

"The people are our only hope. But how can I alert an unsuspecting city of thousands to come to the *patriarchum* tomorrow to elect a new pope?"

"You alone can do little, but come inside and let's discuss your conundrum. Many wise men sit at my humble table."

"There's no time. I must do something now. Where can I turn?"

"To us. I said you could do little since scarce time remains, but that doesn't mean naught can be done. I entreat you to join us and rest while we debate the problem. If a miracle can be discovered, I'm sure we can find one together."

Avraham led the priest into the kitchen, where a dozen bearded rabbis sat on benches around the long table. They rose as one, bowing, "Shalom." Then they began to offer condolences, but the Rosh Yeshiva stopped them. "There will be plenty of time to express our sympathy. First, we need to discuss a matter of great urgency, but I beg you, no debates. An answer must be found, and we must find it tonight."

"Where were you?" Baraldus huffed. "I've been looking everywhere. Have you heard the election has been called for tomorrow?"

"Yes."

"Well?"

"Well, what?"

"What are we to do?"

"All that can be done has been done. It's in God's hands and in some other, unlikely ones. Now I'm exhausted and I'm going to bed."

Johannes retired to his cell as the front door slammed and Baraldus barged out into the night.

16
The Election

Rome's aristocratic families flocked to their clans in the *piazza* facing the *patriarchum*. They congregated around tall poles flying colorful pennants held aloft by pageboys. Nearest the palace stood the most ancient family of Anacii, whose patriarch stood self-importantly in the center. Next to the Anacii was Theophylact's clan, the Tusculani. Behind them, the Crescentii, Frangipani, and Pierleone had staked out their places. Lesser nobles formed a rear guard.

Clergymen tried to squeeze to the front between the clans, but the aristocrats closed ranks, as if on cue, to block their way. Johannes and sturdy Baraldus gave up trying and wedged themselves into a gap far from the ceremonies. The great palace doors swung open. *Vicedominus* Adrian and Archdeacon Nicholas filed onto the terrace, staffs in hand, followed by Theophylact and Archpriest Pietro di Porca. Straining his eyes, Johannes barely made out Anastasius, who had stationed himself in the shadows just inside the door.

Vicedominus Adrian began with a wordy blessing of the crowd, then an interminable prayer of thanksgiving. After long minutes, the throng, shuffling and agitated, would have no more. A voice rang out, "Give us a pope!" When Adrian tried to continue, others added their voices. Soon the entire crowd chanted, "Give us a pope!"

Silenced, old Adrian retreated, leaving Theophylact to take his place. The tall, glowering Count held up his hand and the crowd quieted. "Citizens of Rome, noble brethren. "We elect our pope by popular acclaim according to the *constitutio romanum*. Your raised voices will name the new Holy Father, and I know of only one man in Christendom who merits Peter's Holy Chair. He's a Prince of the Church who fills the poor with joy, traveling even to their miserable slums to sing his hymns. He's patrician of blood, as befits the Pontiff, and we find him without equal. Therefore, I put forth the name of my beloved uncle, Cardinal and Archpriest Pietro di Porca!"

The noble families cheered while behind them, the astonished clergy whispered to one another in disbelief, "Hogsmouth?" Grumbling from the rear grew to a low rumble, then ominous thunder as defiant Romans chanted derisively, "Hogsmouth, Hogsmouth, Hogsmouth," which quieted the aristocrats. They turned to glare at the disagreeable priests. Nevertheless, Theophylact was an expert at crowd control despite his youth, having commanded panicked soldiers. "Calm yourselves!" He shouted. "Quiet, I say! If you have a name, put it forward. Yet I hear nothing but jeers. Do you malign your betters? Shame on you. No one is so deserving as my blessed uncle, and if any man says otherwise, let him face me. What, do I hear no derision now? If there's another, make him known. If not, I demand a vote, and I say Pietro di Porca will be pope."

Anastasius stepped onto the porch, challenged by frowning stares from the *vicedominus* and Archdeacon as well as the assembled cardinals. But the fiercest glare came from Theophylact. Johannes' heart sank as he realized his master was about to destroy his life in the church. The *primicerius* tried to speak, but the nobles drowned out his voice, shouting, "Pietro! Give us Pietro!"

Clerics in the crowd responded with a louder chant of, "Fie on Hogsmouth!" On the uneven border between patricians and priests, skirmishes erupted, with shoving and curses hurled back and forth. Even Theophylact could no longer control the mêlée which threatened to spiral into a riot. Then a wave of quiet washed over the astonished mob. Every head turned in the direction of the city.

Over the crest of the Caelian hill marched a multitude of commoners garbed in homespun tunics, headed purposefully for the chaotic election. Half an hour passed as thousands pressed around the assembly. A reed of a man who donned ill-fitting rags, a capuchon pulled low over his face, jostled and squeezed between people who grumbled at his rudeness until he forced his way next to Johannes.

Theophylact seized on the calm to reassert his nomination. "Good people of Rome," he sounded more uncertain. "A single name has been submitted." The count pulled a red-faced Pietro forward by his sleeve. "I demand that we elect him and unite Rome."

No voices came from the buzzing crowd. Aristocrats and priests alike turned to gauge which way the wind blew with the capricious, dangerous rabble. Anastasius had positioned himself next to Theophylact and raised his hand. The slight man next to Johannes raised his in response. Hands rose at various parts of the sea of commoners, like sentries signaling. Someone nudged Johannes in the ribs and the man next to him muttered, "Deacon John." Twenty paces away a disembodied voice also said, "Deacon John." Military Sentries all over repeated, "Deacon John," louder and louder until the multitude picked up the refrain crying out as one, "Deacon John, Deacon John!"

The congregation of clergy took up the chant, flooding the air with the name. Nobles hollered "Pietro" in response, but their appeals went unheard, drowned out by the roar of thousands.

From the rear of the pandemonium, voices shouted, "God bless our pope." Someone found John Hymonides, and he was lifted upon broad shoulders. Crowds gathered 'round to kiss the hem of his plain brown robe. The swarm of humanity formed into a phalanx with the deacon raised in the center. They sliced forward into the blockade of nobles. Aristocratic clans were split apart as the wedge gained momentum, thrusting to its mark like a slow but unstoppable spear.

Hogsmouth sobbed on the porch as a glowering Theophylact barred the *patriarchum* door. He was thrown aside by a torrent of commoners, their human flood bursting in and delivering John to the foot of the papal throne. Turning to the congregation, tears rolled down John's face and dripped on his robe. The palace filled to overflowing as Rome's humblest citizens mingled with clerics caught up in the surge.

Johannes elbowed his way to the front just in time to watch Anastasius raise the golden papal tiara. Gasps from awed parishioners echoed against stone walls as he lowered the crown reverently on his friend's head. Anastasius took a step back and dropped to his knees. "Your Holiness." The throng also kneeled and said as one, "God bless Pope John."

In mid afternoon near the prayer hour of None, the congregation began to file out of the *patriarchum*. Johannes felt a nudge from behind. He turned to face two men in cloaks, their hoods pulled low. Their mysterious, dark capuchons reminded Johannes of the angels who had appeared to Lot in the city of Sodom. He recognized the small man who had stood beside him in the courtyard speaking Deacon John's name, which had started an avalanche of voices. The man raised his bowed head to reveal a frizzy white beard encircling a beaming smile.

"Rabbi Avraham!"

"Shhh." The Rosh Yeshiva put his finger to his lips. "I'm not sure we're welcome here." The rabbi's son, Elchanan, also revealed his face to Johannes.

"So it was you who worked this miracle," the priest said.

"I have long wished to see the inside of the *patriarchum*." He flashed his sly grin, "but we played only a small part."

"How did you do it in less than a day?"

"We're humble Jews, yet have many customers and suppliers in Rome, along with friends who were delighted to help. Nevertheless, this thing could not have been done without your indefatigable and resourceful Baraldus. He procured these marvelous costumes, although how he did it in the middle of the night is truly miraculous. Do I not look like a gentile?"

"More even than the most pious pilgrim. But how—?"

"Our people did what we could and it was a great deal, but it would not have been enough. Nonetheless, word spread like wild-fire throughout all of Rome. Your Lombard knows every innkeeper, trader, and soldier, as well as most of the merchants in the city. The man is a veritable one-man message service."

"Yet I watched Anastasius give a signal and you appeared to repeat it."

"That was Baraldus' idea. We were spread out in the crowd, but a fire needs a spark at just the right time. Your assistant said Anastasius was the only man who would know it and could get access to the dais."

"How I can ever repay you?"

"There's no need to repay goodness except to pass it on to others, and that I know you shall do."

"Thanks to you and Baraldus and God's own grace, we've won."

"Have you? Rejoice today and then take care. Be wary of the dangerous days ahead, Scholar. Be neither too sweet unless you would be eaten up nor bitter lest you would be spewed out. Find the middle road. But if you wish to repay a debt, come visit me and eat my cakes." The Rosh Yeshiva pulled his capuchon low and took his leave with Elchanon at his side.

Thousands of commoners lazed in the *piazza*, singing songs and hymns they had committed to memory accompanied by lyres, lutes, and fipple flutes. Crowds formed around impromptu musical ensembles, clapping and dancing. Fires were lit in the late afternoon to warm the winter gathering, giving the wide courtyard the festive atmosphere of a holiday celebration.

Johannes walked among the crowd, smiling as he basked in the fraternity of people who rejoiced in a new pope who had sprung from their own humble masses. Passing from group to group, he nodded to calls of, "Bless you, Father," or, "God bless the Holy Church," or, "Bless Pope John Hymonides." Winds of change blew in Rome, and ordinary citizens refreshed themselves in its cleanness.

The Lamps had been lit in the Papal Palace when Johannes made his lighthearted way to the *patriarcum's* Basilica for evening prayers. Pietro di Porca, the *vicedominus* and Archdeacon, who descended from patrician families, were absent from Vespers, as were the obe-dientiary officers. It seemed an obvious slight to John and a rebellion against the changing of the guard, but that would change as time passed. If not, John could appoint an administration of his own.

Johannes took his place next to Anastasius, who showed only the slightest hint of a conspiratorial grin before they fell comfortably into the first of four psalms of Vespers. The *secundarius* recited automatically, his mind wandering. He would insist that Anastasius and Baraldus relate every detail of their parts in the magnificent coup. They finished the *kyrie eleison* and had just begun the *Christie eleison* when a low-pitched rumble invaded his reverie. *Thunder*, he wondered as it reverberated closer. *No*, he realized. *Hooves*.

Shrill screams and the clanging of battle cleaved the peace outside. The basilica doors burst open and warhorses charged into God's house. Hooves clattered on pavement stones, flinging priests hither and fro. Theophylact led troops, swinging his broad sword as panicked clerics scattered. He spurred his charger into the central nave, galloping up its length to the altar while foot soldiers with long pikes rushed behind and herded priests to the outer walls of the basilica.

The mounted Count pinned Pope John to the altar with his charger. It snorted white spume on John's face and robe. John tried to flee, but the well-trained warhorse lunged and blocked his escape. Theophylact dismounted, death blazing in his eyes, his blade gripped at his side. Discerning his master's step out of one fiery eye, the giant horse clopped backward, relinquishing the attack to the count. Theophylact seized Pope John by the collar of his habit and dragged him to the ground. "So you would be pope, would you?" Venom dripped from his words. "You son of a whore from the filthy streets." He raised his broad sword high over his head. Pope John stared, unflinching, into the count's murderous eyes.

"Stop!" The shrill voice from the back of the basilica. "Please, nephew, I beg you." Pietro di Porca wrung his soft hands at the entrance. He stood sandwiched between *vicedominus* Adrian and Archdeacon Nicholas. They had accompanied the small army to the *patriarchum*.

Theophylact's lethal trance was broken, and he came to himself. He scanned the basilica. Priests and soldiers alike stared, aghast, at the scene.

Even nobles shook their heads in horror. Johannes thought Hogsmouth had won a reprieve for John until he heard his voice say, "Do it outside."

"Seize him," the count said. Two sergeants grabbed Pope John by his arms and dragged him behind Theophylact down the nave. The foot soldiers, all of common stock, watched as horrified as the priests.

A young soldier holding a pike to Johannes' chest, mouth agape at the Pope's humiliation, lowered it unwittingly. Johannes leapt over the shaft and charged forward to block Theophylact's retreat. "Enough," he barked in the count's face with his youth's green voice. "How dare you touch His Holiness?"

Taken aback at this affront for but an instant, Theophylact struck the *secundarius* with the hilt of his sword, knocking him to the floor. "The next one who tries to stop me will feel the bite of my blade," he said. He motioned the sergeants forward but Johannes, hunched over and spitting blood, threatened Hogsmouth, "Pietro, if you allow this, then, by the saints, there'll be no music archive."

"I can do nothing. It's the will of God," Hogsmouth said.

"Then I swear I will never teach you harmonies and I will discredit your music with every stroke of my pen. Your songs will be ill regarded and forgotten before you're even dust in the grave." Johannes' icy glare pierced the Archpriest's soft exterior.

"I am to be the rightful Pope, and I will order you."

"If you can do naught, so too can I do nothing. I will be a humble priest or even a layman. That you cannot stop. But you won't have your music, and I'll write of the wicked pope who murdered a pope to seize his crown. Your legacy will be most foul and your songs will be unsung and forgotten, I swear."

Noble cardinals who hated Pietro's songs smirked. Common priests, aghast at the sacrilege of the holy *patriarchum* defiled by blood and armed troops, murmured in agreement. Even the soldiers, fearful for their immortal souls, nodded hopefully.

Hogsmouth grasped that if he allowed John Hymonides to be slaughtered, his papacy would indeed be stained: power without authority.

Worse, he would be forever beholden to Theophylact. He had but one chance to free himself from his nephew's rapacious bullying, and it was now. "If I spare John's life, will you obey me?"

Johannes glanced at Anastasius, but found no advice in his gaze. He turned to Pope John Hymonides and detected no fear, but also no counsel. "I'll do whatever you bid."

Hogsmouth's voice trembled as he spoke to his nephew. "Release him, I beg you."

Theophylact was furious. "I give the orders here!"

Pietro's trembling turned to resolve and his quivering voice congealed to ice. "No, nephew, in the Holy See, it is I who command."

"You, Hogsmouth, dare to defy me?"

"I'm grateful for your assistance, Uncle. Nonetheless, in the *patriarchum*, I sit on the throne. I order you on pain of your everlasting soul to release Deacon John." Pietro added with cruel glee, "Unless you fear neither God nor excommunication in front of these assembled witnesses." The tide had turned and Pietro, ever the politician, sensed it. "Any man, be he noble or common, who harms a priest or a hair on Deacon John's head will be excommunicated and face damnation in Satan's Hell." Soldiers lowered their pikes and nobles slid swords into scabbards. Fearful whispers filled the church, and Pietro knew they would obey him.

Theophylact fumed, but his rage waned as the assembly obeyed Hogsmouth. "I will not see this false pope, who would purloin Saint Peter's throne, set free to work his wickedness."

Archpriest Pietro grasped that his nephew had left an opening for compromise, and he would give him an accommodation so he might leave with some scrap of honor. "So he shall not. I order that henceforth, Deacon John shall be banished to the monastery at Monte Cassino far from Rome, where he will serve God and not his own ambition."

Theophylact spoke politic for the crowd, "Then we are satisfied that justice has been done. Release the prisoner." The assembly heaved a collective sigh. "I will not leave, however, until the rightful pope has been crowned."

Johannes, still bleeding and dabbing at his mouth with his sleeve, intervened indignantly. "The Pope may not be consecrated until he's been confirmed by Lothair. It's the Emperor's lawful right."

The count's hackles raised at the priest's continued impudence. "Lothair is not here and I'll permit no further mischief. I demand the Pope be consecrated now! I will deal with Lothair."

"As you wish nephew," Pietro di Porca said. "Surely the Emperor will understand that in this state of rebellion, an immediate consecration is necessary." He sauntered to the church altar, glancing left and right at his brethren, a gloating smile on his double-chinned face. He turned to the assembly, smug and satisfied that his lifetime ambition had been realized.

The *vicedominus* hurried forward to pick up the conical tiara that had been knocked to the ground and placed it without hesitation or pomp on Hogsmouth's head. There were no cheers, no prayers of thanksgiving, and no psalms recited. Priests, nobles, and soldiers alike felt somehow defiled.

Pope Hogsmouth rose imperiously from the throne of Christendom. "I will no longer be Pietro de Porca, for no pope is worthy of the Apostle Peter's name. Nor shall I suffer further the indignity of being called Hogsmouth. I henceforth take the name Sergius after an illustrious and pious pope, and I shall be the second of that name."

It had never been done before, that a Pope changed his name to call himself by that of another. Many of the priests who witnessed the night's violence grasped the irony that Pope Sergius II took the name of a Syrian who had purchased the papacy for one hundred pounds of gold. Few knew, however, save Hogsmouth, that the first Sergius had likewise been raised and trained in the *schola cantorum*.

17
1969 Citroën

Colonelo **Del Carlo** and *Capitaine* Desmoulins had forbidden Father Romano from leaving Paris without their express permission. As he sat in the emergency room lobby while the Hébers were being examined, the priest brooded over the last twenty-four hours that had dismantled his quiet life of refuge in the Holy Church. *Why did I take the Psalter*, he asked himself. *All of this could have been avoided.*

Well, not all. The Pope's trusted Secretary and his confessor would still be dead, murdered by some arcane group. And these unknown assassins would still be after the Psalter, which was in reality a great deal more than a mere prayer book. Nevertheless, the Hébers would not have been assaulted and the Archive receptionist would still be alive. So what did he have to show for the last forty-eight hours? A ruined career, a sore groin, and the sole responsibility for the theft of the most valuable manuscript in Christendom. It seemed a ruinous way to learn the virtues of obedience.

Nevertheless, Romano was sick of obedience, at least the kind that turned otherwise intelligent people into simpletons as their ideology trumped intellect, and the librarian felt no better than they. He was one of few with unlimited access to hidden writings in the

Secret Archives, and he was tired of hiding knowledge that should belong to the world so they could judge for themselves. Two billion Christians echoed the official creed, but hardly a soul raised a voice for the suppressed writings, at least until Giovanni.

Romano sat in a plastic chair, head bowed. A hand patted his shoulder. "Are you in pain?" Pascal leaned over, purplish blotches spotting his cheek where he'd been struck.

"My groin aches a little."

The corners of the linguist's mouth curled up in an impish grin. "They don't make bandages for such an injury."

The priest's face turned from self-pity to concern. "How's Isabelle?"

"Concussion, but the doctors say she'll be fine."

"I was shocked to see her get up after the blow she took. I've seen football players sidelined by less."

"My daughter possesses remarkable willpower. Of course, there's a fine line between willpower and stubbornness, and Isabelle lives on the edge, a family curse, I fear. They're keeping her for the night as a precaution. She made the mistake of telling them she'd been knocked unconscious. I told the doctor our attacker hit like a little girl. I think he believed me because he's letting me go home. Let's get out of here before they change their minds."

Pascal poured an infusion of herb tea into china cups that made the apartment smell like a summer garden while the priest righted overturned furniture. "Leave it for tomorrow. I'll call the cleaning lady in the morning." He glanced at his watch. "I suppose it is morning. The sun will be up in an hour or so. Drink some rose tea. I brew this for Isabelle when she suffers from cramps. She would berate me if she knew I told you. Perhaps the herbs will help; it's in the same general area, no?"

Pascal's jests made brightened Romano's spirits a bit, although a foreboding still enveloped him like a cheerless fog. The tea relaxed the spasms in his nether region in a way the ibuprofen did not. "I've made a mess of this," he said in a piteous voice.

The retired professor rose from the overstuffed chair to sit beside the heartsick priest. "This isn't a tragedy of your making. Sometimes when one rushes to great heights, every setback seems like the end of the world. Your scholarship and intuition led you to uncover the most significant scriptures in two thousand years. How can it be, how did you put it, a mess?"

"If I hadn't taken the book, none of this would have happened. Now it's lost forever."

"Had you not brought the Psalter to Isabelle, you might never have uncovered the text, and the words are not quite lost." Romano looked at him, not comprehending, as Pascal pulled folded sheets of paper from the side pocket of his cardigan. "I took the liberty of copying the photograph to recheck some of the more obscure words. It's Aramaic, an exact copy, but I can translate for you." The smile on the professor's face grew larger.

"No one will believe a word, especially if I tell them what the book says. Like the Bible, without an original, there would always be doubts and accusations."

"People are hard set to give up their beliefs, even those founded on nothing more than myth or old wives' tales. Some would doubt and accuse you whether you had the original or not."

"I must still face the Vatican. At the least, I'm certain to lose my job in the Archives. Even if I'm allowed to remain a priest, which I doubt, I'll likely be assigned to some obscure position in a remote backwater so I can do no more damage. And if I dared reveal to the public what I discovered, I'd be discredited, even targeted for retribution."

"Is the Pope's Secretary ill regarded because he fell prey to these criminals? Did he not remove the book from the library as well? He was unable to stop them, and neither could you. One man against a well planned attack?"

"Father Mackey didn't question the doctrines of our faith."

"The words in the Psalter are Thomas', not yours. You would simply be reporting what you discovered."

"Someone else said the same thing to me not long ago." Romano thought of his last conversation with Father Mackey. "But I've been down that road before. I don't think the church will make a distinction."

"You're burning bridges before you reach them. If I understand correctly, you face three choices. You can do nothing, in which case the church will believe you're ignoring their authority and they'll impose their decision on you, an unfavorable one, I would imagine. Or you could quit the priesthood, return to the outside world, and your career in the church will come to an end. So will your quest for the original scriptures."

"They'd never allow me to be a researcher again," Romano said.

"Perhaps, and maybe it's likely. But your only hope, if it's the path you desire, is to return to the Vatican and explain what happened. You have nothing to hide. Your motives are honorable even if the church views them as rash. We all err, but our intentions make us who we are. How can the search for truth be dishonorable? Of course, you're forgetting the most important point."

"What?"

"If you want proof of your discovery, you'll not find it in Paris or anywhere in the outside world. You will in all likelihood discover what you're after in the libraries of the Vatican, beneath the prayers and psalms of Giovanni. Personally, I'd like to hear what Jesus' twin brother has to say. Now, I believe we need some sleep. I've had a long day, and I don't know how you can keep your eyes open."

Pascal awoke to the sound of a distant voice and the blessed aroma of coffee. His room was still dark although it didn't seem possible nighttime had come again. He pulled back the drapes to look into the courtyard. The sun was veiled by a thick haze. The damp air seeped into his old bones. His head throbbed and his neck ached as though it had been wrung like a chicken. He glanced at the windup clock on the nightstand: almost noon. *Not so bad. Still morning*, he thought. Then he gazed in the mirror. A bruised, swollen face stared back, and the reflection made his head ache even more.

Romano spoke into the telephone, nodding to Pascal as he passed. The retired linguist microwaved a bowl of milk and added coffee. He sipped café-au-lait and nibbled on a crust of day-old baguette while the priest joined him in the kitchen's dining nook. "I spoke to Isabelle. They're releasing her this afternoon."

"How is she? Was that her on the phone?"

"She says she's fine and ready to get out. Evidently the food is insipid and no, I was speaking to Colonel Del Carlo. I talked to your daughter earlier."

"Why did the Colonel call?"

"He didn't. I called him. I've decided to go back to Rome, and I needed permission. *Capitaine* Desmoulins isn't too happy since the murder investigation is ongoing, but Del Carlo appears to be running the show."

"I was certain you were a fighter, and not just with your fists."

"Nothing to be proud of."

"It was handy last night," Pascal said. "Where did you learn to box?"

"Father Mike, the priest who took me in. Before that, I was a punk who went for the soft spots—kidneys, throat, Glasgow kiss."

"Glasgow kiss?"

"Head butt to the nose."

"Sounds up close and angry."

"That's what Father Mike said: fight with your wits, not from the angry place."

"When will you leave?"

"Tonight. I booked a late flight from Charles de Gaulle Airport. The Colonel's making the arrangements."

"Good. We can pick up Isabelle together."

Romano looked a different man from the unshaven rumple of a priest who had arrived in the world's fashion capital only the day before. Pascal lent him a razor and while the priest soaked in the tub, the professor, who delighted in cooking and laundering for his daughter, ironed his black suit. He also hand washed the well-lived-in shirt and pressed it dry. When Romano emerged from the steaming bathroom, his clothes were draped from a hanger on the doorknob. He fairly gleamed as he appeared in the living room. "I scarcely recognized you, Father. You're positively chic."

"You've been very kind to me, Monsieur Héber. You and your daughter."

"Nonsense, this is the best adventure I've ever had. The mind gets rusty with the routine of aging. A little excitement makes me feel young again."

The priest shook his head, "Much more excitement and we'll be carried to our graves." They laughed out loud together.

Pascal led Romano to an underground garage a block from the apartment. He unlocked the doors of an antique blue Citroën DS. As he turned the key, the engine whirred to life and the car levitated on hydraulic shocks. He pulled on the shifter that extended from the dashboard, and maneuvered it into first gear. The old DS glided up the circular ramp. Turning onto a cobbled street, Pascal spoke while negotiating scooters and Smart Cars zipping by in nonexistent traffic lanes. "Father, you remind me of Jacob and the Angel."

"Which one am I?"

"Cute. You've been wrestling against a power stronger than yourself all of your life and it's maimed you, yet still you hang on. Isn't it time to let go? You've paid far too much whether you owed anything or not. Time to fight *for* something instead of *against*."

Romano pondered his censure by the modern Inquisition and their threats to end his career. What drove him to push on when he was ordered to stop? Mostly, he thought about his depraved punishments as a child. He caught the lump in his throat and swallowed.

"This is a 1969 Citroën," Pascal said. "One of the few things I bought new. It was a marvel of engineering. Did you know if you get a flat tire, you can take off the wheel and drive on three until you find a garage? Rather like limping along until you can get back on track. When you turn the steering wheel, the headlights move in the direction you're going. I'm surprised no one thought of it before. People prefer to look where they've been instead of where they're going. Maybe they're terrified to glimpse what's ahead, but that's how we avoid accidents, no?"

"I thought you were just a linguist. I didn't realize you were a philosopher as well."

"Philosophy? Rubbish. I was talking about the car." One eyebrow arched and the corners of his mouth turned up.

Pascal pleaded with his stubborn daughter as the nurse pushed her wheel chair to the exit of the emergency room. "You should go home and rest," he said. "You suffered a nasty concussion."

Romano chimed in. "He's right. Concussions are dangerous."

Isabelle scowled. "So is starvation. Take me to the nearest bistro before I swoon."

She had eaten the entire basket of sliced, crusty baguette and drained her goblet of table Bordeaux even before the *paté* appetizer arrived. "More bread, please," she asked the waiter.

"She has a good appetite," Romano said.

"My skinny daughter does everything with gusto, especially eat, although you can't tell by looking at her."

Isabelle was unapologetic as she turned her attention to the *paté* and cornichons. "Getting beat up takes a lot of energy." The exotic archivist finished her *paté*, *plat du jour*, salad, and dessert before relaxing. Romano looked on, impressed at her ability to consume a vast quantity of food, while Pascal took pride in his lovely daughter's sensual savoring of her meal. "Now a hot cup of tea, Papa, and I'll be perfect," she purred.

They ordered tea and sipped as the priest spoke with concern, "I wish you would ask *Capitaine* Desmoulins for protection."

"We have nothing to fear, Father," Isabelle answered before Pascal could cut in. "They took what they wanted and destroyed my ability to retrieve a copy. You're the one in danger. Only you can get more copies of *Thomas* if they exist. Now that you know where to look, in the palimpsests of Giovanni, you can be sure they'll be back. I think you're making a mistake to return to Rome. You're much safer here under the watchful eyes of the police. You'll receive no such protection in the Vatican."

"One would think that after getting beaten up together, you could call me Mike instead of Father, and don't underestimate the Swiss Guard. They may wear funny uniforms, but they're just for show. I assure you, they're the match of any elite police in the world."

"Father...Michael," Isabelle took his hand. "No one doubts the Swiss Guard, but someone knew the Pope's Secretary had the Psalter. They also knew you brought it to Paris and that you went to the National Archives. And they knew enough to convince poor Eugène to let them in. You must accept that somebody inside the Vatican is responsible." Isabelle realized she held the priest's hand and pulled hers back.

It was inconceivable to Romano that anyone in the Vatican might be involved. Priests were called to Rome for their faith, their skill, but most of all their fidelity to the church and His Holiness. Every one of the Swiss Guard was handpicked at a young age after painstaking background checks. There was the staff of course. Some were nuns, but even the lay employees were subjected to rigorous investigations. Nevertheless, Isabelle's point rang true. Now, it seemed quite urgent to return home.

Pascal interrupted the priest's reflection as he spoke to his daughter. "*Chérie*, Michael understands what he must do."

"I can't thank you enough," Romano said, "and you've received poor payment for your help. At least let me pay for lunch." The priest pulled out his wallet to retrieve his credit card. "I think I should be going. I'll just grab the Metro at the corner." Romano started to say his goodbyes, but was stopped short.

"Don't be ridiculous," Isabelle said with mock scorn. "We'll take you to the airport. Won't we Papa?"

Having already checked in at the Alitalia desk and now standing in front of the security checkpoint, the priest turned to say farewell to the two who had stood by him, even though it nearly cost their lives. He had come to feel closer to them after a few days than anyone he had met in all his years as a priest, except Father Mackey. Yet they didn't even share his faith. He extended his hand to shake Pascal's, but the old man pulled him close and kissed him on both cheeks. Isabelle likewise kissed him in the French manner, and when the priest started to turn away, she added an extra two. Romano blushed, not sure if four kisses was usual.

He was just about to thank them one last time when another voice addressed them all. "I thought I might find the three of you together." Del Carlo's words held a nuance of sarcasm. "I decided to take the same flight home. That way, the good priest and I can chat."

𝕴𝖘𝖆𝖇𝖊𝖑𝖑𝖊 𝖆𝖓𝖉 𝖍𝖊𝖗 father said not a word to one another on the ride home, not on the autoroute nor the *périphérique*, the highway encircling Paris, nor through the narrow streets to their apartment. There was no need. They could almost read each other's minds, though they were deep within their own private thoughts. The archivist knew she had to face the Director General, but she would claim Mike Romano was a professional colleague and she had been demonstrating their newest technology. He was now sort of a colleague. Anyway, Philippe was a tolerant boss.

The loss of the hard drive was another story. She would requisition a computer, but it would take time to receive and reinstall the IsyReaDeT software, and she was severely backlogged. "I'm exhausted," Isabelle said to her father as he unlocked the door. "I think I'll go to bed early."

"I wish you would, you need rest," Pascal said, kissing her and watching her walk down the hallway until she disappeared into her bedroom. He went to the salon and eased into the overstuffed green chair. Exhaling a long, tired sigh, his eyelids drooped, fluttered, and finally shut. He snored ever so softly as indistinct images crept into his sleep, swirling and vague, then becoming lucid.

The leaves in the woods were bright, multicolored hues of orange, yellow, and red. A brisk wind whipped across the treetops, blowing them to the ground. They were dry and crackled as he stepped on them. The wide path led through a forest of beech, oak, and poplar as the boy wrapped in a woolen coat walked, a spring in his step, toward the light from a clearing. The branches vibrated and the tree trunks passed faster and faster until they were an ashen and russet blur.

Pascal looked down at his feet. He walked normally, yet the forest flew past. As he approached the clearing, the trees on either side slowed and came into focus. Everything appeared normal. The woods gave way to a meadow of dry grass. A low-roofed brick house stood in the middle. The door was open and a familiar old man waved from the threshold, urging him forward.

The man had set brown cakes and tea at the end of a never-ending table in an ancient but cozy kitchen. The boy sat on the long bench as the bearded sage held the platter in front of him, smiling. He seemed to be saying something and Pascal leaned closer to listen, watching him mouth words but uttering no sound. Yet an image of letters began to form in his mind as though he viewed the words rather than heard them. Unshaped and out of focus, their outlines grew sharp and he made them out at last: ו ה ו.

He jerked into wakefulness to find himself muttering letters from the Hebrew alphabet, "*vav hei vav.*" Shaking away the sleep, he picked up the telephone and dialed a number from memory. A receptionist answered, then passed the call to a secretary who placed him on hold for several minutes. Pascal was a patient man and the wait didn't irritate him. He simply closed his eyes until a familiar voice on the other end said, "My dear friend. I wondered when you'd call. I hear you've had a bit of excitement in Paris."

"Does nothing escape your ears?"

"I manage the largest network of spies in the world, so little escapes me. They saved you one day long ago."

"I'll never forget. Now I'm begging another favor."

18
The Prefect

The nose of the Alitalia jet levitated and the fuselage floated off the runway. Romano settled into the wide leather seat. He had never flown first class. Closing his eyes he thought, *Del Carlo's perks must include quite an expense account. The Secret Archives budget would never allow for such extravagance.* "You're kind to pay for my ticket home. I usually take the train."

"Not at all, Father. I thought of taking the train so I could put you under the bright lights for a good fifteen hours. But I don't think my back would survive, and my wife insists I hurry home." The colonel forced a laugh.

"Do you have any suspects?" Romano hoped to head off the questions he knew would come. "Or do you still think the Children of the Book are the culprits?"

"We don't have a lot to go on. You gave a vague description of the two men who attacked you. Can you remember anything else?"

"It was dark and I only got a look of one of them, but I can tell you about the size of his boot. I caught one in the groin." It was now Romano's turn to feign laughter. "I didn't see the other one. I only heard his voice."

"Hum...you said boot."

"Yes."

"Did he wear boots?"

"Painful ones."

"What kind?"

"I'm not sure. I can tell you how they felt, but I don't…wait a minute…" the priest said. "They were black."

"How can you be certain if it was dark?"

"When we circled one another, I waited for him to strike. I used to do a bit of boxing."

"So I've heard," the colonel said.

"Well, I remember his silhouette, and his pants were definitely tucked into the tops, like military boots. The moonlight or streetlight made the toes shine. I can't think of anyone who wears pink or blue. They might've been brown, but I'd bet they were black."

Del Carlo put his hand to his chin. "If you saw his shape, how did he wear his hair?"

"Crew cut."

"Perhaps he was bald," the detective said.

"Nope, the top of his head was flat, not round like skinheads, but more…"

"Like a military haircut?"

"Yes."

The colonel nodded as though he understood. "And the other one. You mentioned that he shouted something."

"I don't remember exactly. I think he said, 'I've got them.' I'm sorry, but when you're getting kicked in the…"

"That's not important. The one who did the shouting, did he speak with an accent?"

"Sure did, foreign. Well, foreign for Americans."

"European?"

"No."

"Middle Eastern?"

"Maybe, but different," Romano said. "Definitely not Arabic, more like French. It might have been Farsi."

"Iranian?"

"Persian is a European language," not Semitic like Arabic, and Farsi is also spoken along the Iraq border."

"Well, Father, you would make quite a detective. You have excellent powers of observation."

"Why didn't you ask these questions last night?"

"Witnesses recall more if they're relaxed, and you seemed uncomfortable. You're sure the one who attacked you said nothing?"

"He only spit on me as he left."

The colonel almost jumped out of his seat. "Were you wearing this shirt and jacket?"

"The shirt, yes…"

"Father, we might have DNA."

The priest shrugged. "I am afraid *Monsieur* Héber washed it this morning."

"Damn. I thought we had him."

The interrogation was not at all what Romano had imagined. He would have gladly offered the information, and Del Carlo had a knack for making one recall forgotten things, things which seemed insignificant. Of course the priest wanted to help. He wanted the culprits arrested. They murdered the Pope's Secretary, his friend and counselor, as well as the Archive receptionist. But he feared the questioning because of the foolish part he played.

"What's your opinion of Cardinal Keller?" Del Carlo stared intently at the priest.

"What do you mean?"

"Do you like him? Do you trust him?" The colonel emphasized the word *trust*.

"I think he's…an honest man, but I don't know him. I met him for the first time in your office."

"You choose your words carefully, Father. If you just met him, how do you know he's honest?"

"He's a cardinal in the Holy Church." What Romano didn't say was that every priest in the church feared the Defender of the Faith on some level. He had been a hardline enforcer for the last twelve years. And while his title had been euphemized from the original Grand Inquisitor, the function of his office was the same: to discipline church dissidents and uphold official church policy against attempts at modernization and reform. Those at greatest risk were liberal and activist priests, especially those who published or advocated change. Even those who merely supported activists found themselves on shaky ground. Issues such as contraception, stem cell research, homosexuality, ordination of women, or opposition to celibacy polarized priests into camps. The ultra-conservative Keller used threats of sanctions to remind the clergy that only the Pope's express policies would be tolerated. Of course, the modern Inquisition was nothing akin to the Middle Ages with imprisonment, torture, and burning at the stake. Nevertheless, sanctions still covered a broad range of punishments, from censure to defrocking or the ultimate penalty: excommunication. And every priest realized a simple censure could be career ending.

"I will share with you, Father, that I don't trust him," Del Carlo said. "In my office you were very open. The cardinal, on the other hand, measured every word as though he was hiding something."

"I'm the one who kept something from you, *Colonelo*. You asked if I noticed anything peculiar about the Psalter and I lied to you."

"Of course, Father. I read it on your face, but I operate on intuition. You have an honest face and I believed it was an honest lie."

Romano couldn't help but grin at the colonel's oxymoron.

"You would have told me when you were ready."

At Rome's Leonardo da Vinci Airport—which Romans still called by its old name, *Fiumicino*— no one manned passport control. The anti-terrorist colonel shook his head in disgust. "All this European Union modernization caused a big hole in our security." They passed into Terminal C, lined with boutiques and restaurants. "I would be happy to drop you off at the Vatican."

Father Romano was just about to accept when he caught sight of a black cassock emblazoned with a bright red sash. A lump rose up in his throat. "Thank you for your kindness, *Colonelo*, but…"

The policeman turned instinctively toward the cardinal. "Why, your Eminence, what a pleasant surprise—and no coincidence, surely."

"*Colonelo,*" the Grand Inquisitor said dryly.

"I would like to ask who informed you we'd be arriving, but I suspect you wouldn't answer, not directly at least. Well, Father," the colonel turned back to Romano and handed him a business card, "next time, please call me before you contemplate taking evidence out of the country. Cardinal..." He let his address trail as he spun on his heels and disappeared into the asymmetric weave of hurried airport travelers.

Romano met Keller's icy glare for a moment, then lowered his gaze. Despite the twinge of humiliation from Del Carlo's jab, he suspected the colonel had chastised him in front of Cardinal Keller to help somehow. The silence between the priest and the Defender of the Faith was more oppressive than the rebuke Romano knew was eminent.

"Are you ready to come home, Michael?"

Romano tried to read the Grand Inquisitor's face, but it was an impenetrable mask. "Yes, Eminence."

The chauffeur had been replaced by a Swiss Guard wearing a blue, work uniform, and a sergeant rode shotgun. The paleographer's heart raced. *A show of force?* he wondered.

As though he could read Romano's mind, the Grand Inquisitor said, "The Guards aren't here to enforce my will. Obedience is for you to choose...or not."

"Had I not chosen to submit to the church, I'd still be in Paris. I've come back to be judged."

"Do I detect defiance in your voice, or pride? It doesn't sound like contrition."

The Librarian's heart sank. *Here it comes*, he thought.

"It's not for me to judge you, Father, although I wish it were. Others have already decided. I'm not sure I agree but, like you, I obey. Your return to the church's authority does you credit, and I must say I'm surprised. I thought you might be more...independent minded. My job would be easier if all of our brethren followed the first tenet of the church, obedience." Then Keller hesitated as though he measured the words which would decree the priest's verdict and sentence.

Romano knew he was about to meet his fate, so the seconds while the Grand Inquisitor paused seemed like eons. *If the worst happens and I'm defrocked, I can always teach*, he thought. The Institute of Medieval Studies had begged him to stay on as the Professor of Paleography before his transfer to the Secret Archives. He could possibly regain his old job, if only as a Lay Professor. But Romano loved the church and prayed that if he was allowed to remain, he would accept whatever bitter pill was offered. *I'm about to receive my punishment*, he thought and closed his eyes to await sentencing.

"You're being transferred to another position. The Library's had a vacancy for a number of years and you are to fill it."

The paleographer's heart leapt. He would remain a priest. He wondered now what penalty the cardinal would levy, but whatever it was he would accept it, even if it was censure. He would start his career over at the bottom and would likely to amount to very little, but at least he would be in the Library.

"You'll be working directly for the Cardinal of the Apostolic Library, Paolo Minissi."

"Directly?" he asked, unbelieving.

"I pray his influence will keep you out of trouble." The Grand Inquisitor didn't smile. "You are to be co-Prefect of the Vatican Library in charge of Technical and Scientific Management, which includes security. As head of security, perhaps you can prevent our books from being stolen."

Romano ignored the dig. "Prefect? Are you serious?"

"As I said, I don't necessarily agree with the decision to promote you, second only to the Library Cardinal, but it was not mine to make."

"What about the Psalter?"

The Grand Inquisitor shifted in the limousine seat to face Romano, looking more grave than stern. "Father, men are dead and a valuable codex was stolen. You're not the one who committed these abominable sins. As far as I can tell, you transgressed neither against the church nor God. Still, you ran off unprotected without telling anyone, even your own cardinal, with a book so sought after that people have killed for it. The church doesn't punish priests for stupidity, although perhaps we should."

They rode in silence for long minutes along the twenty-five kilometers of freeway from the airport to Vatican City until the priest screwed up enough courage to speak again. "Do you want to know what I discovered about the Psalter?"

"No. I'll leave that to you and the police."

"But..." The glare from the Grand Inquisitor put an end to Romano's reply, and he let his voice trail off into an uncomfortable silence. For some reason, the cardinal preferred to be left in the dark, as though he strategized to remain ignorant. On reflection, the priest felt relieved. He wanted to reveal everything, but telling the Grand Inquisitor about the contents of *Thomas* would have been excruciating.

The black Vatican limousine pulled up in front of the priest's apartment in the Apostolic City. "I'll drop you here, Father. Please meet with Cardinal Minissi in the morning. He's expecting you." Romano wanted to thank Cardinal Keller, but the Swiss Guard shut the door and the black Mercedes rolled off toward the *Palazzo del Sant'Uffizio*. The question Colonel Del Carlo had asked on the flight repeated itself in the priest's mind: *do you trust him?*

Back in his apartment the paleographer had nothing to unpack. His backpack had been stolen. He mourned the loss of the Psalter, but more so that a young man with his whole life in front of him had been murdered. He realized he hadn't caused the boy's death. Nonetheless, it nauseated him that he had been involved in the sordid affair.

Seated at his desk, he unfolded the sheet of paper Pascal had penned. It was a copy of the single page written by Jesus' twin brother, Thomas. Men killed for this page. The killers surely realized others existed. In the Vatican Library, many more prayer books waited to be investigated, and the priest resolved to do just that.

Romano fingered the perfect creases ironed on his black trousers as he draped them through a hanger. He wrapped his suit jacket around and hung them over the wooden dowel in his tiny closet. He thought of Pascal's kindnesses, but as he turned down the covers on his spartan bed, it was thoughts of Isabelle that made his heart race.

19
Protector of the Vatican Library

Father Michael Romano passed under a Roman arch and through heavy red doors into the Vatican Library. Only yesterday, his career had been in shambles. Yet this morning, he found himself promoted to a single step beneath cardinal, a Prince of the Church, in the foremost museum library in the world. He hesitated a moment to reflect on the statue of Hippolytus, the third century Bishop of Rome, as Pascal's words about Jacob and the Angel came to him. Then he walked into the foyer.

Broad, sweeping marble stairs led to reading rooms adorned with frescoed ceilings and walls. He visited the Library often because there was regular interaction between Library and Archive business, but he viewed its grandeur through new eyes. "Good morning, Father," a voice spoke from behind. "The cardinal is expecting you."

A young priest led Romano to Cardinal Minissi's offices. A middle-aged secretary, whose dark face and graying hair Romano had seen often, welcomed him. "I'm Father Sabella, the Cardinal's Secretary. Please go in."

As Romano entered the office, Cardinal Minissi labored to push his frail body from the chair. He offered his trembling hand, and Romano bent to kiss the ring. "Your Eminence," Romano greeted the *Protector of the Vatican Library*, the honorary title held by the cardinal. "Sit, Father, since an old man tires easily. I recognized your name, of course, when I was informed you would be the new prefect, but I couldn't put a face with it. Now that I see you, I'm sure we've met."

"Yes, Eminence, more than once in the Secret Archives. You came with Father Mackey." Romano saw the pain that the mere mention of the Pope's Secretary caused the *Protector of the Library*.

"Poor man, a tragic business. Of course, I remember now. You were the *custodes* of the Archives and Director of Paleography."

"Yes," Romano said.

"I once held the position." Cardinal Minissi waved his hand in the air. "Many decades ago. I loved studying ancient manuscripts, my favorite job. Alas, His Holiness had other plans for me. Now my misfortune is to shuffle paper from inbox to outbox, a mere administrator. You must be sad to leave."

"I would have been content to spend my career among the church's secrets, but I never imagined I might be lucky enough to assist your Eminence at the Library. I had no idea I was being considered for the job."

"You weren't my first choice." Minissi realized what he had said. "Oh, I am sorry, Father. I didn't mean to impugn you, but Father Mackey was to have had the post."

"He would have been a better prefect."

"Oh no, you're wrong, although I wished your position for him, even more than he did himself. I mentored him for most of his career until he became the Pope's Secretary, and I loved him as though he were a son. Sentiment clouded my judgment, however. I read your file, several times, in fact. I had heard of your accomplishments in passing, but now God's will is clear. You're truly the man for the job."

"You're too kind, Eminence." Romano felt the cardinal's genuine warmth.

"It's not my intent to flatter you. God in his grace has let an old priest get a peek at His will, and I'm a witness to the wisdom of His choice. Now tell me: Michael Romano isn't your name, is it?"

"Of course it is."

"Your school transcripts say Michael, yet the birth certificate says Peter."

Romano seemed confused. "I've always gone by Michael."

"Why don't you call yourself Peter?"

"I don't know." Romano hated the name. It was part of all he'd left behind when he ran away from home and from a succession of brutal foster homes. Like everything else from the life which now only filled his dreams, he'd blocked Peter out. He was Michael, the name he'd taken from the priest, Father Mike, who found him as a boy sleeping in a cold church. "I'm not Peter. Anyway, to use the name of the apostle and the church's first Pope seems arrogant."

Cardinal Minissi's face brightened. "The first cleric ever to change his name when he became Pope was also named Peter."

"Is that so?"

"Yes indeed, in the ninth century. He said the same thing: that taking the name of the Apostle would be presumptuous. Since then, no pope has taken Peter's holy name. What a shame, such a powerful appellation. He wasn't a good Pope, the one who changed his name, of course. I'm not supposed to say such things, but old men get to say what the young cannot. We're forgiven our offences more easily. You realize that Peter Romano means Peter the Roman."

"Someone reminded me recently."

"Names hold power, don't you think? More so when they're spoken in Latin as they were intended, *Petrus Romanus*. Would you mind if I called you Peter?"

Michael winced at the sound. Like the Pope the cardinal mentioned, the name seemed presumptuous. Mike was more to his liking.

"It obviously makes you uncomfortable, so I shall call you Michael. Now tell me Michael Romano, what exactly was written underneath the palimpsest?"

Cardinal Minissi had put Romano so at ease that he caught him off guard.

"Oh you needn't be surprised," the *Protector of the Vatican Library* said. "I discovered the book many years ago in the Library. We didn't possess the technology to view what was underneath, but I realized from the stylus marks that the pages had been overwritten. The original had been erased so well, I couldn't even read a fragment. I could only make out a few characters, Aramaic, first century." The old man's eyes gleamed.

"You're correct, Eminence, and I would put the date at fifty A.D., plus or minus."

"I knew it!" The cardinal shouted, his face beaming. He sprang from his seat, spry again despite his advanced years, and shuffled around the desk. He sat in the chair next to Romano. "Did you translate the text?"

"Yes, Eminence. The first page, anyway."

"Was it scripture?"

"In a manner of speaking, but not one of the canon."

Cardinal Minissi rubbed his chin. "Well, which book then?"

"*Thomas the Contender*, the lost *Gospel of Mathaias*."

The cardinal's eyes widened and his mouth gaped. "Jesus twin brother. I should have guessed."

"You've read *Thomas*?"

"Of course. Oh, I realize *Thomas* is a heretical book, but he was revered in the early years of the church until Emperor Theodosius banned his texts. Many thousands of Christians also believed in *Thomas*, and with good reason, it appears. If any of the heretical Gospels were the true words of our Lord, I would have guessed they were written by *Thomas*."

"Why?"

"Because theologians still debate whether *The Gospel of Thomas* predates the New Testament Gospels. I always thought the book had as much right to be included in the Bible, more. Then there's the whole *Doubting Thomas* nonsense. Someone simply had to disparage the Apostle to discredit his authority and authenticity."

"Eminence, do you realize what this means?"

"Naturally. Our view of Jesus might be incorrect. Is that so surprising? Jesus' family led his followers after the crucifixion. His brother James took over, and he wasn't even an Apostle."

"What about the church?" Romano's voice raised a notch.

"What do you mean?"

"Our teachings might be called into question."

The Library Cardinal placed his hand on Romano's shoulder. "Fortunately for you and me, that's not our department. We deal in knowledge, the discovery and preservation. Let's leave the implications to the Defender of the Faith and His Holiness. For the moment, we don't need to sort out the issue. *Thomas* is lost."

Romano hung his head. "And I'm to blame."

Cardinal Minissi patted the priest's shoulder. "Don't reproach yourself. The Psalter was stolen from you, just as it was from poor Father Mackey, and by the same people who killed him, I suspect. Now, I have a task for you, Father, which requires the utmost discretion."

Romano arched his eyebrows. "You mean secrecy?"

"Quite."

"As Prefect of Technical and Scientific Management, you must install a system like the one used to decipher the Psalter. I want to translate all of the palimpsests housed here."

"Eminence, the job would take decades, tens of thousands of man hours."

"I think not. You know what you're looking for." Cardinal Minissi grinned.

"Then you've discovered Giovanni?"

"Is that what you call him? Remember, I once held your position. I was fascinated by the scribe with the foreign handwriting who had a singular devotion to copying over heretical scriptures. He seemed to have discovered something both wonderful and terrible and concealed the originals by erasing scrolls and writing over them so they wouldn't be utterly destroyed."

"That's what I felt."

"Well, I think I can give you a head start. Follow me." The cardinal led Romano to his bedroom, past the bed, to a tall, narrow bookcase covering the wall. Religious texts filled the shelves along with a collection of detective stories whose main character was a priest from the Middle Ages, a Medieval Sherlock Holmes in a cassock. "It's most unscholarly of me," Cardinal Minissi said as Romano pulled one down and thumbed through the pages, "but I can't get enough of them." Then he gave the shelves a push and the bookcase spun on a swivel, revealing a hidden room. "I think you'll find most of what you're looking for in here."

The chamber was small, no more than the size of a washroom, but floor-to-ceiling bookcases containing nothing but Psalters covered the walls. Romano slid one from the shelf and opened the leather-bound cover. The script was unmistakably Giovanni's. His face lit up. "Are they all Giovanni?"

"Of course. Forty-nine of them. I've been collecting these since I figured out what the old scribe was up to. When Father Mackey and I realized you had discovered him as well, we redoubled our efforts to collect as many as we could before you got very far. Most of them were in the Vatican Library. How some ended up in the Secret Archives, I can't imagine. I thought I had collected them all when I worked there. It seems I missed more than a few. I told you that you were the right man for the job. Now that we can read the original scriptures, you need to get started straight away."

"It's like a dream."

"There is, however, a more pressing task to attend to with all urgency."

"Anything, Eminence."

"Someone else discovered Father Mackey had the Psalter and that the book was one written by, how did you call him?"

"Giovanni," Romano reminded the cardinal.

"Of course. They knew precisely when he left my office and where he was going. What do you know about bugs, Father?"

"Bugs?"

"Listening devices, isn't that what Americans call them?"

"Yes, but I understand very little of the technology used to read palimpsests and even less about bugs."

"Then you'd better learn. How else would anyone know Father Mackey had the Psalter?"

𝔓𝔯𝔦𝔢𝔰𝔱𝔰 𝔤𝔞𝔴𝔨𝔢𝔡 𝔞𝔱 the raven-haired woman in the inner sanctum of the Vatican Library, accompanied by the new co-prefect. Astonished eyes scanned her collar to make sure she wore a visitor's badge. "I scarcely hoped you would agree to come," Romano said to Isabelle Héber as they walked to his office, "but I didn't know who else to turn to."

"I needed to get away for awhile anyway. Every time I went to the Archives, I imagined poor Eugène's body. Philippe suggested I take some time off, so I'm thinking of this as a working vacation. Besides, I've always wanted to visit the Vatican."

"I'd be proud to be your personal guide."

The cardinal's secretary, Father Sabella, raised his eyes and dropped his pen as he spied Isabelle with Romano. When the cardinal said a technology expert would be visiting, he hadn't mentioned that the specialist would be a beautiful young woman. Romano held the door for Isabelle and as she sauntered by, he caught the secretary ogling—or perhaps he only stared from shock. After Isabelle entered the room, the secretary's gaze passed to Romano, who furrowed his brow. Father Sabella's eyes recoiled to the pile of papers on his desk.

Isabelle pulled a wand with a metal loop from her bag. "This isn't my forté," she said. "Security had to explain how the thing works, but they assured me this would get most of the bugs. Nevertheless, you should really call an expert."

"I can't. No one must know we suspect a spy might be in our ranks. Officially, you're helping me install a document preservation system like IsyReADeT. It's not as important to find every bug as it is to figure out whether the offices are bugged. But shouldn't we be whispering or writing cryptic notes so they won't learn we're on to them?"

"You've been reading too many spy novels. If we find any devices and remove them, they'll realize we are, as you said, on to them."

"Good point."

Isabelle went straight for the telephone on the cardinal's desk. She lifted the base and passed the wand underneath. A low synthetic hum sounded as the gadget passed by the phone, but grew no louder. She pulled a screwdriver from her purse and removed four screws that fastened the phone's cover. Removing the plastic shroud, she inspected the circuit board but saw nothing unusual. She clipped an ohm meter to the line and turned the dial. The needle measuring voltage didn't move, and she shrugged her shoulders. She changed the dial to another setting. The needle remained unchanged. Isabelle scanned the room, paying particular attention to lamps and the chandelier as she'd been instructed, but still found nothing. "I don't detect a thing."

"Strange. The Cardinal sounded so certain."

"Like I told you, I'm no expert. You should get someone who's experienced in this sort of thing, but unless I missed something altogether, I'd say the cardinal's offices are clean."

"I'll tell his Eminence. Somehow, I don't think he'll be relieved," Romano replied perplexed.

"Why not?"

"If someone outside is listening, then we don't need to suspect those of us on the inside."

"Look, Mike, if we found bugs in the office, someone had to install them."

"But not necessarily one of us," Romano said. "Workers come in all the time."

"You don't need a listening device in the room to hear what's going on."

"What do you mean?"

"All kinds of equipment could spy on you from the outside and you wouldn't even know, like a *big ear*."

Romano knitted his brow. "A big ear?"

"Sure, a parabolic antenna like a satellite dish, except it amplifies sound."

"I've never heard of such a thing."

"Welcome to the modern world, Father. We're in the information age, and information is power. People will do anything to get data, like hackers or phishers who troll the Internet to get passwords to bankcards and credit card numbers."

"Priests don't have much credit."

Isabelle laughed, and her face sparkled. Romano couldn't help but be charmed. He felt uneasy around women, but Isabelle was different. "Speaking of credit, why don't I treat you to lunch? As the new co-prefect, I'm allowed an expense account."

"You mean in a refectory on hard benches with hundreds of priests?"

"No, I mean a café down the street that makes terrific cannoli. Welcome to the modern priesthood, Doctor Héber."

"This is the best cannoli I've ever tasted," Isabelle marveled.

"It's delicious, but not the best. A place in New York makes the best. So tell me, how's your father?"

"He's fine and excited that I'll be working in the Vatican restoring documents. How did he put it? *You're finally doing something worthwhile with your life.* He asked me to give you his regards and demanded you call on him the next time you're in Paris."

"I'd love to visit Pascal, but after losing the Psalter, I'm not sure the church will let me out of her sight, at least for a while."

"Yet you're now the Prefect of the Vatican Library, a big promotion, no?"

"Co-Prefect, and in case you hadn't noticed, I'm in charge of security and technology. I think they're trying to keep me away from the books."

"More likely, they want someone who recognizes the church's most precious manuscripts so they can be preserved forever."

"What's considered valuable depends on who gets to decide. One person's treasure is another's trash. Now, let's talk shop for a moment. I want you to photograph a number of manuscripts."

Isabelle became animated. "You mean palimpsests?"

"Exactly."

"Are these written underneath Psalters like the one stolen?"

"Yes," Romano said.

"Then you're looking for more first-century scrolls in Aramaic like *Thomas*."

"Yes."

"Are you trying to prove the church wrong?"

Father Romano pondered the question for a moment then said almost to himself, "I'm trying to find the truth."

20
Lothair's Revenge

Scraping, hammering and the bustle of workers echoed throughout the *schola cantorum*. "I don't know how you can work in this infernal racket."

Johannes looked up from architectural drawings spread across a plank table. "Rabbi Avraham, what a pleasant surprise."

"I've been looking for you these last months, but, alas, no illustrious priest. I end up feeding my cakes to the dogs. They like them well enough, however our conversations are rather limited. Are you so famous that it's beneath you to visit an unremarkable rabbi?"

"You know as well as I that the songs people sing about me are absurd. Anyway, I hold a new position as *primicerius* of the library, and the construction takes all my time."

"The ballads about the priest who defied a count are not as farfetched as that and not just any count, but the formidable Theophylact."

"It's rubbish." Johannes was embarrassed.

"So this is what you paid for Deacon John's life, monuments to Sergius."

"It's a small enough price to pay, I suppose."

Avraham admired the workmanship of the plasterers who stood on wooden scaffolding and tile setters who fashioned colored tiles and glass into works of art. "I had no idea that in addition to your many talents, you're a builder."

"His Holiness in his dubious wisdom placed me in charge of this construction, although I know not a whit about it. But the job is not difficult. I let master craftsmen advise me. Then I ask the workers if their counsel is true. The stonecutters are only too willing to tell me how the masons should do their jobs. And the masons seem to know more about carpentry than the carpenters themselves. They all agree that the architects are muck-brained miscreants. I'm getting quite an education."

The rabbi laughed out loud, cleared his throat, and asked, "May we speak privately?"

Johannes peered into Avraham's eyes not wanting to hold this conversation. "Of course." He led the rabbi to a small cell in the *schola* he used for a study and offered his own chair while he squatted on a stool.

The kind rabbi put a comforting hand on the priest's shoulder. "You have naught to fear from me. I come to offer counsel because I worry about your safety. It was one thing when you were an insignificant novice or even one assistant among many, but now? You hold a position of responsibility and your deeds bring you fame. You've captured the imagination of the entire city, indeed all of Christendom, but you put your life at risk."

Johannes could not hold Avraham's gaze and stared at the floor. "Sergius is no threat, if that's what you mean. He needs me to build his music archive. The idea is not without merit, although featuring his songs demeans the intent." He chuckled half-heartedly.

"Look at me," the rabbi said kindly. Johannes raised his eyes. "Your bravery is beyond question, yet your foolishness dumbfounds me. What would happen if you're undone?"

"Everyone already knows which side I'm on. There's little else to reveal."

"You've disguised yourself thus far, but you cannot hide forever. Leave this foolishness behind. There are many places where you can learn—Byzantium, Antioch, Alexandria. You've surpassed all in Rome. Why not teach, instead? Universities would jump at the chance to employ such an illustrious personage. Reclaim your life in another part of the world."

"Perhaps you're right. Then I could finally remove this knot from my bowels."

A slave boy in a knee-length tunic rushed into the room unannounced and shouted in a thick accent, "*Primicerius,* come at once to Saint Peter's. The sextons need you." Before they could ask the emergency, the boy fled.

Johannes led the Rosh Yeshiva up the road to the basilica. The field in front was littered with carts filled with sticks of furniture. Wounded bodies lay strewn across the plaza, pleading for mercy. Ragged and filthy children wandered about, wailing for their mothers. An unending column of battle-broken refugees trudged up Vatican Hill, flooding into the yard and begging for asylum.

Johannes and Avraham pushed their way through the doors of Saint Peter's, stepping gingerly around piteous souls with livid wounds and hacked limbs, laid out on the cool pavement stones. Linus, the frail old sexton, triaged, directing priests who attended the wounded as best they could. "Brother Linus, what's happening?" Johannes asked.

Large tears puddled in the priest's dull eyes. "There are tales of murder and mayhem from the north, villages pillaged and sacked, mothers and daughters raped, their men slaughtered like spring lambs."

"The Norse?"

"Would that it were those godless heathens, for their souls are already damned. Alas, Emperor Lothair's son, Louis, exacts his father's revenge on Italy. He carves a wide swath as he makes for Rome and for Sergius."

"Sergius?"

"All say that the soldiers' battle cry is Hogsmouth the usurper."

"Do our allies not rally to our defense?"

"The cowards run like startled sheep, leaving the defenseless to fend for themselves."

"I'll send to the hospitals to come to your aid, Father," Johannes said to the sexton.

Avraham added, "I'll make for the Trastevere to marshal our physicians. We're closest." He turned on his heels.

"Tell His Holiness to mount the defenses." Father Linus said. "The apocalypse is at our door."

Sergius's brother, Benedict, sat on the throne in the *partriarchum* with *vicedominus* Adrian at his side. One of Sergius' first acts as Pope was to name his brother Bishop of Albano and put him in charge of administration of the Papal Palace. Kneeling before him was a man in his mid-thirties with long brown hair that curled at his shoulders, who was dressed in the fashion of the Frankish gentry. "Five hundred solidi is my last offer and even that is larcenous," he protested.

Benedict looked away, appearing bored, "A thousand I said and not a *sou* less."

"I won't pay," the Frank said.

"As you will. There are many who wait in the atrium who would pay twofold for such a fine bishopric. The tithes are copious and I understand the women in that part of Louis' kingdom are quite distracting." Benedict feigned a leer and gave the kneeling Frank a sly wink. "I would take the position myself, but alas, my labor here is never ending."

"Done," the sour noble growled.

Benedict arose and grasped the holy scepter leaning against the throne. He pointed it at the Frank. "Arise and do God's work, Bishop of Reims."

Johannes shoved his way through cardinals who shepherded visitors to their audiences with Benedict, who in turn busied himself lining the *patriarchum's* pockets by selling church positions. Priests in the treasury were amazed that their vaults filled as never before with gold and silver, although they grumbled that some vanished only to reappear in Theophylact's coffers.

"How dare you interrupt these proceedings, Father Johannes," Benedict said. "We do the church's business here."

"Forgive me, Bishop, but I must speak with His Holiness."

"He's indisposed. Make an appointment with the scribe and you may have an audience with me. Now, you're wasting my valuable time. See the *primicerius* out."

"You fools!" Johannes lost his temper. "Prince Louis marches on Rome, burning and ravaging the country. Refugees flood Saint Peter's even now as you do your… your business. Where's Sergius?"

Benedict bolted off the throne. "Louis? What did we do to offend the Prince?"

"Have you forgotten that the Emperor alone holds the right to confirm the Pope? You thumbed your nose at him, and this is his reply."

Benedict fled the great hall without a single word. "Wait," Johannes called out. "Where's Sergius?"

"In the cardinal's dining hall atop Zacharias' Tower," the *vicedominius* answered, scampering after Bishop Benedict.

Would-be purchasers of rank took flight like a flock of swallows swooping left and right, seeking a path out of the *patriarchum*. Johannes shoved his way through the stampede to a side door. He ran across the alley to the tower.

Running up stone steps two at a time, he rushed into the dining hall to find Sergius lying on a couch wearing only a white linen surplice hiked to his knees and moaning in pain. His Saracen slave boy dabbed at his brow with a moistened cloth while Pietro drank from a jeweled goblet. Ruby blotches stained his garment. "Fair Johannes, thank the Lord you've come to comfort me in my misery." Sergius was drunk. "God is punishing me for my wickedness. I fear I'm dying."

The librarian gaped at the Pope's feet. His ankles were red and bloated like pomegranates. "And so you will if you keep this up." Johannes snatched the cup from his hand. "Have you sent for a physician?"

Sergius moaned. "They say I suffer from an imbalance in my bile and blood. I've been bled twice."

Johannes pushed up a wide sleeve to reveal fresh wounds from razor incisions. "The dunces."

"Do you also practice the healing arts, young scholar?" Sergius slurred his words.

"Of course not, but anyone with eyes can diagnose what ails you."

"Is my death at hand?" Sergius began to weep.

"Hardly, and you have no time for this foolishness." Johannes turned to the slave boy and handed him the goblet. "Take away the wine and meat. Every scrap of food, out!"

Hogsmouth pleaded, "It's my only relief from this agony."

"Listen to me, Holiness. The strong drink and rich foods cause your distress. You suffer from a malady of indulgence, the gout."

"Impossible. That's the sickness of the wealthy and idle."

"There's no time to dispute. Set your drunkenness aside if you can and listen." Johannes held Sergius by the cloth of his surplice as he explained that Louis scourged the land, making for Rome to dethrone him.

Hogsmouth sobered, realizing he was in mortal danger. "What must I do?" He shivered.

The Crescentii, Pierleone, Frangipani and the other aristocratic families gathered up their households and bolted for their country castles or to relatives in the south, leaving Rome undefended. The Count of Tusculum had thought of opposing Lothair once and for all. But with his allies deserting en masse, there was no possibility of a practicable resistance, let alone victory. In the end, he, too, fled to his castle in Tusculum on the northern edge of the extinct Alban volcano.

The patrician clergy also took flight with their families. Benedict abandoned the *patriarchum* to seek Theophylact's protection. Only common and foreign priests were left with the exception of Sergius, who was bedridden.

Louis crossed the Tiber north of Rome on the Milvian Bridge. Marching south on the *via Flaminia*, the Frankish army punished Roman citizens as they fled the city, hacking the men and children to death and raping women, young and old. Prince Louis rode ahead of the macabre scene on his steaming charger, clad in gleaming armor like an avenging angel.

Poor civilians, taxed heavily for protection, received none. They took the brunt of the villainous attack as is common in every war, no matter how righteous. Fires broke out along the road, set by the arsonist army. Johannes tracked Louis' advance from the aerial banquet hall by the plumes of smoke creeping ever closer.

He clambered down the steps of Zacharias' Tower and crossed the alley into the Lateran Palace to give an account to Sergius and what was left of the clergy, which included Anastasius. Doors were barred from the inside with stout wooden beams. "Louis makes for the Flamina gate and will be here before midday prayers," he reported between breaths.

Sergius had recovered somewhat from his debilitating gout thanks to an enforced regime of cherries and tea, but paced gingerly on painful ankles. Even in his terror, he was lucid enough to realize his life depended on Lothair and Louis' pleasure. "We must send soldiers to man the battlements," he said to Anastasius.

"Holiness, few men at arms are left in the city. I ordered the gates shut and barricaded. The Aurelian walls are strong and will keep Louis at bay for a while, but if he lays siege, he'll breach them soon enough. Little can be done to stop him."

Sergius sobbed, then shouted at Anastasius, "You're the emperor's man. Don't deny it. You and your uncle Arsenius do his bidding. Go parley with Louis. Make him listen to reason. Tell him I'll excommunicate him and his whole vile family!"

"I doubt if Louis would heed my words or anyone else's. Lothair seeks vengeance, not accommodation."

"I order you to meet with him. Do something, for mercy's sake."

Anastasius sought Johannes' gaze. "Any suggestions, friend?"

"There are few chess pieces left on the board. Nevertheless, if you would plead with the prince, you won't be alone. I shall go with you."

The streets were empty, the shops shuttered and locked. Even the rowdy inns which never closed were shut up tight. An eerie quiet hung over the city as the two priests made their way through deserted neighborhoods. The hooligans and their sycophants, troublesome fixtures outside the Colosseum, were nowhere to be found.

Crossing the ox pasture which had once been the Forum, they turned north following the bourgeois *via Lata* until it became the long and straight *via Flaminia*. At last, the Aurelian wall came into view. Only a few soldiers still manned the ramparts at the Flaminian gate. They were supported by commoners, armored in dented helms and worn leather jerkins. One without rank, who seemed to be acting as sergeant, addressed the pair as they approached. "Hold, good priests. You shouldn't be here. Get yourselves to a church for the emperor's army arrives to lay siege."

Anastasius called up to the acting officer, "Nay, protector of Rome. We act on orders from His Holiness to treat with Louis."

"Madness, folly," the soldier said. "And with what will you bargain?"

"With God's good word."

The acting sergeant burst into a hearty laugh. "Then come up and welcome, priests, for you're even more foolhardy than we few."

They watched together in silence as Louis rode at the head of a column of despoilers flying military banners. The sun glinted from polished breastplates and pikes. Helmets shined like halos in the distance.

Prince Louis halted a hundred paces from the wall. He held up his gauntlet, signaling the army to hold while he rode forward, an armored captain on either side. Looking up at the paltry defenders, he mocked, "Why, good Anastasius, I see you're protected by the city's elite guard."

"There are none braver, majesty." He bowed his head to the prince in obeisance.

"At least one is left in the city who respects his liege Lord."

"More than one, sire. All are not of the same mind."

"Like Lot, God's one servant in Sodom, looking for a few righteous souls are you?" Louis smiled, pleased with his allusion.

"Many here bow to the Emperor's rule, yet your men slaughter everyone, making no distinction."

Louis' smirk turned to a scowl. "All of Rome will pay for this treasonous pretender to the papacy."

"Even the Emperor's faithful servants?"

Louis was chastened. "Perhaps my men were overzealous in meting out Lothair's judgment."

"Murder is foul no matter what you call it."

"Tread softly, priest. I give you that we have exacted vengeance, but on my lord's orders. Soldiers are soldiers and once loosed follow their bloodlust. At the end, they mind their master. Whom do you obey?"

"His Holiness."

"And who might he be, John Hymonides or Hogsmouth? Lothair has not confirmed anyone, thus I know of no pope."

"Let's not dispute like enemies, Louis, for we're not. Instead, why don't we treat to the satisfaction of your father and my emperor?"

"Then open the gates so we may speak with no wall between us."

"So your men can ravage Rome as they did the countryside? I will not aid you in committing unspeakable sins."

"Have you the courage then to meet me on the plain undefended?"

"Unarmed I am, but not defenseless. God protects me."

The poorly clad guards lifted the heavy beam out of the sockets and opened the gate, letting four pass through the walls of the city. The self-appointed sergeant and a soldier acted as honor guard, leading Anastasius and Johannes. Wooden folding chairs were unpacked and set in the open field, and Lothair's and Louis' standards flapped in the warm breeze.

Louis saluted the sergeant. "Tell me, soldier, how would you fight me with your dozen men?" he chided.

Redfaced, the soldier stammered in unlettered, vulgar Italian, "We have only a handful posted at every gate, but in truth I…I know not sire. Nevertheless, my duty is to defend the city."

"Yet the lords and officers, even your comrades, abandon their posts, do they not?"

"That's their affair, Majesty," he said. His voice held no hint of disrespect.

Louis turned to his captains. "I could vanquish the Norse and the Saracens with a company of men such as this. Attend to their needs, the best wine and provisions, and for mercy sake, find them some proper armor." Louis bowed to the sergeant. "What's your name?"

"Pelas, sire."

"A Greek? Well, Pelas, if you tire of your post, I would commission you as an officer in my army and welcome your comrades also."

Louis poured the wine as he spoke familiarly with Anastasius. "Who's your young companion?"

"May I present Father Johannes Anglicus."

"The English priest who clipped Theophylact's rooster tail and saved Deacon John's life?" Louis roared with mirth. "In truth, I'm amazed that Rome's greatest heroes are the most unlikely. You're nothing like the songs. Why, you're not much more than a boy. Is it all a fantasy?"

Johannes blushed while Anastasius defended his friend. "The lyrics might exaggerate Johannes' physical stature, I'll grant, but the deed is true."

"Then all the more heroic. You have my respect, young Father." Louis nodded his head. "Well, now, Anastasius, to business. You and your uncle Arsenius are friends to the Emperor and me. So how do we right this wrong?"

"Lothair's claim is just, and a great injustice was done to him and to John Hymonides as well. The good Deacon was elected by Rome's commoners, who defied the nobles, even Theophylact. Yet you would punish those very people. I thought you sought justice for your father?"

"You cut to the quick."

"One pope has already been deposed, and you would upend another. The Holy Church must know some peace, as should the guiltless of Rome."

"And my father is owed respect for his rights. As for me, I would smite these Roman nobles who thumb their noses at their liege lords. I cannot and will not leave without satisfaction."

"If I may, sire," Johannes said. "You have already exacted a bloody price. Surely the emperor would be content with the payment. But if you seek the obeisance of the church and nobility, have Sergius, who springs from noble blood, crown you king of Italy with his own hand. Then Theophylact and the nobles would not dare deny your right as their lawful lord. Sergius shall swear allegiance to Lothair, and you will have procured all with your army. The victory and the fame will be yours."

The Prince regent pondered the idea for a moment. "I believe my father would be satisfied. Yes, by the saints, if all will submit, the empire would be pleased." Louis grew solemn. "But we desire a pope the emperor can wholeheartedly embrace. We want you, Anastasius."

"I'm young, your majesty, only thirty and seven years. Sergius is old and ill and will not be long on Christ's throne. Then I shall stand for the Holy Chair."

"I demand John Hymonides' freedom. Sergius must agree to that too." Louis turned to Johannes. "Your reputation as a scholar is well earned, Johannes, as is your bravery. I would be gratified if I could count on your loyalty."

"Sire, my fealty was never in question. It's to God first, and then the Emperor and you."

"Perhaps one day we may even be friends, you and I."

The 15th Day of Junius in the Year of Our Lord 844

Sergius hastened by litter under the cover of darkness to Saint Peter's Basilica. He snuck into the church while Louis' army slept in their encampment below the Vatican on Nero's plain. He only half-believed his life might be spared. Ordering the entrance shut and barred, he shivered as he waited for the appointed hour of the coronation.

A sharp banging of metal on the wooden doors of the basilica, like the hilt of a sword hammering, reverberated off the stone walls. Sergius fairly jumped out of his kidskin boots. He whimpered through a crack, "Who seeks to enter God's holy house?"

A furious, disembodied voice replied. "Louis, son of Emperor Lothair, your lawful lord. Open, I command in his name and mine!"

Sergius cowered. "The doors will open only if you mean the church no harm."

"You will come to no harm by my hand if you do what was agreed. But if you would be Pope and have me spare your miserable life, open up!"

Louis was crowned that warm June day by Sergius' own hand, and the Emperor's right to confirm the Pontiff according to the constitution was restored. The incredulous aristocracy returned to the city to find it saved. They gave all the credit to Sergius, whose reputation as the most skillful negotiator in Rome soared. Even Theophylact gained a grudging respect for his uncle and no longer called him Hogsmouth in public. But among the common people, the shopkeepers, artisans, farmers, and in the Jewish ghetto of the Trastevere, the names Johannes Anglicus and Anastasius were revered as much as the loss of Pope John Hymonides was mourned.

21
Saracens

August was a month of celebration. With the hay cutting finished and the harvest of wheat, oats and barley well underway under the hot summer sun, granaries filled faster this year than most. Aged Romans remembered the famine years of seven hundred ninety-two and -three during the reign of Charlemagne, when Romans starved. However, these were fat days with plentiful rain and abundant crops.

The opening festival was the feast of Saint Peter in Chains. Priests held special masses to venerate Christendom's first pope, and the city buzzed as people filed out of hundreds of churches and made their way to merchants' stalls to buy provisions, then off to the fairs which had sprung up all over Rome. Farmers who tilled the church's farms or the nobility's demesnes brought crops they grew in their spare time to sell for hard cash.

The theater, nearly dead during the dark ages, had been resurrected in the simple but poignant passion plays performed in the squares. A new play authored by exiled Deacon John Hymonides, who some still called the true Pope, was popular among the populace. In his seclusion in the monastery at Monte Cassino, John had developed a passion for the written word and added short plays to his repertoire of histories and commentaries.

Acrobats leaped and tumbled, and jongleurs sang tales of epic battles, holy saints, and legendary lovers for a few bronze coins. Most Romans, however, clamored to hear stories of the humble English priest, a meek but wise scholar, who had bested Rome's powerful count unarmed and alone, saving the life of the beloved Deacon John. The following days celebrated Saints Eusebius, Irenaeus, the Virgin Mother, Pope Sixtus II, and various minor saints. Thus, for ten days, Rome bustled with fairs and fêtes. Children kicked balls fashioned from inflated pigs' bladders, shot marbles, or jousted on hand-made hobbyhorses with toy lances whose tips were capped with tiny windmills that spun in the breeze. Men swilled cheap wine as they played bocce, which had become a Roman obsession.

This festival day, the tenth of August, was perhaps the most sacred to Johannes: the feast of Saint Lawrence. In the year of our Lord two hundred fifty-eight, Pope Sixtus II and two of his deacons were beheaded by order of Emperor Valerian. Then four more deacons were executed, which left Lawrence, the last of seven, as the city's senior cleric.

Rome's prefect ordered the confiscation of the outlawed church's treasures. Lawrence begged to be allowed three days to collect them. But instead of submitting to Rome's demand, he distributed what monies were left to the needy and spirited away the archives, which included the names of church leaders and their congregations. At the appointed time, Lawrence appeared before the prefect, bringing with him Rome's poor and sick, whereupon he announced that these were the true riches of the church.

A furious prefect ordered Lawrence's body chained to a gridiron and roasted over a flame. Now, six hundred years later, the instrument of his execution, the very gridiron, lay in the basilica of San Lorenzo, which was erected over the martyr's tomb. Ever after, Saint Lawrence would be revered as the giver of alms and keeper of the church's treasures. However, Johannes venerated the martyr for his supreme sacrifice to save the church's library. For him, the Deacon would always be Saint Lawrence the Librarian.

Alone in the Lateran basilica after *Matins*, he said a special prayer to the saint, beseeching his wisdom in the completion of the new library, which was nearly finished. He was interrupted by a gentle hand on his shoulder. "Anastasius?"

"Forgive me, Brother. I would not interrupt your prayers, but I must speak to you. Can you meet with me in my cell?"

"I've just finished and nothing awaits me but more filing in the library."

They left together through the arcade, walked down the steps and into the *scrinium*. Anastasius closed the door to the chamber and pulled a folded scrap of parchment from his wide sleeve.

"What is it?" Johannes said.

"A letter from Deacon John. Read."

Johannes glanced at the salutation and skimmed the script written in the style of the monastery at Monte Cassino. It appeared that John had become friends with the Abbott, which explained how he was able to send out his writings. Arriving at the body of the letter, he saw the emergency and read aloud for emphasis.

> Our Abbott received an alarming communiqué from Count Adelbert of Corsica. A Saracen force captured the naval base at Misenum in the Bay of Naples. Their fleet numbering seventy-three ships carrying five-hundred horses and eleven hundred foot soldiers is anchored at the mouth of the Tiber even as I write. It can only mean that they will make for Rome.
>
> God bless and protect you. Can you send more Greek histories?
>
> John Hymonides

Johannes' jaw dropped. "But the *schola cantorum*, Saint Peter's, all of the Vatican, we're unprotected. The Aurelian walls only surround Rome and not us. We must send for help. Can Lothair get here in time?"

"If the Arabs plan to attack, we have just days, a week at most. It will take a rider that long just to reach Lothair's capital in Aachen. I sent riders to alert the Emperor's garrisons, but they're few in number, no match for a force this size. "

"Theophylact then. Surely, he can field an army."

"Sergius pleaded with him and the other nobles, but they still sting from Louis' rebuke. To a man, they said that if the Emperor wishes to assert his right to rule, he is obliged to defend the city. Even now they're packing up. We'll find no help there."

"We'll be defenseless."

"Not quite, Brother. You must move to the *patriarchum*, behind the walls, where we can defend ourselves."

"What about the library? I can't leave it," Johannes said.

"Books can be replaced, but not your skin. Besides, we don't know whether they will attack Rome. This is a skirmishing force, only eleven hundred men and five hundred cavalry. It would take more than that and many months to lay siege to Rome. The Arabs know it. Most likely, they'll pillage the surrounding villages."

"Then the books must be taken inside the walls."

"Brother, there's not enough time." Anastasius put his hand tenderly on the young man's red hair. "I, too, want to save everything here, but if you hired every litter in Rome, it would take a month. Romans abandon the city. No one is left to help."

Johannes set his jaw. "I will not see the holy writings fall into foul hands. I'll move as many as I can back to the grotto under Saint Peter's. At least there, they'll be hidden. If the immortal souls of dead popes cannot defend them, I can bar the door from the inside and may Saint Lawrence protect me."

Anastasius gripped his former protégé by his shoulders. "If these heathens break in and find you, as surely they will, your death won't be pleasant. Do you know what they do to priests?"

"I have heard tales of beheadings, but I don't care."

"Well, I do, even if you do not." His stern look into Johannes' deep blue eyes softened, and he touched his still-beardless cheek. "You've become dear to me, and I couldn't bear to see you hurt— or worse."

Johannes wrapped his arms around his former mentor's waist and held him tight. Anastasius returned the embrace and kissed to top of his tonsured head. Catching himself, he pushed away. "I...I don't know what overcame me," Anastasius stammered, staring at the floor. "I swear Brother, such a thing has never happened before."

"The fault is mine, Father. I promise it won't happen again." Red blotches on Johannes' pale face told all.

"I claim my portion of blame and beg your forgiveness." Anastasius stared at the pavement, then turned on his heels and fled, leaving a dumbfounded Johannes watching him disappear.

Baraldus fairly ran his legs off, moving scrolls and codices from the *schola cantorum* back to the subterranean grotto under Saint Peter's, He worked tirelessly, and Johannes was certain his plump *secundarius* had lost weight. Muscles bulged in his forearms and his double chin had disappeared, showing traces of a square jaw. His robe hung loose around a sturdy frame that had once been a captain in the army.

Sergius lent the use of his prized Saracen slave boy, his main concern being his music. They commandeered a bier from the cemetery grotto to use like a litter, hauling fifty at a time instead of a few. Still with only three, the going was slow and they worked late into the night when the other priests had gone to their beds.

Ragged refugees brought news daily as they sought shelter behind the twelve miles of brick-faced walls built by Emperor Aurelian. The Saracens had indeed landed at the mouth of the Tiber and overwhelmed the fortress city of Gregoriopolis in a matter of hours. The men were slaughtered along with the elderly and infirm, while women and children were seized for slavery. Everything of value was looted. Church altars were ripped from their foundations and toppled. Every cross was smashed, and the city put to the torch.

Nobles from nearby Porto took flight with their squires, attendants, and men at arms, leaving those who counted on their protection to fend for themselves. Defenseless commoners followed in a panicked exodus, abandoning the city except for a tiny force of soldiers from the foreign *scholae*, foreigners who banded together into guilds. They refused to leave and vowed to protect what they could.

A bitter Spanish captain who had lost his wife and children during the Arab's recapture of the Castilian city of Léon commanded the outnumbered force. He stood fiercely in front of his troops as they met the Saracens' first attack, a crushing cavalry charge that smashed through the city gate. The small band repelled them, standing their ground in spite of overwhelming odds.

It seemed the momentum of battle had turned to favor the few *scholae* troops as they inflicted heavy, unexpected casualties on the invaders. Battling in the passage through the city's wall, the tiny militia forced the Saracen knights back as they slashed at their snorting horses and toppled riders, which infuriated the turbaned emir who fumed from a safe distance.

The next morning after an eerie wail of Muslim prayers, the Saracen infantry took up the attack, rushing past the broken gate into the passage, fighting more effectively in the narrow confines than the less mobile horsemen. Hacking with axes and slicing with single-edged scimitars, they formed a wedge in the defenses that pushed inch by bloody inch through the portal toward the vulnerable city.

Just when the ragged remnants of defenders resolved that all was lost, muttering their last prayers between thrusts and parries of blood-stained weapons, a battle horn sounded in the distance. The stunned Saracens beat a hasty retreat to the protection of their own encampment. A centuria of eighty soldiers from the Emperor's local garrison arrived in the nick of time to save what was left of the dogged defenders.

Their jubilation was short-lived, however. The commander of the Emperor's troops convinced the steadfast Spaniard that outnumbered ten to one, their only military options were to fight and die in a city which no longer held strategic value, or fall back to the defenses of Rome. The Spanish captain wished to stay and meet his death, killing as many hated Saracens as possible. His spent but loyal men would have fought to the end at his side had he asked. But surveying their haggard, bloodied faces, he could not bring himself to require any more of their deaths.

News of the heroic battle of Porto preceded the gallant soldiers from the foreign *scholae*, and all of Rome cheered as they marched through Saint Paul's gate and past the pyramid of Cestius. The commander of the Emperor's troops allowed the Spaniard and his militia to lead the Empire's soldiers so they might receive the praise of the people. Rome's grateful citizens threw garlands of flowers to the brave men who had not cut and run like the city's nobility. The celebration, however, turned to terror as the Emperor's commander reported that the Saracen force followed and was not far behind.

𝕭𝖆𝖗𝖆𝖑𝖉𝖚𝖘 𝖆𝖓𝖉 𝖙𝖍𝖊 brown slave boy ran up and down stone steps through the *Door of Death* to the papal cemetery beneath Saint Peter's, delivering books to Johannes, who arranged them in piles by subject between the silent tombs of past popes. Then Anastasius appeared, carrying an armload of heavy scrolls. "Can you use my help, Brother?" He smiled sheepishly.

Johannes had not seen him since their humiliating embrace days before. "Should you not be at the *patriarchum* preparing for battle?"

"All that can be done has been. I find myself without a task and thought I'd help if you would have me."

"I should like nothing better." He regretted using those particular words as soon as they left his lips, but his heart knew that the nearer the threat drew to Rome, the closer he wanted his mentor about him. Anastasius' mere presence made him feel safer as they worked in an uneasy silence, stashing books on their appropriate piles.

The sun climbed toward its apogee, nearing the hour for the prayers of Sext. Baraldus dropped his latest load and looked sidelong at his master, eyebrows arched. "Yes, I know," Johannes answered his unspoken question. "It's near midday. You must be hungry. Go say your prayers and take the boy with you." He turned to the master of the *scrinium* and added, "I'm going to work through Sext and dinner as well. Don't worry, I'll be alright."

"I would prefer to stay." Anastasius said.

Johannes smiled inwardly. "As you will."

Baraldus called from the floor above, "Master, you have visitors."

The two librarians bounded up the stairs to find Avraham

HaKodesh accompanied by his son Elchanan, who looked more like a legendary warrior than a humble tanner. He wore a leather hauberk over a short tunic, with a tarnished helm on his head and old metal greaves. A sword hung at his side.

Avraham flashed a white smile through his frizzy beard. "The Saracens have been sighted and make for Rome. It's time for you to leave."

"This is my place. I'm not leaving."

The rabbi shook his head. "This fight is not for such as you. Will you defend what you cannot?" Anastasius, who was frustrated by his friend's pig-headedness nodded in agreement.

"Our books must be protected and someone has to bar the grotto door from the inside. I'm the *bibliothecarius*. The responsibility falls to me."

"Books can be rewritten. Great minds are rare," Avraham said.

"The writings of the Apostles and their followers and the history of the church are here. They could never be replaced. But you should go inside the walls with your people, for the *Trastevere* is as exposed as the Vatican."

"Many of my people flee, but I'll stay with my son. I suppose I'm as foolish as you. At least we have a militia. Our armor may be decrepit, but the sting of rusty swords is as deadly. Alas, we're few, just enough to protect the temple. If you need an escape, seek the synagogue. There we will be."

"I'm grateful to you, but I must safeguard what is the church's. I know I cannot do this alone and pray that God and our saints, with the assistance of a stout beam against the door, will thwart these barbarians."

"Don't mistake Saracens for Philistines. They're neither godless nor stupid. I've received intelligence that their army is commanded by none other than Prince Ahmad ibn Muhammad, the Emir of Ifriqiya's nephew. He comes from a long line of lawyers and theologians and is a scholar like yourself."

Elchanan added, "Ahmad taught religious law in a college for Islamic jurisprudence. He's known to have a brilliant mind. And on the battlefield, he's an ingenious tactician. He can do with a thousand troops what others cannot with ten times that."

"Thank you for your counsel, but I won't be dissuaded."

Elchanan shrugged his shoulders.

"And you, Anastasius?" Avraham addressed his onetime conspirator. "Will you not seek the walls of Rome or at least come with us?"

Anastasius looked at Johannes, who avoided his glance. "I'm a librarian like my young brother. My place is with our books."

"Then I shall pray that He Who Cannot Be Named protect you both." Avraham kissed Johannes on the cheek and took Anastasius' hand, then he and his armored son were gone, leaving the librarians alone.

"You need not stay," Johannes said to Anastasius. "It takes but one to bar the door."

"I could be the one, but I know you wouldn't leave even if I asked. Neither shall I go. We'll do this thing together."

22
Prince Ahmad

Ahmad ibn Muhammad ibn Al-Aghlab, the Crown Prince of Ifriqiya, which now included the recent conquest of Sicily and a foothold on the Italian mainland, anchored at the port of Ostia with a fleet of galleys that had transported horses, troops, and war materiel. Accompanying the transports were fustas, shallow-draft miniature galleys with fewer oars and a single mast with a lanteen. The ingenious fustas were favorites of North African raiding parties and invaluable for an attack on Rome. Not only could they ferry men up river, but in a hasty retreat, they could easily outrun pursuing armies.

After the fall of Porto, Prince Ahmad left the supply ships in the bay. He headed up the Tiber at the head of his cavalry while the infantry rowed upriver in the fustas. They anchored outside the Aurelian walls, offloading troops and weapons while Ahmad studied the massive ramparts and compared them with drawings in his outstretched hands. "The walls must be thirty feet high and at least twelve feet thick," he said to himself.

"What is it, my lord?" a captain asked, not hearing his words.

"This won't be like Gregoriopolis or Porto, Captain. Look at the fortifications. They have covered pathways on top, with arrow slits for archers. There are fortified towers every hundred feet, and the gates are narrow. Were we to attack the wall, we'd be showered with arrows and missiles. If we did breach a gate, even a small force could keep us at bay for weeks or months, plenty of time for Lothair to send reinforcements."

The captain pointed with his dagger at the western part of the city. "There're no defenses there."

"That's the river. Are you suggesting we row past the battlements?"

"Why stop here when we can put our men inside Rome?" the captain said.

"With archers shooting from the towers and infantry lining the banks? And did you notice that we can't get our cavalry inside to flank the enemy while our men disembark? Not one man would reach shore alive."

"With all due respect, Sire, we can't go home empty handed. We'd be disgraced and we can barely control the soldiers as it is. Berbers chafe against Turks, and a Shiite wounded a Sunni with his dagger last night over some insult. They must get their reward, and soon, or you and I will be the ones fleeing for our lives."

"Straight to the point as usual. We need plunder for the troops. They have families to feed and I have an army to pay." Ahmad looked closer at the map. "I've heard that much of Rome's riches adorn the churches. Saint Peter's and Paul's lie in this rural area called the Vatican, where no wall protects them. Send scouts to reconnoiter what army remains."

Johannes trotted with one last armload of codices and two scrolls up the dusty road from the *schola cantorum*. Anastasius had begged him not to, but to no avail. He had forgotten some important writings, which included the mysterious Gospel of Thomas. The quarter was empty and silent. Even the chirping birds seemed to have abandoned the Vatican. He had the atrium of Saint Peter's in sight and slowed to a fast walk.

I'll deliver this last load, then try to convince Anastasius to make his way to Rome's walls, he thought when three horsemen cantered into the road, blocking his path. They reined in their mounts. The sun flashed off steel plates riveted to their leather cuirasses. Time stood still as the *bibliothecarius* watched the sweat-dampened horses prance in place.

He spun on his toes, hugging his precious cargo, and ran toward the *schola cantorum*. Shouts of "Allahu Akbar" came from behind, and hooves at full gallop thundered. The pursuers devoured the distance between them, but Johannes made his final dash to the *schola* door. He leapt for the steps, too late. A charging horse rammed its withers into the priest and launched him into the air. He crashed on compacted dirt, skidding on his side and losing skin from a forearm and cheek yet still hugging the books.

Johannes rolled to his knees, jumped up and started again for the door. One of the Saracens spurred his mount forward and Johannes collided into its flank. A kick from a boot caught him in the shoulder and drove him back down. He staggered up and ran the other way, but the riders herded him to the middle of their circling ring. One grabbed his collar, lifting him off his feet, and dropped him to the ground. Johannes watched the rider dismount. He tried to rise, but a powerful hand yanked his short hair and pulled him to his knees.

The priest's head was jerked backward by his red hair, stretching his scrawny neck. The Arab smiled, baring teeth through a black beard. He drew a curved scimitar from a scabbard slung on his back and raised the blade high. Johannes wanted to pray, but could only whisper, "God forgive me." The Saracen loosed his grip and collapsed in a heap.

Johannes recoiled as a helmeted head rolled on the dirt. A brown-robed hulk thrust his sword at another Saracen knight. The horseman pulled back hard on the reins to avoid the attack. He spun his mount to dodge the robed swordsman, but the stout, gray-haired priest was astonishingly fast on his feet. He leapt at the rider with the power of a lion, yanking his boot from the stirrup, hoisting it up and toppling the Saracen out of the saddle.

"Baraldus," Johannes said.

The Lombard swung his sword down on the unhorsed Saracen.

The ring of steel on steel split the air as the enemy parried the blow. Baraldus feinted a backhand slice. As the Arab raised his scimitar to block the blade, the priest spun like a top and hacked deep into the enemy's throat. Blood sprayed from the severed neck. The priest, turned army captain once more, leapt to meet the last attacker.

The remaining horseman faced the steely-eyed cleric who brandished a dripping sword and jerked on the reins. The charging horse sat on his haunches, skidded to a stop, and flailed with its forelegs. Dark hooves knocked the blade from the Lombard's fist. Baraldus dived to retrieve his weapon, rolled, and sprang cat-like to his feet. The wild-eyed horse spun and galloped off in retreat. The priest wheeled, looking for more of the enemy.

Johannes touched his shoulder and the Lombard jumped, raising his sword. "They're gone," the *primicerius* said.

Baraldus circled again to be certain, then faced his master. "I didn't think I would reach you in time." Tears filled the corners of his eyes. "God must've carried this fat priest to your side."

"Maybe you haven't noticed, but you're hardly fat anymore. You're terrible, fearsome...wonderful."

"I am again what I thought I'd never be; may God forgive my bloodthirsty nature."

"You saved my life."

"And I'd do it a thousand times over."

Johannes grinned, and droplets of blood oozed from his grimy cheek.

Baraldus dabbed at the abrasion with his sleeve. "Those were but scouts. The main force cannot be far behind. We must get to safety. Let's make for the walls."

"I told you, I'm staying in the grotto."

"Foolishness! I'll not allow it!" Baraldus shouted, his blood still hot.

"Brave captain, Anastasius awaits me there. He won't leave until I return. If you would save someone, save him, for I'm not leaving."

Anastasius' eyes fixed on the stain on Baraldus' sword. "I was within a hair's width of having my head chopped off," Johannes said, "had it not been for Baraldus. He bested two of them and sent the third packing."

The *secundarius* crossed himself. "God forgive me, they were but boys and stood not a chance against an old hand."

"So they're here," Anastasius said, wide eyed.

"The scouts reconnoiter," Baraldus replied. "The main force will not be far behind. We must get to the protection of the walls."

Johannes shook his head.

"Can you not make him see reason?" The Lombard entreated Anastasius.

"I've tried to no avail."

"At least take my sword." Baraldus held out the weapon to Johannes.

"That will be of little use to such as me. Keep it and take Anastasius with you."

Anastasius shrugged his shoulders. "I'm staying, too."

"You're both lunatics," Baraldus said. "Bar the entrance and the door to the grotto, then hide yourselves. Defenseless as you are, your only protection will be stealth."

Baraldus turned to leave, but Johannes caught his sleeve. "Thank you for my life."

"I fear it has been for naught." The Lombard choked on his words then he fled across the portico.

Prince Ahmad crouched over the headless body, the scout at his side. "You say a mere priest bested you?"

"He wielded his sword like a master. I never saw such a display."

The prince mocked the soldier. "Then let us pray we don't meet the Pope." He rose and spoke familiarly with his captain. "Send riders down every street and behind every building. I don't want any surprises from the rear, like Porto."

"Your will be done, Lord." The captain raised his arms and horsemen split from the column, galloping down the side streets.

Ahmad marched up the street at the head of his army. He alone wore no armor. His khuff, a knee-high leather stocking, cinched loose pantaloons, and a red sash wound around his short tunic, accentuating a thin frame. An open, sleeveless robe hung to his calves and billowed in the breeze. His head was wrapped in a turban of yellow and blue linen, the end of the material falling to his shoulders. Climbing the steps to the basilica, he twisted and pulled the iron ring on the door. "Break it down," he commanded.

The heavy oak doors burst as the battering ram tore hinges from the wall. They fell inward and crashed on the pavement stones. Ahmad raised his eyes to the high ceilings and was taken aback by the splendid architecture. A shiver from the chill inside scurried up his back, and he shuddered. *The church is beautiful*, he thought, *but its heaviness is so unlike the airiness of a mosque and it oppresses my heart.* His superstitious troops tiptoed in, speaking in muffled whispers.

One spied the Altar of Saint Peter. "Silver," he cried, "and gold!" Men rushed forward, passing Ahmad on either side as a river torrent is split by a single stone. The prince only smiled and continued his silent inspection of the holiest church in the empire of Christ. "We have found what we sought, Captain." The captain who followed grinned in response, showing his relief.

Arab, Berber, and Turkish soldiers pried golden plates from the walls. They used axes and spears as levers to strip silver sheets from the doors. A golden balustrade was torn from a stone staircase it had adorned for five hundred years.

Thirty men pounded on Peter's altar with the hilts of their swords. They levered with spears, but the structure didn't budge. Frustrated and overwhelmed by greed, they led in six mounts and lashed ropes to the saddles. They tied the other ends around the altar. The horses slipped and stumbled to their knees on the slick stone as riders whipped their rumps. A loud crack echoed off the walls as the altar tilted and crashed to the floor.

Anastasius and Johannes huddled together as the destruction above assaulted their ears. "We must find somewhere to hide," Anastasius said.

"I've prepared a place at the back." Johannes led him to the far recesses of the grotto.

"In a tomb?" Anastasius rolled his eyes.

"Don't worry. Whoever was here is long gone, taken to the catacombs. It's almost empty."

"Almost?"

Johannes forced a smile. "This is where I hide the heretical books I want to archive."

Anastasius shook his head. "I should have guessed when you said you were setting up shop here."

Johannes had stashed a pile of scrolls and stacks of papyrus codices in the rear of the stone sarcophagus. "I didn't know how long I'd be here so I stored jugs of water, bread, and a straw mattress."

"But how can we close the tomb from the inside?"

"Baraldus has seen to that. He greased the edges with lard and oil. Look, the stone moves easily." They climbed in and slid the cover nearly in place, leaving a crack so they could listen to the bedlam above. A loud crash from the ceiling sent plaster raining down on the tomb. The whole chamber shook.

"They've knocked something large to the floor," Anastasius said, peering out the crack.

"Perhaps God struck them down," Johannes said hopefully.

"More likely the altar. They're after gold and silver." As he spoke, a thunderous boom resounded from the far end of the cavernous grotto, then another and another. "They've found the *Door of Death*." They guided the stone cover to its final place and all turned black inside the stifling tomb.

Saracens rampaged through the underground papal cemetery. They pried stone covers from sarcophagi, searching for plunder. Anastasius and Johannes could only wait as the tide of grave robbers drew nearer. The pandemonium seemed to subside, however. "They'll find nothing of value in the tombs," Johannes whispered. "The only jewelry the Popes possess is the ring of the fisherman, and it's taken from their fingers upon their death and broken. That's why I chose a tomb at the back. They'll tire of their labor when they find only rotting bones for their trouble."

"I would never have thought of that."

"It was Baraldus' idea, not mine."

The Arab captain left the frustrated troops as they desecrated tomb after tomb, finding only moldering robes and old bones. He pulled a codex from a pile and opened the cover. The writing was foreign and incomprehensible, so he cast it back. Lifting a large scroll, he slid off the leather sheath and rolled it open. The script was the same, and he threw it on the pile as well. He walked deep into the grotto and struck the side of a sarcophagus with the hilt of his sword. A hollow ring resonated from within the crypt. When he reached the wall at the farthest end, he turned to retrace his steps then stopped. "Sergeant," he said.

"Yes sir," one of the men answered.

"All of these books, take them out."

"Sir?" The sergeant looked dumbfounded at his commander.

"Don't question me. Follow my orders."

Shrugging his shoulders, the sergeant barked orders to men who began hauling books up the stone steps. Then the captain's trained military mind processed something out of place. He cocked his head, trying to focus on what it was. He returned to the rear of the grotto and scanned the scene until his eye caught what seemed impossible. A tomb seeped a viscous liquid down the side. He rubbed the fluid between a thumb and forefinger, and raised his hand to his nose. *Lamp oil*, he thought to himself, *and the putrid smell of animal fat.* "Filthy Christians," he said and turned, but stopped in his tracks.

He spun and shoved at the stone lid with a great heave. The cover slid and fell to the floor with an earsplitting crack, fracturing into pieces. Two brown-clad priests crouched inside, surrounded by books and scrolls. "Out," he said in Greek. As the pair rose slowly, the crowd of Saracens at the other side of the mausoleum edged closer, swords at the ready. Then they burst into laughter.

"Our books!" Johannes cried out in Latin. He turned to the captain and said in Greek, "You're stealing our scriptures." The captain poked the point of his sword into the priest's ribs, "Up the stairs."

"Hold your tongue, Johannes," Anastasius whispered harshly. "If we can gain any mercy it'll be by our wits, not your hasty words."

The Saracen officer pricked Anastasius' back with his blade. "Silence, priest!"

Prince Ahmad collapsed on Saint Peter's throne. He surveyed the looting of the basilica with satisfaction, but was mostly relieved. He had barely been able to control his men. *In truth, they weren't his men,* he contemplated. *More a loose confederation of mercenaries, warring tribes and religious sects who hated one another almost as much as they hated Christians.*

Ahmad ibn Muhammad descended from a long line of scholarly emirs, the dynasty of the Aghlabids, who followed the Hanafi law, the most tolerant of Sunni Islam. The Aghlabids sought to bring peace and unification to all Ifriqiya. But while Ahmad's family taught tolerance for others, his men were mercenaries and only had respect for their own sect and for gold. Many of them were followers of the Fatamid dynasty that sought to overthrow Ahmad's uncle and impose their rigid brand of Islamic law.

This was an uneasy alliance of warriors that Ahmad led into battle unified by two things, money and land. The Crown Prince held them together, as did his uncle, by conquest and spoils. *I'm a scholar,* the prince thought while sitting on Peter's ancient wooden chair. *Must I waste my mind on incessant stratagems for raids and plunder?*

Troops glanced up from their pillaging to mock the two priests as they were marched at swordpoint toward the seated Crown Prince. "Kneel before the Prince," the captain barked. He seized Anastasius by his collar and jerked him to his knees. The Saracen ranks cheered. Johannes dropped at the same time, hoping to escape the abuse, but received a boot between his shoulder blades anyway. "On your face, infidel," the captain bellowed.

"Well, well, what have we here? Two priests? I hope they're unarmed, Captain. Otherwise my whole army might be in danger."

The troops' faces went sour at the insult. They grumbled and returned to their burglary.

"My lord," the captain bowed his head. "They were hiding in the tombs below."

Prince Ahmad's eyes narrowed. "Are you spies?"

Johannes looked up at the Arab seated on the throne of the Apostle and his mouth gaped. "You're sitting on…"

Anastasius pushed Johannes' head to the floor, silencing him. "My lord, my brother is young and knows not respect for his betters. Forgive him, I beg you."

"One can learn much from the impudence of the young. I wish to hear what you would say, priest. What's so important that you would risk your miserable life to address a prince of Islam thus?"

"I'm sorry, Sire," Johannes could scarcely contain his outrage. "But you're sitting on one of our most sacred relics, the throne of the Apostle."

Ahmad sprang from the chair. "This old wooden seat is the famous throne of Saint Peter?"

"Yes, my lord."

"Upon my word, I'm the one who should ask for forgiveness. A man should not desecrate another's sacred things."

Johannes' outrage was replaced by the observation that he was prostrated before a thoughtful man. "Forgive me for speaking plainly, yet you defile our holiest church and plunder its sacred treasures."

Ahmad laughed. "Sacred to whom? The church was not built by Peter, but a Roman emperor, and a bloodthirsty one at that. And you adorn this holy place with graven images. Is that not a sin even according to your own scriptures?"

"You've read the Bible?"

"Not all. Now, I've answered your questions. I should like an answer to mine. Are you here to spy on us, perhaps our troop strength or our tactics?"

"No, my lord," Anastasius said. "You can see we're priests. We remained behind because we're librarians."

Ahmad reflected, "So you stayed to protect your sacred books, a noble purpose. And do you wish to fight us for them?"

"If I could, I would," Johannes blurted out before his mentor was able to stop him. "Alas, we're not soldiers. We stayed to bar the door to the grotto."

"Some of your priests fight like soldiers. You, young man, have you the heart of a warrior or do you just puff up your delicate self like a bantam rooster?"

"I apologize for my outburst, but I'm the librarian of the Holy Church and you're stealing scriptures that I'm charged to protect. Should I not be outraged and fight, though it might cost my life?"

Prince Ahmad nodded. "I suppose I should expect nothing less than your disdain."

"So will you return our holy books?"

"I fear I cannot. Books are worth their weight in silver, and you possess a vast treasury. I can pay my army for years to come with the price these will fetch."

"Then let's bargain for them. Rome has gold. Sell the books back to us."

"Will you not negotiate for your life instead?"

"These are the true riches of the church," Johannes said. "Without them, my life is not worth a denier."

"Then let us discover whether we can strike a deal."

23
The Bargain

It's a trap, Holiness." Sergius' brother, Benedict, said. "These Godless heathens are nothing more than pirates. Once they get their filthy hands on our gold, why should they give back our holy books? Besides, words can be rewritten, but the church's treasure is hard earned."

"I'm so fatigued, I can't think straight." Indeed, Pope Sergius' pallor was gray.

"Send these ignorant unbelievers packing. I wouldn't pay a single solidi for a room full of books."

"You would trade the Papal Palace for thirty pieces of silver if it would make you a profit. Do you think I don't know that you sell holy offices and anything you can get your hands on?" Sergius shouted, then slumped back in his seat, exhausted.

Benedict bowed his head in feigned contrition. "Dear brother, I sought only to make the church powerful, and money is power. We now possess a treasure to match even the Emperor's."

"You siphoned much for your own use."

"Mine aren't the only desires quenched by pleasures a coin can buy."

Sergius was weak and ill from a lifetime of overindulgence. He felt weighed down as though the earth pulled at him to join his brethren. The old names called to him again, Pietro di Porca and Hogsmouth. The Pope shrank from their memory. Nevertheless, he sensed his time on earth was short. With his remaining days, he resolved to fight against Hogsmouth and be Sergius to the end, penance for a dissipated life. "There are Holy Scriptures in the library written by the Apostles' own hands. These must be restored to us, and I won't allow the church's music to be lost forever. The profits from your avarice will buy them back."

"Your stupid songs again," Bishop Benedict said. "Those insipid tunes are not worth the parchment they're written on."

"Out, I say. Get out!" Sergius gasped as he sprang from his chair. "I never want to lay eyes on you again."

Benedict rushed from the chamber, malice contorting his face.

Anastasius helped Sergius back on the throne. "Holiness, these are neither ignorant nor Godless men, and I believe their leader is an honorable man. Their beliefs are not ours, but their word is sacred to them as our holy oaths are to us."

"Yet they hold Johannes hostage."

"Not so. Prince Ahmad offered to release him as well, but Johannes refused to leave. When I left the basilica, he was guarding your music." Anastasius silently asked God's forgiveness although it was not a total lie. He had left Johannes inspecting piles of books hauled out of the Grotto, which included Sergius' compositions.

"Our beloved brother Johannes," Sergius said. "There is not one so good and refined in all of Christendom."

"Everyone in Rome shares your opinion, Holiness."

Bishop Benedict sat astride a warhorse next to Theophylact on the far side of the Tiber behind Hadrian's sacked and spoiled mausoleum, just out of view of the Sant'Angelo Bridge. He had once again donned a colorful tunic instead of his priest's robe and covered it with a knight's hauberk. Theophylact wore a light breastplate, and his head was protected by a mail *coif* that left his face exposed.

Behind them was a long column of the count's men in battle armor, armed to the teeth.

"You were wise to come to me, Uncle. I won't forget this."

"I'm certain we can profit one another, but how can you be sure they won't cross the Vatican Bridge instead?" Benedict said.

Theophylact smirked inwardly. His facinorous uncle had many useful talents, but tactics and reconnaissance were not among them. His were the stratagems of frontal assaults on a woman's virtue and surrounding an unsuspecting purse. "Nero's old bridge is the direct route, but they wouldn't dare haul carts laden with gold and silver over the rickety thing. A breath of wind could knock it down."

At that moment, Theophylact spied the train of carts in the distance. He recognized Anastasius astride a donkey at the procession's head, but didn't recognize the stout priest at his side who looked more like a soldier than a man of God. Priests prodded the oxen with cane rods as the beasts labored under heavy loads, and no men at arms guarded the defenseless clerics. *So much the better*, the count thought to himself. *It would hardly be politic to kill soldiers in the service of the Pope.*

When the last cart lumbered past, he nodded to the officer behind him who waved a banner, and the column of cavalry surged forward, galloping on either side of the heavy carts. Theophylact loped to the head of the wagons to face Anastasius and Baraldus.

"You have no business here, Count," Baraldus said.

"My business is wherever it may please me, priest."

Anastasius put a calming hand on the Lombard's shoulder to entreat his silence. "We're on an errand in his Holiness' name. You have no right to stop us."

"I retain an army," Theophylact said. "That's my right, and I've been informed of your mission. You're giving the church's gold to the heathens."

Anastasius glowered at Benedict, knowing their betrayal had come from him. "We give nothing. We're paying the ransom to buy back the church's dearest possession, our Holy Scriptures."

"Is this one of the Emperor's tricks, to bankrupt the *patriarchum* so he can exert his own control?"

Anastasius shouted so the troops might hear, "The Pope has sworn allegiance to Lothair and even you, Theophylact, are his vassal. I do the Pope's business, and in this matter, you enjoy no standing. So why are you here?"

Theophylact rankled at the Emperor's man broadcasting the count's subordination to Lothair. He instinctively reached for the hilt of his sword but caught himself. Instead, he chided Anastasius. "Where is the Emperor? Does he defend the church? No, he languishes at his capital in Aachen and his few troops hide behind Rome's very walls."

"Nevertheless, you didn't answer my question. What's your business?"

Theophylact spotted the trap. "Why, dear Father, I'm here to save the church's wealth, the tithes of its parishioners."

"You're here to steal the gold."

"Not steal, protect."

"You forget that the Saracens hold our scriptures and a priest hostage."

"Ah yes, Johannes the *bibliothecarius*. It would be tragic if he were to die by the hands of filthy unbelievers," he sneered. "Fear not. We'll save your precious books and the librarian if we can, and Sergius' treasure in the bargain."

"You'll do nothing of the sort," Anastasius said. He turned his head so Theophylact's men could hear him well. "Anyone who interferes will face excommunication, I swear by the Holy Virgin." Gasps were heard from the ranks.

Theophylact grabbed for his sword to jerk it from its sheath, but Baraldus leapt from his donkey in the same instant and gripped the count's hand in his own giant fist. The count struggled to free himself. However, his strength was no match for the powerful Lombard, who crushed Theophylact's fingers against the hilt, making him wince in pain. Then Baraldus felt a prick at his throat, and warm droplets oozed from the cut.

"Loose him, Brother," the voice said dispassionately. Benedict held a long dagger.

"Father Baraldus," Anastasius said, "nothing will be gained by this." Benedict pressed the point deeper, drawing more blood. Finally, Baraldus loosed the count's throbbing hand ever so slowly until Theophylact could yank it free.

Rubbing his bruised fist, the count shouted, "Seize the carts," but not a soldier moved. "I said, seize them!" Soldiers glanced at one another, not knowing what to do.

Benedict remounted and slid his dagger into a sheath underneath his hauberk. He stood in the stirrups and faced the immobile troops. "I'm Benedict, Bishop of Albano, and Pope Sergius' brother. We're here to do his will, and the brave Count of Tusculum speaks truly. We shall save our Scriptures and the church's treasure, and even noble Johannes. No man will face excommunication. You have my sacred vow."

The soldiers appeared skeptical. They knew Anastasius' goodness, and Benedict's reputation for avarice was also well known. Theophylact ordered again, "Commandeer those carts." This time they drew their swords. Theophylact turned to Anastasius. "As I said, I'm in command here. You and your friend may return to the Lateran and tell my uncle that I have things well in hand."

Prince Ahmad joined Johannes, who inspected scrolls piled outside Saint Peter's on the open field. "I'm truly sorry about the library. It must grieve your heart sorely. Our Qur'an holds the words of Allah, and my people would weep and tear out their beards if our holy books were stolen. You store many scriptures here, tens of thousands."

"They're not all scriptures, of course. Some are commentaries from the finest scholars, church histories, and even heretical books."

"What are these heretical books?"

"Scriptures we don't accept as orthodox."

"Then why do you keep them? They should be destroyed if they're false," the prince shrugged.

"I'm not sure all of them are."

"They're either the word of God or they're not."

"It's not quite that easy. After our Messiah was crucified, more than thirty Gospels had been written, and they contradicted each other. One of our early church fathers, Irenaeus, decided there should be only four since there are only four points of the compass and four directions of the wind."

"Can such a thing be true?"

"I can't say how he chose them, but that was his justification," Johannes said.

"Many must have disputed his unscholarly argument."

"Most Christians at the time thought his claim was absurd and continued to study heretical Gospels for another two hundred years until they were banned."

"Which of your prophets forbade them?"

Johannes chuckled. "No prophet. It was Roman Emperors Constantine and Theodosius."

"An emperor ordered which scriptures would be true and which would be false?"

"Theodosius commanded that all outlawed books be destroyed and anyone who possessed them executed. Within a few years, all dissent was crushed."

"Who wrote these heresies?" the prince asked.

"Early church leaders, followers of the Apostles, perhaps the Apostles themselves."

"Yet they were destroyed by an emperor? A king may not tell a holy man what is just. How would he know? He's but a king."

"Something had to be done," Johannes said. "Many scriptures were altered by over-zealous monks. Entire books were composed to oppose earlier writings."

"You mean forged? Blasphemy! By the beard of the Prophet, I don't understand you Christians. How can you judge what's true and what is not?"

"That's why we ordain priests. We study to find the truth."

"It's one thing to search for truth in the words of Allah and quite another to seek it out amidst a haystack of lies. Moreover, a Christian must discern which priest speaks falsely and which tells the truth? Your religion is too complicated for a simple man like me."

Creaking and rumbling reached their ears from the lowland below the Vatican. Prince Ahmad spied the long line of carts with priests walking beside the oxen. They trudged up Vatican Hill led by two armed men of rank. He spoke to Johannes in a suspicious voice. "I said no soldiers."

Johannes strained his eyes. "There're only two. Surely that can't be a threat." But the priest noticed the knights were nobles and wondered who they might be. "Maybe they've come to direct the exchange?" Yet even as he spoke, he didn't believe his own words.

"Perhaps." Ahmad turned to his captain and said something in a dialect Johannes didn't understand, even though he was familiar with many Arabic words. The captain barked orders to his sergeants, who scurried to their troops. The encampment disintegrated into organized chaos as soldiers rushed to their appointed positions.

Standing next to the Prince, Johannes strained his eyes as the wagon train approached. Finally, he made out the two nobles, and a lump grew in his throat.

"I detect trouble in your countenance, priest."

Johannes turned to face Ahmad. He felt the prince's dark eyes probing his own as though he was burrowing into his soul. He thought about lying. Certainly it could be no sin to lie to an unbeliever who was intent upon stealing Holy Scriptures or the church's treasure. Johannes surprised himself as he opened his mouth, only to discover the truth spilling out. "The armed men who lead the wagons are no friends of the church, although one's a priest. I fear you've been betrayed, but I know not how."

The prince gave a satisfied nod. Then he ordered horses brought to them. "Let's investigate what deception has been planned."

Sleek Arabian stallions were led to Ahmad and Johannes. "Join me, priest."

Johannes looked around, but spied no other troops. "Just the two of us?"

"Your wagons are defended by two warriors, and we also shall be two."

"You don't understand. These are devious men. You won't be safe."

"This is a war. No one is safe in a war. Allah will either protect me or require my death. His will be done. Shall we?" Ahmad motioned down the Vatican Hill toward the column, and they trotted off.

Theophylact held up his hand to halt the slow-moving carts as Ahmad and Johannes reined in their smaller horses. Benedict's eyes narrowed as he peered down on Johannes from his massive charger and addressed him in Latin. "Are you here to interpret, *bibliothecarius*, or have you converted to Islam?"

"I still wear my priestly garments, yet you don a knight's armor," Johannes said. "Which are you?"

Ahmad interrupted the exchange, speaking in perfect Latin, which caused Benedict's mouth to gape. "The priest is here in good faith to reclaim the Christian scriptures. Are you?"

"Enough." Theophylact halted the verbal joust. "We're here to trade. We brought your gold, as you see. Where are the books?"

"They lie in the courtyard of your great church in plain sight, but I don't see any gold, only carts. I would first have evidence that you bring what was promised."

"And I must confirm that our Holy Scriptures are undefiled." The count smiled shrewdly.

"There's no obstacle, sir. By the prophet, I swear the writings are undamaged. You may enter the Vatican freely and take your priests with you to verify the truth of my words."

"And fall into a trap? No, thank you. Bring them here."

"The books are there just as the Prince says," Johannes said. "I have the prince's word the exchange may be done in peace. No one will be molested."

"You believe a common thief?"

Ahmad eyes flashed. "I demanded that no soldiers come, yet you are here. Do you think I need to set a trap for priests? What game do you play? I have no wagons to haul your books. If you want them, you must take them from where they lie. First, you will pay the price. I'm not here to haggle."

Theophylact dug spurs into his charger's flanks. The warhorse leapt forward as the count drew his sword and swung it down on the prince's head. Ahmad loosed his scimitar in a flash from the sheath on his back and deflected the heavy blow with an earsplitting ring as the count's warhorse charged by.

Theophylact reined to the side, but the charger was no match for the smaller, nimble Arabian, and Ahmad was on his heels, closing. He extended his scimitar to deliver a slicing coup de grâce when the sword flew from his hand. Benedict had struck the blade in mid-blow and turned backward in the saddle as he passed. He sliced at Ahmad's throat. The prince ducked as the steel whistled by. The turban flew from his head.

Reining his stallion hard, the prince faced three columns of armored cavalry charging up Vatican Hill from both flanks and the middle. Theophylact and Benedict had turned their mounts and attacked ahead of the mounted troops. Ahmad's blade lay on the ground, out of reach. Blood flowed from his brow.

They'll be on him in an instant, Johannes said inwardly. "Flee!" he shouted. The prince wiped blood from his eyes and looked frantically for an escape. He swayed on his mount and seemed addled. At the last moment, Johannes wrested the reins from his hands and tugged. His stallion lurched sideways in a big crow hop. Ahmad held on to the saddle with all his might, rocking back and forth.

Johannes led Ahmad's mount by the reins and raced for the protection of Saint Peter's. Looking behind, Theophylact and Benedict rode just ahead of their cavalry in full attack. He put distance between them on the faster Arabians, but the prince slumped in his saddle. He could not hold on much longer and if he fell, they'd be lost. Approaching the Vatican, columns of Saracen riders galloped from behind the buildings, passing them on either side, followed by a horde of infantry shouting and waving axes and scimitars. Ahmad's captain flew by, his angry eyes flashing as he looked at the bloody prince. He turned toward the immediate threat and spurred his mount, racing to his place at the head of his men.

The air split with the clanging of steel and horses screaming as the two armies crashed headlong into one another. The horrible sound pierced Johannes' ears as he reined in the wild-eyed mounts in front of Saint Peter's. He leapt to the ground just in time to catch Ahmad, who fell but clung to his horse's neck. Johannes pulled Ahmad's arm over his shoulder and they stumbled up the basilica steps into the coolness of the Narthex, where he laid the Saracen prince gently down.

Johannes tore a strip of cloth from the hem of his brown robe and dabbed at the livid gash above the prince's eyebrow. Ahmad opened his eyes and whispered, "Priest, you're a wonder." Then he closed his eyes and sank into unconsciousness.

24
Sacrilege

Johannes fetched a sleeping pallet from one of the sexton's cells. He lay Ahmad down and covered him with blankets. The prince had lost much blood and shivered as warmth drained from his body. Finding a needle and thread, Johannes had lowered his hand to stitch the livid gash that stretched from eyebrow to temple when the sound of boots running across the stone pavement caught his attention.

"Will he live?" Ahmad's captain panted as he knelt beside Johannes.

"The wound is not lethal, but it's to the bone and must be cleaned and closed."

"Shall I hold him?" the captain asked.

"I've numbed the gash with an unguent of opium. With luck, I'll finish before he regains consciousness." Johannes noticed a tear in the corner of the captain's eye. "I know you love your prince. I'll be as gentle as I can."

"He's not just my prince. He's my brother."

"Fear not. I'm no doctor, but I've sewn many a cut, although few so deep as this." Johannes drew the needle to the brow to sew the first stitch as a hand grabbed his wrist.

Ahmad did not open his eyes and spoke hoarsely. "Was there a battle, Captain?"

"Yes Prince, but not much of one."

"And the gold?"

"Please, Brother, let the priest attend to your wound then we can talk."

"Captain?"

"It was a ruse. The carts were filled with stones and branches. The priests ran as soon as you were attacked. Then the cavalry came from their concealment and chased you up the hill. They would have caught you, too, if not for the priest."

Ahmad opened his eyes and cast them on Johannes. "Go on."

"We engaged them hard, although ours was the smaller force. When they saw we wouldn't run, they were the ones who cowered. They fled like women."

"Dead and wounded?"

"A few minor wounds, a drunken Turk fell from his horse and broke an arm, and a Berber's horse bit a sergeant in the arse." The captain tried to make his brother laugh, but Ahmad didn't even grin, so he continued, "As I said, it wasn't much of a fight. They were probably an expeditionary force. A larger army may attack in the morning."

"Very wise, Captain, and what do you think, Priest? You saved my life although I'm your enemy. Could I trust you to tell me the truth?"

"I didn't do it for you. I wanted to save our scriptures."

"Again, you speak without deceit. Will they attack tomorrow?"

Johannes hung his head to hide the misery that overwhelmed him.

"I think not," the Prince of Ifriqiya said. "These men had no intention of rescuing your holy books, did they?"

"The force was led by Count Theophylact and the knight at his side was a priest although he debases our order. Land and money are their business. I fear it was only a show, and the church has lost."

Ahmad put his hand on Johannes' arm to comfort him; however, the librarian felt little. "Perhaps things will not be as bad as you think. After all, I owe you my life. Attend to my wound and then we can talk. And priest, make the stitches small."

"I can ease only some of the pain. Are you so vain that you're worried how the scar will look?"

"I'm the leader of men. Many have had battle wounds stitched. This is my first. I want them to witness that pain is nothing to me so sew the stitches small, very small."

"As you wish."

Saint Peter's Basilica looked more like a ruin than the holiest church in the world. Saracen soldiers and Turkish mercenaries camped on the stone floor, their fires burning in every niche and filling the building with acrid smoke. They spoke in muffled voices, and their hollow laughter echoed off sad, bare walls. Johannes tucked blankets around the prince, avoiding the accusing eyes of his enemies.

Ahmad's younger brother had returned after seeing to the men and knelt next to Johannes, inspecting Ahmad's flushed face. "Will he be able to travel?"

"He's running a fever. He may have an infection."

"What can you do?"

"Nothing for the moment. We must let him sleep."

"Do what you can for we leave at first light."

"Ahmad needs rest if he's to recover."

"I have to think of the troops now. We must escape before your armies regroup."

Johannes awakened with a start. He had drifted into an uneasy sleep on the chill basilica floor, watching Ahmad's face contort in pain and then ease. Having mixed a draught of opium and mandrake dissolved in wine to make him sleep, he was stunned to find the pallet empty. Forcing his stiff cold bones to rise, he found himself alone in the church. A commotion of shouting men came from outside.

Ahmad barked orders to the men who hitched horses to wagons abandoned by Theophylact. They had draped some kind of strange collar Johannes had never seen around the horses' necks, and lashed the collar to the wagons. Troops scrambled atop the carts, emptying branches, straw, and rubble. A group of Berber mercenaries grabbed handfuls of books and tossed them irreverently into an emptied wagon. Ahmad shouted an incomprehensible order, obviously a rebuke. The Berbers shrugged their shoulders and sat on the end of the wagon.

"You're awake at last, Priest."

Johannes placed his hand on the prince's forehead. Cold, damp sweat moistened his palm. "The fever has broken. There's no infection."

"I'm taking your scriptures, and all you can think about is my health?"

"If I begged you to leave our books, would you?"

"Would that I could. As ungrateful as it sounds, I need the dinars they will bring. My people survive by plundering our enemies. However, we're commanded to take neither from Moslems nor lands that pledge us fealty. So we raid further and further afield to find gold and silver. The armies which make us powerful drain our wealth like ravenous dogs. I must pay the men in my service. If I can't, they shall be master and I slave." Ahmad put his hand on Johannes' shoulder. "But I'm shamed before you, Priest. You showed me kindness when I deserved none. You saved the life of a prince of the tribe of Bani Tamim. So I held my men, who are anxious to flee, at bay until you awakened."

"For what reason?"

"To repay you in some small way, and perhaps I can do your faith a service as well."

"What do you mean?"

"You said these books were filled with forgeries and all manner of false writing, is that not so?"

"True."

"Would you not wish to be rid of the lies?"

"Of course."

"Although I don't know you, your heart is plain to see. So I will allow you to choose the words of the Prophet Jesus that shall remain and which writings will come with me."

"I don't understand." Johannes furrowed his brow.

"We leave in one hour. I can give you until then to pick as many books as you wish. Those you select, you may keep. The rest, I must take. I've instructed my captain to assist you."

"You're asking me to decide what's true and what's not?"

"No," the prince replied. "I am granting that you may keep what you want."

"It's the same thing."

"For an honest man, I suppose it is. It's a great burden. I realize that now."

"I don't possess the wisdom."

"Then you must find some and if you cannot, I counsel you to follow your heart. It served me well. I've read that Christians are commanded to love their enemies. You obeyed your God and showed me love. I'm sure He will now show you the answer you seek. When the sun rises, we leave. You have an hour." Ahmad turned, shouted some orders, and was gone.

Johannes ran amongst mounds of books and scrolls stacked in front of the basilica, trying to make sense of what might be in the piles. Saracens gaped at the crazy priest as he opened one book and another, glancing inside, then casting them aside. Many mocked or aped his frantic spinning and scrambling to the amusement of their comrades, laughing out loud and running in circles only to fall to the ground howling. Johannes ignored them. He had but an hour to save what he could.

Ahmad's brother didn't join in the merrymaking. He dutifully followed the frantic priest, catching books tossed to him and handing them to sergeants who passed them to the soldiers who had formed a sort of bucket brigade. They, in turn, passed the scrolls and books man-to-man and heaped them on the basilica steps.

At last, Johannes found the pile that held the most promise and dove into the middle to the astonished guffaws of his audience. Books flew in the air like a fountain, and soldiers broke into even louder laughter.

"Silence," Ahmad finally shouted. "Load these." He pointed with an angry glare to the stacks Johannes had left behind. Men rushed to their work throwing seven hundred years of Christendom's testimonies into emptied wagons. Finally, soldiers began scooping at the hill of books surrounding Johannes as the first rays of morning sun loosed their brilliant arrows.

Johannes, exhausted but still frenetic, felt a hand on his shoulder. "Your time is up," Ahmad said.

"A few more," Johannes said.

"We can wait no longer. We must retreat."

The librarian plopped down on his backside, legs splayed, as the last of the church's writings were snatched from around him. An uncomfortable lump prodded his skinny rump and he pulled out one remaining book, a Psalter. He hugged it against his chest. "I don't know whether to curse you or thank you," Johannes said to Ahmad.

"You may do either, or neither, or both, as you wish. You've earned the right. In your place, I think I should curse you. However, I don't have your courage. Only exceptional men, and most women of course, possess such bravery to carry on when only tragedy and hopelessness reign, doing what must be done when all seems lost. It's far easier to fight and die rather than carry on." Prince Ahmad surveyed Johannes with his thoughtful regard. "You're no woman, so I'm proud to know an exceptional priest."

Johannes felt as though he should thank Ahmad, but he found little thanks in him. Still, he was grateful for the few hundred or so books he'd been granted. Looking at the wagons filled with gold and silver pilfered from Saint Peter's as well as the church's library, he stood wearily clutching the Psalter. "How can you haul such a load? Horses can't pull heavy wagons. The harnesses will strangle them. You need teams of oxen hitched to wooden yokes." *Perhaps God had sent a miracle after all*, Johannes thought, wondering if Ahmad's lack of planning might yet save the day.

The prince stared for a moment, reflecting on what the priest said, then shouted to one of his men who retrieved a large, oblong object from one of the carts. The soldier carried it to Johannes and dropped it on the ground. "A parting gift, Priest. It'll make you rich if that is what you desire. My men spent the night fashioning them." Ahmad clasped Johannes' narrow shoulders with large hands. "I've taken a liking to you, although I'm not sure what my people will think when they discover a priest saved my life. Write to me and let me know what you do with the collar, and tell me which scriptures you spared. Send the letter to Sicily. It will find its way to me."

With that, Ahmad climbed on his stallion and waved as he raced to the head of the cavalry while the infantry boarded their fustas, pushing away from shore with oars. Mounted Arabs, Berbers, and Turks advanced, and the wagons lurched forward, rumbling.

The horses did not strangle as they would had they pulled the loads with the throat-and-girth harnesses Italians used. Johannes marveled as he watched them pull the wagons much faster than oxen could. Yet he wept bitterly as Rome's Holy Scriptures disappeared down the road to Ostia.

Johannes labored all morning and into the afternoon, carrying the books back to the shelves in the grotto. He had taken but a moment to decide that he should protect what he had saved rather than running to the *patriarchum* to raise an army. Theophylact commanded Rome's military, and the church would receive no help from him. Most likely, he was busy hiding the gold he had stolen. No one could divine where the Emperor's men were, but as usual, they were not where they were needed. In the end he saw only one logical choice: to save the scriptures.

Scribes could begin their copying once again with what he had saved, but had he found enough? He had rescued the oldest copies of the Gospels and the letters of Saint Paul, as well as the apocalyptic Revelations. He had salvaged many complete Bibles in Latin and the earliest Greek ones, written long before Jerome's translation. For himself, he retrieved as many heretical scriptures as he could find. These heresies, he returned to their secret place in the sarcophagus, and he resolved to find a new stone cover.

Dirt lined his face in streaks where rivulets of sweat had deposited it. Weary and sad beyond belief, he sat on the marble steps of the violated basilica, rocking back and forth. He knew he should make his way to the *patriarchum*, but fatigue welded him to the spot. Only now did he hear troops marching quick step from the direction of Rome and spied heads wearing dissimilar helms and breastplates that neither gleamed nor did one soldier's armor match another's.

At the head of the disorganized column tramped Anastasius

and Baraldus. Beside them was Avraham's son, Elchanan. An odd assortment of troops followed the three, wearing different uniforms. Some of their weapons were merely old, while others were antiques. Yet despite the lack of orderliness, the men looked ready to fight, and some limped as though they had seen battle already.

The soldiers were neither Lothair's nor in the service of the city's nobles. They were a ragtag army of guards from the foreign *scholae*, various confederations of Greeks, English, Frisians, and dozens of other foreigners as well as a battalion of Jews. Together, they had defended the city, led by Baraldus after Theophylact and the other nobles fled.

At first the guards of the *scholae* laughed and mocked the Lombard who looked ridiculous in his priestly robe cinched to his knees, wearing a steel helm too small for his head and waving a short sword. But as he shouted orders and cuffed men on the ears who scoffed at his authority, all realized that this was no ordinary cleric. He took command as easily as a parish priest says mass.

Jews were used to having no protection for their poor quarter in the Trastevere. Thus, every able man belonged to a militia organized for their defense. They beat back the Saracens, who had come to pillage their Temple, led by Elchanan the tanner.

Baraldus and Anastasius ran to where Johannes sat. "Are you well, brother?" They squatted beside him.

Johannes did not look up.

"Where are you hurt?"

"In my soul," Johannes said. "They've stolen everything. The golden offerings, the vestments, anything of value, they've taken. They even tore down the silver altar over the tomb of the Apostle, leaving his bones scattered on the floor." A sob broke the priest's voice. "And they've stolen the library."

"Our books?" Anastasius replied, astonished. "How do you steal a library?"

"They loaded them on carts and wagons and took them."

Baraldus' cheeks and ears turned bright red. "We'll run them down and smite the heathens for their wickedness." The Lombard thrust his sword into the air.

"You won't catch them," Johannes said.

"We'll march all night and fall upon them as the sun rises on the morrow."

Johannes hung his head. "They're on horseback and in their boats, and you're on foot."

"Too true, Master Johannes, but they tow wagons, and men can march faster than plodding oxen."

"Oxen don't pull their wagons. Horses do."

"Your brain is addled. Impossible."

"I tell you that teams of horses pull the wagons, and they galloped away with little effort."

Baraldus shook his head. "Horses cannot last long pulling such weight. We'll catch them. We must." Turning to Elchanan he said, "Your men are the best fighters I've seen in many a day. Nevertheless, this isn't your fight, but the church's. There's no shame if you would go back to your families."

"We started this day with you, and we will finish it with you. Jesus was a Pharisee, a prophet, and a Jew. We'll fight for Him and for you and our friend Johannes."

"Thank you," Baraldus said to his new comrade-in-arms. He shouted orders to the rabble of soldiers, and the column trotted off down Vatican Hill toward the port of Ostia, kicking up a choking dust.

Anastasius consoled his protégé. "They'll catch them."

Johannes laid his head on his mentor's lap on the steps of Peter's holy church as despair and fatigue overwhelmed him.

25
Normandy

Rashid al-Ansar guided the Renault minivan out of the rental lot at Charles De Gaulle Airport. He drove around the loop, past the terminals, and entered the freeway toward Paris. Next to him, Hassan lit a cigarette and punched a button on the radio. He exhaled a fog of smoke as an Arab rap tune blared from the speakers.

"Open the window," Rashid said.

"It's freezing outside," Hassan shot back.

"Then put out the cigarette."

Hassan smirked as he cracked the window. "You should have rented something flashier. My grandfather drives a nicer car than this piece of crap."

"We're not here to waste the community's donations, although we could spare some cash for better clothes," Rashid said.

"What do you mean?"

"You look like an army deserter with your camouflage pants and military boots, and what's with the US Army t-shirt?"

Rashid grew defensive at the criticism. "It's the latest style—urban combat. I'm not wearing a suit or some Bedouin dress. I'm a soldier, and I'm going to dress like one."

"You're conspicuous. How about something casual, slacks or blue jeans? We need to blend in."

"Hah," Hassan scoffed. "If you want to look like them, I'll get some bleach for your hair and skin. You're such a pain in the ass."

"Me? You almost bungled the job. You let a priest beat you senseless, a Christian priest!"

Hassan scrunched down in his seat. "He sucker punched me."

"You hit an old man and a woman for God's sake. What did you expect?"

Hassan pulled a box knife from his pocket and pressed the flat of the blade against Rashid's neck. "I'm doing all the dirty work while you keep your hands clean."

Rashid stared straight ahead. The steel was cold on his skin. "Nothing is unclean in our holy mission. Does not the Qur'an say to smite the unbeliever's necks? The blood sacrifice atones for their sin."

Hassan pushed harder, digging the point into flesh. Rashid lifted his chin, but set his jaw. "Next time, get a real razor. You couldn't even cut his throat properly."

Hassan slid the cutting edge back into the metal handle. "We got the job done."

Rashid realized he was holding his breath and exhaled slowly so Hassan wouldn't notice. His palms sweated as he gripped the steering wheel. "It was messy. I said to keep them occupied. That's why I gave you the pistol. If you can't take care of an old man, a woman, and a priest without causing a riot, I'll get someone else. You made a hell of a racket."

"That was no ordinary priest," Hassan said.

They drove in silence around the *peripherique* and exited at the autoroute toward Normandy. The freeway narrowed into a two-lane highway and the congested city soon became a series of towns. The towns gave way to villages, and they rolled past brown, dormant fields hibernating in the winter gloom.

Not far from the coast, Rashid turned the minivan off the main road. A country lane bordered by tall hedgerows wound around fields cultivated for a thousand years and more. The single-car lane was walled by skeletal beech trees stripped of their leaves.

"Please tell me we're not going to be stuck out here in the backwoods with cows and chickens waking us up at dawn," Hassan complained. "I want to be in the city where we can have some fun."

"We're on a mission, and that's our only concern. Seek your diversions on your own time."

"Why we can't do both?"

"Because we're commanded to come here," Rashid snapped at his friend, frustrated at his obstinacy.

At the end of the lane, they approached a heavy iron gate supported by two brick pillars. Rashid parked the minivan, stepped out, and walked toward the barrier. A video camera on top of a pillar followed his steps. He spotted a tarnished brass speaker at the side of the gate and pressed the button below the mouthpiece.

A voice spoke from the speaker. "What do you want?"

"It's Rashid, Rashid al-Ansar."

"Who's with you"?

"Hassan."

"Enter and peace be upon you." The gate opened automatically, but no one was visible inside. Rashid drove the Renault into the gravel courtyard toward a two-story, half-timbered house. Large brick outbuildings with gabled roofs on either side formed a U-shaped compound. One of the buildings might have been a barn once and the other stables, but they had been modernized and appeared to be living quarters.

The farmhouse door opened and an Arab in a white ankle-length robe stepped out. He raised his arms, and a large smile spread on his face. Rashid sprang from the car and ran to his master, who held him by his shoulders and kissed his cheeks. "*Salaam Aleichem*, peace be upon you."

"And you, Imam."

The imam turned to Hassan, who stepped from the minivan. "Welcome Hassan the reluctant."

Hassan lowered his head. "Salaam, Imam."

"You're just in time for the afternoon prayer. You've been through an ordeal which clouds the soul, but your spirits will soar once you pray." Then, turning to Rashid, he narrowed his eyes and whispered, "Did you bring the book with you?"

"Yes." Rashid smiled proudly. "I'll get it."

"Later, after you've prayed. First, you must purify yourselves with running water and put on clean clothes. Let me show you to your rooms."

The compound included no mosque, but one of the brick buildings had a large room set aside for services. The congregation numbered only eleven or twelve men and they seemed like hard men, hardly what one would expect in a holy community.

The imam led prayers for the assembly. As he recited verses from the Qur'an, Rashid sensed the presence of God. He faced east with the others toward the city of Mecca, while the imam preached. Then he bowed, crouched on his knees, and laid his head on the floor. Finally, he prostrated his body, giving himself over to Allah's divine will.

With the *fard* or obligatory prayers complete, he continued to sit, meditating long after the others had left. His heart opened to the overwhelming presence of God and tears moistened his eyes. How could one not be moved by the words of the Prophet? He had faith that God guided his life on the holiest of missions.

Rashid sucked in a large breath and returned to the physical world. He felt refreshed and morally whole. The imam was right, prayer was necessary to restore the spirit, like being *born again*, as the Christians said. He rose and turned to leave. The imam stood in the open doorway, beaming. "Truly, Rashid," he said, pleased at the young man's devotion, "Allah has a special place in heaven for a faithful son. Now, let's see the book."

The imam thumbed the pages, pressing his face close to the ancient script, peering at the text through half-moon spectacles. Occasionally, he mouthed a word. "This is the one. You saved it and restored our honor."

"What's the importance of this Latin book?" Rashid asked.

"Ah, my son, the meaning is of little use to us. The significance lies in a great sin committed by our forefathers."

"What sin is that?"

The Imam breathed a gloomy sigh. "One that obliges us to protect the book until the Mahdi returns and brings the golden days of justice."

"I don't understand."

"Of course you don't, but understanding will come sooner than you can imagine. You're part of the plan. It's your heritage."

"Can you not tell me what that is?" Rashid chafed at the arcane answers.

"Not yet, but when the time is right. First, you must deliver the book to someone."

"I'll tell Hassan to get ready."

"No." The imam stopped Rashid with a hand on his shoulder. "This is a task for you alone. No one else must know. Hassan has his special talents, but this job requires precision and subtlety. Those are not his strengths. After all, he's not one of us." Surprise covered Rashid's face and made the imam laugh. "Oh, don't think for a moment I don't understand Hassan completely. He's a brute and his faith waivers in the slightest breeze, but he has skills I need. However, only our family can do what has to be done. Now you must take the book to Paris."

"We've just come from there." Rashid was confused.

"Of course, and the book must go back, but somewhere else in the city."

"What's the address"?

"I'll call you when you're on the road, but go now," the imam said. "Under no circumstances can you return here. Leave the rental car. One of the men can deal with it. I bought a used car from a local and haven't changed the registration. One can't be too careful."

"Is something wrong?"

"No Rashid. All is as it must be. No more questions; time to go."

"You're not leaving me here." Hassan threw himself on the bed, exasperated. "Where are you going?"

"I was told not to say."

"Oh come on, I swear I won't tell."

"I can't, Hassan."

"Well, what am I supposed to do, milk cows?"

"There are no cows."

"You know what I mean. We're in the middle of nowhere and when I tried to walk through the gate, the guards stopped me. They say I'm not allowed to leave without permission from the imam. Can you imagine? This is worse than living at home."

"You knew what you were getting into when you signed on."

"All I wanted was a ticket out of the desert. I didn't expect this. Please take me with you. I'll do anything you say, I swear."

Rashid was sympathetic to his friend and spoke deferentially. "I would if I could, but it's not possible."

"Come on, we're a team. We've been one since our days in the camps, remember? Who helped you finish early morning runs when the instructors were on your ass and you barfed your guts?"

"You," Rashid admitted.

"Who spent late nights showing you how to take apart and reassemble machine pistols and AK-47's when you thought you were failing out? And you would have blown yourself up when they tried to teach you how to make explosives if not for me. I laughed my ass off watching you get gel all over your hands. So what if we're from different tribes? We're brothers to the end, remember?"

"I'll never forget, but I still can't take you with me. Orders."

Hassan jumped from the bed in a rage that Rashid knew was more act than ire. "You're an ungrateful bastard, Rashid. Don't ever ask me for anything." He stormed out of the room, slamming the door.

He hated to hurt his friend's feelings, but the imam was right: Hassan was not one of them. Rashid had grown up destitute in the desert on the Iran-Iraq border, where his village recognized no manmade boundary in the land Allah had given his people. The youngest of several sons, he was mostly uneducated until his twelfth birthday, when his father had led him to a Mosque and turned him over to the care of the imam. From that day forward, his life was never to be the same. Indeed, the imam transformed him completely. He sent him to school to learn the Qur'an and, when he was lettered enough, began to tutor him personally in other books, foreign books with ancient writing. The Aramaic was easy since it was like Arabic, but Latin and Greek were bizarre, written the wrong way, from left to right as though they were in opposition to God. Hassan knew nothing of these languages and less of the burden placed on Rashid's people, the *Children of the Book*.

After his education, he was sent to a camp in Lebanon to learn how to fight. That's where he had met Hassan, who became his fast friend and helped him train during those grueling days when he was brutalized by merciless instructors. After Rashid finished his training, his first assignment was to open a safe house in Rome. He chose Hassan to be his assistant since they had forged a bond of loyalty in the desert, a connection only soldiers understand. Now, for the first time in ages, they'd be separated.

Anyway, his task was confusing and he couldn't explain what it was to Hassan because he didn't know himself. First they seized a book in Paris and now he had to return it, all very cryptic. The job would have been much easier if they had just dropped it off in the city. Then their mission would be over and they could go back to Rome. But soon, the imam had said, all would be revealed.

Rashid saw Hassan's sullen face in the rearview mirror as he steered the rattling Peugeot 206 through the open gate into the early evening. Hassan was selfish, easily provoked to violence and devoted to his worldly distractions, but they had a past together. *I'll buy him something in Paris*, he thought. *Maybe an MP3 player or some rap music.* Then he drove into the tunnel of trees lining the narrow lane that was illuminated only by the dim, dirty lights of the creaky Peugeot.

26
Ḥalawa

Colonelo **Del Carlo** poured over copies of ledgers the forensic accountants of the French counter terrorism unit, the GIGN, had prepared. They showed a complex series of financial transactions, but the number crunchers had sorted them out. Money from financiers with links to terrorist groups was transferred from accounts in Saudi Arabia to Lebanon and Jordan. Then the cash went to banks in Dubai, which obeys few international banking regulations, and was wired to Muslim charities in Europe.

More difficult to trace was money from Islamic charities whose source was legitimate, but was diverted later for illicit purposes. Virtually impossible to follow was a system of cash transfers used for hundreds of years. Known in Asia as *chop* or *hundi* in India, in the Middle East *halawa* was a network to move money without banks. A code was sent from one country to another, often simply a password by email. Then the receiving party collected cash from a businessman who lived in the country. No bank transfers and no records.

Legitimate banking institutions had a hand in money laundering, as well. Bankers who charged fat fees turned a blind eye because their bottom line mattered more than shutting down cash pipelines to terrorists.

The ledgers made clear that an imam in France had used laundered money to buy a farmhouse and the surrounding land. According to *Capitaine* Desmoulins, an attorney had negotiated the deal while keeping his client's name hidden. The residents eventually found out and filed suit to keep the transaction from being concluded. However, the imam claimed in court that the farm would allow young Muslims to escape city slums and spend their vacations in the countryside. He had played the racism card and the French court ruled in his favor, finding no legitimate reason to nullify the sale. Of course, the courts had not been able to trace the source of the money used to buy the property. *Too bad*, Del Carlo thought.

The Colonel read several statements from locals that gunfire often came from the farm and laughed out loud. *Did the imam truly think he would find anonymity in Normandy, one of the most conservative regions in France?* The imam claimed that rifles and shotguns were fired only during hunting season or for target practice, and refused to allow police to search the premises. Nevertheless, residents lodged lots of complaints—hundreds, in fact. The local cops passed reports to the GIGN, and they had ended up on Desmoulins's desk. He theorized that the farm was being used as a training camp.

The reports fascinated Del Carlo, but he wondered why Desmoulins had sent them to him. An attached note requested that he call after his review. His interest piqued, he dialed the direct line to the GIGN captain. "Hello, *Capitaine*. Del Carlo here."

"*Bonjour, Colonel*, a pleasure to hear from you. How's your American priest?"

"Fine, as far as I know. I heard he received a fat promotion, in charge of Technology and Security at the Vatican Library."

"Security? After the fiasco in Paris?" *Capitaine* Desmoulins was incredulous. "You're kidding, surely."

"Who can fathom the workings of the church?"

"Did you read the report I sent you?" Desmoulins asked.

"With great interest, and I appreciate your courtesy in keeping me informed, but I don't grasp the relevance to the dead priest or missing prayer book?"

"Do you recall Father Romano's description of his attacker?"

"Sure do. I thought it might be a paramilitary operation," Del Carlo said.

"Me too. Not many Europeans dress in military fatigues. Imagine my surprise when a surveillance team spotted a man on Interpol's Terrorism Watch List dressed in secondhand army clothes, complete with boots and a crew cut. So I did some checking. He's a known associate of a radical imam and flew from Rome to Paris the morning of the break-in. Are you interested now?"

"Of course. I would never have guessed Arabs. Is he at the farm with the imam?"

"Yes and we've planned a raid. I thought you might like to observe," the French captain said.

"You bet, but..."

"What is it, *Colonelo*?"

"Well..."

"Come on, spit it out," Demoulins said bluntly.

"Father Romano might be of some use. How would you feel about him joining us?"

"You must be joking!"

Romano was incredulous as he answered the colonel. "What use would I be on a raid of a terrorist compound?"

"It's a hunch, Father, but if these are the men who attacked you, there's a good chance they have the Psalter with them. It might be our only chance to examine it."

"Couldn't you bring it here?"

"Father, this is a French operation. If the book is there, I doubt *Capitaine* Desmoulins would release it to me and certainly not to you."

"I get your point. I'll have to ask my cardinal for permission."

"If he agrees, will you come?" The Italian colonel asked.

"I wouldn't miss it."

Romano told Isabelle he had to attend to some business out

of town and would leave her in the charge of Cardinal Minissi's secretary. Father Sabella was a quiet priest with a keen intellect and unswerving devotion to the Library's Cardinal. His was the theology of efficiency, and he used his quick mind to carry out Minissi's instructions to the letter with robotic zeal. He balked at having a woman in his charge, admitting it made him uncomfortable. But when Romano explained Isabelle's mission, to install a digital photography system that could detect scriptures long erased, he became enthusiastic to be even a small part of the task.

For her part, Isabelle said she wouldn't have the time to miss Romano since she had thrown herself into researching which system would be best for a massive Library with such a miniscule budget. Unfortunately, IsyReADeT was proprietary, and the beta software was on loan to the French National Archives. She mused that IsyReADeT would have been perfect because the system practically ran itself. Instead, she would have to choose something more labor-intensive, and that meant a good deal of training.

Unmarked cars from the French GIGN raced down National Route Fourteen, blue lights flashing, followed by four large vans loaded with strike units from the Paris gendarmerie attached to *Capitaine* Desmoulins. Romano sat between Del Carlo and Desmoulins. He felt out of place and ill at ease. He knew that even though the church had forgiven him for losing the Psalter, these two professionals regarded his actions as amateurish at the least and more than likely incompetent. He squirmed in the little space he had.

Approaching the turn to the farm, Desmoulins spotted a beat-up Peugeot turning onto the highway from the narrow lane. He ordered the driver to slow. Through binoculars, he read the license plate and keyed the number into his notebook processor. The car was registered to a local farmer.

"You understand," the French captain said to Del Carlo and Romano, "you're observers and must remain in the car until we've secured the site. Then I'll send for you."

"Of course," Del Carlo replied. "I have but two interests, the prayer book and the men who stole it."

"Then we're agreed, *Colonelo*, you'll be responsible for Father Romano?"

"Yes."

"Good. I'll rely on your professionalism."

Capitaine Desmoulins gave instructions to his lieutenant, and the operation was set in motion. Elite military police from the gendarmerie dressed in black with MP5A3 submachine guns and wearing night-vision goggles scaled the stone walls surrounding the compound. They dropped to the other side and ran across the courtyard. Gravel scrunched under their rubber-soled boots as they surrounded the farmhouse and brick dormitories.

A dog barked from inside one of the houses. A light flicked on in one of the upstairs windows. "*Merde*," Desmoulins swore, then shouted into his walkie-talkie, "*Allez, allez, allez!*"

On cue, gendarmes pried open ground-floor metal shutters with crowbars and tossed stun grenades inside. They detonated with a percussive bang. Three teams of gendarmes burst through doors and windows. They screamed at the occupants, who rushed downstairs in boxer shorts and t-shirts, waving rifles and shotguns.

One of the Arabs fired a blast from his double-barrel. Pellets splattered the wall, sending plaster flying. The French team flopped to the ground and sprayed the stairs from prone positions. Two Arabs plummeted over the banister, crashing to the floor with lifeless thuds. Another slumped on the steps. Gunfire erupted in short bursts from the other buildings.

Desmoulins ordered the sergeant at his side to open the gate. He produced a battering ram and with a second gendarme, they swung hard. The gate resounded with a metallic clang but didn't budge.

"Blow it," Demoulins said. They placed a small plastic charge on the lock and retreated behind the cars. The sergeant pressed a red button on a miniature black box and the detonation shattered the lock. The gate limped open. Desmoulins marched, in alert and focused, his Beretta automatic pistol gripped in his hand. He knew his team was mopping up by the chatter on his radio. They dragged out men still in their underclothes, arms behind their backs and secured with plastic tie wraps. Police pushed prisoners to their knees, then onto their faces.

The lieutenant, seeing his captain in the courtyard, ran to his side. "Report," Desmoulins said.

"No casualties, *mon Capitaine*. They have three dead and two wounded."

"Where's our imam?"

"Inside. He hasn't been roughed up or humiliated, sir."

"Good. I don't want any martyrs…and our suspects?"

"They haven't been found, *Capitaine*. We're searching the buildings now."

"*Merde*! Very well, Lieutenant, carry on." Desmoulins walked back to the gate, proud of his men. Once again, they'd been lucky; but Desmoulins's definition of luck was when skill and nonstop training met with opportunity. His teams were skilled and he trained them relentlessly. Their dangerous assignments provided all the opportunity anyone could desire. Still, he was troubled that two had flown the coop, and he thought again of the Peugeot 206. He was making a mental note to contact the owner when he was jerked backward by the collar, the barrel of a gun shoved under his chin. "Make a sound and I'll blow your face off," the voice from behind hissed as the captain was pulled to the stone wall. "And drop the pistol."

"Calm yourself," Desmoulins said with difficulty. "My men are everywhere. You can't escape."

"We're leaving together or we'll depart the earth together. The choice is yours."

The GIGN captain registered deadly intent in the passionless voice. This man felt no fear and no emotion. That was truly dangerous. He didn't fit the profile of someone who negotiated. For the first time in his life, Desmoulins knew his odds weren't good. His only hope was to help the man escape. Yet once free, Desmoulins would be a hindrance and eliminated without so much as a passing thought. The faces of his beautiful wife and two little daughters rushed into his thoughts and he was grieved to think of tears in their lovely eyes.

"Drop your weapon!" Colonel Del Carlo shouted, pointing his service Beretta at the attacker from an acute angle. He edged closer to get a more direct shot, but Hassan had his back against the wall and shielded his front with the captain.

"No, you drop yours." Hassan shoved the automatic harder under Desmoulins' chin, making him wince. "Or I'll blow his brains out."

"Don't do it, Colonel," the French captain rasped.

"Shut up," Hassan said.

"Shoot, Colonel."

"I don't have a shot."

"I'm ordering you."

Del Carlo moved the barrel micrometers back and forth, searching for a better angle.

Hassan squeezed his trigger finger tighter and Desmoulins felt the hand flex. "Shoot now, for God's sake!"

"I said shut..." Hassan was saying as the gun fired. The discharge burned Desmoulins' cheek, and he fell to the ground. His eye stung and he caught only glimpses of a man in black, spinning.

Romano had jerked the barrel from Desmoulins's chin with his right hand, and his left delivered a crushing blow to Hassan's ribs. The Arab doubled over, yet managed to hold on to the automatic. They struggled for the gun, whirling and jerking until Hassan headbutted the priest, striking his cheekbone. Romano saw stars, but knew from his days on the streets what it was like to have his bell rung, so he held on. He clenched the Arab until the netherworld between consciousness and a knockout passed.

Hassan struck him in the mouth and followed with a short hook to the chin. He cocked his arm for another punch. A spark of light revived Romano's senses. He ducked and countered with a combination jab to the nose and roundhouse to the temple. Hassan staggered, his legs rubbery. Romano grabbed the automatic's barrel, but Hassan yanked with all his might and wrenched it from the priest's hand. He leveled the gun at Romano.

Three shots rang out in rapid succession, and Hassan's eyes bulged. He slumped to his knees with an expression of wonder, then fell to the ground. Romano spun as wisps of smoke rose from the barrel of Del Carlo's gun. He rushed to Hassan's side and knelt. A trickle of dark blood oozed at the corner of the Arab's mouth. The priest recognized him as the attacker in the Héber's apartment and wanted to ask why, but the young man's time was up. Romano made the sign of the cross as Hassan's eyes went blank, his soul's last breath fleeing to whatever heaven awaited.

The lieutenant rushed up with three gendarmes, machine guns at the ready. Del Carlo inspected the burn on Desmoulins' face. "I'm alright," Desmoulins reassured him. "Have some men fan out outside the wall. We still have one bird loose."

"I'm sorry, *mon Capitaine*." The lieutenant was horrified that the operation had not gone flawlessly and his captain nearly paid the price.

"The fault is mine. I didn't think to leave men outside. Now, go find the other one." Turning to Del Carlo, he said, "I ordered you to shoot."

"You would've died."

"Perhaps, but we would have dictated the situation, not him."

"Sometimes *Capitaine*," Del Carlo grinned, "you have to play defense." He helped Desmoulins to his feet.

"Is this the man who attacked you in Paris?" Desmoulins asked Romano.

"Yes."

"I thought you couldn't see his face."

"I can tell by the way he moved. He telegraphs his punches."

Desmoulins frowned. "I told you to stay in the car."

"I'm not very obedient," Romano said.

"I misjudged you, Father. I've never met a priest who was a man of action, not just prayers. You have my thanks and my respect." He held out his hand. "If you ever decide to change jobs, call me."

"My boss wouldn't approve."

The lieutenant sprinted back. "I think you had better look at this, *Capitaine*, in the basement."

Desmoulins expected to find automatic rifles, perhaps AK-47's, the weapon of choice for terrorists because they were cheap and effective. He also thought they might discover plastic explosives or perhaps more sophisticated gel. Since they were in farm country, manure and ammonia could be procured easily to create low-tech bombs with massive power. Instead, the basement housed garden tools, bottles of water, and shelves of canned goods. A rack on the wall secured a row of shotguns and a second one held hunting rifles.

What captured his attention however, were maps, photographs, and handmade sketches of a nuclear reactor on the coast. On another table lay a schedule of ferry crossings from nearby Dieppe to Newhaven, with photos of ferry interiors, particularly the hold that carried automobiles. "Oh my God," Desmoulins said, "the reactors, the ferries." Turning to the lieutenant he ordered, "Notify the port authority."

Desmoulins allowed Romano in the basement. The priest had earned his trust, and Romano walked around the room glancing at the guns and shelves holding supplies. He noticed nothing unusual until a stack of photocopies on a work desk attracted his attention. Leafing through the pages, he called to Del Carlo. "*Colonelo*, it's the Psalter."

"Are you sure?"

"They're only copies," Romano replied, "but I would know the script anywhere. The book is definitely here. At least, it was."

27
Sayyid

Rashid sat with his head resting on the steering wheel in the old Peugeot, deep in despair. He had pulled off the freeway at a rest stop outside Paris. Tractor trailers filled the parking lot, and light from the café spilled out on the sidewalk. Phosphorescent hands on the car's dirty clock pointed to nine forty-six. *Forty-five minutes late*, he thought. *The imam was supposed to call before nine p.m. with instructions. Something's happened. Those police cars surely went to the farm. Now, all is lost.*

Rashid hadn't wanted to leave without a definite plan or at least directions, but the imam had insisted he leave immediately. He must have known disaster was about to fall and wanted the book and Rashid gone. Yet now, he had no directives, no contacts, and nowhere to go. Perhaps he should poke around the Mosque, but he had been warned to stay away.

He stared at the ancient book wrapped in wax paper. *A clue might be inside*, he thought. He set the bundle on his lap and tugged the paper free. Opening the faded red cover, worn through in places, an ornate illustration depicted a gaunt, bearded man hanging from a cross, wearing only a loincloth. Spikes had been driven into his hands and feet, and his head hung down. Blood dripped from his brow, pierced by a wreath of thorns. Rashid loathed that Christians revered such a gruesome execution scene.

Jesus had been a martyr like Mohammad's cousin, Ali, who had also been murdered by his own people. Muslims, however, didn't make paintings of executions. *Not only were such images disgusting*, he reflected, *they were forbidden, even according to the Bible*. He turned the pages and skimmed the Latin words drawn in elaborate calligraphy. *Maybe instructions had been slipped inside*, he thought, turning brittle vellum sheets. He was about to give up when an electronic chime made him jump. He fairly shouted into the phone, "imam, are you alright?"

"Listen to me, Rashid, and don't hang up. The imam has been arrested." The caller spoke in Farsi.

"Who is this?"

"Are you listening? I need your complete attention," the caller said.

An overwhelming impulse told Rashid to press the *end call* button.

"Don't hang up if you want instructions."

"Who are you?"

"Will you listen now?"

Rashid didn't answer.

"I'm the one who called the imam to warn him the police were coming. He was sending you to me to deliver the book."

"Why didn't he save himself?"

"He knew he could not. Besides, the book is more important."

"Who cares about a silly old book? We must save the imam."

"So we will, but the book isn't silly and plays a crucial role in the imam's plans," the caller said. "Weren't you taught this? Are you not a *child of the book*?"

"Yes," Rashid said.

"Then don't blaspheme it. You must bring it to me now."

"How can I tell whether these things are true?"

"Who gave me your telephone number? How would I know you possess this book?"

Rashid thought for a moment. "I don't know."

"Yes you do, Rashid al-Ansar, and I was also told you're to be a warrior in the days of justice. Now listen, and I'll tell you where you're to meet me."

He was to rendezvous with his contact at a bistro not far from Paris' Mosque, which made Rashid uncomfortable. The imam had drilled him to avoid places where Arabs congregated, except at the busiest times, when he might find anonymity in a crowd. It would be nighttime in the fifth arrondissement, one of the expensive and chic districts in Paris. An Arab would be conspicuous even though the mosque was only a few blocks away. Fortunately, he wore slacks and had fetched a black sport jacket from his bag so he could blend in better. Still, his skin crawled with uneasiness as though every eye watched.

He sat just inside the door rather than at one of the small sidewalk tables and ordered an espresso from a waiter who eyed him suspiciously. He had arrived fifteen minutes early because he wanted to size up his contact. After all, he was turning over the book that held such enigmatic importance, and there could be no mistakes. He would make no mistake.

The appointed time came and went. Another ten minutes passed and still no one. Rashid scanned the sidewalk as the waiter carried wicker chairs and tables inside and stacked them. He went over every point in the caller's instructions. He was at the right bistro at the right time.

Rashid stood up and stepped outside. He looked up and down the street, but realized the futility. Sitting back down, the waiter gathered up his demitasse and asked if he wanted another espresso. "No," Rashid answered, looking at his wristwatch. He must have misunderstood or the caller had decided not to come.

Rashid felt a hand on his shoulder and jerked in surprise. "Do you mind if I sit?" The dark man had appeared from nowhere. Actually, he came from the one place Rashid hadn't suspected, deep inside the café. "You are indeed Rashid al-Ansar, are you not?" the man asked.

"Yes."

"Forgive me if I startled you."

Rashid noted the man's dark face and curly graying hair, and recognized the Lebanese accent. "I expected you earlier."

"I was already here when you arrived but wished to be prudent. The imam said you were clever and wouldn't be followed, but one can't be too careful."

Rashid found himself oddly reassured that the man displayed such wile. "Would we be less conspicuous if we spoke French? I'm sorry, how should I call you?"

"You may call me sir or monsieur or *sayyid* and we can speak in French if you like, but our work is better done in private, and Farsi will give us that."

Rashid narrowed his eyes. "You seem to know a lot about me."

"The imam described you well."

"Shall I give you the book now?"

"Tell me first, have you read it?"

"A few lines, Latin prayers I think." Rashid knew the text was Latin and understood the little he had read, but he didn't wish to sound smug.

"But you have no idea what it's about?" the man probed.

"No, but it's very old."

"Indeed, over a thousand years. Since the imam told you nothing, I shall be the one to reward you for your obedience. You carry a common Christian prayer book of no particular importance except for what's hidden underneath the words."

Rashid was intrigued. "What do they hide?"

"Secret things."

"Have you read these secrets?"

"Oh yes, Rashid. I have."

"Tell me what they say."

"They tell us how to destroy the false Christian religion."

Rashid lifted the Psalter from his lap and laid it on the table. "Read it to me so I may learn how to wipe out these infidels."

Sayyid scooped up the book with one arm. "I don't need to. I already know what it says and so shall you, very soon."

It was nearly midnight in Paris as they drove up the wide *Boulevard Magenta* through the intersection with *Boulevard de Rochechouart*, passing the Metro then rolling toward *Château Rouge*.

The sidewalks were still full of North Africans and West Africans and Arabs who overflowed into the cobblestone streets. Vendors stood on corners, hawking corn on the cob grilled on braziers set in the baskets of metal shopping carts. Drunks huddled together on curbs with large cans of beer, while the occasional beggar squatted against a stone building. Rashid spied a wrinkled man in a *thobe* and short vest, fingering prayer beads and muttering what were surely scriptures from the Qur'an.

Sayyid had ordered Rashid to leave his car near the mosque and drove him here. "You won't attract attention if you stay in this quarter. Did you bring clothes that are a little more...foreign?"

"Of course."

"Blend in. This will be your home for awhile."

"Won't the police be looking for me?"

"I think not. You weren't identified. Nevertheless, don't draw attention to yourself."

Sayyid pulled onto a narrow unlit side street and double-parked the car. The apartment building was old, not like the upscale Haussmanians or the eighteenth- and nineteenth-century buildings. These apartments had been built in the 1920s and '30s and were old because they were uncared for like their occupants. Faded paint peeled from the walls in curls and aging shutters had missing slats or hung precariously from a single hinge.

Sayyid led Rashid up a steep, circular stairway one flight then two and three to the top, sixth, floor. He pulled a key from his trousers, slid it in a lock, and turned twice. The latch clicked and the heavy door creaked. Flipping a switch, the single bulb hanging from a wire spread a dim light as dingy as the walls.

"It's only a studio," Sayyid said, "but I've bought everything you'll need. Towels are in the bathroom and soap and disposable razors. Sheets and blankets are on the bed, but you'll have to do your own shopping for food. Do you have money?"

"Some."

"Here's five hundred Euros." Sayyid handed Rashid a stack of small bills.

"Five hundred. How long will I be here? I need to get back to my job in Rome."

"Perhaps two or three days, but we'll speak often. We're going to be allies and I hope good friends because we share a common cause."

"And the imam, we must help him escape." Rashid said.

"He won't be in jail long, so we don't need to do anything for the moment."

"How can you foretell these things?"

"Because, dear Rashid, all has been accounted for, nothing left to chance. Now give me your cell phone." Rashid pulled a black phone from his jacket pocket and handed it to Sayyid, who dropped it on the floor and stomped.

"Hey, what're you doing?"

Sayyid offered him a shiny silver one. "This one uses a prepaid card, no names, no identification. When you run out of time, buy another card. Use cash."

"My friends, my contacts, they were programmed in the phone."

"Don't call your friends until we've finished our mission. Do you understand?"

Rashid nodded. Sayyid was right, although he was galled that this complete stranger gave orders and felt he could somehow replace his master. However, the imam had trusted him enough to give him Rashid's number. "Just what is the operation?"

"A little more patience. I realize this is hard. Your imam was arrested and you're forced to listen to someone you've never met. But notice I said, *your imam* and not *ours*. He and I follow the same master, but not the same path."

Rashid thought of the Mahdi, the guided one, the redeemer of Islam, but said nothing.

"Give me a few days and you'll be able to judge for yourself whether I speak the truth. Until then, trust me because I'm keeping you safe."

"I suppose I have no choice," Rashid said with resignation.

"One always has a choice. You can choose to follow the will of your imam or you can turn from the path of righteousness."

"I'll give you your few days, then I'll see for myself."

Sayyid laughed. "Well spoken. Now tell me, have you been trained?"

"Yes."

"Completely?"

Rashid answered with confidence, "I can do whatever is required."

"Then I'll leave you for tonight. Sleep well and put your mind at ease because we'll change the world in ways that will astound even the most cynical unbelievers. Good night, Rashid al-Ansar."

Sayyid drove toward the airport, pleased with himself. The imam would be out of the way for awhile and now he had his most valuable operative under his control. Best of all, he had the Psalter. He steered the rental car with one hand while pulling a white plastic tab from the side pocket of his jacket and sliding it into inserts in the collar of his black shirt.

28
Yokes and Plows

Pope Sergius sat glumly on a cushioned chair, his sagging chins resting on his fist, listening to Benedict and Theophylact recount their heroism in the bloody battle with the Saracens. The *patriarchum* was filled to overflowing. Priests crammed into every corner and deacons lined the walls. Cardinals sat in the center, spellbound by Benedict's magnetic voice. Sergius, however, listened with increasing skepticism. "So where is the church's treasure?"

"Alas, Holiness, the wicked Saracens are liars and deceivers. They feigned a parley then attacked, catching us unaware. They have stolen the gold and silver. Our men fought like Romans of old, but the heathens had the superior force. We were lucky to escape with our lives. I know I disobeyed your Holiness, but I hope I've redeemed myself with my valor. Had we left unarmed priests to the task, they would have been slaughtered to a man."

"Yet you have not a single wound between you," Sergius said.

"The Lord protects the righteous."

"Is the library saved or lost?" the Pope leaned his aching body forward.

Benedict turned to Theophylact, not knowing what to say. The count only shrugged. "Dear brother, it's surely safe, for how would they carry all those books? So in the end, we've succeeded. We must have, although we had hoped to save our treasure as well. Alas, I fear our beloved brother, Johannes, is dead."

The assembly gasped in shock.

"He was brought to the battlefield as a hostage, yet he fought them like a lion. Then we lost sight of him."

"I witnessed the heathens seize him and take him from the field," Theophylact said. "They surely butchered the poor soul, but he battled courageously. As well as any soldier."

Priests wept at the loss of their dearest brother; however, Sergius was unconvinced. "Johannes is a cultured man of letters, unskilled in the use of weapons. With what did he fight?"

"He fought with…his bare hands, Holiness, and with…great courage," Benedict sounded less confident.

"Frail Johannes attacked, on horseback, with no weapon against Saracens armed with swords? Did he strike fear into their hearts by chasing them like a game of tag?"

Benedict searched for a plausible parry to Sergius' thrust when a shout came from the back of the Papal Palace, "Lies, they're all lies!" The assembly separated down the middle, opening a pathway from the throne to the door where a dirt-caked Johannes stood with Anastasius at his side. Cheers arose from the assembled clerics and cries of, "He lives," and, "Our brother's alive!" filled the great hall while Benedict shrunk and Theophylact glowered.

"As all can see, I wasn't butchered by Saracens and I assure you I was never taken hostage, nor did anyone seize me on the field of battle. I feel remarkably well for a dead man," Johannes said. Anger rose like bile in his throat and made him forget how tired he was.

"Brother Johannes," Benedict said. "Confusion reigns in the heat of battle." Now Benedict's voice grew sinister. "It only appeared you were taken captive."

"Wicked liars!" Johannes walked down the aisle. The much taller Anastasius kept pace with him.

"How dare you call me liar?" Theophylact gripped the hilt of his sword.

"Liar and thief!"

"Calm, dear Brother," Benedict said. "You're spent from the battle."

"What battle?" You were unprovoked yet attacked a lone man who came to trade in good faith."

Benedict stepped away from the approaching Johannes. "Brethren," he addressed the congregation, spreading his arms like an orator. "Johannes is addled. He knows not what he says. We fought for our Holy Scriptures, I swear."

The assembled priests grumbled their doubts. Their murmuring reverberated through the hall.

"You had no intention of trading the gold for the library. You didn't even bring it." Turning to Sergius, Johannes said, "They offloaded the wagons and filled them with rubble. They still have the treasury hidden, likely in Theophylact's castle."

The count drew his broad sword over his head and rushed for Johannes. But priests mobbed him, flinging themselves from all sides and disarming him of his blade.

"Thief," Sergius cried out, lifting his considerable bulk from the chair.

"No, Brother, we sought only to protect the church's fortune, so we hid it from the vile Saracens who would have surely taken the gold and our library, as well."

"Did you not say they were the ones who stole the gold?"

Sergius stepped toward Benedict, who backed away, cowering. "Well...I..."

"False priest, liar. Avarice is your sin. You have no truth in you."

"You hypocrite," Benedict snarled back, "glutton and drunkard. You would've given away our treasure to pagans who desecrate the offerings with their filth."

Sergius glared at his brother. "Instead, you debase what is holy with your greed. You're not fit to live in our brotherhood."

The grumbling of the clerics grew louder, their faces grim as they formed a circle around Benedict. "Wait, you know me," he said. "I'm the Pope's own brother, a noble like you."

"You're no brother to me." The ring of brown robes closed smaller, tighter like a noose. They fell upon Benedict and Theophylact, hoisting them aloft. "Cast them out," Sergius said.

Priests echoed, "Cast them out!" over and over as they passed the two helpless souls over their heads as though they were tossed helplessly on storm-churned waves. The raging current of hands washed them to the door and flung them out on the stone porch. Then, a dozen priests slammed the heavy doors with a resounding clang.

The assembly heaved a collective sigh as if they had relieved themselves from aching bowels. Sergius hugged Johannes as a father would his son and begged him, "Tell us what happened, dear brother."

The crowd surrounded him pleading, "Give us a true accounting."

"I'll reveal everything, but the telling grieves me. The loss is measureless for us all, for the world."

"You mean our gold and silver?" Sergius said. "Fear not. Theophylact and Benedict will return the lot or I'll excommunicate them for this foul deed. The treasury will come to its rightful home."

"Not the *patriarchum's* treasury. The Saracens took the silver altar over the tomb of the Apostle Peter and all of the gold. Indeed, they pilfered everything of value from the basilica and from the cathedral of Saint Paul as well. I watched them load perhaps three tons of gold and thirty of silver. Father Baraldus is in hot pursuit with troops from the foreign *scholae* and the Jews. Yet the Saracen retreat was swifter than you can imagine. I doubt they can be overtaken. Pray, Brothers, for we need a miracle."

Pope Sergius felt his knees buckle. Two priests rushed to support his massive weight. Johannes took the Holy Father's weakened hand. Sergius probed the depths of the *bibliothecarius'* eyes and asked, "Is there yet more?"

"Saints preserve us, the worst hasn't been told."

"I must know. Tell me all."

"They've stolen our library, the Scriptures, every document and every page. I was allowed to keep what few I could collect. Everything else is gone."

"My beautiful music, my compositions. Barbarians would have no use for my music."

"They've taken that as well."

"No," the Pope said hoarsely. His eyes bulged and his legs gave way. As he slumped, the priests lowered him to the floor. Convulsing on the cool stone, he gripped his tightening breast with one hand. The other lay lifeless. One side of his face sagged and drool dripped from the corner of his mouth. "No," he whispered again as his eyes rolled.

"Get him to his bed," Anastasius said. "He's afflicted by a seizure."

𝔖ergius languished unconscious, murmuring incomprehensibly with his half-paralyzed mouth. Doctors from all over Rome went to his bedside. They checked his pulse and measured his breaths, examining and postulating, then consulted even more doctors. The second-century Greek doctor, Claudius Galen, was still the medical authority in Rome, and his treatises were read over and over until a diagnosis was unanimously delivered. His Holiness had fallen victim to evil humors transmitted through the air by unclean barbarians. These foul humors had weakened his *vital spirit* and caused an imbalance of blood, yellow bile, black bile, and phlegm, weakening his heart.

A course of treatment was agreed upon. First, the evil had to be expelled. Thus, a regimen of bloodletting three times a day was prescribed until the poisons had been drained. Then a medicine of herbs would be administered to restore the internal balance of the natural humors. Rabbi Avraham had come at Johannes' urgent request, accompanied by the finest Jewish doctors, who abhorred Galen's outdated therapies. Though they already attended most of the nobility and cardinal priests, they were refused admittance by suspicious senior clerics who oversaw the Pope's treatments.

Johannes found himself idle for the first time in his life. He had no construction to oversee, no library to sort and catalogue. He delivered what canon scriptures he had saved to Anastasius, who had charge of the *scriptorium*, so his scribes might begin their laborious copying. Of course, he had kept the heresies hidden in the papal crypt beneath the basilica. Nevertheless, he was now reduced to a librarian in name only, in charge of perhaps the world's smallest library.

The basilicas of Saint Peter and Saint Paul were a shambles, stripped of their finery. Tombs were hewn open, and the remains of popes and saints scattered. Altars and niches had been used as privies, and now priests and workmen labored to clean the filth so repairs might begin. How that might happen seemed a mystery. The church found itself destitute and with Sergius lying delirious on his sickbed, no authoritative threat of excommunication could be leveled at Theophylact or Benedict. Nevertheless, the details of their deception had come to light as soldiers in the service of the count repented to parish priests, confessing their part in the profane theft.

Three days had passed, yet Baraldus sent no runner. Johannes made his way to the Trastevere to the house of the Rosh Yeshiva. He carried the odd horse collar that Prince Ahmad said could make him rich, although he had not divined how that might be. A horse pulling a wagon faster than oxen would be a great gift and more efficient for hauling goods. Still, horses were much more expensive, and swifter transport would make no man rich.

"Any word from your son, Elchanan?" Johannes asked at the door before greeting the rabbi.

"And good morning to you, too, Father *bibliothecarius*," Avraham said, bowing low with a mocking courtly sweep of his arm.

"You're quite right, my sincere apologies. Good morning, Rosh Yeshiva. How are you today?"

"Come in, come in. I'm eager for news like you. That's how I am. How's Sergius?"

"I fear his condition is the same, but those attending him will say nothing. What news from your son?"

"Not so much as a rumor. Still, I have faith that they can handle themselves."

"Against Saracen cavalry and infantry?"

"A battle is fought in many ways. They will do what they can, but sit you down. Enjoy some tea, and what in heaven's name is that thing you carry?"

Johannes sat at the long table. He leaned the collar against the wall. "It's a harness of some sort, for a horse."

Avraham eyed the object as he poured tea. "For a horse, you say?"

"Yes, and I watched the Saracens use it. They hitched their small Arabians in teams to stout wagons and hauled them away like child's play. I wouldn't have believed it had I not been a witness."

Avraham lifted the collar, turning and examining it at various angles. He placed it on the table and stood back as though he might understand better from a distance. Finally, he put the contraption around his neck and let it rest on his shoulders. Bending over at the waist, he trotted up and down the kitchen, hollering, "clip-clop, clip-clop."

Johannes stared in shock at first then burst out in laughter as the old rabbi played horsey.

"How simple," Avraham said. "The collar rests on the beast's withers and pulls against the sternum instead of bearing on the trachea, so horses can haul great loads without strangling. What a fine gift, a grand improvement over the throat-and-girth harness. You say the Saracens used them to pull their wagons?"

"Yes."

"How did you come by this one? Did you steal it?" The rabbi feigned an accusatory stare.

"Of course not. It was given to me by their prince. And he said the oddest thing, that it could make me rich."

Avraham scratched the top of his balding head and knitted his brow while he pondered. "I wonder." He turned without taking his leave and walked out of the room. Johannes had become accustomed to the rabbi's odd flights of fancy and simply sipped his tea, waiting for him to return. "Johannes, come here," Avraham called to the priest.

"Where are you?"

"In my study."

The priest followed the sound of his voice to a room whose walls were lined with shelves loaded with ancient scrolls and books. The rabbi had rolled out a scroll and traced the sentences with his finger.

"I knew I had heard of such a thing although I couldn't remember where, but it has come back to me."

"What are you reading?"

"The Roman historian Pliny the Elder. He had a voracious mind."

"What could a historian possibly say about getting rich with a newfangled type of horse collar?"

"You've obviously never been a farmer," the rabbi said.

"No."

"Then you can't be expected to see the possibilities, so let me explain. Oxen are stupid beasts. Two years are required to train a team to the yoke to pull carts and wagons, but more importantly, a plow. Then their working life is only another two years, so farmers must constantly breed and train new teams; and oxen are also slow and plodding. Of course, they have their benefits. Ox meat is delicious. On the other hand, horses last twenty years and can be trained in a few months."

"That's certainly more efficient, but how would that make a person rich?"

"Because my learned friend who knows not a whit about agriculture, a horse walks three times faster than an ox, and a horse or team of horses can pull a plow three times faster than oxen."

Johannes began to catch on. "So a horse would plow more fields in less time and triple the yield."

"Now you know the potential for such a simple invention. Just one problem remains."

"That is?"

"A farmer would need to triple the size of his farm."

Johannes shrugged his shoulders. "Why not clear more land?"

"That's the answer, of course, but clearing new land is slow and difficult with our light wooden plows, and that's what made me remember Pliny. Look here." Avraham pointed to a portion of the scroll. "He describes a heavy plow mounted on wheels in use hundreds of years ago in Gaul."

"The wheels would certainly make plowing easier because the farmer wouldn't have to toil to hold it upright."

"Indeed, but there's an even greater benefit. With wheels supporting the weight, the plowshare can be raised and lowered to change the depth of the furrow, depending on the crop. Such a plow on wheels could do everything from clearing land to shallow furrows for vegetables."

Johannes arched his eyebrows. "A new plow pulled by horses? Our poorest people would be awash in food."

"And in wealth." Avraham thought for a moment and added, "But you must take care."

"Why?"

"Wealth is power, and the powerful guard their privileges."

Not only was there discovery in the visit with Avraham, his words dispensed their usual wisdom. Johannes resolved to build these new rigid collars and heavy plows so they would be available to all, but he dare not do it in the church. That he knew, for word traveled faster in the *patriarchum* than a loosed arrow, and the inventions would fall into the hands of the wealthy while the poor lost their benefit. The librarian who had no library had to find a way to use these marvels for the poor. Still, the greatest landowner in Christendom was the Holy Church and for his church, he would find a way to use the collar and plow to earn back the money that had been lost.

29
Corruption of the Flesh

Johannes inquired daily on the condition of Pope Sergius. Cardinal priests replied in vagaries, saying he was "as well as can be expected," and "the learned physicians do everything humanly possible," or "it's in God's merciful hands."

"Is His Holiness getting better or worse?" Johannes demanded, to which he would hear the infuriating reply, "Only God knows. Nevertheless, the physicians are hopeful but cautious." Johannes deduced from their downcast spirits, however, that Sergius worsened.

Weeks had passed since the Saracens fled with the church's library, yet still no word from Baraldus. Johannes spent his time in the Jewish quarter with Avraham making drawings from Pliny's description of a heavy plow on wheels.

They gave the rigid horse collar to artisans: a carpenter, blacksmith, and harness maker to manufacture a copy. Having disassembled the prototype Johannes had provided, each crafted exacting reproductions of their part. The carpenter made a frame of wood. The harness maker copied the leather cover, and the smithy forged metal buckles for the collar to attach to the traces. However, they had not thought about who would assemble the parts. In the end, they took their jealously guarded pieces to the furniture maker, who fashioned padding from flax fibers and straw bound with linen and fitted them together while the others offered unwelcome suggestions.

Johannes and Avraham were walking from the Rosh Yeshiva's home to the furniture maker to inspect the finished product when a loud commotion came from all around. People fled their homes and workshops to the streets, making for the Ponte Rotto and the city. "They're coming, they're coming!" the crowd shouted as they hurried past. Avraham stopped an old woman who tried to keep up with the horde. "Who's coming, mother?"

"Why, Rabbi," the woman grinned from ear to ear. "It's my son and your son, Elchanan. All our sons return in triumph."

Tears escaped Avraham's shining eyes, and he grabbed Johannes' arm for support. Together they merged into the river of Romans rushing down the street and flowing across the bridge.

A long column of horsemen on sleek Arabians had already entered the city through the *San Paolo* gate, followed by the wagons that had left Rome laden with books and gold and silver from Saint Peter's and Saint Paul's. Only now, they were filled with naked, pitiful Saracens chained and shackled or bound with leather thongs.

At the head of the convoy rode Baraldus, looking weary and uneasy on his mount with Elchanan by his side, sitting ramrod straight. Next to them was a captain wearing the uniform of the Emperor's army. The mob surrounded the column, searching for husbands and fathers and sons and brothers. Avraham held his son's hand as he walked beside his horse, gazing up at him.

"Baraldus, you old warhorse," Johannes greeted the Lombard. "You look miserable."

"I hate horses," he said, "and this beast has thrown me twice. I'm an infantry man, fought on the ground with real men, may God forgive me. I've got blisters on my arse the size of walnuts. Here, you ride and I'll walk." With that, he hopped off and laced his fingers together so Johannes could climb up.

"You sent no word, nothing. We were worried sick. You might have shown a little consideration."

Baraldus hung his head. "I had only evil tidings and didn't want to be the one to tell of our misfortune."

"But you won. The Saracens are in chains and you recovered what they stole."

"Nothing of the sort, we lost…everything."

"I don't understand. The enemy is defeated and you ride their horses."

"Oh, I can't say it even now." The hulking priest, who sported a steel helm and bronze breast plate over his brown priest's robe and who had commanded a ragtag army against the Saracens, began to sniffle.

"I suppose I can tell the story best," Lothair's captain said. He was bruised about the face and his left arm was supported by a sling. "We first engaged the Saracens as they fled Rome, pillaging and burning villages on their retreat to the port at Ostia. They were the superior force and routed us. Nonetheless, we followed. Like wasps, we stung the stragglers but scarcely slowed them down. They loaded their stolen plunder on ships and set sail while we watched, helpless."

Elchanan took up the tale, "We arrived only to watch their sails catching the wind."

"But how did you stop them?" Johannes asked. "Was it our navy?"

Baraldus choked on his words. "God's own wrath rained down His vengeance."

Elchanan comforted his new friend with a hand on his stout shoulder. "They sailed out of the harbor, heading south when a great storm descended, tossing their ships like toys. Every ship sunk and not a single one was left afloat. We spent the week gathering survivors along the coast."

Johannes gasped, "Our library, our treasure, Saint Peter's silver altar…,"

"At the bottom of the sea in God's own care." Baraldus wept.

They walked in silence through the streets of Rome. The crowds cheered the soldiers of the foreign *scholae* and Jewish militia, but insulted the emperor's troops. "Where were you when they raped our churches? You steal our taxes and leave us defenseless, you defenders of nothing." However, the mob hurled their worst taunts and jeers at the naked and trembling prisoners shackled in the wagons. They spat on them, threw stones, and drenched them with the contents of their chamber pots.

No one raised a hand to stop the angry Romans who desired nothing less than revenge for the humiliation they and their holy basilicas had endured. Even Johannes, who had not a coldhearted bone in his body, did not raise his voice to calm the people. For the first time in his life, he felt hatred and also thought of revenge.

The Jewish contingent split from the column for the Trastevere to decommission their militia and return to their families. Elchanan HaKodesh took the Lombard's wide hand in his own, squeezing it with respect and newly felt brotherhood. "Shalom, Baraldus," he said, feeling the priest's pain. "If you ever need a man at your side, seek us out and we'll stand with you." For his part, Baraldus was still choked up and barely mouthed an inaudible thank you. Then Avraham walked home beside his mounted son, holding his hand.

The column continued until the Emperor's troops broke off to take the prisoners to the dungeons and seek the comfort of their own barracks. Baraldus and Johannes stayed with the guards of the foreign *scholae* until they, too, dropped off at their neighborhoods after praising a teary-eyed Baraldus. The various militias shrank until only Johannes and the Lombard remained. At last, they made their way in silence up the Caelian hill to the *patriarchum*. The story of the church's immeasurable loss would be theirs alone to tell.

"His Holiness has been asking for you," Archdeacon Nicholas impressed on Johannes outside Sergius' apartment. His blue eyes were moist and reddened. "You must go to his side at once. The physicians say he has little time left." Johannes turned to the door, and the elderly deacon grabbed his arm. "Sergius was such fun when we were boys. We played and laughed together. He was my favorite, you know."

"Favorite?"

"Like Sergius, I'm *Tusculani*. Pietro is my cousin. I beg you, for his sake and mine, don't tell him the tragic news. Let him leave this life of sorrows with one less pain."

Sergius' eyes fluttered as the librarian closed the door behind two aged physicians in black robes who shook their heads as they exited. "Who is it?" he whispered through his sagging mouth. "Have you found the *bibliothecarius*?"

"It is I, Holiness. Johannes."

"Thank the Lord," Sergius' voice trembled. "Draw closer so I may gaze upon you."

Johannes dragged a stool to the Pope's bedside. He was horrified by the hollow face that stared back, one side sagging. "I'm here, Holy Father."

"Good Brother Johannes. I couldn't rest 'til I saw you again. Did the army rescue my music? I know you at least will tell me the truth. They're all liars here and speak in riddles."

Johannes couldn't bring himself to look Sergius in the eyes. "Yes, Holiness, brave Baraldus defeated the Saracens and brought everything back to its rightful home."

Sergius' dull eyes brightened until he read the librarian's face then he sighed. "That's good," he said, understanding the lie. "Then hear my confession."

"Holy Father, you need a proper confessor. I'm not…"

"I haven't been a good pope," Sergius whispered.

"Nonsense."

"You needn't protest. I know what I am." His whisper grew slow and halting and he gasped for air between words. "I strived to be Sergius. Alas, I knew I was just Hogsmouth. Yet I tried to be good at the end. Can you see that?"

"You were brave, valiant. You stood up to the most powerful man in the land, that villain Theophylact, and defeated him by God's grace and the power of your will."

"Do you think so?"

"The church will tell the story for a thousand years."

Sergius' eyes grew wide as though he saw something in the distance. "I just wanted make music, but they wouldn't let me."

"It was the most beautiful music."

"Do you remember my songs?"

"Of course, Holiness. Am I not your own *bibliothecarius?*"

"Will you sing one?" Sergius' faint whisper weakened still.

Johannes thought for a moment and began, "*O admirabile Veneris ydolum….*"

Pietro's mouth shaped some of the words until it could not. His contorted face relaxed, returning to its natural shape as he drifted from the physical world into oblivion. He languished for months, drifting in and out of consciousness until a frigid January morning when his breath fled with his soul for the very last time.

The body of the Pope should have lain in state at Saint Peter's like the popes before him, and that would have been Sergius' fondest desire. However, the basilica was a desecrated ruin. Thus, he rested on a bier in the cathedral of Saint John Lateran's next to the Papal Palace while the Duchy of Rome, indeed all Christians, wondered when His Holiness would be interred. At length, they begged that he be buried or at least moved to another place so they might celebrate mass without suffering from the putrid stench. Despite the unguents and oils mixed with ground coriander seed and wreaths of mint covering Sergius' robed hulk, citizens avoided the *patriarchum's* basilica, choosing to frequent the other churches.

Weeks turned into a month and one month became six, yet still Sergius lay rotting in his place of honor. Suspicious whispers raced on the wind. It was rumored that a Saracen magician had cast a spell upon the Pope's body and try as they might, no one could move him. Rome grew anxious and grumbled for a Holy Father. Nevertheless, one could not be elected until Sergius was buried. Christendom held its collective breath as the faithful waited for a new Vicar of Christ.

There was, however, no magician's spell. The truth was found in politics. Anastasius wrote of Sergius' death to Lothair, as was his duty, and to his uncle Arsenius. Then he sent a letter secretly to Deacon John Hymonides, still in exile in Monte Cassino, writing his histories and plays. He suspected some new stratagem from the nobles although he wasn't able pry a word from the cardinal priests.

He also complained that the church had been beggared. Worse, farmers' rents were doubled by Benedict, who continued to rule the Papal Palace in the absence of a Pope. Not a single cardinal dared oppose the Bishop of Albano who sold indulgences to any and all for a price. The *patriarchum* had become a common marketplace, with sins forgiven or church offices bought for a few coins or many.

For farmers who tilled the Apostolic farms and sharecroppers who toiled on the nobles' demesnes, life was a horror. Crops lost much of their value, and a copper piece was the rarest thing in the land. Artisans were forced to barter goods for food to survive since no money was to be found. Anastasius didn't know, however, that the Papal Palace was closely watched by Theophylact's spies, who intercepted all dispatches. Nothing escaped the Duchy that was not read first by the count or Benedict. Anastasius' letters never left Rome.

July was hot, and sunset came as a welcome relief. Johannes walked in the cooling air from the Vatican to the Caelian Hill to sup with his old mentor in Anastasius' tiny apartment in the *scriptorium* next to the Papal Palace. He had come to inquire what news might be had since there was naught but wild speculation in the remote Vatican.

They should have eaten in the refectory with the other brothers of their Benedictine order, but the hall was empty. The reek of Sergius' body had infected every hall in the *patriarchum*. Cardinal priests and bishops of noble birth took to eating their evening meals in the airy dining room atop Zacharias' tower to find relief from the oppressive smell and to parley in secret.

"They're planning their next move," Anastasius said. "I listen to them disputing and laughing while they dine up there."

Johannes walked to the narrow slit of a window to peer out. The tower was just across the alley from the *scriptorium*. The racket from the top sounded more like a boisterous banquet for a foreign dignitary than a serene evening meal for holy fathers.

Anastasius watched him at the window. "Believe me, they have no intention of allowing another election upset. I'd give anything to know what scheme they're hatching up there."

"Surely the people will elect Deacon John again and Theophylact wouldn't dare overthrow him a second time."

"Don't count on it. The Emperor will demand that his own man be pope. If another is elected, Lothair could care less what happens."

"Are you still his man?"

"I'm afraid so."

"You do not wish to be the Holy Father?"

"Of course not," Anastasius said.

"Truly?"

"It's my uncle's fondest wish and the Emperor's demand, but I harbor no such desire, although it may be the only way."

The knock on the apartment door startled Johannes and Anastasius and they looked at one another blankly, wondering who would be calling at this hour.

"Uncle!" Anastasius was flabbergasted at the unannounced visit. "Come in and rest yourself. Did you just arrive from Orta? Why didn't you write you were coming?" Anastasius kissed his uncle's cheeks and helped him with the traveling satchel draped across his shoulder.

"Didn't you receive my letters?" Bishop Arsenius looked perplexed.

"I've received nothing, and what about mine?" Anastasius was equally confounded.

"You wrote to me?"

"Of course and to the Emperor as well, the very day His Holiness passed to his reward."

"Those scoundrels," the bishop said disgusted. "Up to their old tricks, and has Sergius not yet been buried as the rumors say?"

Anastasius shrugged. "No, and all of Rome wonders."

"They'll stop at nothing. Well I have a little surprise for them."

"What are you saying?"

"It can mean only one thing, and I'll get to the bottom of it." Arsenius stormed out of the *scriptorium*, Anastasius and Johannes in tow. He marched across the alley to the tower. Soldiers bearing the crest of the Count of Tusculum guarded the doors. When the three priests tried to enter, their way was barred. "What's this?" Arsenius boomed in a throaty bass voice.

"I'm sorry, Father." One of the guards recoiled at the bishop's commanding tone, then recovered and replied, "Cardinal priests and bishops are conferring. No one may enter, orders."

"Whose orders?"

"My Lord Theophylact's," he said.

"You dolt," Arsenius was vexed. "I'm a Bishop, Arsenius of Orta, and I'm here to speak with my brethren. You're on church property. If you wish to guard something, retire to Theophylact's den of thieves and guard that." Arsenius shoved the soldier aside, and the three priests passed by.

They climbed the rectangular stairway that abutted the plastered walls and entered the banquet hall through an arched doorway. The scene looked like an ancient Roman Bacchanalia, with clerics reclining on couches as they were served succulent dishes by slave boys and youths sent forcibly into the priesthood by their parents.

The animated diners grew silent and every eye turned to the three, as though they had been caught in some off-color jest. At the far end of the hall at the head table, Benedict stood glaring at Johannes and Anastasius. "How dare you...I mean Bishop Arsenius, I didn't recognize you. What a pleasant surprise, but this assembly is for the cardinals and bishops and your nephew and Johannes are not..."

"They're with me." There was no polite tact in Arsenius' voice.

"Of course, Bishop, come in and welcome."

"That's my intent, welcome or not."

"Dear Bishop, your ire is misplaced here. Are we not a fraternity of love?"

"Don't bandy words with me, Benedict. I know who you are. Why is Sergius not buried?"

"We thought to wait until Saint Peter's was in a better state of repair so we..."

"Yes, yes out with it, so you could what?"

Benedict's words stumbled out, "Well, perhaps you know that the Saracens stole…"

"I've heard all; too much, in fact." Arsenius turned left and right to address the reclining governors of Christ's church. "Does Theophylact's puppy speak for you all? Is there not a voice amongst you except his?"

Cardinals and bishops sat up on their couches, yet no one answered.

"Dear Arsenius, you have no call for this reproof," Benedict said.

The Bishop of Orta narrowed his eyes. "Very well, Benedict." Arsenius curled his lip. "Since all are mute save you, when's the election?"

Benedict looked to his brethren, pleading voicelessly for their support. "As I said, the Saracens attacked us and His Holiness died from the shock. We've been left without a pope in our greatest hour of need and…"

Arsenius recognized the elderly man in the seat of honor next to Benedict, hanging his head in shame and squirming more than most. He wore a robe of white cloth. "In heaven's name, what have you done?" He said. Then his voice thundered, "What have you done?"

Benedict was no longer politic. "Are you a man of God or the Emperor's?"

"I'm a priest, you scoundrel, yet I owe to Caesar what is his, as the Bible commands. By what right have you named a pope without a lawful election?"

"Lawful, you say? Where was the Emperor when the Saracens attacked Rome and stole our holy treasures and our scriptures? Where was the law then?" The cardinals grumbled their agreement. "And where is he now? It's been six months and we've heard nothing yet the church is a pauper."

Arsenius' face flushed with fury. "If you're in need of donations, the church's money lies in Theophylact's coffers as you well know, Benedict, you thief."

"How dare you call me a thief? I'm a Roman of noble blood and answer to no foreigner."

"You answer to the Emperor." The Bishop of Orta pulled a folded page from inside his sleeve and held it high. "This is a decree from

Lothair, Emperor of the Holy Roman Empire, to whom you owe lawful allegiance." Arsenius shook the sheet and it unfolded for all to see. "It names me, Bishop of Orta, as the Roman *missi*. I'm the Emperors' representative at the *patriarchum*. When you address me, you're speaking to Lothair. The Emperor has arrived."

Benedict's mouth gaped in fear. The elderly man in papal robes next to him shot up from his seat. "I didn't want to do it, Brother Arsenius. I refused the nomination just as I have in the past, but they were going to name Benedict, and I couldn't let that happen. I had to agree."

"I do know you Leo, Cardinal Priest of the *Santi Quattro Coronati*. We've been friends for many long years. You were wrong to break the law, and you'd be wise to submit to the will of the Emperor. His will shall be done and his rights defended."

Leo's shoulders slacked, and he lowered his eyes to the floor. "You speak truly. It's for Lothair to confirm me and if he chooses otherwise, I shall step down."

30
Cardinal of the Domus Cultae

$\mathfrak{T}$hough they call him pope, there was no lawful election and no confirmation," Bishop Arsenius told his nephew. Johannes scarcely believed what he was hearing as they stood together in the *scriptorium* among scribes who labored to copy what had been left to Johannes by Ahmad. Stacks of parchment lined the walls, and priests hauled in piles of blank sheets, seeking out empty nooks in which to cram even more.

"So Leo is not the Pope. We've won," Anastasius said.

Bishop Arsenius shook his head. "Leo shall be Pope."

"Uncle, I don't understand."

"The people have waited for a pontiff for half a year and must wait no longer. Lothair believes the church cannot survive another scandal like the overthrow of John Hymonides, and I agree."

Anastasius grew agitated. "What could be worse than denying Romans their vote?"

"Civil war, and in such a fight, Lothair finds himself in a weakened position. Not only does he face Saracens to the south and Vikings in the north, Romans still blame him for the desecration of

Saint Peter's and Paul's. They feel no love for the Emperor just now, and he would change that before he exerts his will. Leo is an old man and won't be pope long. Besides, if he does a bad job, Lothair can claim his authority was usurped and unseat him."

"Politics and, once again, the people lose."

"What's all this nonsense about the people? Can you not grasp, nephew, that they will never hold any real power?"

"Isn't that why the Constitution was written? So ordinary citizens might choose their own Holy Father?"

"Of course not. Pope Stephen had no authority to end elections as they have always been. His decree simply handed the Papacy to the Roman nobility. But commoners don't speak with one voice, so they could never choose a pope. If they tried, Theophylact wouldn't allow it, and if Theophylact failed, Lothair wouldn't allow it. The papacy is money and power. So forget this nonsense. Besides, I bring good tidings for you."

"How can any of this be good?"

"Patience, nephew. The Emperor rules still, and he wishes that his influence should take root in the *patriarchum*. So you're to be one of the church's newest cardinal priests."

"I'm to be a cardinal?"

"Yes, and with your own church."

"Can this be true?"

"It's all arranged." Arsenius said.

"What do you mean *arranged*?" Anastasius looked askance at his uncle.

"The Emperor will not press for his right to confirm the Pope, and in exchange, you're to be a cardinal."

"So neither did God in his grace choose me nor did I earn the position. My post and my church are an accommodation, purchased for the indulgence of the Emperor."

"Why should you care?" Arsenius shrugged. "You deserve San Marcello and much more. Are you not the most brilliant mind in Rome? Haven't you excelled beyond the greatest expectations, only to be knocked down by these rapacious nobles who play at being priests?"

"San Marcello, on the Quirinal hill? That's the other side of Rome. Don't you see? They scheme to get rid of me, a promotion to get me out of the Papal Palace."

"Of course," the bishop said. "You're a threat, just as I want you to be. I agreed to San Marcello for a reason. It's a venerated church in a chic quarter of Rome, the *Lata,* with aristocrats and wealthy merchants as parishioners. You're already popular with the commoners, and now you'll be seen among those who hold sway. You'll be a powerful voice in the *patriarchum.*"

"I'm not displeased uncle, but I would have had it otherwise. Nevertheless, I'm grateful for your intercession." Anastasius held his uncle's shoulders a long moment, then kissed his cheeks. Arsenius' face shone at his nephew's affection.

"I bring good news for you also, young Johannes."

"For me? Why would the cardinals reward me? It's well known that I side with Anastasius and John Hymonides and consort with Jews."

Bishop Arsenius chuckled. "Too true, and everyone in the Papal Palace shakes their heads in mirth at your ignorance of political wile. Nevertheless, all witnessed your dedication to the library and to Sergius, which was no easy task, and risking your life by remaining with the Saracens to protect our scriptures resounds throughout Rome. More importantly, you're English and no Roman, so you're not a threat to the nobles, even if you are a thorn."

"You said Anastasius was but one of the new cardinals. Am I to be a cardinal too?"

"Yes, and none of my doing, although I'm well pleased," Arsenius said.

Johannes' face beamed with excitement. "Which church is to be mine?"

"No church. You're to rule over the church's farm colonies, the *domus cultae.*"

"The church's lands?"

"Indeed. The Holy See is bankrupt and in desperate need of money. Oh, I'm sure we'll get something back from Theophylact and

Benedict, but I'm just as certain they won't return it all. Leopards don't change their spots, although they might be skinned alive."

Johannes was downcast. "Then they've heard already about the horse collar and plow."

"Did you imagine you could keep these things secret?"

"Long enough figure a way to get them into the hands of the peasants where they're needed most."

"Too late," Arsenius said. "The church needs the wealth your remarkable inventions can bring. The *scriptorium* suffers from a critical shortage of parchment, and I'm told you're an expert in their procurement and manufacturing. Crops and animal husbandry are to be your cathedral, but you shall retain the title *bibliothecarius*. There's not much of a library left, and the cardinals agreed unanimously that you should be in charge of what you saved. Now, I would ask you a question and have you search your heart and mind. Isn't it clear that supporting the Emperor is the only way to loosen Theophylact's iron grip on the throne of Saint Peter?"

"It's one way, I'll grant you, Bishop, but you want me to side with one master over another, and both pursue their own interests. Only the people wish to serve the church, not control her."

"At least, can I count on your loyalty to my nephew?"

"Anastasius is my mentor, Brother, and even now I think of him as my master. Most of all he's my friend. How could I ever be disloyal?"

"That's all I require of you, Johannes Anglicus."

Johannes made his way from the *patriarchum* in misery. He, too, was being moved out of the Papal Palace, away from his books and scrolls and ink-blackened fingers, everything he loved. He was to be a farmer. Worse, he couldn't even take pleasure in a day's hard labor in the field. He would instead be the overseer of the greatest landholder in the world, a sort of Baron in a priest's robe. The thought made him shiver and he said to himself, *This isn't why I came to Rome.* Yet even as the voice in his head faded, another took its place, saying, *Learning is learning and not all comes from a book.*

The wide *piazza* in front of the Colosseum was filled with merchants and artisans, nobles and landowners, even priests. The crowd was abuzz, shouting and laughing as they flocked around the wooden platform that held cowering Saracens stripped to their brown skins except for linen loincloths that provided the barest of modesty. The army was selling slaves. The practice was barbaric to Johannes, even though slavery was acceptable to Bible authors who admonished slaves to obey their masters. Saracens were no better. They took Christians as booty. Children were sold for labor, and the women kept as concubines.

Johannes found this more revolting even than his new position. The bidding for flesh and the carnival atmosphere made him sick, and he was about to turn away when one of the slaves caught his eye. The naked wretch knelt beside the stage shackled by a heavy iron collar attached to a chain. His hands had been bound behind his back by a leather strap that cut at his wrists. Raising his puffy face, his gaze met Johannes' for an instant then broke off. "Prince Ahmad," Johannes whispered, unbelieving.

Ahmad turned away as far as his chain would allow, shuffling on bloodied knees. Johannes wedged his way through the packed crowd of Romans who were anxious to make a purchase or who simply enjoyed the spectacle of revenge meted out upon the defilers of the basilicas. "Turn away, Father," the guard said to Johannes who knelt next to Ahmad. "This is no place for you, and these Arabs are a dangerous lot."

"I'm just inspecting, sir. I might need a new slave."

The guard remembered Johannes from the march through Rome. "Father Johannes, I didn't recognize you. Of course, take your time, but this is a skinny one. The best are yet to come. We even have cabin boys from the ships who've been trained to serve. If you like, I'll speak to my sergeant. I'm sure he would make a special price for the friend of the illustrious Baraldus." The guard sauntered off, leaving Johannes with the miserable slave.

"Are you here to gloat?" Ahmad rasped through a parched throat. "If you have any pity after what I've done, leave me to my fate. Allah has chosen my punishment."

Johannes placed a hand on the fallen prince's bare back, but

Ahmad recoiled. The priest rose without another word to seek out the guard. "Name your price and bring him to me. I reside in the *schola cantorum*."

"It shall be done, Father," the guard said.

Johannes arranged his meager belongings in his new apartment, books and two heretical scrolls, the *Gospels of Thomas* and *Mary*, he had retrieved from the papal crypt beneath Saint Peter's. He was folding his scant extra clothing when a loud rapping came from the heavy wooden door as from the haft of a spear or hilt of a sword.

"Who is it?" he called out.

"We've brought your slave, Father."

Johannes lifted the beam barring the door and it swung open, the bolt having been broken by the Saracens and not yet repaired. Two guards led in Ahmad, who was still shackled by a chain attached to a metal collar. Giving the chain a powerful yank, one of the soldiers forced him to his knees. "Are you alone, Father?" The guard appeared concerned.

"Yes."

"I wouldn't have brought this miscreant if I thought you were by yourself. He's far too dangerous. I can take him back."

"That won't be necessary. Baraldus will join me in the morning. Leave him bound and he can sleep on the stone. He deserves no better."

"Very well. Baraldus will have little trouble handling this scrawny one." The soldiers left with salutes across their breasts, and Johannes replaced the beam after them.

He retrieved a thin dagger he used to cut meat or break wax seals on letters and hovered over the forlorn prince. "Go on, I beg you," Ahmad said. "Send me to Allah and end my humiliation."

The *bibliothecarius* stood immobile like a statue until the fallen prince glanced up. Johannes knelt and raised the blade. Ahmad bowed his head once again. The priest sliced the edge across the leather thong that bound his wrists and held a cup to his bleeding lips. "Drink this."

"Better to let me die."

"Not today." Johannes pressed the cup to the naked prince's mouth letting ruby drops wet his cracked and scabbed lips.

Ahmad clasped the beaker and poured the liquid down his throat, spilling rivulets of wine from the corners of his mouth. "Water," he pleaded.

"Finish the wine first and your pain will be eased." The priest disappeared, then returned with an earthenware pitcher and his own traveling cloak, which he wrapped around the naked Ahmad. He trickled water from the jug into the emptied cup. "I can't unhook the collar. It's welded with a rivet."

Ahmad quaffed the water. "Another," he said, and Johannes poured again. This time, the prince sipped and let out a sigh of relief. "Why do you show me this kindness? Do I not deserve your wrath?"

"It's for God to judge you, not me. We're commanded to forgive our enemies, and that I must strive to do, although I confess I wished evil upon you and your men."

"Allah heard the prayer and judged us all for my sin. God's word is his Holy word no matter which prophet writes it. I've committed a sacrilege by treating it as mere booty. I know that now and am humbled."

"I didn't find your brother. Did he survive?"

"He's not among us. He paid the price for my iniquity and his was the better heart. It's hard to recognize the justice in Allah's will."

Johannes wrapped his arm around a distraught Ahmad, who recoiled from the priest's compassion. Then the Prince heaved a woeful sigh and his breaths became softer. "Lie on my pallet," Johannes said. "I put a sleeping potion in the wine. You'll feel better on the morrow."

"What can you be thinking, Cardinal?" Baraldus scolded. "He might have slit your bony throat. Have I protected you all this time only to watch you take such foolish risks?"

"Why would he kill me? I saved his life and he showed me a kindness in return. Is that the mark of a murderer?"

"Any man would kill to escape his prison. Believe me, I've seen it."

"I'm his only chance, and he knows it," Johannes said.

"For what, a life of slavery? No man who falls so far could accept such a fate. If he doesn't harm you today, he might tomorrow."

"Well then, you must make sure he doesn't."

"I? What do you mean?"

"I want you to work for me once more."

"As a farmer? No thank you very much," Baraldus shook his head. "I'm getting old and I just want to get fat again and lazy."

"I need you to be *primicerius* of the church's farms."

"Me, an unlettered Lombard?"

"You're an expert at the making of parchment, much better than me. You know farming and can count. Men respect you, and you were born to command. I can't do without you, and the church needs you. Will you not say yes?"

Baraldus' gruff face turned sheepish. "As though I'd refuse you anything, master."

"After all these years, can you not call me Johannes and friend?"

"You're my friend, but I cannot call you by your name now that you're a cardinal. It wouldn't be proper. I'll call you by what's seemly and by what you are, my brother and my master."

The smithy removed Ahmad's iron collar, striking off the rivet with a hammer and chisel to Baraldus' frustrated protests. As they walked toward the *Trastevere*, the Lombard kept close to the Arab, poking him with his elbow and pointing at his short sword. Johannes only shook his head. Baraldus had his safety at heart, but the bullying seemed unnecessary. Nevertheless, the newest cardinal was not completely sure of the prince, even though he counted himself an excellent judge of character.

"Ahmad ibn Muhammad ibn Al-Aghlab," Avraham stroked his whiskers as he reflected a long while. "Your uncle is Muhammad Abul-Abbas, Emir of Ifriqiya, is that not so?"

"The same, blessed be his name, although he would rather be

known as a jurist and scholar and for the honor he brought our people. I bring my people only shame."

"This is a cruel blow to you and to Christians also. Yet who can know the mind of God? He Who Cannot Be Named chose to deliver you into the hands of your enemy. But surrender yourself to His will, for I do not believe He would silence a man such as you forever."

"I'm a prisoner, a slave. I have little choice," Ahmad said bitterly.

Avraham smiled through his frizzy beard. "We can always choose."

Elchanan joined them, and they sat around the large table in the kitchen eating cakes Avraham had baked, as was his daily custom—meditation, he called it—and sipping tea. The Rosh Yeshiva's son took turns with Baraldus, frowning and glowering at the Saracen slave who was treated as a guest at his father's table.

"This is wrong," Ahmad said, pointing to the buckles on the collar. "They must be in such a place where they can be hitched to a plow or wagon. And the plow's coulter has to be steel, not merely an iron strip over wood. It will break clearing new land."

The corrections were sketched on paper and Elchanan and Baraldus discussed what changes would need to be made as Cardinal Johannes squirmed in his seat. "What's wrong, young scholar?" Avraham asked. "You wish to add something?"

"I'm not sure how to say it. It's not a plan, really, and I don't know if such an enterprise could be accomplished. I wouldn't even know where to begin."

"Just tell us," Avraham said.

Johannes pondered what he wanted to say for a moment. "Well, artisans can manufacture the collar and plow, but at considerable expense. Only the church and nobles possess money enough to buy them."

"Yes?" Avraham replied, anxious for Johannes to make his point.

"I had hoped these inventions might help the lot of the poor who till the fields, slaves to their lord, to the land, and to their poverty. They will make their labor easier perhaps, but not their lives. However, if they owned a plow and a horse, they would be masters of their destiny."

Baraldus gazed on Johannes as a world-wise father on an idealistic but impractical son. "Where would farmers get enough coins to buy horses and complicated plows? All they own is what's on their backs, their paltry implements, and such beasts as they can breed. They have no money."

Avraham, too, perceived no answer for Johannes' munificent wish. "Gold and silver are now so rare, it would take two season's harvest to pay such a price."

"I don't see the problem," Ahmad said under his breath as though the answer was as plain as the cakes on the table.

Baraldus glared at the Saracen. "What do you know, pirate? These men are your betters, scholars and writers of books and have the world's knowledge in their heads."

Everyone turned to Ahmad.

"And you call us barbarians." Ahmad shook his head. "My people were illuminating manuscripts when yours were drinking from skulls and painting your bodies blue, Lombard."

Baraldus leapt from his seat, his ears red.

"Calm yourself, captain of the city's defenses." Avraham made a point of honoring the stout priest in front of Ahmad to soothe his rising bile. "We seek solutions, not quarrels."

Ahmad reminded himself, feeling his bruised face and burning wrists, that he was no longer a Prince of Ifriqiya. He was a lowly slave in a hostile land. "Forgive my effrontery. I only meant to say...what baker would not desire to receive double payment for a loaf of bread?"

Everyone at the table shook their heads, not comprehending, and Baraldus seated himself, just as confused.

"It's quite simple. Give the farmers a plow, a collar, and a horse. Then they pay with their crops as they can, but the price is double. If they triple their yield, they could repay the debt in a year. Two years would be easier and they would stockpile more food than they ever had, plus enough to give their lord as rent and still more to sell for cash. Allah forbids the charging of interest, but in his wisdom he did not mention what price may be demanded."

All at the table *aahed* as the concept struck home.

"On my word," Ahmad said. "Did you never hear of banking?"

31
Council of Laodicia

Johannes soon understood Leo's desperate need for money. Theophylact and Benedict had returned but a portion of the church's treasury, and only on threat of excommunication. However, had the whole sum been recovered, it would not have been nearly enough. Tithes flowed once again into the holy coffers, but they were a fraction of what was needed to finance Leo's grandiose plans. Emperor Lothair contributed offerings from the imperial treasury to rebuild the devastated Saint Peter's and Saint Paul's and for the raising of a larger army to protect Rome. Yet still more was required, much more.

Pope Leo committed to the diocese, to the clergy, and to God that the most sacred site in Roman Catholicism, Saint Peter's Basilica, would be grander and richer than ever. Moreover, he vowed that such a sacrilege would never happen again. Thus, he embarked upon a construction the likes of which Rome had not seen since the third century. Leo resolved to build a colossal wall to surround the rural Vatican and enclose it within the confines of the city.

Workers would have to be fed, artisans paid, and raw materials purchased. While all Christendom would contribute, a large portion of the monies had to come from the *patriarchum's* farm colonies, from Johannes. Rome's youngest cardinal priest felt the pressure. Planning daily with Elchanan, Baraldus, and Ahmad, it was clear that a virtual army of laborers would be needed and there was not nearly enough land under cultivation to feed them and their families.

Baraldus was a natural commander, and he viewed the farms as a battlefield to attack strategically. He divided the workers into two teams, with the stouter men clearing the woods and breaking virgin ground with the revolutionary plows drawn by stronger, albeit slower, oxen. The second team cultivated farmland with less powerful but faster horses, turning the soil with incredible speed and finishing in a third of the normal time. Then they joined the crew clearing and sowing yet more land. The work progressed at an ambitious pace, and Johannes had already planned a fall crop.

Elchanan managed the supply line, overseeing Jewish artisans in the production of the rigid horse collars and heavy plows on wheels. Ahmad adeptly controlled the money, disbursing payments to craftsmen and horse breeders. He also oversaw the distribution of equipment to unbelieving farmers who marveled that they were simply given a plow, a horse, and a collar. All they had to do in exchange was to make their mark on a piece of parchment with words they could neither read nor understand. They grasped, however, that upon a handshake and an oath, they would own their tools and become their own men.

After months of working around the clock, weary Johannes found himself missing his mentor and fellow bibliophile, Anastasius. May was already hot, yet just enough rain had fallen and the crops ripened. Hay cutting would begin in four or five weeks, and he would have no time at all until the harvest was finished and the wheat, barley, and oats stored in the granaries. So in the evening, at the hour between last light and dusk when the shadows were longest, he left his labors and crossed the Tiber on the Sant'Angelo Bridge, traveling near the river through Rome's most populated quarter, the *campus martius*.

Since the barbarian invasions had cut the city's aqueducts, many commoners were forced to move from the hills to the river's edge.

Artisans and merchants followed to serve the new residents. The *campus martius* swelled further with pilgrims longing to pray at Saint Peter's, pilgrims who had brought money from the four corners of the earth. Poor shopkeepers and relic hawkers were only too happy to help them lighten their purses.

Bishop Arsenius had been shrewd in choosing San Marcello for his nephew. While the church's governors in the *patriarchum* thought they were rid of the troublesome Emperor's man, in reality, Cardinal Anastasius was now the pastor of Rome's most populous parish and to its wealthiest citizens, voting citizens. Johannes turned north on the fashionable *via Lata* to visit his friend, an ancient scroll of the heretical *Gospel of Thomas* tucked under his arm. *A theological discussion is what I need to distract myself from this bone-tiring work,* he thought.

"I agree with you. Nothing in Matthew, Mark, or Luke says Jesus was anything but a mortal man," Anastasius said as they sipped sweetened wine. They sat by the narrow window digesting their dinner, hoping for a breath of a breeze. The *Gospel of John* makes the difference."

"But why was *John* added to the Bible and not the *Gospel of Thomas?*"

"Because Jesus would have been different." Anastasius tapped on the open scroll for emphasis

"My point exactly." Johannes leaned forward, his eyes bright, driving home his line of reasoning. "Not only were parts of the Bible forged or altered to promote a particular belief like the virgin birth chapters in *Matthew*, books were cobbled together for the same effect. Had *John* not been added, Jesus wouldn't be God. If *Thomas* had been the fourth book, Jesus would have been only a man with a twin brother who God adopted.

"Yes, but *John* was chosen and not *Thomas.*"

"Obviously." Johannes rolled his eyes. "And other books were rejected, and not because they didn't deserve to be included?"

"But why do you keep mentioning *Thomas?*"

"Look at the handwriting. The book was written at the same

time as *John*, after Jesus' generation and yet another had passed. Both books must have been authored by someone other than the two apostles. One wanted Jesus to be a God and the other believed he was a mere man. My point is that neither Jesus nor the Apostles decided our beliefs; rather it was anonymous men propagandizing their own beliefs. Finally, Roman emperors used their power to decree our doctrines just as an Emperor and Theophylact now fight to impose their requirements on the church."

Anastasius squirmed, uncomfortably. "Are you suggesting that our church isn't legitimate because Jesus isn't God?"

"No, I'm saying that the truth matters and I don't know what the truth is. This I do know: *Thomas* and the suppressed books must be preserved until someone with more knowledge than you or I can understand them. Until then, we have to resist the efforts of the Empire or the nobility or even church leaders to use our faith for their own interests."

The two cardinals leaned back in their chairs, pondering and perspiring as the still heat chafed. Johannes hiked his priestly frock above his knees to cool his slender legs. "I need to use the privy," he announced, but took several moments to pull himself from the comfort of the chair.

Anastasius was grateful for his onetime protégé, a mind that matched his own even at his young age. An educated and cultured foreigner, the Englishman viewed everything from a different per-spective. His Greek schooling had taught him to view historical events as clashes of opposing ideas rather than battles between good and evil. The pastor of San Marcello heard a table rattle. The legs scraped along the stone floor. "Light a candle, Johannes. It's dark out there," he called but received no reply. "Are you all—"

His words were silenced in mid-utterance as his voice was squeezed from his throat. He tried to slip a finger underneath the leather thong wrapped around his neck, but the attacker jerked tighter still. Frantic, Anastasius clawed at the garrote, standing and spinning, driving backward with all his dissipating might, crashing their bodies against tables and chairs and slamming into the wall. The thong loosened for an instant and he squeezed two fingers through and pulled the strap away from his constricted neck. Not enough; he was losing consciousness. With a last, desperate effort, he flung himself to the center of the room, tumbled over a toppled chair and crashed to the floor. The faceless killer held his grip, squeezing tighter as peace descended on the cardinal and he floated away.

Anastasius' chest inflated in a sudden great heave and he gulped for breath like a baby's first taste of air. Blood flowed once again to his brain, flooding in spurts that pounded in his temples. His unwilling eyes opened and a muffled distant sound grew louder, calling, "Oh come back. Come back to me."

Johannes held Anastasius' head in his lap, rocking back and forth and sobbing until he looked down at dazed eyes staring up. "Thank you God. Thank you." He smothered the face with kisses.

"Oh my aching head." Anastasius rubbed his temples with the palms of his hands. "What happened?"

"He tried to kill you," Johannes said.

"Who?" He looked over at a body lying in a pool of blood, a dining knife thrust in the throat. Pulling himself up on trembling knees, Johannes supported him as they wobbled away from the corpse. "I need to lie down."

"We can't stay here. There might be more of them." Johannes led him out the door, looking left and right and straining his eyes in the darkness.

"Where're you taking me?"

"To the *schola cantorum*."

"I don't think I can make it," Anastasius said.

"Lean on me. It's downhill."

The exertion and air revived Anastasius and after fifty paces, he walked under his own power although he had not completely regained his sense of balance and leaned on the *bibliothecarius'* shoulder. Each person they encountered in the narrow streets seemed suspicious, and Johannes followed their every move until they disappeared around a corner or moved to a safe distance.

They neared the *schola cantorum* and Anastasius began to tremble. Johannes wrapped his arm around his friend. "I need to get you into bed." He pushed open the door to the *schola* and pulled his mentor through. Leading him to the bedroom, he laid Anastasius on his own pallet and covered him with a blanket.

The room was warm and stuffy, yet Anastasius shivered. "I'm so cold." His teeth rattled.

Johannes lifted the covers and slid in, rubbing him all over, trying to pass heat from his body to his friend's. It seemed to be working. The shivering subsided and Anastasius relaxed. His breathing came easier and he sighed in relief. "You saved my life tonight."

"I killed a man." Johannes' lip quivered.

"You had no choice."

"I could have hit him or struck him with something, but I stabbed him without thinking. No, that's a lie. I thought he was killing you and I wanted to hurt him, kill him." Tears flowed from Johannes' reddened eyes, and he began to weep.

"You did what you had to do."

"Thou shalt not kill."

"You took a life to save one, mine. The scales are balanced."

Johannes weeping grew into sobs. "Oh, I don't care. What would I do if I lost you?"

Anastasius turned on his side and pulled his young friend close, holding his body tight with one hand, wiping the tears with the other. "Please don't cry. You committed no sin."

Johannes reached out his own hand, touching his companion's cheek with his fingers, and gazed into his eyes. "To lose your dear words, I simply couldn't bear it." Unthinking, he pressed his lips to his friend's, kissing him softly at first, then harder.

Anastasius recoiled.

"I'm sorry," the young priest said, realizing what he had done.

He tried to push away but Anastasius held him close. "I share the same desire although I can't explain it. Some priests in our brotherhood consort with men. I've never felt such yearning, not before I met you or even after. Only with you have I craved these things. I try to resist, but cannot."

Johannes pulled Anastasius to him, kissing with closed lips at first, but opening them finally to his friend. They held each other close until Anastasius bowed his head. "I can't. I want to. God forgive me, I do. I desire a part of you more than anything on earth… but I don't wish to be with a man."

Johannes gazed on his friend's sweet face; however, Anastasius would not meet his eyes. "Can't you love me for who I am?"

"I do, but I don't want to make carnal love with you."

"Is it my body?"

"Yes."

"Then let God's true creation be revealed." Johannes rose up to his knees and untied the cincture binding his robe. He slid it over his head and pulled off his linen shift. "Let this robe never come between us. Can you not at least look at me?"

Anastasius raised his eyes, and his mouth gaped. "Oh my God!"

Johannes broke into sobs once again. "I should've told you. I never meant to deceive. I wanted to learn and it's forbidden for us and I…"

"You're a woman!"

"Can you ever forgive me?"

"Forgive you? I love you." Anastasius kissed her passionately, uninhibited. He laid her down on the pallet. Gazing into her eyes, the cardinal rolled on top, spreading her thighs, touching the sweetness of her soft skin. "I don't even know your name."

"Of course you do. I'm Johanna. Joan, not John."

"Who would believe it?" Anastasius said smiling, fulfilled, even amused at the idea. "A woman cardinal."

"Oh dear heart, I never meant for it to go this far. I wanted to learn what I could, only a year or two, then I planned to leave. But

I received interesting jobs and I believed the church needed me and what I did was important."

Anastasius laughed. "Let me see," he said. "The woman Junia was a priest during Saint Paul's time, a bishop even, and many argued that Mary Magdalen was an Apostle. In fact, the scriptures call her the Apostle to the Apostles. Of course, Bishop Theodora was a woman and Priscilla a priest who worked with Saint Paul, and Paul tells us Phoebe was a deacon. You might be on solid ground."

"You're teasing me." Johanna poked Anastasius.

"The early church had many female priests, but oh yes, I remember now: the popes put an end to it. Women were forbidden to hold the priesthood in the fourth century at the *Council of Laodicia*. Then the *Council of Chalcedon* forbade women under the age of forty from being deacons. That rule is quite confusing because anyone holding the title of deacon has the right to be a priest as well. On the other hand, I haven't heard of any women deacons lately."

Johanna wasn't nearly as amused as Anastasius. She shook her head as he continued his reflection while they lay in each other's arms. "In truth, one might argue there's no legitimate prohibition against women being priests. All the same, I don't think I'd advertise it just yet."

"If only I had been born a man."

"And where would that leave me? I thought I had become a Sodomite. How did you keep it hidden all these years?"

"The worst was my monthly cycle. Thank heaven I worked alone most of the time, but hiding the evidence was a chore. I was sick every month believing I might be discovered."

"We've all been fools. How did we ever believe such beauty as yours could be a man?"

"Oh, sweet Anastasius, what am I to do?"

"Do? You're to do nothing and say nothing. You're right. The church needs you, and I need you. Now that I've found you, I'll never let you go."

"What if I'm discovered?"

"You guarded your secret these many years and I believe God will protect you just as he has seen fit thus far. I swear I'll find a way for us to be together, every second of every day."

"Oh no, impossible. You must flee today."

"Leave? What are you saying? Don't you love me?"

"More than my own life and that's why you need to go." Johanna caressed Anastasius' cheek with her palm. "Don't you understand? Who do you think tried to kill you tonight?"

"I don't know, a thief perhaps. Rome has many poor and destitute."

"Did you not see the assassin's clothes? He was no pauper. This is Theophylact's doing, and likely the cur, Benedict. They don't intend to allow the Emperor's power to grow in the Papal Palace. And now they have you where they want you, isolated at San Marcello, where you're an easy target."

"Uncle Arsenius supports the Emperor as well. Will they not try to kill him? I can't leave him unprotected."

"They wouldn't dare touch the Emperor's *missi* at Leo's palace and risk Lothair's wrath. You have no such protection. They've seen to that. You must flee. I'll be your eyes and ears in the *patriarchum*. When it's safe, I'll know. Then we can be together."

Anastasius grabbed his beloved Johanna's hands and pulled her close. "What am I to do without you?"

"You're to get you out of Rome, far from Theophylact's reach. Make for the border of the Frankish country where Lothair can protect you. I'll come to you, but first, I must farm the apostolic lands and earn the money Leo needs for his wall. Until then, you're to stay alive and love me as I love you."

32
Heresies

Isabelle Héber scanned the images on her computer screen at the desk provided for her in the Vatican Library. Father Sabella had been more than accommodating and supplied her with everything she required. He avoided her at first, but once he discovered she would be deciphering early Biblical scriptures, the librarian in him overcame his suspicion of an outsider, and a woman to boot. He even acquired the habit of hovering around her desk while she installed her equipment. She explained everything to him solicitously at first, but lately had to shoo him away to get her work done.

Isabelle had purchased a digital-imaging software program used mostly by professional photographers and graphic artists. However, finding a digital document camera had been difficult. In the end she bought the best camera she could find in Rome and added a macro lens and colored filters.

Photographs were easily downloaded from the camera to the computer, and a colleague had emailed her a dictionary of first-century Aramaic that interpreted the words she uncovered. Pages had just begun to appear when the doorknob turned and the hinges creaked. "Please Father Sabella," she said, "I'm at a critical point…"

"Sorry if I'm interrupting."

Isabelle jerked around to the welcome sound of Michael Romano's voice, then her jaw dropped. "Oh my God, what did you do to your eye?"

"I didn't do anything," Romano countered. "This was done to me."

"By who?"

"It's a secret."

Isabelle's intuition told her the priest's black eye had something to do with the men who had attacked them in Paris. "Does your shiner have anything to do with a raid on terrorists in Normandy?"

"How did you hear about that?"

"So I'm right?"

"I promised not to say."

"You just did. Anyway, it's not much of a secret since every newspaper and TV station is running the story. But what would Arabs want with Psalters?"

"I don't have any idea," Romano said. "I feel like I should, but I can't put my finger on it."

"Sit here while I find some ice." Isabelle rose from her chair and pushed Romano into the seat.

"You're a little late; the damage is done. What might interest you, since you've guessed already, is that the man who gave me this is the same one who assaulted us in your apartment."

"Are you positive?"

"I'd recognize his punches anywhere," Romano said.

"You mean actual terrorists were in our home?"

"I don't think they'll be bothering you. The one who attacked me was killed, and the others are in jail."

"Did you find the Psalter at least?" Isabelle was hopeful.

"No, but it had been in the terrorist's compound. I found photocopies of the pages. The police are still searching."

"Oh Michael, I am sorry. But this might cheer you up. I've got a rudimentary system up and running, and I just translated the first pages of a Giovanni Psalter."

"Is this the page on the screen?"

"Yes, although some of the words are missing. I need to find more filters, but I think enough is legible to tell which book this is. If I'm not mistaken, Giovanni copied over the text in the exact order it was written."

"An entire scroll was cut and bound into a single codex?"

"I'm pretty sure," Isabelle said.

"That's never happened before. Monks cut scrolls into pages and they ended up in many different books."

"Maybe I'm mistaken, but as I loaded photographs on the computer, the sentences continued from one page to another. I don't read Aramaic, but the script appears to be unbroken."

"That would mean Giovanni intended to keep the contents of the scroll whole. I've always had a hunch about this monk." Romano eyed the digitized image of Aramaic writing.

Isabelle reached over him. Her hair brushed against his face as she tapped the enter key. The ancient writing disappeared and English words reappeared in their place. "Do you recognize the text?"

Romano grimaced as he stared at the computer monitor. "The sentence construction is confusing. We could certainly use your dad to translate but yes, I know the verses," he said.

"Well?"

"The Gospel of Mary Magdalene."

Isabelle was flummoxed. "I had no idea women were Apostles."

"They weren't, according to the church. But there's been a lot of debate lately. Some of the early church fathers called Mary the *Apostle to the Apostles*. Even Paul referred to a woman named Junia as 'foremost among the Apostles.' Women certainly held positions of authority, but later popes suppressed their roles. However, they continued to be ordained as late as the fourteenth century."

"If women were priests, could they also marry?"

"I suppose," Romano said. "The early church had no restrictions on marriage. Some of the Apostles were married, but in the fourth century, marriage began to be forbidden, although the prohibition wasn't absolute. By the fifteenth century, half of the clerics continued to marry. Even popes had wives and children, but I've never heard of priests marrying each other."

"So you and I might have been married if we lived in the middle ages." Isabelle gently touched the black ring under Romano's eye.

Michael clasped her hand and brushed the fingers against his cheek. He stood and wrapped his arm around her waist. His lips moved toward hers, and she closed her eyes. He whispered in her ear, "You'd better get the ice," and turned to open the door.

"Are you leaving?"

"Yes?"

"Why?" Isabelle asked.

"You know why. Do you think your dad would help you?"

Isabelle pleaded on the telephone with her father to come to Rome. "Please Papa, I need you. Michael needs you."

"So he's Michael now, not Father Romano?"

"Really Papa, we're colleagues and we've become close friends."

"I'm teasing. Romano's a good man. I meant no harm."

"Then you'll come? Can I tell Michael you will?"

"I have too much work," Pascal said.

"You're retired."

"I do a lot for the university and I chair some committees. How would it look if the Chairman was absent? It would be easier if you brought the codices to Paris. There's better equipment at the Archives. You said so yourself."

"Impossible. The church would never release their Psalters after what happened, and it would be dangerous for us. The terrorists know where we live. If they got wind we had more Psalters in our apartment... Well, I don't want to think about it."

"You said they'd been arrested."

"The police aren't sure if they found them all and the Psalter hasn't been recovered, so someone's got the thing."

"So lock them up in the Archives," Pascal said.

"Oh, sure and work on them while I'm imagining what happened to poor Eugène. No thank you very much. They broke into the Archives too, remember?"

"They connived their way in and that's not likely to happen again. How many books did you say you'd uncovered so far?"

"Five, but we've only deciphered the first pages, enough so Michael can tell which ones they are. I'll finish all of the photographs in a few weeks. Then the computer dictionary won't take long to translate them and you can fill in the gaps."

"Computers, bah!" Pascal groused. "They can't comprehend syntax, idioms, metaphors."

"Why do you think I'm calling you? This is the most meaningful job I will ever do and you could be a part. I don't understand you. Religion was always more important to you than me."

"I suppose I might rearrange my schedule. I've missed meetings before, the absent-minded professor excuse."

"I love you, Papa."

"You better be ready for me when I arrive so I'm not hanging around all day with a bunch of priests. I may be old, but even an aging Frenchman needs a few pretty girls in the picture."

"What about me?"

"You're not pretty, Isabelle, you're beautiful; but you're my daughter and daughters are different."

The two Thomases aren't the same at all," Pascal explained to his daughter as he poured over printouts in Aramaic. They had managed to squeeze another chair into her postage-stamp office which was already crammed with a computer and camera mounted on a desk-top stand, and Pascal had to share half of her desk. "I wish you'd paid more attention in catechism. This would be much easier."

"It had nothing to do with paying attention. I decided I was an atheist as a teenager, remember? I played hooky from catechism."

"Now you're paying the penance. You're forced to listen to me instead of the long-suffering curé. As I was saying, the *Gospel of Thomas* says he's Jesus' twin brother and Jesus told him the secrets to salvation, which are available to anyone, provided, of course, they can interpret them." Pascal glanced at his daughter to gauge the impact of what he'd said, but Isabelle's thoughts had drifted elsewhere. "Hello," he raised his voice, are you home?"

"I'm sorry, Father. What did you say?"

"I said you're not listening. You're not even here. You want to tell me what's going on?"

"No."

"I've never seen you like this. If I didn't know better, I'd say you'd fallen in love. But where would you find an eligible bachelor in the Vatican?"

Isabelle burst into tears. "I don't know how it happened. I'm not sure if it did. Anyway, the whole thing's impossible." She wrapped her arms around her father's shoulders.

The door opened and Father Romano's head popped in. "How's everything going, you two?"

Pascal and Isabelle's heads were pressed together as though they were hatching some sort of conspiracy. Isabelle sat up ramrod straight, looking like a guilty schoolgirl, and wiped her eyes.

"We're just talking heresy," Pascal said.

Father Romano shrugged. "I suppose it's impossible not to with heretical writings scattered around your office. What're you working on?"

"The *Gospel of Mary Magdalene*."

"Anything new?"

"No, only what we've already uncovered—except the words are in Aramaic."

"So how do you interpret the book?"

Pascal had a sly look about him. "Mary's a women's libber from the Bible days, maligned by traditionalists for her progressive ideas and the most subversive of philosophies that struck fear in the hearts of every man."

"What philosophy?" Romano asked.

"That mere women would dare to be as spiritual and as smart as men, and that they dared to be equal."

"Is that why you believe Mary's Gospel was excluded from the Bible?"

"It should be obvious," Pascal said. "Men, bah! They think they know everything. I realize you see the scriptures as divinely inspired, and perhaps some are. Nevertheless, many were composed simply to support a position during the religious infighting after the crucifixion. One sect said Jesus was God, while others asserted he was merely a man. Books like *Mary* claimed women were equal to men, but traditionalists insisted on their subordination. To add authority to words, the authors declared their books were actually penned by Apostles. These guys were not so unlike political propagandists who fabricate stories to support their side and malign the opposition."

Romano raised his eyebrows. "I wish I had the time to dispute your fanciful interpretation, but I have an appointment. What a shame this is only a fragment. I would like to read the rest."

Pascal was disappointed Romano didn't take the bait. He wanted to have a man-to-man talk with him, or at least a verbal joust. Alas, he provoked no game today, not even a mild theological defense, and he frowned pitifully, stretching the corners of his mouth down and down like a caricature, a mime, the essence of sadness.

"You're making me feel wretched, Pascal," Father Romano laughed, "but I'm late for an appointment. Tonight, no holds barred and you can make as many jabs as you like, and I promise a spirited repartee."

Pascal turned his lips up in an equally exaggerated infectious smile, making Isabelle and Michael laugh out loud together. "Now, seriously, Isabelle, can I take some of the translations? I need to meet with my cardinal to explain our progress."

33
Vengeance

I am glad you called, Desmoulins," Del Carlo said to the GIGN captain as he looked back and forth at the pages of a report prepared by his lieutenant, Moretti, which were scattered across his desk. "I have some interesting developments to tell you. Money is flowing into Rome from Islamic charities and much of it is going into a brass plate company called *Crescent Rural Schools*. Of course it's a front. Guess whose?"

"The imam's?" The French captain said.

"How did you guess?"

"Because *Colonelo*, I'm looking at the same reports."

"Why are you interested in Rome? This is my jurisdiction."

"Just a hunch. I thought I would do some checking before I called you."

"Into what?"

"I'm sorry to be the bearer of bad news, *Colonelo*, but the imam was released from jail."

The Italian colonel was flabbergasted. "What! You can't be serious."

"Believe me, we tried our best to keep him behind bars, but he has powerful attorneys. Most of all, he broke no laws. He had only shotguns and hunting rifles, which are completely legal, and he claims no knowledge of how this Hassan got hold of a pistol. His testimony is that Hassan was a newcomer and wanted to enjoy pastoral peace, meditation, and prayer like the rest of the visitors."

"But the photographs of the ferries and reactors, the drawings…?"

"The imam claims they were planning vacations," *Capitaine* Desmoulins said.

"Bah! Ridiculous."

"Of course. However, his attorneys insist we're just a bunch of racists, and it gets worse. They filed wrongful death lawsuits, claiming our search was based on misrepresentations and is therefore invalid. I'm afraid it's become rather a mess, so I decided to follow the money laundering route."

"What did you find?"

"Nothing yet."

"Then why did your attention turn to Rome, *Capitaine?*"

"Which brings me to the second reason for my call. The imam booked a flight to Rome for Friday, and I thought you might be interested. On a hunch, I investigated whether any unusual money transfers had come your way. You may want to find out if this *Crescent Rural Schools* company is legal, but our imam is a shrewd customer and I'd bet it is. There's one more thing."

"Yes?"

"Money from the same charities is flowing into another account, a numbered Swiss one."

"Are the Swiss cooperating?"

"I'm afraid not." *Capitaine* Desmoulins said. "At least not yet, but I'm about to turn up the heat and make things quite nasty if they don't. They want evidence the money is laundered or involves terrorist activity. I pointed out our suspicions about the imam, but he was cleared by our own courts and the Islamic charities are legitimate, according to the Swiss."

"You said the imam arrives Friday?"

"An Alitalia flight."

"Perhaps I can have a chat with him," Del Carlo said.

"*Bonne chance.* I hope you meet with better luck than I did. If you need anything at all my friend, I'm at your service. I'm haven't forgotten that I'm indebted to you."

"You owe me nothing, *Capitaine*. You'd do the same."

"Oh, I almost forgot," Desmoulins added. "Did you hear the Hébers are in Rome?"

"Which one?"

"Both."

"Thank you again, *Capitaine*." Ringing off, Del Carlo pressed the button on the telephone's intercom. "A minute of your time Lieutenant Moretti." Two short raps sounded on his door a moment later. A tall, uniformed officer entered with no formalities. "Excellent report as usual," Del Carlo praised his subordinate. "I've been informed that money from these Islamic charities is also going into a numbered account in Switzerland. I want the name of the owner."

"Swiss bankers are tough."

"So are you, Moretti. Don't take no for an answer."

"*Si, Colonelo.*"

"And Lieutenant, I want the answer yesterday."

Moretti didn't look back as he exited through the door. "As usual, *Colonelo.*"

"Not at the apartment," Sayyid told Rashid on the anonymous cell phone. "You'll find a café across the street and down a little. We'll have lunch together, say forty-five minutes?"

"Do you truly mean forty-five and not an hour and a half?" Rashid replied sarcastically.

"If you go now, you can see if I've already arrived," he laughed. "Don't be so suspicious." Sayyid's attempt at familiarity irritated Rashid.

"Which café?"

"That side of the street only has one."

The *rue Jean* is a public thoroughfare in the middle of Paris's 18th *arrondisement* in the center of the *Goutte d'Or*, but the road might as well be blocked off to traffic, for the immigrant merchants and residents have nearly confiscated it. Shops move their wares to the sidewalk, forcing the flood of pedestrians into the street. The sweet smell from the green grocer's fruits and vegetables mingles with the odor of blood from the butcher's beef and wafts to and fro like a toxic cloud. Arabs hawk sunglasses and wallets, and African women plop plastic sacks of strange purple tubers onto the pavement to sell to passersby.

Occasionally, police in small groups wander down the lane. Everyone can tell when they've arrived because vendors scoop up their goods in a flash and flee in the opposite direction. Woe to the hapless automobile that makes an inadvertent turn onto the one-way street. No one moves aside despite toots on the horn or revving engines. The driver must simply fall into line with the mass of slow-moving, unconcerned immigrants inching forward until arriving at the far end of the road to make a hasty escape.

Rashid navigated the block, weaving around African women whose gleaming ebony skin was wrapped in bright robes of blue and black or green and orange, their headdresses of matching cloth piled in complicated folds. He dodged teenage girls poured into skin-tight jeans and push-up bras and perched on high heels, and men in slacks or ankle-length cotton robes of beige or black.

Sayyid was right. The other side of the street had only one café. It was sandwiched between a wig boutique and travel agency offering discount flights to Algeria, Tunisia, and the Ivory Coast. Seating himself in back, he could monitor the front and everyone who entered the café. Next to his table, a narrow passage led to a back room and door. He grasped the strategic advantage of sitting in the rear where he might examine customers who came in, yet those entering had difficulty seeing the back. Better still, the escape route was right next to him. He could be out the door before anyone noticed. *Yes*, he thought to himself, *Sayyid is a clever customer. He understands this business. I could learn a thing or two, but perhaps I won't trust him just yet.* Rashid ordered hot tea and added a copious spoonful of sugar, stirring as he waited.

Sayyid made a great show of looking at his wristwatch and tapping the face as he walked toward Rashid. "I'm right on time and now you're the one who has been watching out for both of us. Are we safe?"

"I've noticed nothing unusual."

"You're a quick study, Rashid, as the imam said you would be."

"How do you know him?" Suspicion coated Rashid's voice.

"We're not old friends if that's what you mean, and I'm not part of his congregation. We're more like…business associates, shall we say."

"What is your business?"

"To strike at the heart of the infidel and you're going to help me."

"You're presumptuous. I didn't agree to whatever your plan is."

"Oh, I think you will," Sayyid said.

"Why should I? I don't even know you, let alone trust you."

"Because, my young colleague, I bring sad tidings."

Rashid was in a panic. "The imam, what did they do to him?"

"Fear not, the imam is safe."

"Then what is it?"

Sayyid placed his hand over Rashid's. "Dear Rashid, Hassan is dead."

"How can that be?"

"He was killed the night you escaped."

Rashid was caught off guard. Of all the things he might have suspected, he didn't expect that. His comrade was gone. As reckless and worldly as he was, Hassan was the only person he could call a friend in Europe. Tears welled up in his eyes and he wiped them before he was shamed by their rolling down his cheeks, like a soft schoolboy.

"There's no indignity in weeping for a friend, but you should be rejoicing, for Hassan died a martyr. Even now, he reaps his reward."

Rashid sniffed, "I hope Allah in his infinite goodness saved the most beautiful virgins for Hassan. He would be overjoyed and mock me for not joining him."

"Is that what you wish, to be one of the holy martyrs?"

Rashid's eyes grew cold like steel. "I want to avenge my friend."

"Perhaps you can do both."

"I'm not ready to be one of the *ishtishhadi*, a suicide bomber, if that's what you mean."

"Of course not. The *ishtishhadi* are called by Allah to give the supreme sacrifice. Should you be summoned, you'll know."

Rashid nodded, but he knew it wasn't the whole truth. He had seen boys in the camps schooled by their teachers when he was being trained to serve the will of the imam. While they were taught the Qur'an, their lessons were filled with fanciful stories of the glorious *istishhadi*, lone warriors against the armies of the infidels and the apostate. It was forbidden, of course, to send anyone younger than fifteen; however, these boys were trained from the age of five to fulfill Allah's divine plan, and they revered the martyrs.

Yet Allah was not the one who chose them, but commanders of the resistance. All too often, Rashid witnessed unquestioning youths sent out to kill fellow Muslims in their own public marketplaces, where guilty blood intermingled with the virtuous. And was it not a sin to attack the innocent? Certainly women and children deserved protection and not bombs.

The choice to be a martyr was supposed to be the *ishtishhadi's* alone. However, Rashid had seen the brainwashing firsthand, peer pressure and chidings from the trainers. *These poor boys enter the camps eager to learn the Prophet's words. Their unwitting parents only want an education for their children to break the heavy burden of poverty. Yet when they pass through the gates, they're doomed.* "No, Sayyid, I don't wish to be a martyr. I still have battles to fight. Nevertheless, Hassan deserves justice."

"We can avenge him without your needless death," Sayyid said.

"How?"

"I know who killed him."

"Who?" Rashid leaned forward, piercing Sayyid's eyes with his own.

"An Italian colonel named Del Carlo and a priest."

"A priest?"

"The one in the apartment who beat Hassan."

Rashid grew excited, focused. "He's here in Paris. We can strike now."

"He's not in Paris. He's at the Vatican."

"Then I'm going home."

"Of course you are, and I can show you how to get to the priest and the colonel as well."

"Tell me?"

"Certainly, but you must understand that this is a divine plan. First the mission, then the priest and the colonel. Allah shines His light on our path. It's a sign."

"*Allahu Akbar.*"

"Yes, Rashid, God is great and now is the time to make our move, my young friend."

34
Saint Malachy

Pascal folded the sheet of paper in half lengthwise, then the corners at one end in forty-five degree angles to fashion an aerodynamic nose. He added creases along the sides for wings and small bends at the rear for elevators. He flicked his wrist and launched his missile. The paper plane banked in a semicircle as it soared to its zenith, floated for an instant, then plummeted and crashed on Isabelle's computer keyboard. She rolled her eyes. "Really, Papa, you're acting like a child." She crumpled the plane in her hand and tossed the wad into the waste bin.

Pascal embellished a sigh. "There must be something for me to do?"

"I'm going as fast as I can. Revise one of your translations. Surely they could use another glance."

"They're perfect, more than perfect, ultra perfect. I'd rather stab myself in the eye than read them again."

"I need a couple of hours to finish this one. Why don't you get a coffee?"

"What're you working on?" Pascal leaned over her shoulder, squinting at the screen.

"How should I know? I can't read Aramaic."

"Go to the top so I can figure out who claims to be writing."

"You're driving me crazy." Isabelle scrolled up the page. Faint words grew darker or lighter as she digitally painted, erased, and repainted the area.

"Stop, that's good enough," Pascal said as his mind translated the Aramaic. "*Jesus said to them, My wife...she will be able to be my disciple.* An unheard-of Gospel of Jesus' Wife!" He turned his head toward Isabelle and grinned. "Somebody's not going to like this. Can't you go a little faster?"

"Not if you keep interrupting me. Get out for an hour or so and give me some peace. What did you say about a wife?"

Pascal stood and stretched his wiry frame. He was about to reply when the door burst open.

Two Swiss Guards in blue uniforms stormed into the room. The taller guard who wore captain's bars barked, "Please, Madame, stop what you're doing and move away from the computer."

Isabelle spun her chair. "Get out, we're working." She tried to sound stern, but her words squeaked and she wished she could say them over.

"You hold no authority here, Madame Héber. Now if you please."

"On whose orders do you dare—"

"On my orders." A tall, gray-haired priest wearing a scarlet sash and zucchetto eased into the office. "We don't need to be so military, Captain. I'm sure the Hébers will be cooperative." Cardinal Keller challenged Pascal with a haughty glare.

"Who are you and what do you want?" Isabelle demanded.

"I'm sorry, *Mademoiselle*. You're quite right to be offended. Please forgive our atrocious lack of manners, but we're accustomed to working among men. We seldom host such lovely guests. I'm Cardinal Keller, the Defender of the Faith, and we're taking possession of the Psalters and your computers, as well as everything in this room."

"You can't. All our work."

"Don't fret. You'll be fairly compensated and yes, we can. Indeed, we can."

Blood rushed to Isabelle's cheeks. "Who are you to give us orders?"

"Isabelle, please," Pascal interrupted their exchange. "The good cardinal is what we Jews called the Grand Inquisitor. He's second only to the Pope. Vatican City is a sovereign country and he can do whatever he wishes. I believe he wishes to hand us our walking papers."

"An unfair sentiment, Pascal. We've simply decided that for security's sake, we must protect the church's treasures until we develop adequate precautions. I'm aware of the unfortunate incidents at your apartment and the French Archives. Of course, you should interpret nothing I've said as impugning either your credentials or integrity, which are illustrious." Cardinal Keller looked at them imperiously, confident of his unquestionable authority.

"Can't we appeal?" Isabelle said. "Who are the *we* that made this decision?"

The Grand Inquisitor narrowed his eyes. "The *we* is me. Now, if you please, the captain will escort you to the gate, and I hope you'll accept the gratitude of the church for your contribution."

"What are you going to do with the Psalters, our translations? You can't hide them away. They must be—"

Cardinal Keller simply turned to the captain. "You have your orders. They may take nothing from the room." Under his breath but loud enough to be heard, he added, "Search them before they leave."

"Efficiently German of you, Herr Cardinal," Pascal said.

The cardinal bowed and walked out.

Romano struggled to reassure Isabelle as he sat next to her at the kitchen table in her small apartment while Pascal paced. "I tried, Isabelle. Keller won't even see me."

"But all of your work, everything's gone," she said.

"We can't be sure."

"I think we can, Michael." Pascal sounded disgusted.

"I'll appeal to His Holiness."

Stopping in his tracks, the professor faced Romano. "You can't believe the Pope is unaware? More likely, the fan on Isabelle's new-fangled computer scarcely stopped its infernal racket before he knew each and every word she uncovered. Trust me, the Pope knows more about what we're doing than we do ourselves. Nothing will happen until he decides what to do with your discovery and issues some sort of Papal Bull or whatever you call it." He waved his hand in the air pretentiously, as though he was delivering an oration. "If history is any judge, his pronouncement won't happen in our lifetime. I told you Isabelle," Pascal shook his finger at her. "We should have taken the Psalters to the Archives. Anywhere but here."

"Despite what you might think, the Pope is a just man, and I believe I can get an audience," Romano said.

"Is that so?" Pascal said. "Have you actually met him?"

"No…I'm sure he doesn't even know who I am, but my cardinal is a personal friend and one of his closest confidants. I'm certain he would speak on our behalf."

"Pardon me if I don't hold my breath, and I'm not going to stay here as a tourist. My work is piling up in Paris."

"Drink your tea while it's hot, Michael." Cardinal Minissi patted him on the hand.

"Eminence, he was heavy handed." Romano protested to the Protector of the Vatican Library.

Cardinal Minissi shook his head. "The old rascal thinks he can bully everyone, his Prussian upbringing. He should have spoken with me first, but I think he loves the drama."

"What can we do?"

"What do you mean?"

"We need to get the Psalters back," Father Romano said.

The cardinal shrugged. "It's a setback I admit, but rather insignificant in the scheme of things."

"How can you say such a thing?"

"Don't you recall that I'm hiding a cache of Giovanni Psalters? We must simply be more discreet."

Romano arched his eyebrows. "Are you saying you would keep our secret from His Holiness?"

"Of course not, but I don't intend to tell Keller. I assure you."

"Don't you think that's how Cardinal Keller found out? His Holiness probably told him."

"Impossible." Minissi shook his head.

"How can you be sure?"

"Because I haven't spoken with the Pope yet."

"Then who told him?"

"Who can say? Keller has spies everywhere, but don't waste your time worrying about him. You must carry on."

"Where will we work? Cardinal Keller banished the Hébers from the Vatican."

Minissi rubbed his chin. "That does present a problem. Keller has his nose all over."

"Only one option is left," Romano said. "We must take the Psalters outside of the Vatican."

"Oh no, it's far too dangerous. I can't allow it."

"Eminence, we have no choice if we're to discover what Giovanni has hidden. Otherwise Keller will confiscate everything."

"Listen to me." Minissi leaned forward in his chair. "I realize how important it is for you to translate these books. However, your life cannot be jeopardized."

"I'm ready to risk my life for God's word."

"I fear you will one day, Father Romano. It's your destiny, only not today."

"What do you mean?"

"Can't you guess? Don't you realize who you are?"

Romano stared at his newest mentor, feeling as though his skin was being peeled back to reveal his hidden self, stripped bare not of his clothes, but the mortal shell that shrouds the soul.

"Didn't you wonder why you were promoted so quickly, the youngest professor of paleography at one of our most prestigious universities, then *custodes* of the Archives? Now you're co-Prefect of the Library. Look around. We're all old men and you're so young."

"I've worked hard for the church and I thought..."

"You thought that stealing a book from the Library and having it stolen from you would get you another promotion? An interesting career move, but I wouldn't recommend it to just anyone. But then you're not just anyone, Peter Romano." Cardinal Minissi emphasized the priest's name as though the mere mention would help him come to some sort of epiphany.

"I don't understand what you're trying to say," Romano was perplexed.

"Father, we brought you here to protect you."

"From what? More assassins?"

"Assassins, spies in the church, from everything, even yourself, so you can take your rightful position when the time comes, and I believe the time is near."

Romano stared blankly at his boss. "What are you trying to tell me?"

"Do you know the prophecies of the medieval priest, Maelhaedhoc Ó Morgair?"

Romano shook his head.

"Drink your tea and I'll tell you a story. You might be familiar with his Latin name, Father Malachy."

"I heard it from an unlikely source."

"He was an Irish priest in the twelfth century who had come to Rome to give an accounting of his diocese. Yet when he arrived, he fell into a trance and had a vision of the life of every pope right up to the last one, and he wrote it all down."

"There's a list of every pope until the end of the papacy?"

"One hundred and twelve of them," Minissi nodded.

"He lists them by name?"

"Not their names, he called them by arcane titles like *Religio depopulata* or *Fides intrepida*. At first, no one understood what the designations meant. Over time, we began to understand that they described their lives or a significant event in their reign."

"People see what they want in a prophecy," Romano said. "They're so nebulous."

"Saint Malachy called Pope John Paul I *from the half moon*. He was pope for only a month? He was a wonderful man, loved books.

Did you know his papacy began at the half moon and he died during the half moon?"

"No."

"Or that His Holiness John Paul II was called, *from the eclipse of the sun.*"

Now Romano's interest was piqued. "Don't tell me John Paul II was born during an eclipse."

"He died during one as well. Each pope had some event or personality trait linking him to the name Malachy had given."

"Where does the list end?" Romano asked.

"The last pope will be the 268th since the Apostle Peter."

"But His Holiness is the 267th. Are you saying the next pope will be the last?"

"That's what Malachy said, but he says even more. He prophesied that during the reign of the last pope, Rome would be destroyed and our Judge would pass judgment upon his people."

"Really Eminence, this sounds like the ravings of medieval crackpots."

"Please, Father Romano. Malachy was no crackpot, as you put it. He was a brother and a Saint. Do you think Pope Pius X was a crackpot as well?"

"Of course not."

"Pius predicted that *The Pope will leave Rome and, in leaving the Vatican, he will pass over the dead bodies of his priests!* Other modern popes had similar visions and they weren't medieval crackpots."

"Forgive my poor choice of words," Romano said, chastened, "but what you're saying is too fantastic to believe."

"You must. Do you remember the Miracle of Fatima?"

"Every Catholic knows the story."

"Ten-year-old Lucia de Santos was visited by the Virgin Mother in 1917 and given three prophecies. She kept the last vision a secret. She wrote everything down and sealed the account in an envelope, saying the Virgin had given instructions that it not be opened until 1960. When the time came, Pope John read her vision and fainted. Why? Because Lucia repeats the same visions as these Popes and Malachy.

I have a part of it right here in my drawer." Cardinal Minissi pulled a page from his desk and wiped it smooth with his hand. He pointed with his finger at the words, mumbling as he scanned. "Here it is."

...the Holy Father passed through a big city half in ruins and half trembling with halting step, afflicted with pain and sorrow, he prayed for the souls of the corpses he met on his way; having reached the top of the mountain, on his knees at the foot of the big Cross he was killed by a group of soldiers who fired bullets and arrows at him...

"Do you understand now why you must be protected?" Minissi stared intently at his protégé.

Father Romano had no idea what his cardinal was driving at. "What does this have to do with me?"

"Because, Father, for one hundred and eleven popes, Saint Malachy gives no name, just a description. The only name on the list is the last pope, *Petrus Romanus.*"

"So...?"

"In English, you would say Peter the Roman or Peter Romano."

"But you're saying I'm to be the next pope? Popes are elected by secret ballot in a conclave, not because they have the right name."

"I am well aware of how they're chosen since I'm a member of the College of Cardinals who does the electing. We've been watching you for some time, or, rather, watching for you. The name Michael threw us off the trail."

Romano's breathing quickened. "It can't be. I'm not worthy to be Pope. I'm not sure if I'm good enough to be a priest."

Minnissi squeezed Romano's shoulders and spoke to him in a soothing, paternal voice. "We all suffer from our shortcomings and failures. We're Human."

"What should I do?"

"You must do exactly what you have been doing, Father *Petrus Romanus.* The Psalters will remain within these walls and you with them. Together, we'll find a way to keep them from Keller's snooping."

35
State Secrets

This isn't a simple bomb," Rashid emphasized to Sayyid as they sat in a small, empty warehouse near Rome's Termini train station. "It's a complicated operation. Strapping on plastique to blow up a few people is one thing, but a building?"

"You don't need to destroy the structure, only the contents," Sayyid said. "You told me you'd been trained?"

"Roadside bombs or improvised explosive devices, nothing of this magnitude."

"Can you do it or not?"

"I'm not sure. What's inside?"

"Books."

"Are we going to blow up a book shop?" Rashid said.

Sayyid laughed, "A library, the largest and most corrupt on earth." He rolled out map on the workbench and pointed to a building in Vatican City. "This is our target, the Library."

"You want to blow up the church's library?"

"Yes."

Rashid shook his head. "To what end?"

"We'll strike the heart of the infidels."

"How does bombing a Christian library hurt the infidels?

Christians are not evil nor is their religion. Crusaders who attack
Islamic countries, prop up dictators and occupy our holy lands are
the corrupt ones. However, it's wrong to destroy religious books."

"Wrong, you say?" Sayyid raised his voice. "Did not Allah forbid
the making of images, yet more paintings of the Prophet Jesus and
God himself are in this wretched building than anywhere else on
earth. The vile place is a repository of forbidden works."

"Are not the words of the Jesus also in the library? We're the
Children of the Book, not the destroyers. Wiping out His words would
a sin. We should find and protect them as I've been taught. I tell you
I don't like this one bit."

Sayyid glared at his protégé, then his face became soft.
"Sometimes, we must do things that are distasteful, that in another
time might even be a sin. But today, we're the vanguard of the holy
battle to bring about the golden days of justice. The imam said
you would understand. This is his will. Do you not wish to follow
his plan?"

It was true, Rashid thought, *the imam had promised I would be
a warrior in the battle against the infidels. He also put his trust in this
man who waged war on the crusaders. If this is indeed the will of the
imam, who am I to question?* Had the words come directly from him,
he wouldn't hesitate, but Sayyid was no imam. "For a job like this,"
he began slowly, "we'll need incendiary devices as well as explosives,
a great many."

"You were well chosen, Rashid al-Ansar. A fortune will be placed
at your disposal for whatever you need, but where can we buy explosives in Italy?"

"You don't know?" Rashid looked disappointed.

"I can provide financing, but I'm not much of a procurer."

"No matter. I'll make them."

Sayyid pulled a notepad and pen from his jacket pocket. "What
do you require?"

"To begin with, paint thinner, antiseptic, and toilet bowl cleaner.
I'll calculate the amounts."

"Are we going to clean the Library before we blow the thing up?"

Rashid smiled at Sayyid's lack of in-the-trenches training. "Triacetone triperoxide is one of our favorites. We use TATP to make shoe bombs: powerful, unstable, and easy to hide. While I mix the chemicals, you can hunt down as much aluminum and iron oxide as you can buy without drawing suspicion."

Sayyid furrowed his brow. "Can't we simply buy pipes or drums?"

"Oxide is metal powder. I'll mix the powders to make thermite. You want to burn the place down. Thermite will burn through armor plate at four thousand degrees. A few million books will be an appetizer. I'll also need magnesium strips for a fuse."

"How can we get everything into the Library?"

"I know a way," Rashid said.

Two police officers from the *Carabinieri* intercepted the imam at the gate as he stepped off the Alitalia flight and escorted him to the *douane*, the customs window. "*Passaporto, signore*," the officer said. The Islamic cleric pushed his passport through the window and an officer scanned it into a computer, then picked up the telephone.

The *Carabinieri* escorted the bearded imam through a nondescript door into a sterile waiting room with a large mirror. One of the officers pulled back a chair from the table and ordered him to sit.

From behind the one-way mirror, Del Carlo stared patiently, searching every part of the imam's facial expressions through his graying curly beard. The imam revealed little of what he might be thinking or feeling. The colonel cocked his head as he glimpsed the corners of the imam's mouth turn up ever so slightly. *Could be grinning?* He asked himself. Turning to his lieutenant, who also watched at the colonel's side, Del Carlo said, "If two large policeman escorted you to an interrogation room, what would you find amusing, Moretti?"

The lieutenant shrugged his shoulders. "Perhaps he wants us to see that he doesn't fear the police."

"Then he'd wear a big smile. This one is for himself."

Del Carlo stepped into the secure room and closed the door,

leaning against it as he waited for the imam to acknowledge him. The imam stared straight ahead as though he was in a trance. "Well, imam, you decided to pay us a visit."

No response. Del Carlo walked around the table. He stood behind the seated cleric for a long moment before continuing, heels clicking, step by step, on the linoleum floor, until he came to a chair on the opposite side. "You're not very talkative." Still no answer. "I hope you won't mind answering a few questions." Del Carlo sat.

"You need only ask, *Colonelo*." The imam looked him squarely in the eyes, unafraid and uninterested.

"So you can speak."

"I'm not a mute, but since you've detained me against my will, I have no desire to offer anything. Nevertheless, if you require an answer, I shall do my best."

"I'm glad you're going to be cooperative. We're already aware of your Italian bank accounts and phony business."

The imam only stared.

"If this is how you'd like to play, then I'll ask and you answer. You've had a business license in Rome for some time now and fat bank accounts that are getting fatter. Yet there's no commerce, just money moving in and out. We call such a farce a brass plate company."

"Truly? Interesting description. I don't know what it means."

"I'm quite sure you do. They're companies in name only, used as a front to launder dirty money. It's against the law."

"I've broken no laws, *Colonelo*."

"Where's the money going, and why are you passing it through a nonexistent company? Can you explain that?"

"Of course," the imam said impassively. "I acquired a business license in Rome, a bit premature, but I'm sure it's not against the law. I receive revenue in my bank accounts from all over the world, and that, too, is no crime. The issue is threefold: is the source of the income from illegal activities? Will the money be used for unlawful purposes? And are assets hidden from the government to avoid taxes? The answers are no, no, and no."

"What is this premature venture?"

"I owe you no explanation for the nature of my company. I've consulted my attorneys on this matter, but I shall tell you so you know where I stand." The imam glowered at Del Carlo with eyes that changed in a flash from disinterested to hot and piercing. "I intend to buy farm houses in rural areas all over Italy, as I did in France, so Muslims can experience the joy of country life outside the squalor and bigotry of the ghettos where they live." He leaned forward on the table, challenging the colonel. "Where they can be taught and trained in the true path of Islam—a good thing, don't you think? Such purchases require considerable money." He sat back in his chair, looking serene and impenetrable once again. "We'll teach Allah's will in tranquil, rustic settings far from prying, prejudiced eyes."

"It sounds like a veiled threat. Should I be afraid?"

"Why, *Colonelo*, how can peaceful Muslims vacationing in the country, listening to the true words of Allah be a danger to you?"

"I don't know," the Del Carlo said, "but I intend to find out. What's your interest in medieval prayer books?"

"Many prized copies of the Qur'an from the years you call the Middle Ages are displayed in museums. Their value is beyond measure."

"I'm talking about a Christian book of Psalms written in Latin."

"Such a book would hold little interest for me," the imam shrugged.

"Truly? Then why did we find photocopies of this type of book at your farm?"

"How should I know? Perhaps Hassan brought them. Why don't you ask him?"

"Clever, and this Hassan, whoever he is, or rather was, came to your compound with another man. Oh yes, you've been under surveillance for some time. Who is this man, and where is he now?"

"I am afraid I can't help you. I don't keep track of the comings and goings of our guests. I leave such things to our administrative personnel. My pursuits are strictly spiritual. In the area of the soul, I can help, but I'm not the reservations desk."

"Guards," the colonel called. "Please escort our guest to his cell."

"Am I under arrest?"

"Not for the moment."

"Then on what grounds are you holding me?"

"Did you forget? Men were killed, shot to death."

"I've not forgotten," the imam scowled. "They were Muslims and defended themselves against an illegal assault by the French police. Yet we're in Italy, not France."

"You're right, and in Italy I can hold you for twenty-four hours without charges or an attorney. I think we can find something in a day, perhaps an obscure law that was broken."

"In that case, I take my tea strong, *Colonelo*."

Del Carlo paced in front of Father Sabella's desk, hands behind his back, making Cardinal Minissi's secretary a bit frazzled. "I'm sure Father Romano will be here any moment," he said. "He's quite busy, adjusting to his new position."

"I'm in no hurry, Father," Del Carlo answered, continuing to pace while taking in the layout of the office.

Father Sabella tried to concentrate on the papers in front of him but glanced up furtively, hating that Prefect Romano was not on time for his appointment. The door finally opened and the librarian glided through, hand extended, "I'm happy to see you, *Colonelo*, and in more pleasant circumstances."

"How's the boxer today?"

"Out of shape." Romano patted his belly.

"I don't believe that for a minute. The eye looks a little better, though."

"I got beat up much worse in school. Come this way." Romano led the GIS chief through the door and down the hall to his office. "Would you like a coffee?"

"No thanks, Father, and I want to thank you again for what you did in France. You were brave to put yourself in harm's way."

"It's our calling, to help our fellow man. I only wish someone didn't have to die."

"It's unfortunate, but, after all, he was going to use the gun. I assure you, once he had escaped, he wouldn't have let *Capitaine*

Desmoulins live. He was a professional. They don't leave loose ends."

"Any death is a tragedy, no matter whose. The whole affair left me feeling tainted."

"No man is untouched by a killing. I suppose it's part of the job, like a black eye in the boxing ring. I'm sorry you were involved. On the other hand, Desmoulins is quite happy."

After the salutations and requisite small talk, Romano got down to business. "Well, what can I do for you?"

"How do I say this without sounding suspicious?" the colonel asked tentatively.

"What?"

"I believe you've discovered more books."

Romano was taken aback. How did the colonel know? Did he employ spies in the Vatican?

"So I'm right? You needn't look surprised. It didn't take a genius to figure it out. Isabelle and Pascal Héber were listed on separate flight manifests from Paris to Rome, and I'm betting they're still here. So why would two experts who specialize in ancient manuscripts be visiting Rome? A friendly visit?"

"You hit the nail on the head once again," Romano said. "I did discover more Psalters, and they came to help translate. You're quite a good detective."

"It's in the job description. What did you find?"

"I should decline to answer." Romano hesitated then added, "It's confidential."

"Father, you have a job, but so do I. A priest is dead, along with suspected terrorists. One of your Psalters was stolen and everything is somehow related. I'm just trying to connect the dots before anyone else gets killed."

"I'm afraid I can't offer much assistance."

"Why will you not help?"

"I would if I could, but the books were confiscated."

"Taken? This is becoming a habit," Del Carlo said. "By who?"

"The Defender of the Faith."

"Cardinal Keller? Why?"

"If I tell you," Romano said, "I must have your personal assurance that you won't divulge what you hear."

"State secrets?"

"Something like that," Romano nodded.

"Father, this is a murder investigation and evidence is evidence."

"Naturally, but you have none, and neither do I. I'm not asking you to hide anything you discover, only to keep what I'm about to say in confidence."

"You have my word," the colonel said.

"Did you ever hear of Saint Malachy?" Father Romano began.

36
The Borgo

Prince Ahmad crept through the front door of the *schola cantorum* between the prayers of Lauds and Prime, in the hour before dawn when the city begins to stir and cast off its nighttime covers for the labors of the day. He hung his cloak and removed his metal collar, which wasn't really attached. Johanna had seen to that. The iron was just for show, for Ahmad's safety she told him.

"You're empty-handed." Johanna looked dumfounded. "Did you meet with trouble?"

"Not I, but I fear Cardinal Anastasius is about to. San Marcello is swarming with soldiers. They found a body in his cell." Ahmad nodded in Anastasius' direction.

"He didn't kill the man. I did," Johanna admitted.

"He was an assassin," Anastasius said, "and would have killed me had Johannes not struck."

"You need explain nothing to me," Ahmad said blithely. "I'm but a humble slave."

"No such thing," Johanna replied. "At least not within these walls."

Ahmad bowed. "In any case, a chafing collar didn't cause the burn on your neck." Ahmad turned from Anastasius to Johanna. "The body was clothed in a fine leather hauberk. He was no ordinary killer; he was an officer. Lucky for you your knife found his neck, otherwise the leather might have turned the blade."

"You got close enough to see the body?" Johanna shivered.

"The moon doesn't reflect a brown face as it does pale ones. I looked through the window and listened to what Bishop Benedict said to Count Theophylact."

"They were there? How did they find out so quickly?" Johanna appeared dumbfounded.

Ahmad deduced the answer. "They would know if the assassin was their man. But you're quite right, Master; Anastasius must leave now, on the hour. They'll search the city and are certain to come here." Then turning to the Cardinal of the San Marcello, he apologized. "I'm sorry, but I couldn't collect your belongings. I would have been found out."

"You've taken a considerable risk, and I give you my thanks. My meager things are worthless and can be replaced. All the same, I wish I had a few books for the road."

Johanna wrapped her traveling cloak around Anastasius' tall shoulders. It was too small and made him look like a comic minstrel mocking the priesthood in a passion play. She tucked her own Psalter into his hand and bid him farewell with a peck on the cheek, and he blushed in front of Ahmad. Ahmad looked down as though he hadn't seen. "Lead him through the alleys as far as Nero's plain, and protect him so he meets no harm." Her instructions sounded like a prayer.

Ahmad slipped a long dangerous dagger into his belt and pulled his own cloak around. "Everything you ask, I shall do."

Then Johanna pushed them out of the door, sank to her knees, and wept.

Pope Leo ordered Anastasius' arrest on a charge of murder, but was forced to retract the warrant when Johannes testified that it was she who killed the assassin to save the cardinal's life. Benedict raged and argued for a trial anyway. An officer commissioned by

Count Theophylact had been stabbed to death, and a killing was no trifling matter.

"Truly," Johannes answered his charge, "and just how did you happen to arrive at San Marcello with Theophylact and his men in the dark morning hours before Lauds to discover the dead soldier? Did a soothsayer reveal this foul deed in a dream?"

Benedict cowered, taken unawares, wondering desperately what Johannes had heard and how he might have heard it. "Who said I was about?"

"I do. Do you deny it?"

"I...I spent the evening at the home of my nephew, Theophylact, when word came of the murder."

"Did Theophylact tell you, or did you give the news to him? Perhaps we should question the count separately to find the truth?"

In the end, Benedict withdrew his objection and Leo declined to uphold the charge after Bishop Arsenius reminded him that the Emperor would be incensed if a cardinal in his favor should be falsely accused.

Nevertheless, Benedict would not be denied. Three weeks later, he charged Anastasius with abandoning San Marcello and his parishioners. Once again, Arsenius came to his nephew's defense using all of his diplomatic skills, as well as threats of the Emperor's wrath. When his arguments were exhausted, he pleaded for mercy, saying that Anastasius wasn't safe within the walls of the city. Johannes reminded the assembled cardinals and bishops that a cardinal of the Holy Church had been attacked by someone who wanted his influence silenced, permanently. She glared at Benedict the whole time she defended Anastasius, while the Bishop of Albano squirmed uncomfortably in his chair.

Benedict wasn't cowed for long, however, and countered that the assassin, if indeed he was one, was dead and no evidence had been presented to show that any further threat existed. Nevertheless the rules of the *patriarchum* were clear: no priest could abandon his duties for a period longer than three weeks. Therefore Anastasius, the Cardinal of San Marcello, was excommunicated from the church.

Johanna was disconsolate and dreaded sending her beloved the terrible news, but Bishop Arsenius appeared unconcerned. "This isn't a major setback," he said, "only a bump in the road. Theophylact and his supporters fear that the Emperor extends his power within the Papal Palace, and they wish to nip it before his influence can take root. They believe they've won," he laughed. "No such thing. Their authority doesn't extend past the diocese of Rome. Anastasius is safe at my house in Chiusi where Lothair rules, just beyond their reach."

"But he's been deprived of his priesthood."

"This is a political move not a religious one," Arsenius said. "Anastasius will be a priest in Lombardy until he can return to Rome. Excommunications are just words. They can be pronounced but also withdrawn. Never fear for Anastasius. His excommunication will be undone, but you are the one who should take care. You stand in Benedict's way. What they tried to do to my nephew, they are sure to visit upon you."

"Are you saying they would try to assassinate me? I'm no favorite of the Emperor's."

"It wasn't wise to stand up for Anastasius and expose Benedict in the bargain. Benedict can't fathom how you undid him, and I should like to know as well. I won't ask, for we all need our secrets. But while he doesn't vie against you for power, for you possess little, Benedict is vexed the other cardinals listen to you. You revealed that you're audacious enough to thwart his ambition."

"I only wished to defend Anastasius," Johanna said.

"Yet you've made Benedict fear you. Poor judgment, I must say. You'd do well to remember that in the Papal Palace, there are only two kinds of clerics: those who hold power and those who wish to take it from them. It's not advisable to let people see which one you are."

"I'm neither. I simply want to serve the church in the best way I can."

"Um, too bad," Arsenius said as he surveyed Johanna's soft, hairless face. "I think you might be the cleverest of all. No matter, I'll tell you where you must get for the time being. Leave the *schola cantorum* at once, or you won't live many more days. Find a place outside the city walls where allies can watch you. There's strength in numbers."

"Where would I find such a place and still perform my duties as Cardinal?"

"Are you not English by birth, Johannes Anglicus?"

"Yes."

"Then you should move to the Borgo. There's an Anglo-Saxon school and a hospital as well as a church, *Santo Spirito in Sassia*, I believe. You would be with your own people where neither Benedict nor Theophylact nor any of their spies can enter without being spotted. Get you to the Borgo, Johannes Anglicus. You'll be safe there."

The Borgo, which was the old fourteenth district of Imperial Rome, lay sandwiched between the Vatican to the north and the Jewish ghetto in the Trastevere to the south, with the Tiber on the eastern edge. Its inhabitants were mostly Anglo-Saxons, but also Lombards, Franks and Frisians, and not a single Roman. King Ina, the monarch of the West Saxons, had founded the *schola Anglorum* in the Year of our Lord 727 with the blessing of Pope Gregory II. Attached to the *schola*, he built a church dedicated to the Virgin Mary to serve the spiritual needs of English pilgrims.

Yet many who made the arduous pilgrimage across the channel from Wessex to Francia, then crossing Burgundy and Italy, were the lame and infirm, who hoped to pray for a miracle at the tomb of Saint Peter. Alas, many prayers received no answer, so King Ina set aside a cemetery for their earthly remains. Later in the eighth century, the Anglo-Saxons' most powerful sovereign, King Offa of Mercia in the English midlands, added a hospital to the *schola Anglorum*.

Around this island of English transplanted on the alluvial sands between the Tiber and the clay hills leading to the Vatican, a community of expatriates had grown. They set up shop to serve like-minded immigrants who flocked to Rome for a new life in the capital of Christendom.

Thus did the Borgo become a safe haven for foreigners across the river from the city. Bishop Arsenius was right, neither Benedict nor Theophylact cast any influence here. In fact, Romans avoided the outsiders, who they considered to be of low caste. Those few who dared venture into the Borgo were watched with resentment and mistrust.

Not only did Johanna find safety among her own people, but Prince Ahmad could wander without his metal collar, unshackled and unmolested. Baraldus reveled in his newfound celebrity with his Lombard countrymen and guards of the foreign *scholae*, who he had commanded in the defense of Rome. They hailed him as savior of the city and bought him drinks in the taverns in exchange for tales of his exploits in the days when he was a captain in the army of the Empire. As for Johanna, the Borgo seemed like the home of her childhood, which she had put out of her mind for years and years.

Unlike Romans who fashioned their homes with flat brick and stone covered by marble veneers, the English built with wood. They constructed their houses and shops in the half-timber style, beams attached with pegs to frame the structure, and planks for the joists. The walls were fashioned in layers called a *cob*. The middle was a mat of branches or reeds woven into the frame and plastered over with a mixture of mud and straw. The floors were earthen or wooden boards, and the roof was thatch. The only stone to be found was the fireplace in the main room, which held a crackling fire that cast warmth and shadows. It was just the comfort Johanna needed, cocooned in the memories of her youth, and only a fifteen-minute stroll to a cup of tea, sweet cakes, and intellectual diversion at the table in the Rosh Yeshiva's kitchen.

Her new home was better suited to her position as Cardinal of the Apostolic farms since the Borgo adjoined the Trastevere. A short stroll and Johanna could survey the Jewish craftsmen who worked with an industry and efficiency that dumbfounded her. Plows, rigid horse collars, yokes, and harnesses were manufactured by the hundreds, along with spades and scythes.

Baraldus, for his part, commanded the tenant farmers and freemen as he would a brigade, ordering which fields to plow and which to leave fallow; when to harvest, and which crops to rotate. He purchased the choicest cows, bulls, ewes, and rams like a shrewd hand. Then, running roughshod over the husbandmen in the raising of the beasts, the offspring bullocks, heifers, and lambs were sold to the fleshmongers.

Crops and cattle flooded Rome, and a large surplus was exported to the Frankish lands, Lombardy, Frisia, and Germany. Plows and farm implements were hauled to the port of Ostia and loaded on ships bound for foreign ports, even to the Saracens in Spain and Sicily. The great city of Rome that had fallen upon desperate times became prosperous and proud once again.

Laborers came from all over Lothair's Frankish empire to build Leo's new wall, and the finest artisans worked on the restoration of Saint Peter's and Saint Paul's as well as the ruined *schola cantorum*. People labored and laughed and played. Everyone was content; everyone, that is, except Johanna, who for long years lived inside her longing letters to her love, Anastasius. She took care, of course, not to post them with church's couriers, for she knew they would be read. Instead she gave her dispatches to Avraham, who entrusted them to Jewish traffickers, traveling north to sell their goods in Chiusi's markets and fairs.

Her visits with Avraham became as frequent as her letters and today she handed him the latest, lingering as usual to accept the hospitality of his cozy kitchen.

"What troubles your soul Johannes," Avraham said. "You come to talk, yet are quiet. In truth, I think your body is here but your thoughts are far, far away."

"I don't know what ails me. It's just that I feel rather useless, like I'm not needed."

"Ridiculous. The farming is a great success. All of Rome is astounded by what you've done. Your genius is the talk of the city. Coins flow into everyone's hands like water. Craftsmen and artisans can hardly keep up with their orders. Farmers are flush with crops and hard cash, yet their burden is eased. Money fills the church's coffers once again, and Leo has the finances to build his wall, which even now spreads around the Vatican. Masons and carpenters rebuild your cathedrals grander and more glorious than before. This is a revolution the world has not seen in many centuries. Only the rich grumble. They watch their power slipping away."

"Do you know me so little? I don't care what Rome says about me, good or bad. Baraldus works with the farmers when he isn't spinning tales in the inns. Ahmad's days are full of contracts, finance, and endless ledgers. Even your son is occupied organizing the suppliers, but what do I do? I'm idle."

Avraham pondered his guest for a long moment. "You're right. I have not seen you, but I'm not quite as blind as you might think."

"I don't understand."

"It's easy enough to see if one looks beyond how we wish others to view us."

Johanna's jaw dropped until she caught herself.

The Rosh Yeshiva smiled serenely, "You would fill the days to overflowing so your mind has little time to dwell on the hole in your heart."

"It's only that you all contribute and I do nothing."

"You're the cardinal of the Apostolic farms. You don't toil in the fields and workshops like the others. You hold a position of authority, to make sure all do their jobs well, and you've done it better than anyone might have fathomed. Yet your idleness is not what you lament. Your melancholy is that you miss Anastasius."

Johanna fidgeted in her seat. "Of course I do. He's my dearest friend and I worry for his safety."

The rabbi leaned back in his chair and sighed, "Who would not in your place?"

"I need his help and advice. I'm lost without him."

"Do you need him to help you with your idleness?"

Johanna realized her misstep and searched for an answer.

"I'm sorry, my words were thoughtless," Avraham said. "Who would not long to hold their dearest friend once again and listen to his soft voice and gentle counsel? Do I not miss you when you've been too long at your labors?" The Rosh Yeshiva leaned forward at the corner of the table, bringing his grizzled face close to the priest's. "Still, there's no despair like the longing one feels when they've lost their wife."

Johanna peered into the old man's eyes.

"When my beloved wife died, I believed my world had come to an end; indeed, part of it had. I knew I would never again enjoy the affection and comfort of a woman. My love was gone to me until my time comes to join her."

Tears filled Johanna's eyes and flowed down her rosy cheeks. She flung herself into Avraham's open arms, weeping.

"Now, now daughter. Put your faith in God and pray that he will protect your love and guide him once again to you. I'll say a prayer in the synagogue that He Who Cannot Be Named hears our plea. I'm certain He will."

Johanna sobbed and sniffed, trying to control her crying. "How long have you known?"

"Since the day we met. I'm bewildered you didn't spot it in this old man's eyes."

37
Peripleumonia

The English school's Headmaster was beside himself with joy that such a famous cardinal and distinguished scholar would offer his services as a mere teacher at the humble *schola anglorum*, the English guild's university in the Borgo. Avraham had counseled Johanna to fill her days helping her own people. "There can be no greater gift than education," he had said, "and you possess a surfeit. I've spent my life educating my Jewish brethren about the Torah and its lessons for our lives and souls. No occupation could be nobler than a teacher. Do your scriptures not call Jesus, *Teacher*? Let Him be your example."

Thus did Johanna leave *primicerius* Baraldus in charge of the apostolic farm colonies assisted by Ahmad and Elchanan. They were the real force behind the success of the farms anyway, she told herself.

"But surely you should be Master of the *Trivium* or *Quadrivium* departments," the school's Headmaster said.

"No," Johanna replied. "I wish only to be a humble teacher. I'm well qualified to teach grammar and logic, and perhaps even geometry so my students can measure the length and breadth of their lands and daily work."

Rome's academic institutions, like all those in the Western World, were based on Aristotle's model of education: the *Trivium*, which included grammar, rhetoric, and logic, and the *Quadrivium's* arithmetic, geometry, music, and astronomy. Schools educated children of the nobility or wealthy merchants to prepare them for a life administering their family's lands or business, or a career in law or even the church. Although the English school taught mainly their own people, they educated lesser nobles and less prominent merchants as well. There were also a few students from wealthier families who wanted to be immersed in a foreign language like Frankish or English.

However, Johanna had a new idea. She believed that knowledge was power. Farmers and ordinary people might free themselves from mind-numbing labor or indenture to the church or nobility if only they could be educated.

"If their minds can be freed from ignorance," she told the Headmaster, "then they might devise a way to emancipate themselves from their servitude."

"Education is expensive. Who will pay for it? We're not a charitable institution, and while our classes have not the quality of universities in Rome, they still cost money."

"I will," Johanna said.

"You? Has a priest such a fortune that he can compensate us for our costs?"

"For each man that labors on the farms or on Leo's wall or the restoration of the cathedrals, the church will pay for a child, boy or girl, to be educated here."

"Girls, in the *schola anglorum*? Unheard of!"

"All or nothing, that's my offer. You can either become the largest, most profitable university in Rome, with girl students, or I shall find somewhere else to teach. What say you?"

Johanna began her newest career as a teacher the following week, but, never having taught, she didn't know where to begin. Frazzled, she fled as usual to Avraham, who patiently instructed her in the rudiments of lesson plans, starting from the simplest ideas and building on them to more complicated ones. He assured her that within a month, it would become routine but at the end of two long and frustrating weeks, her head swam. She returned to the Borgo and fell into bed without eating the supper Ahmad had prepared and was sound asleep before Vespers.

She tossed and turned, locked in a dreadful nightmare where she stood in front of her class stark naked as students laughed and mocked her. Worse, her womanhood was stripped bare, and she tried to cover herself with her hands. Schoolboys pointed and snickered while the girls hung their heads in shame. The boys yanked at the girls' hair and lifted their frocks to humiliate them.

One part of her heard the bolt on the door slide and the other did not, and she was scarcely aware that her covers were pulled back and a man had slipped onto the pallet beside her. It was only when her body began to warm that she jerked awake. A hand covered her mouth. "Anastasius!" she cried in surprise and delight, then threw her arms around her sorely missed love, showering his face with kisses.

"I couldn't stay away any longer," he whispered, kissing the nape of her neck and holding her in his large hands.

"Did anyone see you?"

"The streets are empty except for a few snoring drunks."

Their lips met as they grasped and caressed, smelling one another's musky sweetness, trying to crawl into each other's skins, to cleave together physically just as their hearts were already joined. Anastasius brushed back Johanna's short, cropped hair as she clung to him, kissing his lips and finally pulling her fugitive love upon her. They feasted upon one another, giving their passion free rein, worshiping and adoring until satisfied unto exhaustion. Then they fell into a deep slumber, side by side, wrapped safe and contented in the tenderness of each other's arms.

Johanna coughed and choked, awakening to an acrid stench that strangled her. Her eyes stung, and she was blinded by tears. Shoving herself off the pallet, she felt for the clay lamp on her bed stand, knocking it over, and crawled on hands and knees to search for it. The air was cleaner near the floorboards, and her head cleared a bit. The thatched roof sparked and sparkled like fiery stars. Smoke filled the room, and the ceiling burst into flames.

"Anastasius, wake up!" Johanna shook and shook, but couldn't rouse him so she dragged him off the pallet to the ground and slapped his face, to no avail. She pressed on his chest over and over. Finally, he spat and coughed, then retched. They crawled to the door, keeping their noses close to the ground, but thick smoke descended like a fog and they choked and heaved. Holding his breath Anastasius pulled the bolt and shoved, but the door wouldn't budge. He drove his shoulder into the wooden planks with all his might, but it moved scarcely an inch. Starved for oxygen, he slumped over.

Johanna pushed on the door from the floor, but it would open only a crack, and flames crept in when she did, licking at her hands. "Help us," she croaked, gasping for air while holding her palm to her nose. Her head spun and her eyes rolled as she heard a crashing from outside. She could barely utter a whisper and lay down, clasping Anastasius's hand, willing herself to remain conscious.

Outside, Baraldus grabbed burning tables and beams piled in front of the entrance, mindless of his blackened hands. He lifted them effortlessly and heaved them aside like so many sticks. "Master, master," he cried. "Hold on, I'm coming." Grabbing the last burning timber wedged against the entry, he hoisted it on his shoulder, stumbling away as it burned into his robe and singed his ear and tonsured hair.

Ahmad flung open the door. Johanna lay naked on the floor. He was taken aback for the briefest of moments, then stripped his cloak and wrapped it around her. Lifting her, he fled the smoke filled room. "Anastasius," she whimpered. "Anastasius."

Baraldus dropped the heavy timber and stormed into the building as flames clambered up walls, devouring beams and lapping at the joists. Lifting the excommunicated cardinal, he flung him over his shoulder like a sack of potatoes and lumbered out as the burning roof crashed to the ground.

A gale from the coast blew hard on Rome, warming as it passed over land. Gusts rushed up Vatican Hill and flowed down into the Borgo, fanning the flames like a bellows. Sparks and smoldering straw from thatched roofs filled the sky, settling on other roofs and igniting them. Extreme heat from burning buildings ignited the structures next to them, and within minutes, the Borgo was aflame.

"We must get across the Tiber or we'll be roasted alive," Baraldus shouted to Ahmad. But streets and alleys were filled with a frantic mob carrying small bundles or children in their arms, packed together, shoving and grasping, inching toward the river and the safety of Rome. Burning debris rained down upon them. Horses bolted wild-eyed, crashing the carts they pulled into buildings and galloping through the throng. Freed cattle, smelling the water yet having no path to escape, gored and trampled the fallen. Sheep and lambs bleated in terror, their frightened cries adding to the cacophony of the horror stricken.

"No," Ahmad said. "It's folly to fight a panicked herd. The wind blows from the west so let's head south to the Trastevere."

Anastasius coughed nonstop but walked under his own power as they shoved their way across the powerful torrent of frenzied people. Johanna begged to be let down between hacking and gasps for air and Baraldus pleaded to carry her, but Ahmad would have none of it. He carried her in his arms, holding his cloak around her. Stout Baraldus led the group, plowing his way like a rolling boulder into one river of souls after another. He shouldered and pushed people aside, creating a brief space that slammed shut the moment they bowled through. The river of humanity flowed slower the further south they drew, and rivulets of people split off from the surge, scattering into side streets. At long last, they made their way to the narrow alleys of the Trastevere.

The Rosh Yeshiva stood outside his home with his son as Jews filled the streets, watching flames from the Borgo burn toward the Tiber. Avraham strained his eyes, then recognized the singed, soot-stained quartet as they rounded the corner. He rushed forward with Elchanan at his side. "Get to my house," he shouted and led them to his door.

Elchanan fetched the doctor, who ordered draughts of wine into which he mixed a brownish powder. "*Parthenium*," he said. "You call it feverfew. It'll dull the pain and open the airways." Then he tossed hot stones on the fire. "We must steam the smoke from your lungs, or you'll get an infection." Avraham whispered something into the doctor's ear, and the physician arched an eyebrow adding, "I'll put you in different rooms so I can attend you separately." Ahmad's normally inscrutable face heaved a sigh of relief.

Avraham put Anastasius in a pantry and Ahmad carried Johannes to a closet. The doctor used tongs to set searing stones on large, earthenware platters in each room. Towels and a bowl of cool water were brought, and he showed them how to ladle a bit of liquid on the rock to make steam. "You must breathe in the vapor. It won't be easy—inhale and spit. Now strip."

In the kitchen, Baraldus was bare to the waist and winced as the doctor applied cold compresses to his scorched and blistered hands. Yet as each wave of pain descended, he clenched his square, Lombard jaw. "I'll give you something for your discomfort, but you'll suffer for awhile. How did you get such burns? Were you playing with the fire?"

The slave Ahmad smoothed the back of Baldurus's singed, tonsured hair. "If not for the priest, who has the heart of the greatest warrior I have ever known, the others wouldn't be here."

A single tear escaped the corner of the Lombard's eye, but he sniffed and caught the rest.

Avraham led Ahmad into his study while the doctor attended Baraldus. "So you know?"

"I know."

"You were right to come here."

"I knew not where else to go," the onetime prince said.

𝕭𝖊𝖓𝖊𝖉𝖎𝖈𝖙, 𝖙𝖍𝖊 𝕭𝖎𝖘𝖍𝖔𝖕 of Albano, stood alone on Rome's side of the Tiber, a smug look on his face as stampeding refugees poured over the Sant'Angelo Bridge. Pope Leo arrived with the *patriarchum's* cardinals in attendance. He braced himself in the superheated wind as fire raced toward the river from the opposite shore. "Those poor souls," he lamented as the newly homeless sought refuge.

"Poor souls?" Benedict said. "They're foreigners and have no place here. Their shamble of a ghetto might have burned down the whole city. Let them return to Lothair for assistance and see how he likes hosting this rabble. Still, perhaps two of our problems have been eliminated."

Leo looked at Benedict, puzzled. "Let us remember the parable of the *Good Samaritan* brother, when only a foreigner would help. They deserve our pity and our blessing, not our scorn." Leo raised the simple wooden cross he wore on a chain around his neck and held it high for all to gaze upon, to give them hope in their hour of need. He held the crucifix aloft until after Lauds when the sun, a dull orange ball, rose over the hill, until the raging inferno reached the river and burned itself out.

Baraldus, though badly blistered and scorched, would no longer suffer the messy emulsion of opium, hemlock, and lard daubed on his hands. "I'll not stay another minute," he griped, recoiling from the doctor's ministering. "A cup of wine yields more relief and my greasy robe will be the cleaner."

"Please, *primicerius* Baraldus," the doctor said. "Your hands are charred. If scar tissue forms, it'll be painful and you may lose the use of some fingers."

"Balderdash. I'm no scribe that has need of fingers, only these great fists." He held up two blackened claws and started for the door.

"Please," Johanna said as she slouched in a wooden chair, hacking and spitting up darkened spittle into a crockery bowl, "at least take some medicine with you."

"What work can I do with my hands dripping with this muck?" He fled outside.

Ahmad could only shake his head in disgust. "To think this priest once commanded soldiers. Give me the crock. I'll make sure he lathers up, no matter how loud he bellows." The slave followed the Lombard out of the Rosh Yeshiva's house and into the streets of the Trastavere.

Johanna looked dejected as she heaved long sighs that brought on fits of coughing. Anastasius seemed less affected and, while his lungs were burned and painful, the doctor did not fear for his condition. He was healing and his phlegm was clear. Johanna, however, spit blackish green gobs and the physician feared that she had an infection, and *peripleumonia* was deadly.

The doctor took Avraham aside and handed him a pouch with dried herbs that smelled of mint. "Pennyroyal," he said. "Make an infusion with four leaves and have her drink three times a day, but no more. Beware," the doctor put his hand on the Rosh Yeshiva's shoulder, "the medicine is poison. If she's still ill five days hence, you may give her no more, for the cure will kill her."

Johanna's condition indeed worsened. Within two days, she had developed a fever and sweat drenched her bedclothes. Avraham made a pallet for her in his study, and she lay there, delirious. Anastasius refused to leave her side. He placed cold compresses on her brow and patted her hand, assuring her that she'd soon be well.

Yet even in her delirium Johanna thought only of Anastasius and begged him to get away. "Theophylact and Benedict will stop at nothing. You must flee Rome."

"Soon my love, never fear." But he had no intention of abandoning her.

Anastasius communicated secretly with his uncle Arsenius, dispatching letters with Ahmad since he dare not risk sending Baraldus, who was well known as Johanna's *primicerius*. He pleaded for a meeting but his uncle was intransigent, demanding that he depart from Rome before he was undone. Anastasius was just as insistent. Finally, Arsenius agreed to meet clandestinely within the walls of the Colosseum where priests and soldiers seldom ventured, fearing the rabble of the makeshift city. As further insurance, Arsenius chose the tranquil hour of Lauds when the noble cardinals were heavy-eyed and the soldiers fast asleep.

They met in the deep shadows under an arch in the arcade. "This time," Arsenius said, "you have a real chance of being elected. Even if you're not, you're still young and the cardinals must give you a position of authority inside the *patriarchum*. Lothair will accept nothing less. Until that day, you must stay out of the Roman diocese. Leo has hardened his heart against you and Benedict and Theophylact would see you dead."

"Uncle, I'm begging you, I need to remain in Rome."

"You make no sense," Arsenius shook his head. "Death and destruction await you here. Why is it so urgent to stay where you can't even show your face? Chiusi is a beautiful city and you're a cardinal there. Enjoy the Tuscan sun until I send for you."

Anastasius searched for a reasonable argument but found none, and the more he disputed, the more dumbfounded Arsenius became. "Leave now, nephew," Arsenius said. "The sun will rise soon. You take foolish risks for naught."

Despite the danger from every quarter, Anastasius could only think about how to remain in the city. He dared not tell his uncle the truth, and without the truth, his arguments sounded feeble. He couldn't leave, he wouldn't. Yet his very presence at Avraham's home brought danger not only to him and the Rosh Yeshiva, but Johanna as well. Sooner or later, Theophylact would search the Trastavere.

Tiny droplets covered Johanna's face and her red hair was plastered to her forehead, but her breaths came soft and even. "She's worse," Anastasius was panicked.

"No. She's better. The fever has broken and her body cools. Thank goodness because I dare not give her more medicine. Nevertheless, she's weak and needs time to recover from the illness—and the cure as well."

"I'll stay with her."

"No," Johanna's voice was but a whisper. She searched for his hand with her own.

Anastasius found hers and cradled it between his two. "I'm here, darling, and here I'll stay."

"Talk to him, Avraham. I have not the strength."

The Rosh Yeshiva spoke softly, mindful of Johanna's fragile state. "Theophylact's men have been here already and they watch the house.

How you got by them is a miracle, but you can't remain here. You're only safe in the protection of Louis' Empire."

"How can I escape with soldiers outside?"

"All has been accounted for," Avraham said.

At sundown Friday, Jews ceased their work on the plows and collars, restoration of the basilicas, tanning, and all their labors to observe the Sabbath. The next morning they came from throughout the ghetto to attend services at the synagogue. A cantor began singing hymns praising God. Rabbis wearing prayer shawls recited Psalms and chanted prayers. Avraham took the Torah from the ark, and men approached one at a time to read from the scroll.

Finally, Avraham HaKodesh delivered his sermon, which was uncharacteristically short, and the faithful wondered. Then nodding at the front row, he ended the services chanting, "The Lord bless you and keep you! The Lord let his face shine upon you and be gracious to you! The Lord look kindly upon you and give you peace!"

As the congregation filed out of the synagogue, it was enlarged by three unusual-looking Jews even though they wore the mandated dress: hose, caftans and four-pointed hats. One was dark, another stout, and the last uncommonly tall. The three elbowed their way to the middle of the crowd, heads down as they passed Theophylact's troops who spied on the Rosh Yeshiva's house. Then they made their way across the Rotto Bridge, heading north to the Vatican, where the wall was unfinished with many gaps remaining and no gates or guards to pass.

38
Children of the Book

I told you that you were wasting your time." Pascal shook his head in disgust as he and Isabelle and Romano sat on Belvedere lounge chairs in the lobby of their hotel on the *via della Conciliazione* in the district that once was the ancient Borgo.

"It's not the end," Romano said, "just a setback."

"There's only one solution. If you want no interference, take the books out of the Vatican. You should bring them to Paris, out of Italy completely. France doesn't tolerate censorship, and we could translate and publish them before anyone was the wiser."

"I can't do that."

"Why not? You said you had access to many more Psalters. Let's get them out of here before the Grand Inquisitor finds them."

"Look, Pascal, for what it's worth, I agree. I made the same arguments to my cardinal, but he won't allow it. He thinks it's too dangerous. You and Isabelle, more than anyone, must realize he's right."

"Of course, but it's worth the risk. You thought so, too, when you brought the book to Paris. Are you going to let some silly rules stop you now? They didn't before."

"Using one's own judgment, however flawed, is quite different than defying an order."

"So you're going to do nothing?"

"I didn't say that. I just need to find a secure place before I start over," Romano said.

"Bah! So Keller can take our work away again and hide everything in the bottomless pit under the Vatican? No, thank you. I'm going upstairs to pack."

"Don't leave like this."

Pascal turned back to the priest. "I don't blame you. You went ten rounds, but remember Jacob and the Angel? You can't win. The best you can do is to hang on and get hurt in the process. Think of your career. You almost ruined your life."

"That's not fair."

"I'm not chiding you. I mean it sincerely. Truth be told, I enjoyed the fight, reminds me of my younger quixotic days. However, I've seen the church in action, very slow action. I hope I'm still alive to see how this ends, but I do need to get back to Paris."

"You can wait one more day. His Holiness will celebrate a special Mass at Saint Peter's tomorrow for Ash Wednesday, and I brought invitations for the both of you, reserved seats up front."

Pascal couldn't help but laugh out loud. "Reserved seats for a heretical Jew and an atheist? That's rich. How did you arrange it?"

"I didn't. Cardinal Keller did."

Pascal arched an eyebrow. "The Grand Inquisitor?"

"The Defender of the Faith, and yes, I think it's his way of apologizing."

"Isn't Ash Wednesday the first day of Lent, a day of repentance? Is the good cardinal sending us a message?" Pascal grimaced.

"Now you're being cynical."

"Perhaps I can watch one more chapter unfold before I go home, but I still need to pack. I'll see you at Saint Peter's tomorrow and, regardless of the reason, thank the cardinal for me. But I warn you, I'll give up nothing for Lent, and don't expect any repentance. I like my sins just as they are." Pascal shook Romano's hand and headed for the elevator.

Isabelle leaned forward in the Belvedere chair. "You don't believe Keller was apologizing."

"I do, and I hope he's sending a message, also," Romano said.

"What kind of message?"

"That your work in the Vatican is appreciated and perhaps things will change, even if change is slow."

"Father's right. You are an optimist."

"Hardly. I have inside information, shall we say."

Isabelle looked hopeful. "You mean Keller might let us go back to work?"

"Not exactly, at least not for awhile."

"Well, what then?"

Romano tried to avoid answering.

"Tell me what you mean, Michael."

"I'm not sure how to say this, or even if I should."

"Don't leave me hanging."

"Where do I begin? I never expected to amount to much in the church. I've always been a loner, ambitious about my work but not political, and I don't belong to any insider groups. Not great qualities for success."

"You have been successful, and on your own merits."

"I don't believe that's true." Romano shook his head.

"How can you think otherwise?"

"Like I said, inside information. You'll think I'm weird if I tell you everything, but the church has a mystical side not often seen by the public. So let me say that some influential people seem to have a good deal of confidence in me."

"Of course they do. You're a courageous scholar." Isabelle praised the man she had come to adore.

"It's not my work they admire."

Isabelle took Romano's hand. She didn't understand his commitment to the priesthood, but sensed a man in pain. He started to return her affection, then pulled back his hand. "I'm not trying to seduce you, Michael. Can't a priest be friends with a woman?"

"We are friends."

"So why are you frightened? Is it me, or women in general?"

"It's not you." Romano lowered his eyes. "I'm afraid of me."

Rashid passed groups of Pakistanis peddling umbrellas to tourists outside Rome's Termini Train Station. They didn't bother to solicit him as he entered the glass door to take a shortcut through the mall, facing the platforms. The hair on the back of his neck tickled as he passed the boutiques. Stopping at a fashionable men's shop, he pretended to gaze at suits in the window while glancing side to side. He recognized the uneasiness of being followed, but nothing seemed out of place. People waited for trains, shoppers browsed or sipped coffees. Nevertheless, the feeling was oppressive.

He went to the opposite end of the station and exited on the *via Giovanni*, walked fifty paces, then stopped abruptly and backed against the wall. His eyes focused on the door—ten, twenty, thirty seconds—but no one followed. His internal alarm was seldom wrong, yet only the occasional tourist pulling a suitcase exited Termini Station and paid no attention to him.

Crossing the boulevard, he wound his way through the neighborhood between Termini and the Vittorio Emanuele Monument, rounding corners and halting abruptly to peer back. Only businessmen or locals stood on the sidewalk, engaged in conversation. He walked around the block twice. *I must be losing it. Nerves*, he told himself and finally turned the key in the lock at the tiny warehouse where he roomed.

There was still much to do and little time. Standing in front of a long worktable, he shifted his attention to the common cleaning supplies he had divided by the order they would be added to his concoction. He heard a scraping at the door and the clicks in the lock's tumbler. His heart leapt and his hand went instinctively to the Beretta lying on the table. He pulled the slide to chamber a round. The door handle twisted and he held the pistol in both hands, arms extended, looking down the sight.

"Would you shoot a tired, old Muslim?"

"Imam!" Rashid ran to the cleric, taking him in his arms as tears moistened his eyes. "I thought you were lost forever."

The imam patted him on the back. "I knew where I was. What, no kiss for a beloved mentor?"

Rashid kissed him on both cheeks, then wiped tears from his own eyes. "What did they do to you? Were you tortured? How did you escape?"

"Calm yourself," the imam said. "I'm well and no harm has come to me. I may move slowly, but the old fox can still outwit the hounds."

"Did the police arrest you?"

"Of course. First the French, then the Italians, but they can prove nothing. They produced no evidence and had to let me go because they're looking in the wrong place. They're thinking about their precious ferries and reactors in Normandy. Their infidel minds can't conceive of a mission such as ours." The imam patted Rashid paternally on the back. "I see you met your contact. Did you deliver the Psalter?"

"As instructed," Rashid puffed out his chest. "But how did you find me?"

"Do I not own this warehouse? Rome is our destiny, my boy."

"That's what Sayyid said. All has been planned and I'm nearly ready."

"What are you saying? Who is Sayyid?"

"Your colleague, the one I gave the book to."

"He doesn't know our mission, and he's not one of us. He's not even a Muslim. What did he tell you?"

"He said the days of justice were at hand and I had to attack the library in the Vatican."

"What nonsense! Attack the library, for what purpose?"

"To destroy their infidel books."

A look of horror passed over the imam's face. He leaned on the table for support.

"Are you alright? Sit down here." Rashid pulled up a chair and helped the cleric into it. "What's wrong?"

"He would multiply the sins of our forefather. I should have told the fool nothing. A little information can be dangerous."

"What do you mean *our sin*? Is it not time for me to know what this great sin is?"

"Rashid, we're not here to destroy the writings of the Prophet Jesus. We must protect them. We're the *Children of the Book*."

"I've studied these books and their languages, and I had hoped some day I would understand their meaning. But, the knowledge hasn't come to me."

"The truth is not in the books, although they're the words of a prophet. We're the descendants of the greatest Emir of Ifriqiya. I've taught you these dead languages not for understanding, but so you could identify them. Our task is to keep the writings in their hiding place, to guard them to cleanse the sin of our ancestor."

"What sin is this?"

"Our ancestor stole the scriptures of the Prophet Jesus and they were destroyed in a storm, taken back by God in his wisdom. The Prince paid for his crime by protecting those that were left for the rest of his life. Now we, his descendants, must spend our lives defending the ancient writings that are hidden in their secret place."

"You mean we protect Christian scriptures?"

"Not wholly Christian. They're different, but it matters little whose they are. They are words spoken by Allah to a prophet, but the Christians don't listen. So they must remain hidden until the time is right, until the return of the Mahdi."

"Where are they?"

"One escaped, and that's the one we found and returned. Most are in the bowels of Saint Peter's, a hiding place known only to me. Now the location will be known to you as well."

"If Sayyid is not one of us, why do we return the books to him?"

"I thought he believed as we do and wished to return the scriptures to their rightful place. That was not his aim, and I've been used," the imam grumbled.

"Then what are we to do?"

"What did you plan to do with these chemicals?"

"Destroy the Library and burn everything inside," Rashid said.

"Is all prepared?"

"Yes."

"We must not touch the Library, for God's word is God's word. However, we need to make sure once and for all that the old books stay hidden. We will finish what the Emir, Ahmad ibn Muhammad, started."

The GIS lieutenant charged through Del Carlo's door without knocking. "Not now, Moretti. I'm leaving for a meeting."

"*Scùsi Colonelo*, I know who the Swiss bank account belongs to. You're not going to believe it."

"The imam?"

"They refuse to give me a name, but the money is going to a Vatican account."

"A priest?"

"Yes. So I pulled phone records from the Vatican exchange."

"That's not legal, Moretti."

"Calls have been going from the Vatican to the imam in France. We're trying to find out where in Vatican City they came from."

"Damn! The imam was released this morning."

"So I heard. I took the liberty of having him followed," Moretti said.

"Good work. Do you know where he is?"

"Near Termini Station, and he's not alone. A man is with him who matches the description of the one who got away in Normandy."

"Well done, Moretti. Assemble an operational section, thirty men, and put two sniper teams on the roof. I think we will pay the imam another visit."

Colonel Del Carlo's secretary called after him as he rushed by, his lieutenant in tow. "Your meeting *Colonelo*. You have a full day."

The GIS colonel called over his shoulder, "Cancel everything and notify the other teams. I want them on alert."

The narrow street was blocked at both intersections by the *Carabinieri* vans that had transported the thirty-man operational section and snipers. The elite commandos, all volunteers from the

First Carabinieri Airborne Regiment, *Tuscania*, were among the world's best counter-terrorist forces, and *Colonelo* Del Carlo drove them hard to be better than the best. Teams followed pre-planned procedures and surrounded the tiny warehouse on the ground floor of tall apartment buildings. Several four man units ringed the entrance while others evacuated residents, sending them scurrying down the street past the vans.

The two sniper teams found positions on roofs aiming Mauser rifles, equipped with Syncrofire that made the weapons fire simultaneously.

"Everyone's in position, *Colonelo*," Lieutenant Moretti reported.

"Is there a back door?"

"No. The warehouse backs to an apartment."

"Good."

"Do you want the bull horn?"

"No," Del Carlo said. "We need surprise on our side. Bring the battering ram and break down the door."

Two commandos inched along the wall holding the handles of the ram until they came to the entrance. They waited for a signal from Del Carlo. He nodded his head and they sprang into action. Securing themselves on either side of the door, they grabbed the handles of the ram, hoisted it backward, then swung the heavy tube. The ringing of metal on metal echoed off apartment walls, and the door groaned but held. The soldiers swung the ram back again and thrust with all their might. The hinges snapped and the door burst, crashing to the ground.

"Go, go," the lieutenant shouted, and the teams converged on the doorway. A sudden blast shook the building, resounding off the walls as fire and sparks spewed out of the warehouse in a brilliant ball. Soldiers were flung to the pavement. Parts of their uniforms and bulletproof vests ignited with a white, sparkling blaze. Men screamed and moaned as their comrades rushed to douse burning coveralls.

Del Carlo took the force of the blast point blank. He was hurled backward against the opposite wall and crumpled in a heap.

39
Home of the Forgeries

The GIS colonel's eyelids fluttered open, then shut for a few moments and opened again. He tried to focus on the figure above him. "Where am I?"

"You're in the hospital." Romano leaned forward in his chair. "Would you like some water?"

"Yes," the colonel rasped. "How did you find me, Father?"

The priest held a plastic cup with a straw for him to sip. "You must be joking. You're all over the radio and television." Romano waved his open hand across an imaginary newspaper headline, *"Decorated Colonel Hospitalized in Blast."*

"Oh, the explosion, stupid of me. I should've anticipated a booby trap." Del Carlo settled back on his pillow and tried to adjust his position, which made him wince.

The door opened and Lieutenant Moretti poked in his head. "You're back with us." His face was riddled with cuts and contusions and blistered on one side. Del Carlo's eyes went to the sling supporting Moretti's arm.

"Are your injuries serious, Lieutenant?"

"It's nothing, *Colonelo*, a slight shoulder separation and a suntan."

But the colonel didn't laugh. "Give me a report."

"You'll have plenty of time…"

Del Carlo exhaled a heavy breath. "Lieutenant."

"Yes sir. One dead and four wounded. Two serious. Burns, mostly."

"It's my fault. I didn't see it coming." Del Carlo was downcast.

"None of us did. You couldn't know."

"I'm paid to. And what about the suspects?"

"I'm afraid they've escaped," Moretti said.

"How?"

"A tunnel through the floor to the apartment at the rear. They were probably inside when we arrived, but must have armed the bombs and flown the coop."

"What did they use?"

"Please, *Colonelo*," Father Romano said. "You should be resting."

"Later." Del Carlo's body ached, his head throbbed, and heavy eyelids tried to drag themselves shut, but his mind raced. "Explosives, Lieutenant, what were they?"

"TATP and thermite."

"Why would they need thermite?"

Lieutenant Moretti thought for a moment. "They wanted to burn something. Maybe they didn't want us to examine what was inside."

"Possibly," Del Carlo raised his eyebrows. "Where did you say the calls to the imam came from?"

"The Vatican, but I don't know exactly where."

"Do you recall the number?"

"I wrote it down." Moretti pulled a note card from his pocket and showed it to the colonel.

"The number sounds familiar, but my brain's a fog. Do you recognize it Father?"

The lieutenant passed Romano the card, and he stared in shock. "Well?"

"It's mine," Romano said. "At the Library."

"The Vatican Library?"

"Yes."

"Oh my God." The pieces began to fall into place. Del Carlo threw the covers aside and pulled the IV from the back of his hand.

"What do you think you're doing?"

"Get me out of here." Del Carlo tried to raise himself off the bed, grimacing.

"*Per favore, Colonelo*," the lieutenant said. "You have broken ribs and a concussion. Tell me what you want done."

"Find something to wrap these damn ribs and get me out of here."

"What can you be thinking?" Romano asked, unbelieving.

"That if we don't get to the Library in a hurry, it's going to look like the warehouse."

"Neither of you brought a car?" Urgency made Del Carlo impatient. Lieutenant Moretti had arrived at the hospital by cab, and Romano had taken the subway.

"Sorry," the lieutenant apologized.

"Hail that taxi." Romano pointed at the cab pulling up to the curb in front of *Admittance*.

An elderly woman had just paid the driver as Lieutenant Moretti trotted up. "We need to get to the Vatican."

"Sorry, *signore*, but I have another fare. They phoned in."

The lieutenant pulled his identification from his jacket pocket and shoved it in front of the cabbie's nose. "Official business."

"*Si, si.* Get in, *signores.*"

Del Carlo eased into the seat. "Get us to Saint Peter's."

"In the square?"

"No," Romano said, "the side gate on the *via della Stazione Vaticana.*"

"I'm not allowed in," the cabbie turned to Del Carlo.

"Just get us to the gate. *Andiamo*, let's go!"

The plain white delivery truck crawled up the *via della Stazione Vaticana* past the Mercedes-Benz service center and lines of parked cars, toward the open steel gate in the Leonine wall. This was the private entrance for Vatican employees, priests and cardinals of the

Curia and for His Holiness, the Pope. The entrance was surrounded by blue Carabinieri Alpha-Romeos, yellow stripes emblazoned on their sides and lights mounted on the roofs. Uniformed and plainclothes officers milled around, wires dangling from earbuds in one ear. Every eye turned to follow the truck approaching the gate.

"Two of you today?" the Carabiniere guard commented as he looked at Rashid's identification card.

"We have a lot to deliver. I needed some help."

"So you brought your grandfather?" The guard laughed and gave back Rashid's ID. He kneeled to inspect the bearded passenger. "ID, *signore.*" The imam pulled an Italian national identity card and employee ID from his coveralls and handed them to the guard.

"Your first time here?"

"Yes, officer," the imam said, smiling.

"I can usually handle the load myself," Rashid said, "but the company told me to be quick today. Something big is going on."

"That's right. The Pope is saying a special mass for Ash Wednesday in the basilica, so avoid Saint Peter's."

"I'm just making a delivery to the cafeteria in the Museum as usual."

"Drive on."

Rashid pulled forward to the guard shack manned by Vatican City Police. The guard entered the license plate number into a computer. Then he motioned for Rashid to get out. "Open up the back."

Rashid hopped out, walked to the rear of the truck, and opened the double doors with his key. "I've only got sodas in canisters and cans."

The guard eyed the large aluminum cylinders and the boxes of soft drinks. "Don't forget to sign out when you leave."

The gray taxi sped past the *Villa Borghese* heading south toward the *Trevi Fountain* and the *corso Vittorio Emanuele*. "Faster," Del Carlo urged as they turned onto the *corso*. The driver held the steering wheel tight and pressed the accelerator. The little minivan shot forward. Sweat beaded on the driver's bald head. Flying across the *Prince Amadeo* Bridge, the taxi lurched onto the narrow *via della Stazione Vaticana.*

The milling group of Carabinieri officers spotted the speeding taxi simultaneously and jerked Berettas from holsters, holding them at the ready. The driver slammed on his brakes screeching to a stop. *"Per favore, signores.* This is as far as I go." Del Carlo opened his door and tried to get out. Every gun aimed at him. The lieutenant stepped out on the other side, a hand raised, flashing his ID. "Moretti, GIS!" he shouted. Romano hopped out to help Del Carlo stand. The officers recognized the colonel and lowered their guns.

A uniformed major ran forward to meet the Del Carlo. "Are you crazy, *Colonelo?* You could've been shot."

"Later, *Maggiore.* Who came through the gate today that shouldn't be here?" Del Carlo held his aching ribs, half speaking and half grunting.

"No one sir. I assure you."

"Think hard. Who did you not recognize, who's out of place?"

"I need to look at the manifest," the major said. They hurried to the guard shack and the major asked for the sign-in sheet. He scrolled his finger down the list. "These are all employees or contractors, people who come here every day."

"Something must be out of place," Del Carlo said.

The guard in the shack interrupted. "One man I've never seen before, but he had a company ID and works for one of our suppliers."

"What did he look like?"

"Harmless really, elderly with a beard, but he was with a regular. He came to help deliver supplies to the canteen and cafeteria."

"What're they delivering?"

"Sodas. I thought it was a bit odd that they would send an old man to haul something as heavy as cans."

"Where're they from?" Del Carlo asked.

"Sir?"

"What nationality, what race?"

"I don't know. Arab, maybe."

Del Carlo gave orders to the Carabinieri major. "Notify the Swiss

Guard and Vatican Police. Surround the Library, but don't go in. There may be a bomb. I want a helicopter in the air, and ask the Swiss Guard Captain to meet me. And for God's sake, find that truck!"

"But, sir," the guard at the gate said, "they went to the Vatican Museum, to a storage room in the cafeteria."

"That's not where they went." Turning to the major he said, "*Maggiore*, I need your car."

"You're not allowed in. This is Vatican City."

Romano jumped in the driver's seat. "It's alright, *Maggiore*. They're with me."

𝔗𝔥𝔢 𝔖𝔴𝔦𝔰𝔰 𝔊𝔲𝔞𝔯𝔡 Captain stood resplendent in his brilliant blue-and-gold striped traditional dress uniform and cape. He paced back and forth behind a semicircle of cars that surrounded the double red doors at the entrance to the Vatican Library. Romano negotiated the Carabinieri Alpha around the corner and stomped on the brakes, skidding to a stop just outside the barrier of Vatican *Gendermaria* police cars.

"I hope this is a real threat," the captain said to Del Carlo as he eased out of the car. "I'm supposed to be at Saint Peter's, leading the honor guard for His Holiness."

Romano supported Del Carlo by an arm as he hobbled to the captain. The captain looked first at him then at Lieutenant Moretti's battered face and the sling supporting his arm. "I thought you were in the hospital. You look like shit."

"Early release," Del Carlo said. "The men who did this to us are in the Library, Captain."

"The explosion in Rome. You think they're going to do the same thing here?"

"I'm positive."

The Swiss Captain spoke into his radio. "Anything unusual, corporal?" He pressed on the earbud in his ear, listening. "I just talked to the control room. They monitor every part of the Library through the video cameras. There's no one except a few priests. Everyone has left for the mass at Saint Peter's."

"Who's in my office?" Romano asked the captain.

He spoke again into the radio. "Only the cardinal's secretary, Father Sabella."

Romano bolted through a space between two police cars and up the stone steps. He opened the red door and disappeared inside while the Swiss captain, Del Carlo, and the guards stared in shock.

"Damn," Del Carlo grunted and trotted after him.

Romano bounded up the stairs to the second level and sprinted down the hall to the offices of the cardinal and prefect, his own offices. Turning the corner, Father Sabella was pulling the door closed. A briefcase sat on the floor by his foot. Spotting Romano, he grabbed the case and fled in the opposite direction. Romano pumped his arms, rising on the balls of his feet in an all-out sprint, and dove, tackling the priest. The two slid down the marble floor as though they were on a rain-slicked football field.

"Let me go," Sabella bellowed, trying to shake free. But Romano held him down by his shoulders.

Del Carlo, Moretti, and the Swiss Guard Captain, followed by Vatican police, rounded the corner, their mouths open and eyes locked on the two priests struggling. The captain shouted, "Father Romano, what're you doing?"

"Open the briefcase."

"No," Sabella said. "It's mine. You have no right!"

"Open it, Captain," Romano said, glaring into Sabella's dark eyes.

Sliding two buttons, the captain opened the cover and pulled out an ancient leather-bound book, and held it up. Romano grabbed Sabella by his lapels and heaved him to his feet. Turning to the Swiss captain he ordered, "Hold him." Sabella tried to jerk away, but Romano gripped his jacket, pulling his face close. "You did this, didn't you?" Two guards seized Sabella by his arms.

The captain handed the book to the paleographer and Romano flipped open the cover to the first page. He needed only a glance to realize what he held. "This is the stolen Psalter."

Del Carlo faced Sabella, pondering his approach in microseconds. He recognized the haughty defiance in the priest's countenance. "Do you want to confess something, Father? Perhaps your involvement in Father Mackey's murder?"

"You have no authority here. We have our own laws in Vatican City."

Romano held the Psalter in front of Sabella's face. "You killed a brother, a man of God like yourself."

"They weren't supposed to kill him, only take the book. That's all I wanted." His eyes grew wild and he curled his lip at the co-prefect. "We tried to deal with you. You stole everything: land, authority, even the right to the title of pope. For seven hundred years we thought we could make you see reason, but you swindled us with rank forgeries. We Melkites were the original Christians, and you called us names and stole the church from us with lies."

Romano glowered at Sabella. "Who's in this with you?"

"You and Minissi and Mackey. Yes, even him. This is your fault. You think I didn't know what you were doing, were about to do? You dare to question the Holy Scriptures by publishing more lies? I'll stop you once and for all."

"How?"

Sabella stared straight ahead, refusing to answer.

"I said, how?"

"I couldn't discover where you're finding these Psalters, but I'll make sure they never get out again. By the time you figure out where they've gone, it'll be too late."

"We know your plan, Father," Del Carlo said.

"You understand nothing."

"The Swiss Guard are searching the Library as we speak. You planned to burn it down, didn't you?"

Sabella's arrogance turned to desperation. "Get out while you can."

"Brother, why would you destroy the Holy Library?"

"If thine hand offend thee, cut it off. The Gospels can be duplicated. But no more forgeries will escape this wicked place. I'll make sure of that even if I have to destroy everything."

"You would burn the Library for the sake of a few books?"

"It's done. I tried to discover where you found these palimpsests. Oh yes, I know it all. You think you were clever and

Cardinal Minissi with his secret closet, gone all gone."

A crackle squawked from the Swiss captain's earpiece. "Are you sure? Did you check every room? Then seal the building."

"What is it Captain?" Del Carlo asked.

"The Library is clear. No sign of anyone, no explosives, and no bombs."

"That can't be," Sabella said, unbelieving. "I don't believe you, you're lying. I just...."

"Just saw them? I'm sorry to disappoint you, Father," the Swiss captain said. "I'm sure they're somewhere, but they're not here."

Del Carlo turned to Romano. "Are any rooms not monitored?"

"Of course. The cardinal's office."

They rushed to the Administration offices, led by Romano, who dashed into Minissi's office. He pushed on the floor-to-ceiling bookshelf, and the wall swiveled open. The closet's shelves had been emptied, but the *Protector of the Vatican Library* lay bound and gagged on the floor.

Romano bent and untied the gag. "It's alright, Eminence," the co-prefect said. "We caught Father Sabella. I would have never have guessed, an Italian priest in league with Arabs."

"Sabella is not Italian, he's Lebanese. He came to us from the Middle Eastern Melkites who split from the church in the fifth century. I hired him because he's an expert in Aramaic."

Romano reassured Minissi, "It's under control. We know all about the Library."

"You fools," Minissi said, his throat dry from the gag. "Get to Saint Peter's."

"But Eminence," Romano worked on the knot that bound the cardinal's hands. "The library is safe, and we'll get the Psalters back."

"Forget the Library, Michael. Remember the prophecies of Fatima and Malachy. Today is the day of *penance*. They're after His Holiness. Save my friend!"

The microphone crackled again in the Swiss captain's ear. "They've located the truck behind Saint Peter's abandoned, but the Psalters are inside."

"Thank God," Romano said.

"But the intruders are nowhere to be found."

40

Decretals of Isidore Mercator

Pope Leo had indeed hardened his heart against Anastasius. He was infuriated the excommunicated cardinal stayed outside of his reach, too distant to feel the humiliation he would heap on him. So Leo convened a synod to anathemize Anastasius. Excommunications might be pronounced but also removed by any bishop. However, anathemas were the ultimate punishment, complete separation from the church, and could only be meted out by the Pope.

"For what reason do you anathemize Cardinal Anastasius?" Bishop Arsenius interrupted Benedict's list of infractions.

Pope Leo sat on the wooden chair of the Apostle in the lavishly reconstructed basilica of Saint Peter, glowering at the Imperial *missi*. "If you would listen, Bishop, instead of interfering you might hear the charges against your nephew."

Arsenius started to respond, but an agitated Johanna cut him off. "With all due respect, Holiness, we've listened to these accusations and they're the same ones for which Anastasius was already punished. Do you plan to indict him twice?"

"I have proposed nothing yet. We are pronouncing his transgressions against the church. At least, we're trying."

"I submit that Anastasius has been charged and sentenced. Can a man be punished over and over for a single offense? He abandoned his basilica and I say for good reason, for there are those in Rome who plot against him. Yet neither the church nor the nobles give their protection. Nevertheless, he's been excommunicated for his absence. So what's his latest foul deed?"

Leo rose from the wooden throne, his face bright red. "He refuses to return to Rome and accept his punishment."

Arsenius placed his hand on Johanna's shoulder and spoke in a low voice, "This is not the time or place..."

Johanna jerked away, the bit in her teeth. "You've stripped him of his church and denied him communion, and he has accepted your will. What law says he has to live in the Diocese of Rome?"

"I say so!"

"By what authority? This council must first decide whether canon law was broken, some new infraction. Only then can judgment be passed."

"By this authority." Leo held a codex high over his head.

"I know the law better than any here. Tell me which of the canons he violated."

"The *Decretals of Bishop Isidore Mercator*! This is the law that gives me the absolute license over all."

"I recall no such Bishop Mercator. You say these *Decretals* are his? Why do we not know this book?" Johanna faced the assembled cardinals. "Who among you knows this book or the Bishop?" The cardinals looked at one another, dumbfounded, for no one had ever heard of either the cleric or his *Decretals*.

"Do you call me liar, Johannes Anglicus?"

"Far from it Holiness. However, I fear that you aim to pass judgment based on letters and laws you may believe to be true. But before you do, would it not be prudent to let scholars examine them to see if they're genuine?"

"I've examined the contents and I say they are!" Leo placed the purple cope around his neck and sat on Peter's throne, beginning to recite while twelve cardinal priests lit black candles.

"The council has not decided," Johanna said.

"The council advises and I decide, only I. You'd be wise to remember it, Englishman." The Pope read from a parchment page. "We deprive Anastasius, nephew of Arsenius, himself and all accomplices and all his abettors of the Communion of the body and blood of our Lord..."

"This isn't right! You can't do this thing!" Johanna shouted.

"...we declare him excommunicated and anathemized and we judge him condemned to eternal fire with Satan and all his angels and the reprobate..."

Bishop Arsenius tried to put a halt to the pronouncement. "In the name of the Emperor, I protest!"

"...we deliver him to Satan to mortify his body, that his soul may be saved on the Day of Judgment."

Twelve cardinal priests chanted, "fiat, fiat, fiat, let it be done," and flung their black candles to the ground. Leo marched into the *sanctum santorum* and yanked a drape from the wall. A new fresco had been painted, depicting Jesus receiving the kiss of betrayal from Judas.

Johanna recoiled at Judas' face. The likeness was Anastasius'. Her knees buckled and she fell to the floor, unconscious. Only Arsenius knelt at her side to hold her head off the cold stone. The assembled cardinals watched, mortified, but feared to help their beloved brother.

The doctor uttered solemn words in Hebrew to Avraham, who ushered him to the door and thanked him, pressing coins into his hand. Then he padded to his own bedroom, peering in with his smiling, frizzy face.

"Come in," Johanna groaned.

"How do you feel?"

"Like I'm on a ship in the middle of a storm and I want to get off."

"Could you eat some chicken soup?"

Johanna shuddered. "Don't even mention food. What did the doctor say? Is it serious?"

Avraham petted her brow and smoothed the red hair that curled at her temples. "Indeed it is."

"Am I to die?"

"On the contrary, no life is forfeit. One is to be given."

Johanna looked at him, puzzled.

"You're going to be a mother."

As the anthology of letters and documents comprising the *Decretals of Isidore Mercator* was studied by experts, it was evident by the handwriting that they had been composed in Francia. In fact, specialists in monastic script pinpointed the exact location: the monastery of Corbie near Amiens.

Patriarchum theologians noted that the one hundred letters, supposedly authored by popes and bishops during the first three centuries after Christ, gave the papacy absolute power. Nevertheless, it was just as certain that none of the letters had been written then. Each and every one had been penned in the last few years, and all of them at the Corbie monastery. And curiously, many of the passages resembled the writing style of the brilliant author and theologian, Abbot Paschasius Radbertus.

Tucked away in the collection of forgeries was perhaps to most brazen of the church's fakes, the *Donation of Constantine*. The forged *Donation* conveyed colossal power to the papacy proclaiming, among other things, that the Bishop of Rome was Christ's representative on earth and giving him dominion over *all the churches of God in the whole world.*

Leo relied on the *Donation to* command that the title *Pope* would be reserved exclusively for the Bishop of Rome. Bishops the world over were confused, since they were already called pope, which simply meant father, by their congregations. Even priests were often dubbed popes. The Patriarchs of Alexandria and Africa and the Patriarchs of Antioch and Constantinople, also popes, protested the effrontery. Yet in each negotiation, Rome produced mountains of forged documents to support claims of primacy, so much so that for hundreds of years, the Roman Church was derided as the *Home of Forgeries*.

Archbishop John of Ravenna rankled at the exaggerated powers Leo granted himself based on a collection of dubious *Decretals* which had never before existed and had been assembled by a bishop who also didn't exist. Naturally, he rebelled at his own diminished authority. After all, Leo was only the Bishop of Rome and had no sovereignty over any other bishop outside the Roman diocese. However, everything changed with the *Decretals* and the *Donation of Constantine*.

Accordingly, Leo and Benedict and Count Theophylact, accompanied by a cohort of soldiers, journeyed to the Italian capital with the intention of inspiring the Archbishop. The trip was successful, and Archbishop John submitted to the Holy will after Leo's prayers and Theophylact's display of military might. However, the exertion of travel had weakened the aging Leo. And far from calming rebellion, the Pope discovered that another archbishop, Hincmar of Reims, publicly proclaimed the *Decretals* to be obvious frauds and rejected not only their authenticity, but the absolute power they bestowed on the Holy See.

Hincmar bristled at Leo's audacity and claimed the forged *Decretals* were blasphemy. He derided the worst of the one hundred forgeries, a letter attributed to Saint Ambrose, proclaiming that anyone who disagreed with the Holy See was a heretic. Such a profane belief would render the pope infallible. No bishop or cardinal or even lowly priest could accept such a preposterous premise. "Blasphemies like the *Decretals* cannot stand," Archbishop Hincmar preached to his followers, "and such an obvious power grab is based on a pack of lies."

Leo had no other choice but to embark once again on another holy pilgrimage supported by Theophylact and his troops, to the Frankish lands northeast of Paris to inspire Hincmar as he had John of Ravenna. The voyage to Reims in Lothair's territory was much further than Ravenna, and the journey was made more grueling by the heat of the mid-July sun. Leo and his retinue had journeyed but three days when a courier galloped back to the *patriarchum* with an urgent dispatch. Pope Leo IV was dead.

What no one in Rome knew until imperial dispatches arrived from the Empire's capital in Aachen was that Emperor Lothair had fallen seriously ill. He commanded that no Papal Elections would be held until he recovered, upon threat of retribution. However, there would be no recovery. Two months and twelve days later, Lothair followed Pope Leo to his eternal reward. His son, Louis, the avenger of Lothair's honor, now ruled the Holy Roman Empire.

Louis' first order of business was the Papal election. "I shall allow no further shenanigans from Theophylact, nor permit the Roman nobility to thumb their noses at the Constitution," he told his Queen, Engelberga, and his councilors. "The law will be enforced." For the first time in many, many years, there was to be a lawful vote for the Holy Father.

41
Pope of the People

The patriarchium's cardinal priests in their finest robes, emblazoned with red cinctures and scarlet skullcaps, assembled in the *piazza* in front of the Apostolic palace to pay homage to the newest Emperor and his Empress. The two senior clerics, old *vicedominus* Adrian and Archdeacon Nicholas, positioned themselves at their head. Even the Bishop of Albano, Benedict, was in attendance, although he had slunk to the back of the assembly.

Johanna stood in her rightful place next to Bishop Arsenius as thirty-year old Emperor Louis, dressed in tight stockings and a rich doublet of Imperial purple, rode by on a sleek bay stallion. At one side, the beautiful Queen Engleberga sat sidesaddle, garbed in a long, creamy gown gathered at her waist by a silver cincture. Golden curls flowed down her back. They were followed by a column of attendants, grooms, and a cohort of Imperial troops.

Behind the Imperial procession, hordes of commoners from the city trailed the elegant entourage. The assembled cardinals marveled at such pomp and richesse as the parade passed, but Johanna's eyes were locked on the proud, triumphant return of the man in a cardinal's robe riding at Louis' other side, her own beloved Anastasius.

Louis dismounted and faced the assembly as grooms rushed

forward to help the Empress step down. Louis motioned them aside and lifted her himself. Vicedominus Adrian genuflected, and the assembled clerics who ruled Christendom bowed. The show of obeisance pleased the young Emperor and he responded with a courtly wave.

Old Adrian padded unsteadily to Louis' side and took his arm, leading him toward the open doors of the palace. The congregation of cardinals and bishops opened a pathway, and the three passed through. Johanna raised her eyes to gaze upon Anastasius and could not force the loving smile from her face. The anathemized cardinal turned his regard and reached out his hand but brought it back, reflecting instantly on the gesture.

The reception went on all afternoon with a sumptuous banquet and speeches promising fealty to the Emperor as well as Louis' pledges of support for the church. Johanna ate modestly, having little appetite, which surprised Anastasius, for as he cast furtive glances her way, he was sure her thin frame had swelled. At long last, when all were sated from the meal and drowsy from the August heat and endless speeches, Louis proposed they adjourn. For on the morrow, Rome would name a new pope according to the constitution.

"Why did you not tell me you were with child?" Anastasius said as they lay together caressing and touching, locked in seclusion in Johanna's apartment in the restored *schola cantorum*.

"Because you would have come back and risked your life and I couldn't prevent it."

"I missed this time with you while our child grew in your womb and it's time I can never reclaim."

"Our child will come whether you're here or not. However, had you fallen into Leo's hands or Theophylact's, you might never have seen the babe, who would have been deprived of his father."

"It will all be at an end soon. No one would dare harm me with Louis here. But do you not fear Theophylact and his men out in the Vatican?"

"I'm using the *schola cantorum* for my classes until the Borgo is rebuilt. Ahmad and the students protect me. Not a soul can pass who they don't inspect, but what about you? Louis can't stay here forever."

"Too true, but he's raised an army to defend the southern borders against the Saracens and assured me they will follow my uncle's command. If God wills that I'm elected Pope, they'll obey me. In any wise, the army has been ordered to safeguard me, and Louis shall make this known whilst he's here. I'm back and I'll never leave your side."

"What am I to do? I thought about running away, for I fear the child is due soon. The cardinals believe I'm simply getting fat and indeed I am, but I still have work to do. My students need me."

"Is it not time to end this charade and live the life you were born to, as a wife and mother?"

"Then I wouldn't be able to teach nor learn, and I've even contrived to admit girls to the *schola anglorum* to receive an education without having to disguise who they are."

"You're living in a dream. God has protected you thus far, but it's over. How can you hide a child?"

"I've given it much thought. I can give birth in the *Trastevere*, at Avraham's. There are midwives aplenty and we could attend our babe secretly and…"

"Johanna, my love, it's finished. Just as you would not risk my life, I wouldn't endanger yours and the life of our child, as well. Johannes must leave forever. You may hide at Avraham's until you bear the babe and your hair grows out. When you emerge from your confinement, however, you must don the clothes of a woman and be Johanna. We can be man and wife as it should be. I'll bring books and scrolls to our home and you can read and study to your heart's content, but Cardinal Johannes must be no more."

Johanna sighed with resignation. "You're right. I had hoped I might find a way to live in a man's world, but I love you so much that I would now be a woman. The election is tomorrow, then Johannes will leave, never to return. Nevertheless, a movement is afoot to ban clerics from taking wives. You might be on shaky ground if you would marry me. Perhaps if you had a wife before you were pope, but to take one after?"

"I assure you it'll never happen," Anastasius said. "popes have wives, bishops are wed, cardinals and even the lowliest priests enjoy the sanctity of marriage. Why, old Cardinal Adrian has a wife, and a young one to boot," he laughed out loud. "Such a thing will never become law and indeed the canons support no restriction. Anyway, no one will ever keep me from you, my dearest."

Louis was determined the elections should be free and fair and all would have an equal voice as it had been for centuries and as the Constitution of 824 mandated. He further resolved that he wouldn't leave Rome until he personally questioned the pope-elect and found him fit to ascend the throne of Saint Peter. And this time, he would post Imperial soldiers under command of the *missi*, Bishop Arsenius, to guarantee that no one would unseat the lawfully elected pontiff.

Imperial guards were stationed all around the courtyard of the restored Saint Peter's, and Louis forbade the attendance of soldiers from the Roman nobility, especially Theophylact's troops. "They may attend as citizens, for it's their lawful right," he told the heads of the noble families, "but they may not wear their uniforms or the crests of the clans they serve. Neither can they bear arms." His sternness left no doubt he meant business. Theophylact bristled at the admonition, but there was naught to do but obey.

The sun rose large and warm on the autumn morn of the vintage month when grapes are harvested from the vines. Standard bearers claimed their space in the *piazza san Giovanni*, facing Empress Fausta's old Lateran palace. Tall poles flew pennants emblazoned with family crests. The nobles crowded around their family's flags near the doors of the Apostolic palace as lesser noble families moved to their positions behind. Lowly clerics, artisans, merchants, and freemen were relegated to their undistinguished sites at the rear of the multitude.

Count Theophylact had a chair placed in front of the stone

steps where he might be seated during the ceremonies, a symbolic throne of defiance. He hated the low-lying Lateran, thinking the area unhealthy. "At least it's not the middle of a malarial summer," he groused. "If I must be here, I'll be at my ease."

Nevertheless, the rest of Rome was atwitter, anxious to catch a glimpse of the dashing emperor and his comely bride. Of course, they were just as excited to raise their voice for their candidate. This time, though, the citizens told themselves, neither Theophylact nor the Roman nobles nor even the cardinals would hijack this election. Commoners would have their say.

The doors of the Apostolic Palace opened and the towering Emperor robed in Imperial Purple, holding his Empress's hand, guided the procession of cardinal priests onto the wide stone porch to the oohs and aahs from the crowd. Even the noble women could not restrain their exclaims at the sight of Empress Engelberga's rich crimson robe trimmed in white ermine. At Louis' other side stood Anastasius, evidence of Louis' favor. He was every bit as tall as the Emperor, though not as broad.

Archdeacon Nicholas led the congregation in prayer asking God's guidance and blessing on the elections. The stirring crowd fell into a solemn but uneasy quiet. The dais was turned over to Louis, who proclaimed in his deep voice that any Christian, even laymen, could be lawfully elected without regard to class. "I caution every man here," he glowered at the still-seated Theophylact, "before the pope-elect is confirmed, he will swear an oath of allegiance to me as the constitution demands." The sullen noble families grumbled. "People of Rome," Louis said, "name your Holy Father."

Before another candidate could be put forward, however, Louis nominated Cardinal Anastasius. Laymen and common priests cheered, but the assembled cardinals behind the Emperor murmured protests that he had been anathemized. "I said any man," Louis scolded them even louder. The crowd clapped to show their approval.

Count Theophylact rose and the multitude hushed to deathly silence as he climbed a few stone steps toward the Emperor, then turned to face the throng. He raised his arms wide like a Roman orator of old. "In the name of our ancient families, I nominate Cardinal Adrian." The assembly nodded in agreement, whispering that old Adrian was indeed an honorable and pious priest and would make a good Holy Father, even if he was a noble.

Adrian stepped away from his cardinal brethren and walked to the Emperor's side. He bowed to Louis and then the assembled Romans. "I thank the count for the honor. Nevertheless, as I have done in the past, I decline. His Holiness should be one greater than I. I possess neither the wisdom nor the strength to lead the church." He turned and padded back to his place.

Theophylact seemed to have divined that Adrian wouldn't accept. "In that case," the count said, "I'm left with no other choice but to nominate a learned priest of experience and wisdom from the most noble family of Tusculani, brother of a pious pope who governed well during the Pope's illness. I name the Bishop of Albano, Benedict, as our man."

The assembly protested with hisses and shouts of "fie" and "villain", but they were quieted by the Emperor's raised hands. "Citizens, citizens, please. I said any man can be nominated. Let your vote be your protest. So, good people of Rome, I've appointed my candidate and the noble families of Rome have named theirs. It's for you to select the people's choice. If you please, you may choose as many as you desire."

Commoners in the swarm behind the nobles disputed together as names were put forward, only to be cast aside. John Hymonides was proclaimed and his name repeated by many in the crowd. Heated discussions grew into arguments as a cleric was championed by some and rebuffed by others. Then a name began to be shouted at one end and another, from the back and also the middle. Cries of agreement resounded as the people roared with a single voice, "Johannes, Johannes, Johannes!" Farmers chanted Johannes' name as a battle cry, as did artisans and students and merchants. Even the Jews who had no vote raised their voices. Minor nobles who sent their children to the *schola anglorum* took up the cheering, along with guards of the foreign *scholae*. Even some from the noblest families shouted Johannes' name.

Theophylact leapt from his chair, furious, and urged the Tusculani and Crescentii to proclaim for Benedict as he waved his arms upward, signaling they should raise their voices. Nevertheless, the sheer volume of assent for Johannes drowned out the nobles and no sound was heard from beneath their bright blowing pennants. Seeing the overwhelming support for this unknown Johannes, the Emperor did not bother to encourage his loyalists or even his troops to claim for Anastasius. The election was over.

The multitude's shouts softened as voices grew hoarse. Louis finally raised his hands to silence the gathering. "Romans, you have spoken, and I acknowledge your choice. Send forth this man so I may question him to satisfy myself that he meets the requirements according to the constitution."

People looked at one another and behind until a shout from the farthest edge of the horde said, "Make way. He's here." The sea of Romans separated from back to front, leaving an aisle in their middle that led to the steps of Saint John's, just as the sea had once parted for the fleeing Israelites. At the far end stood the small priest with a protruding belly, accentuated by the red cincture of a cardinal.

Johanna's first impulse was to run, but she was transfixed. "Father," came a voice from the crowd. "Holy Father, they're waiting."

As though in a dream, Johanna fixed her eyes on Anastasius, who stood tall on the Basilica's porch. She took a single pace forward, then another and another. "Holy Father," people whispered reverently as she passed and they touched her wide sleeve. Arriving at the base of the steps, a scowling Theophylact stood in her way for a moment. Then he turned aside, allowing the Cardinal to climb.

"Can one so young be wise enough to be Pope?" Louis marveled.

Archdeacon Nicholas answered the Emperor as Anastasius looked on, flushed and visibly distressed. "Father Johannes is the cardinal priest of the Apostolic farms and has been with us many years, Highness."

"So this is the priest who worked miracles with the farms, like

Jesus feeding the multitudes; the one I met on the plain with Anastasius who saved Deacon John from an untimely death."

Johanna bowed her head, blushing and mute.

Nicholas added, "And it was he who rescued our few scriptures from the Saracens. He teaches the poor along with the rich, instructing even girls in his classes."

Empress Engleberga squeezed Louis' arm.

"From which noble family do you hail?" Louis asked.

"I'm not noble, sire," Johanna said humbly.

"Surely you must descend from an ancient Roman family."

"No, sire. I'm an Englishman."

The Emperor looked surprised. "Can it be possible Rome would elect a foreigner as pope? Are we entering a new age or are you so remarkable, Johannes Anglicus?"

"I feel rather ordinary, Highness, quite unworthy."

"Well spoken, but can you swear allegiance to me and obey the constitution of the Empire without reservation?"

Johanna pondered the question, which was more of an unspoken demand. "Our Lord taught us to give to Caesar what is his. I can do no less. Still, I must tell you that I could not put you above our Lord and our God."

"Nor would it be required of you." Louis searched Johanna's face, looking for any hint of deceit. Then he proclaimed, "I find Johannes Anglicus to be more than worthy. The Empire finds him exemplary. Turning to Johanna, he said respectfully, "I will await you at the Papal Palace in the Lateran with the mitre and crook. There I shall confirm you as pope of the universal church."

42
Anastasius

"Why did I let things go so far?" Johanna whimpered as Anastasius held her tight in her apartment in the *schola cantorum*.

"I'm as much to blame. I should've taken you away and we could've been together in Chiusi or anywhere in the world," Anastasius said.

"I was blinded by pride. I believed I was better than everyone else and could change the church."

"You're guilty of no such thing. Only you could have accomplished what you did, but the price is too high."

"What am I to do? Do you think I might actually be the Holy Father?"

"No one would be greater, but what about us and our child? Come, sit and rest." Anastasius helped Johanna ease onto a chair. "Is it so important to be Pope?"

"I never desired to rule anything, least of all the church. Oh, I'm so anxious, my guts are twisted in knots and the spasms make me ill. I think I'm going to be sick." Johanna leaned back in the chair and held her convulsing belly.

An insistent rap came from the door. "Yes?" Johanna called, sniffling and wiping her eyes with the back of her hands. "Who is it?"

"It's Ahmad, Cardinal Johannes. May I come in?"

Anastasius slid the bolt and pulled the door open.

"The cardinal priests wait for you outside," Ahmad said to Johanna.

"Already?"

"They say the time has come to accompany you to the *patriar-chum* for your coronation." Ahmad turned to Anastasius. "I'm also to tell you that you may not join them and neither may you enter the basilica, for you're anathemized."

Anastasius took Johanna by the arms as she rose from the chair. "Don't do this, I beg you. Let's flee now."

"Cardinal Anastasius is right, Lady," Ahmad said. "If you go down this road, you won't be able to turn back. I'll make an excuse so you can have a head start. But you must leave."

"Not just yet." Johanna set her jaw. "First, I'll wear the Mitre."

"I'm begging you," Anastasius said.

"Don't you understand? As Pope, I can remove your anathema. And I'll have the horrid fresco in Saint Peter's wiped clean. Then we can decide how we shall leave Rome."

"I don't care about the anathema or the excommunication. Let Uncle Arsenius or Louis handle that."

"I'll not leave while you're condemned to the fires of Hell. I won't ever be separated from you again. Not in this life or the next."

Johanna left Anastasius and Prince Ahmad standing in the doorway of the *schola cantorum* as she took her place at the head of the procession of the archbishops, bishops and cardinal priests. Nicholas and Adrian held the reins of a donkey. Johanna needed their help climbing on. They led her down the Vatican Hill, across the Tiber, and into the streets of Rome, followed by a solemn parade of red-cinctured cardinals, hands tucked into their wide sleeves. Bishop Benedict trailed at the end, haughty and sullen on a high-spirited white stallion.

Anastasius confronted Ahmad. "How did you know Johannes was a woman?"

"How is it that all of Rome does not?" Ahmad grabbed his leather satchel from the foyer and headed to the door.

"Where are you off to?" Anastasius asked.

"To find Baraldus. Maybe he can talk some sense into her."

"What shall I do?"

"Pack your belongings. I'll send word to you."

The citizens of Rome laid palm fronds on the road in front of the new Holy Father and tossed handfuls of rose petals as Johanna passed on her plodding donkey. The procession climbed the Capitoline Hill toward the ox pasture that was once the Forum. Crowds of Romans lined streets and leaned out windows to catch a glimpse of the Pope. Shouts of, "Bless you, Holiness," resounded off brick walls and mixed with the monotone chanting of the cardinals.

Johanna looked neither right nor left as the donkey clip-clopped into the multitude that swarmed at the Coliseum. She thought only of righting a terrible wrong, and how she might then escape her preposterous dilemma. *Perhaps I can feign death*, she told herself. *If I simply disappeared, would they proclaim it a miracle, claiming I had ascended to heaven? Or would they think I'd been kidnapped? Maybe they'd blame Theophylact and his spell over Rome would be broken.*

She was oblivious to the horde of commoners that pressed on either side to touch the hem of her robe with whispers of, "Bless me, Holiness." Nicholas and Adrian led the donkey into a narrow lane that led to Saint Clement's Church. "Ow!" Johanna gasped as a biting pain wracked her belly.

"What's wrong, Holy Father?" Archdeacon Nicholas reined the ass to a halt.

Johanna held her middle. "It's nothing," she grimaced. "Continue on to the *patriarchum* and quickly."

"Holy Father, we should find a doctor," Nicholas said.

"Go on, I say. My discomfort is passing."

They urged the donkey forward, but had only walked fifty paces when Johanna was gripped again by spasms. She rocked back and forth on her humble mount, groaning in agony. "Help me off." Nicholas and Adrian supported her weight as she slid down the donkey's side.

"Sit against the wall in the shade," Nicholas said and they lowered Johanna to the cool stone, out of the sun. Cardinals crowded around their suffering pope. Fear clouded their faces. Tears glistened on some.

"Fetch a physician," Adrian called out.

"There's no need I say." Johanna tried to sound calm between the convulsions. "The pain is passing." Then she gasped as fluid seeped from her body and trickled onto the cobblestones. Panicked cardinals looked on, horrified.

"The Pope is dying," a shout came from one of them. People hanging out of the apartments overhead screamed and begged, "God, don't take our pope from us." The crowd of clerics prayed and shouts of "send for a doctor" echoed up and down the lane.

Johanna told herself that she would rise and run, but was powerless. An overwhelming force glued her to the ground in the narrow street. Thoughts of being Pope and how she might escape had gone. A voice in her head whispered, *Soon, all Rome will know the truth and I'll be disgraced, humiliated. I don't care*, she agonized, *but please God don't make me deliver my child alone.*

"Eeee!" She screamed and spread her legs wide as she felt the unborn babe force its way from her womb. She sobbed, "Do what you will with me. I don't care, but save my baby." A tiny head appeared between her thighs.

Gasps came from the cardinals and the group who had pressed in to gawk. "It's a miracle," shouted one of the women, staring down from an open window. "God gives us another Holy Child."

The crowd of cardinals was pushed aside by a white steed as Benedict forced his way between them. "It's no gift from God," he said. "Johannes is a demon, a succubus. Observe how he has changed into the guise of a woman." He hopped off the stallion and jerked up her robe to reveal the half-born babe. "This is his wicked spawn with some unwitting priest, or Satan himself."

The cardinals recoiled in unison. They held up their crosses to ward off the evil. "It's true," one of them said. "Johannes has been possessed. Here's the evidence of his sin."

Johanna grunted, breathless and flushed as the babe was born on the hard cobbles. The crowd looked on bewildered as she lifted the newborn from the stone and pressed it to her breast. "I'm no demon," she whispered. "I'm a woman. I've always been a woman."

"He lies," Benedict said. "By who are you with child?"

Johanna shook her head.

"Even now he keeps the secret of his evil master. He must be destroyed and his offspring too, lest their evil infect us all." Benedict grabbed a stone and held it over his head.

"Don't do this," old Adrian said, but Benedict pushed him aside, knocking him to the pavement. His eyes blazed in a lethal mix of fear and hatred as he launched the stone. Johanna rolled on top of her child as the missile thumped between her shoulder blades. An onlooker scooped up a piece of brick and cast it too. The pitch was true and split the back of her head. Blood seeped down the nape of her neck. Bystanders scoured the ground for rocks and stones and hurled them upon the helpless woman. Her body shook from every blow.

"Araghhh!" A booming howl came from outside the mob as commoners and cardinals were thrown aside, bowled over by Baraldus, who plowed his way to Johanna's side. Benedict turned just in time to be knocked flat on his back as the old soldier lunged and sprawled over Johanna and her baby. His body took the full force of the stoning.

Ahmad followed, waving Baraldus' short sword. He thrust the blade at the throng and menaced anyone who reached for a stone. Benedict tried to rise, but Ahmad spun and crashed the hilt of the sword into the bishop's jaw, driving him back to the ground. Grabbing the reins of Benedict's white stallion, he led the horse between the howling pack and a splayed Baraldus. "Get her on!" he cried. The old soldier, bleeding from gashes on his cheek and temple, heaved himself to his knees. He lifted Johanna, who clutched her babe, staggered to the mount, and set her gently on the saddle. "Now you," Ahmad said, facing the angry crowd that edged closer.

Ahmad felt himself hoisted off his feet. He waved his arms

helplessly as he was plopped on the back of the horse behind Johanna. Baraldus slapped the stallion on the rump and it lunged forward, sending priests and citizens scurrying out of its path. Those who were too slow were tossed against the wall or knocked to the road. Free of the mob, the steed charged down the lane. Ahmad turned in the saddle as he passed Saint Clement's to watch a hail of stones and bricks, yet he could no longer spot his friend Baraldus. A lump rose in his throat, for he knew that no man could survive such a stoning.

Elchanan HaKodesh was led by a group of suspicious students to Johanna's apartments on the second floor of the *schola cantorum*. They surrounded him until Anastasius opened the door. "I'm here to fetch you," his voice quivered. "You're to come to my father's house without delay."

"What's happened? Is Johannes alright? Tell me, for the love of God!"

"Father says you must come now," he insisted and offered no more.

Elchanan and Anastasius ran through the narrow streets between the *schola cantorum* and the Trastevere until they came to the Rosh Yeshiva's low brick house next to the synagogue. A rabbi watched for them at the window and opened the door as they approached.

The slave Ahmad stood in the salon, cradling a newborn babe wrapped in white linen. Tears lined his cheeks. Anastasius stepped toward him. "Is this…can it be…?"

"You have a son." Ahmad's lips smiled, but sorrow filled his countenance.

Anastasius touched the infant's cheek with his outstretched finger. The newborn seemed to focus his eyes on his father while he reached for the long finger with a tiny, closed fist. The bedroom door opened and Avraham crept out. His beard glistened with droplets. "You're here at last. She needs you."

"Is she alright?"

"No, she's not," Avraham choked on his words, "but there's no time to explain. Go to her now for she has not long and hangs on to life only for you." Anastasius reached for the door, but Avraham grabbed his sleeve. "Don't show your grief, for it will make her passing harder. Let her see your love for her and the child. Then she can be at peace."

Anastasius sat in the chair at the side of the bed. He took Johanna's small hand in his. She didn't need to open her eyes to know the feel of his palm. "You've come at last," she said in a weak, breathy voice. "I knew you would."

"No power on earth could keep me from you, my heart."

"Have you seen our son? Is he not...beautiful?"

Tears streamed down Anastasius's face. "He's the most beautiful boy ever born, and his hair is red, like yours."

"He is my gift...to you." Johanna coughed, and her wracking brought up blood mixed with bubbling drool. Anastasius wiped the red spittle with a linen towel. He willed himself not to cry. "I would have grown my hair...long for you, but alas...I cannot. You'll never see my curls."

"I care not for your locks, dearest. It's you and our child I love above all else."

"But you would have loved my hair...all the same." Johanna sucked in a breath of air and looked away. A faint smile curled the corners of her lips. "It's time for me to leave you...my love."

"No." Sobs sneaked out of Anastasius' mouth and he tried to stop them, but some squeaked out.

"Fear not, darling. I don't travel alone."

The cardinal gazed into her eyes not, understanding.

"Mother and father," she took another long breath, "are by the window." She closed her eyes for several moments.

Anastasius looked but perceived nothing.

"Baraldus is just outside. He can't quite be here, but refuses... to stay away. They wait to take me."

Tears rolled down Anastasius' cheeks.

"I want to go, but I wouldn't leave until I gazed upon your face... once more. I knew you needed to tell me goodbye." Johanna took in several slow breaths, saving her last bit of strength for her words.

"And when your time comes… dearest, I'll be waiting to walk with you. Take care of our son…and love him for both of us…and raise him unto manhood. Now, kiss me."

Anastasius leaned over and touched his lips to Johanna's. She raised her hand to his moistened cheek, then it fell back to the bed.

"𝕎e didn't know how to find you, Cardinal," Old *vicedominus* Adrian said as he stood at the door with Archdeacon Nicholas. Anastasius had been holed up in Johanna's apartment for days. He had eaten nothing, and his eyes were clouded and red. "Are you ill?"

Anastasius seemed not to hear and looked through Adrian to a far-off place. "Yes, I'm ill."

"Shall we send for a doctor?"

"No."

"Can you walk? Are you well enough to make it to the *patriarchum*?"

"I think so. Why? Am I not still anathemized?"

"Why Anastasius, Emperor Louis awaits you. You're our Holy Father, our new Pope."

43
Season of Penance

Saint Peter's Basilica had stood for almost twelve hundred years, adorned with gold, silver, sculptures, mosaics, and countless works of art crafted by the world's greatest artists and artisans. By the sixteenth century, however, part of the foundation built over Nero's cursed circus had begun to crumble. Pope Julius II ordered the basilica razed.

Nothing from the original church was spared, not a mosaic, fresco, or work of art as laborers tore Saint Peter's to the ground, and the destruction didn't end there. They demolished Countless temples and Roman monuments to provide building materials for the new church. Every single stone and brick and piece of marble was ransacked from the ancient buildings that once were the marvels of the empire.

But after 160 years of construction, a modern Saint Peter's had replaced the worn-out one, more lavish and opulent than its ancestor. The basilica was a magnificent Frankenstein, constructed from the bones of pagan temples and monuments to the glories of Rome. Even the altar over the tomb of Saint Peter was cast from bronze pinched from the Pantheon, temple of the old Gods. Surrounding Peter's altar, where once stood stone columns pilfered from the Temple of

Solomon, metal pillars rose like vines or twisted tree trunks supporting Bernini's magnificent canopy.

All that remained of the original church was the Sacred Grotto,
the burial place beneath the basilica of saints and popes. And underneath the grotto, hidden for seventeen hundred years, lay the Roman
graveyard, cemetery to pagans and gladiators and Christian victims
of Nero's brutal spectacles, as well as the grave of Rome's first Pope,
the Apostle Peter.

"I hate sitting in the front row," Pascal complained.

"Why?" Isabelle replied, hoping her father was not about to deliver
one of his long-winded complaints.

"Because I don't remember when to kneel or stand or clap or any
of the other things you're supposed to do."

Isabelle was touched and tickled at the same time. She seldom
observed her father express genuine self-consciousness. "Copy me,"
she said. "I remember everything from childhood. It's ingrained,
like guilt."

The seated congregation chatted as they waited for the Ash
Wednesday Mass to begin, their voices echoing off stone and marble like
the sound of a rushing stream. The conversations quieted as altar boys
holding large candles entered the basilica. They walked on either side
of a white-robed priest who held up a super-sized book of the Gospels.

The choir began a hymn, and the crowd hushed. Every eye turned
toward the front doors. People crowded against the waist-high aluminum railing that blocked off the center aisle. Archbishops in white
robes and miters followed the altar boys. Hands in the audience
rose, holding cameras and digital recorders, trying to capture even
a fleeting image of the Pope.

His Holiness entered Saint Peter's wearing the papal miter, gold
on white. He held a staff in his left hand and with his right made
the sign of the cross, blessing the assembly. Veering to the rail, he
shared a moment with a few of the faithful to the delight of the
congregation. Adolescent girls squealed in excitement. The multitude
stretched out hands, palms open, as though they could touch some
of the Vicar of Christ's saintliness across the ether.

Cardinals of the Curia followed the Pope. Pascal and Isabelle spotted Keller, the Grand Inquisitor. Pascal whispered to his daughter, "It doesn't feel right to be here. We're not Catholic, so why would he invite us?"

"Shhh. I'm trying to see." In fact, Isabelle strained to find Father Romano, but there was no sign of him.

"He won't be with the Pope." Pascal said.

"What do you mean?"

"Romano's not a cardinal or a bishop and he's certainly not an altar boy."

Yet Isabelle searched the procession all the same. Something told her he'd be there.

"What're you doing?" A *sanpetrini* maintenance worker who multi-tasked as an usher questioned Rashid as he exited the door to the cupola, the dome that rises over Saint Peter's.

"I was showing my co-worker the dome."

"Can't you read the sign? It's closed," the *sanpetrini* said.

"I'm sorry. I wanted to show my colleague before mass starts. He begged me."

The *sanpetrini* scowled. "Did the old man get to the top? It's 320 steps."

"Magnificent," the imam replied. "I'm spry for my age."

"Well, don't do it again or I'll have to complain to your company."

"I won't," Rashid said.

"Get to the basilica or all of the seats will be taken." The *sanpetrini* examined the two as they walked down the path to Saint Peter's. He turned toward the entrance to the cupola just as his radio squawked. "I'm on my way," he said into the microphone.

Rashid squirmed in his seat next to the imam, who sat calm and serene as the Pope and archbishops and cardinals entered Saint Peter's. While everyone in their row crowded to the center rail to get a better view, they sat on the outside near the rear and didn't move. Rashid looked back at the entering procession. "We don't have to be here, imam. I can pull the trigger from anywhere in Rome—or the other side of the world, for that matter."

"Yes, but who would witness the completion of what our ancestor did not achieve? He's in paradise, and I want him to watch us finish his work and be at peace."

Rashid's palms were clammy, and he fidgeted in his chair.

"What is it, my son?" the imam said, patting Rashid's knee like a consoling father. "There's no shame in fear."

"I don't want to be a martyr. Let's leave while we can."

"You believe I intended to sacrifice you? No, that is not to be your fate."

"Then let's get out now."

"Dear Rashid, today's sacrifice is not to be yours. You're to carry on after me. You will be the imam."

"What are you saying?"

"Time for you to leave. I only brought you to this point to be a witness and tell our people what we've done. Take the Psalters and hide them. Allah will guide you."

"No, let's go together. You're the one who must continue."

"Now, now. Give me your cell phone."

Rashid pulled the phone from his pocket.

"How does this thing work?"

Rashid shook his head miserably and tears welled up in the corners of his eyes.

"Who can say what shall be my fate?" The imam said. "That's in the hands of Allah, His will be done. *Allahu Akbar.*"

"*Allahu Akbar,*" Rashid repeated through a moist, choking voice.

"Now, show me."

"The telephone number is programmed here." Rashid scrolled down the list. "Press the green *call* button twice. When the phone rings, the TATP will ignite."

"Is there enough?"

"More than enough."

"Now kiss me and leave. Everything has been provided for you. Don't worry, your path shall be revealed. Get to the truck and wait.

The diversion will let you escape and we'll meet at the warehouse or in paradise."

Rashid held the imam in his arms, then the imam pushed him away. "Go," he said. Rashid walked swiftly to the front of the basilica. He looked behind only once to behold the imam's face one last time.

The guard stopped him at the door as he tried to exit. "I can't guarantee you'll get back in," he said.

"I need to use the toilet."

The guard shrugged. "To your left and down the steps toward the crypt."

Rashid disappeared into the throng. But instead of heading to the bathroom, he turned in the opposite direction, shoving his way through the crowd that stood in the square to listen to the Pope on the loudspeaker.

Reaching the colonnade on the south side, he waited as two Vatican police cruised by in their electric Lamborghini cart, then passed between the columns to the Perugino guard station. He offered his ID. "My truck is in back. I just wanted to get a look at the Pope before I left."

The guard tried to make eye contact, but Rashid looked away. Instead of holding the plastic card under the scanner that tracked visitors, he picked up the telephone and spoke in a low voice. "*Si, Maggiore*, I understand," he said. The guard eased his hand to the holster on his hip to unclasp the snap. He turned to face the open door. Rashid al-Ansar had disappeared into the crowd.

His Holiness sat in his chair in front of the Altar of the Apostle. Wisps of white hair showed beneath the Papal miter. His aged hands trembled as he spread out sheets of paper on his lap and began to read his homily. "As we begin Lent, a time of prayer and repentance," he spoke into a microphone, "let us remember not only the symbol of ashes, for *you are dust, and to dust you shall return*, but also that Lent is a season of penance."

The imam rose from his chair on the outside aisle and walked forward as the Pope's voice filled the basilica over the sound system. One of the *sanpetrini* blocked his approach. "You again? *Signore*, take your seat." The imam tried to step around, but the usher barred his path once more. "Please. I must insist."

"I also insist." The imam put his hand into his woolen overcoat and grasped the handle of a polymer-framed Glock pistol. He pulled the gun out and jammed the barrel into the usher's ribs. "Walk in front of me and no sudden moves." Blood drained from the usher's face as he turned. The pistol prodded his back.

Plain-clothes *Gendarmeria* in black suits spied the two men walking up the side aisle toward the altar and moved to intercept them. Heads from all over the basilica twisted and necks craned to survey the commotion. His Holiness glanced up once, but continued to read.

One of the police ordered the imam, "Drop your weapon."

"I think not. Ask the congregation to leave. Let no innocent person be injured by what happens here."

"Are you crazy?" The policeman raised his voice.

The imam pulled out the cell phone from his pocket and flipped open the cover. "I would rather say that I'm committed."

The *sanpetrini* spoke to the officer in a shaking voice. "Do what you have to do. I'm not afraid."

"No one's going to get hurt," the officer said.

The imam waved the gun at the officer. "Let's hope you'll be reasonable."

The policeman edged forward, challenging the imam. "Just drop the gun and let's be done with this nonsense."

"I have a bomb!" the imam hollered, and the threat echoed off the stone walls." Women screamed and thousands of congregants jumped up, knocking over chairs. A panicked herd stepped over one another, elbowing and shoving. People ran and pushed their way to the double doors at the front of the basilica. The stronger charged for the exit while the elderly and young faltered against the irresistible human flood. They fell one by one, trampled beneath the rampaging herd. A middle-age man bent to pick up a child and grasped him in his arms as he was driven by the torrent toward the narrow escape at the doors.

The Defender of the Faith signaled the cardinals, and they surrounded the Pontiff. Keller opened a small gate at the altar of Saint Peter and motioned the Pope down steps that descended into the crypt. Cardinals who had sworn to protect the Vicar of Christ with their lives followed. Then Cardinal Keller shut the gate and turned to guard the small barrier with nothing to defend the path but his body and his faith.

𝕿𝖍𝖊 𝕾𝖜𝖎𝖘𝖘 𝕲𝖚𝖆𝖗𝖉 captain led Del Carlo, Father Romano, and Lieutenant Moretti through the Vatican Museum to the priests' entrance of the basilica. Entering by the glass door, they spotted the group of officers surrounding the imam. The old imam held them at bay with the pistol and a silver cell phone.

"Don't go near him," Del Carlo shouted. "He has a bomb, and we don't know where it is."

Black-suited police edged back as Del Carlo approached the cleric. "Let the man go. You don't need him anymore."

"You're right, *Colonelo*, provided you know what I'm holding."

"I do. Where's the bomb?"

The imam laughed. "After our little conversations and the warehouse fireworks, do you believe I'll tell you just like that?"

"I think you should stop while you can."

"And you'll let me go? Police are dead, and you'll release me if I stop?"

"We can work something out."

"You're offering a deal?" Turning to Father Romano, he glowered. "This is your fault. The sacred books were hidden for a reason, and they're meant to stay that way. It's not for you to unearth them. It's for Allah alone."

"Do you know where the scrolls are, the original scriptures?" Romano was compelled to ask.

"Of course, but you'll never get them. They're the true words of a Prophet, preserved so one day His message might be revealed. But in His time, the Mahdi's time, not yours."

"And yet you would destroy them?"

"No, I'm here to make sure you don't find any more."

"But if they're the Word of God, they should be available to everyone."

"For what purpose? So you can forge them into what you think they should be? That's not the will of God. His words must remain uncorrupted."

"How do you know these things?"

"This is the commission given us a thousand years ago, to protect the words of a Prophet. It's a task we shall perform until the days of justice, when God reveals his will."

"Who charged you with this?"

"Our ancestor, a true Emir. We have sworn a holy vow to him, and we shall keep our word."

"How do you know it's God's will?"

"Enough, priest! Save yourself if you wish, but no one will stop me from what I'm sworn to do."

Del Carlo's radio squawked, and he could hear rotors from the Carbinieri helicopter over the speaker. "We've spotted something, *Colonelo*," the voice said through the radio.

"What is it?"

"It's difficult to see, but it looks like cans are strung around the dome," the officer in the helicopter reported,

"The dome," Del Carlo said to the imam. "You are going to blow up the basilica?"

The imam raised the automatic pistol and pointed the barrel at Del Carlo's face. "You owe me a debt." The police tensed and aimed down the sights of their weapons.

"No." Del Carlo held up his hand. "Don't shoot."

The officers hesitated then lowered their guns. The imam walked by Del Carlo, still pointing the pistol. "But the payment will not be required just yet," he said in the colonel's ear. He passed between two guards, turned, and stepped backward until he was sure no one followed. Another about face, and he walked toward the altar.

The imam appeared unabashed, like a tourist gazing at columns and sculptures and art, oblivious to the threat around him. However, Romano's heart leaped into his throat. Pascal and Isabelle stood between the imam and the altar. Behind them, Keller had stationed himself with his arms folded across his chest.

Romano bounded over a row of chairs and vaulted the aluminum rail. He ran for the group while shouting at the imam, "Don't harm them. Let them pass." Then he yelled to the three, "Run!"

Isabelle grabbed Pascal's arm and dragged him away, but Cardinal Keller held his ground, rigid, facing the smiling imam who pointed the Glock. "You're a brave man."

"I'm a man of God," the cardinal said.

"As am I." The imam pressed the green call button on the cell phone.

Out on the dome's ledge, an artificial tone from a silver phone chimed. An electric current raced along wires attached to a fuse. Dozens of cola cans filled with unstable gel exploded, rocking the cupola and sending plaster and brick plunging to the marble pavement. Romano shoved Isabelle and Pascal to the statue of Saint Helena, down a stairway leading to the crypt. Wreckage crashed to the floor. The steel chain that held the double-shelled ceiling together buckled and rippled. The egg-shaped structure struggled to stay in place. Then, in the very center, the spire atop the dome plunged like an iron lance. Bricks and plaster followed, imploding as they descended toward the ground like a thundering wave.

For a microsecond, the imam smiled, looking up at the mass of projectiles rocketing down on the bronze altar and on them. Keller lunged with all his aging might, diving and sliding on the marble floor. Plaster and bricks rained on the imam and the cardinal, entombing them in a burial mound of rubble.

The plummeting dome thundered down upon the altar of the Apostle and spread on the pavement stones, sending up clouds of dust. Police, ushers, and hundreds of congregants were knocked down, choking and gasping. Those nearest the destruction lay dead, crushed by bricks and falling columns, debris, and the great chains that had held the cupola in place. Agonized cries filled the basilica as the injured and dying writhed in pain.

Romano lifted his head off the floor and shook it. Plaster powder that burned his eyes and choked his throat drifted to the ground. Iridescent light shone through the gaping hole in the roof and diffused through the billowing cloud of dust. It emitted a luminescent glow, as though the church had become radioactive. Statues had been toppled from their pedestals, and marble columns lay on their sides. Debris had been strewn everywhere.

The spire that crowned the dome had crashed on top of Bernini's canopy, and three of the pillars were gone, disappeared underneath a mountain of rubble. Yet one remained standing like a stout, misshapen trunk supporting what was left of the canopy. It seemed like a cross fashioned from a twisted tree on a hill of destruction. One word pounded in Romano's brain: *Golgotha*.

44
Petrus Romanus

The Pope pulled against the cardinal who held his arm. "Your Holiness," the cardinal pleaded. "We must take you to safety."

"Let me go," the Pope said. "There are those who need us. They need me."

"It's not safe."

"We have to tend our flock, to provide comfort and aid where we can." The Pope wrested away his arm. "Find a stairway that's not blocked," he said.

The Vicar of Christ stepped from behind the statue of Saint Helena, which had somehow escaped the devastation, and onto the floor of the basilica. Sorrow and grief gripped his heart in a vice. He surveyed the destruction as the dust settled enough to view the mayhem and pandemonium. Cries from the injured assailed his ears and he craved to cover them, yet resisted. Instead he choked a prayer, "Please God, grant us the faith to bear this."

Police and rescue workers cleared a path at the front door and the first stretchers were carried in as emergency technicians flowed into Saint Peter's, carrying medical bags. "Holiness," the cardinal called from behind, "help is here. Now will you come with us?"

"No." He spied a figure on the ground in front of him, a dazed man covered in dust and large flakes of plaster, struggling to rise. The Pope hurried to him and grabbed an arm with both hands, helping him to stand.

"Holiness," the man said trying to kneel, but the Pope held him up.

"Thank God you're safe, Father Romano."

"You…you know who I am?"

"Obviously," the Pope smiled. "Are you alright?"

"I'm not hurt, Holiness."

"Good, then let me lean on you and help me get to the pile of rubble over the Apostle's altar."

"It's unstable, Holiness."

"Do you believe it's foolish and would be a risk?"

"Yes."

"Sometimes, my son, great risks must be taken. Of course you know that, don't you? People are hurt, many have died, and more will today. I would soothe their fears if I cannot ease their pain. If they look upon the symbol of their faith, they'll take heart and be comforted. Isn't that worth the risk?"

"Yes Holiness."

"Then help me."

Romano steadied the Pope as they stepped around bodies of priests and parishioners. They scrambled up the hill of bricks and stone and plaster which had once been Michangelo's magnificent dome, but was now a dusty, barren mound save the remaining pillar that supported what was left of Bernini's canopy. They slipped and slid, holding on to each other for balance until they came to the base of the bronze column.

The Pope turned to face those in the congregation who had not escaped: the injured and dead as well as the emergency personnel who rushed to help. Spreading his arms, he said a prayer beseeching God to take pity on the faithful. At that moment, the clouds outside separated to let a brilliant ray of sunlight beam through the gaping maw atop Saint Peter's.

His Holiness seemed ablaze in glory as beams of light reflected off his pure white robe. The dying and the broken and those who labored to save them turned to gaze at his brilliance. Cries of pain and pleas for help softened for a moment as a vision of faith renewed their hope. Heartened, rescuers returned to their work and victims heaved a collective sigh as though come what may, God's mercy was with them.

From the shadows within the Chapel of the Blessed Sacrament, a lone figure stepped over the dead and dying, ignoring pleas as he moved with purpose toward the mound of rubble. Pulling a Beretta from his overcoat, Rashid al-Ansar extended his arm, aimed, and squeezed the trigger. The pistol recoiled in his steady hand.

The Pope staggered as a burning pain seared his side. Loose bricks gave way and he fell at the base of the cross. A crimson spot grew on the gleaming white robe. Romano dropped to his knees beside the Holy Father. The Pope gasped for breath, and Romano put his hand underneath the Pontiff's head to cushion it from the rubble.

Another shot rang out, and a spark flashed next to Romano's face. A sliver of brick struck his cheek and drew blood. Rashid scrambled up the mound. He tried to aim the Beretta as bricks shifted beneath his feet. Romano could only watch in horror as the assassin climbed ever closer. Rashid held the deadly Beretta, ready to strike. Hate blazed in his dark eyes as Romano rose to face him, maneuvering his body between the killer and the wounded Pope.

Del Carlo strained to kneel over an unconscious Lieutenant Moretti. He unsnapped the strap on Moretti's shoulder holster and slid out his service automatic. He broke into a limping trot toward the mountain of rubble. "Move, Father!" Del Carlo shouted, running forward, looking for an opening to shoot.

Rashid smiled and lifted the pistol. He touched the barrel to Romano's forehead and squeezed the trigger. A powder-caked hand rose from the rubble and grabbed Rashid's ankle, pulling him down. The shot went wild as Rashid fell, sliding down the mound. The man tumbled behind him. An avalanche of bricks and plaster followed in a wave as they rolled over and over. The dust-covered man, white from head to toe, landed on the bottom. He gripped Rashid's pistol hand. Rashid jerked free. He cocked the hammer and pointed the gun.

Rashid's head snapped to the side, the force of the kick knocking him off the grimy man. Romano yanked him to his feet by his collar and swung a tight hook to the chin. Rashid's knees quivered and the Beretta skidded across the floor. The Arab grabbed Romano and leaned on him, driving fists into his kidneys. Romano winced, then shoved hard, pushing Rashid away. Romano jabbed with his left. Rashid blocked the jab with his forearm and hooked his arm around the priest's. He drove knuckles into the priest's throat. Romano gasped for air. The Arab punched, striking the cheekbone, and Romano's head snapped back. He thrust his fist into the solar plexus. The priest's eyes rolled, and the lights dimmed. Romano keeled over, stunned and sucking for air, but none came.

Del Carlo watched Father Romano crumble. He leveled the pistol as he tried to steady his throbbing knee, and fired a shot. Rashid jumped, startled by the blast echoing off the basilica's walls. The bullet whistled by his ear. He dropped to his knees and jerked the priest between him and the colonel. He put his arm around Romano's neck, the crook over his Adam's apple as he had been taught, and squeezed to block the flow of blood to the carotid arteries.

Romano grabbed at the wrist with his hands as his strength ebbed away. He jerked hard…no luck…Rashid squeezed harder. The priest's grip loosened. Darkness crept into his peripheral vision and covered his eyes. Peacefulness descended on him, and he went limp.

Out of the blackness, the familiar form from his dreams appeared. The hideous hag slapped his face. She closed her fists and hit the boy. Mike Romano tried to move, to raise his tiny hands to stop her, but he was paralyzed. A far away voice said, "Let him go, or I'll shoot." The words seemed unimportant.

Something splintered and lucidness returned. Not the same consciousness, but another from the past, the angry one, from the place he tried never to go. The little boy could finally move his arms. He blocked the crone's blows and struck back at her. Tears streamed from his eyes and power flowed into his body. Romano swung both fists hard behind his head and boxed the Arab's ears. Rashid loosed his arm lock and Romano grabbed the wrist with both hands, pulling it loose. He jerked his elbow behind and caught the Arab in the ribs. Rashid spat.

Reflexes took over, not the technical boxing drilled into Romano, but older skills, ones learned on the streets. Clenching a handful of hair, he launched his fist into the Arab's gut. Rashid rolled on his side, then stumbled to his feet. Romano dove forward and grasped both legs. He lifted him off the ground and slammed him to the stone floor.

Rashid tried to punch while lying on his back, but he had no leverage. Romano gripped his ears, then smashed his forehead down on the Arab's nose, shattering the bone. Blood spattered. The priest threw a left to the jaw and a right, and another left, over and over. Rage flowed through his fists as he pummeled the unconscious face.

"Father," a faraway voice said, but Romano kept swinging. "Father," the voice grew closer and a hand held his wrist. "Father, enough," Del Carlo said.

The medic gingerly inserted a needle for the intravenous solution into a vein on the back of the Pope's hand while another medic tightened straps securing His Holiness to the gurney. They tried to wheel him away, but he held on to Father Romano's sleeve. "Thank you, my son," the Pope said.

"I didn't do enough. Had I been smarter, discovered more, perhaps this might have been prevented."

"What happened today was written long ago. Don't forget the words of Pius and Fatima. You couldn't stop these things, and you didn't cause them, so get that out of your mind. Nevertheless, they didn't view the future quite clearly, did they?"

"Holiness?"

The Pope smiled. "I'm not dead and you're not the Pope."

"I have no wish to be the Pope, now or ever," Romano said.

"And I don't want to die just yet, although the door awaits us all. Still, no one wishes to be the Pontiff, my son. We're chosen, and it's for us to accept God's will. Who knows, perhaps today is not the day foretold, and my fate awaits me still. As for you, who can tell what your life holds, but I can say one thing for certain."

"Tell me, Holy Father."

"You're not Michael Romano. You're *Petrus Romanus*. Whether you sit on Peter's throne one day or not, you'll never find peace until you accept your true self. No one knows that better than I. Who you once were isn't who you are. As for me, I'm a victim of my own vices."

"Holiness?"

"If I didn't love tiramisu so much, the bullet would never have struck the spare tire I carry around my middle."

Romano grinned.

Again, the medics tried to pull the gurney, but the Pope held fast to Romano's sleeve. "One last thing," he said, turning serious. "Keller is no adversary. He's a friend to you just as he was to Father Mackey. Why do you think he took your books? He tried to protect you."

Romano looked confused.

"He's never recovered from my Secretary's murder. You see, Father Mackey was going to meet Cardinal Keller that dreadful night. I foolishly gave them permission to take the Psalter to be translated." He squeezed Romano's hand, "And so he did everything in his power to keep you from harm, Peter Romano." Then the Pope motioned to the medics, and they wheeled his gurney away, surrounded by cardinals.

𝕱𝖆𝖙𝖍𝖊𝖗 𝕽𝖔𝖒𝖆𝖓𝖔 𝖇𝖗𝖚𝖘𝖍𝖊𝖉 plaster dust from the powder-covered man's face. "Cardinal Keller?"

Keller coughed. "I thought you were a goner. Isn't that how you Americans say it?"

"Yes."

Cardinal Keller shook himself, flapping his arms. The dust

billowed. He rubbed his face, creating streaks of white powder that made him look like a clown trying to remove greasepaint. "I wasn't sure I could get to you in time," he said.

"How did you survive? And how were you able to climb through the debris to reach me? It doesn't seem possible."

"I saw you. Whether with my own eyes or something else, I can't say. But it seemed as though I beheld you and His Holiness through a shaft of light from where I was covered. God must have guided me and given me the strength."

"I owe you my life and an apology."

"You owe nothing, Father. I'm doing my job."

"I believed you were imposing the church's law on me and I thought it was unfair. I beg your forgiveness."

Keller sighed. "The Grand Inquisitor? I know how many feel about me. I'm the Defender of the Faith, not the decider of the doctrine. That I leave to His Holiness and those who have greater minds than mine. People like you, Father. Perhaps one day I'll be your Defender, with my own life if necessary."

"What do you mean?"

"There's no need for a new Pope...at least not today. All the same, I'm watching you, *Petrus Romanus*. Now it's my sad task to make Father Sabella reflect on the error of his ways and provide an appropriate penance."

"Oh my gosh! I'm sorry Eminence," Romano said, trotting away. "I left the Hébers in the crypt."

Romano ran to the statue of Saint Helena, down the stairs to the grotto. Looking in every direction, he spotted no one, but the subterranean altar of the Apostle was a wreck. Three of the bronze pillars from above had been driven through the cavern's ceiling as if by a pile driver. They had plunged through the chamber and the floor of the crypt as well, and only their tips showed above the ground.

The paleographer ran to a gaping hole in the floor. A tiny light shone from below. "Isabelle, Pascal!" Are you there?"

"We're down here," Isabelle called out from below.

"Are you alright?"

"Yes," they both answered. "Come down, Michael," Isabelle said. "There are stairs carved in the stone. Watch the first one, it's the biggest drop."

Romano felt his way down rough-hewn steps, feeling the wall as he descended until dirt was beneath his feet. Looking to his right, he could just make out a shelf carved out of the rock. His eyes adjusted to the darkness that was slightly illuminated by ambient light from above. Bones lay in a niche, covered by a moldering linen cloth. Over the shelf, written on the rock face appeared graffiti scrawled with chalk or white paint. Romano strained his eyes. Finally, he made out the single Latin word, *petreus*, Peter.

"We're over here," Isabelle said.

Romano crossed himself. He wanted to pray, to say something, but his mind was blank. *What does one say to an Apostle*, he thought. He groped his way in the darkness, shuffling deeper into the cavern. Isabelle and Pascal sat on stone blocks beside a tomb that had been broken by falling bricks from above. Scrolls poured out of the sarcophagus and lay strewn across the floor. Pascal used a cigarette lighter to shine a light on one that Isabelle held open. They looked up at him as he stood over them. "What have you found?"

Isabelle and Pascal beamed back at him. Then Isabelle grabbed Romano's hand. "A letter from Jesus' twin brother...and it's in Aramaic. The scrolls are all in Aramaic, except one...in Latin." Isabelle had tears in her eyes.

"What does it say?"

Pascal gazed up at the priest. "You should read it, Father. I think it is addressed to you."

45
Johannes' Testament

Brave and stout Baraldus, the old soldier and priest of fame and faith, lost his life in the narrow lane between the Colosseum and Saint Clement's Church, the same street where I was born and where they claim Mother is buried, although I will not say whether this is true or false. The citizens of Rome ever after called it the *vicus papissa*, street of the woman Pope. Furthermore, since mother gave birth to me there, humiliated before all Rome, every Pope has turned away from the road, although it's the direct route from the Papal Palace to Saint Peter's.

My father, Anastasius, was indeed elected Pope after mother's vile murder, and his first act was to imprison the villain Benedict for his many crimes. But truth be told, he never desired to be Pontiff. The day after Louis left Rome, Theophylact and the noble families named their own Pope, the foul Benedict, even though he languished in his prison cell. The cardinals of the *patriarchum* abandoned their positions until, in the end, Father reigned as Pope over an empty palace.

Emperor Louis sent dispatches demanding that father fight back and enforce the Constitution and Canon Law, as well as the laws of the Diocese. Even Empress Engleberga encouraged him with letters promising her loyalty and affection. Having secretly read them, I often wondered if she had somehow divined the truth of Mother and Father. Women possess eyes in their hearts that see things men cannot.

Finally, Father renounced the papacy and left the governing of the church to Benedict and Theophylact. Louis raged, but soon his fury softened. Engleberga's handiwork was likely the cause. Do not women round out men's sharper corners? Nevertheless, Louis was loyal to a fault and negotiated that, in exchange for Father's abdication, his anathema was lifted and he was readmitted to communion. Thus did Father become known as the anti-Pope.

Yet the happiest day of Father's life came years later when he was named Librarian of the Universal Church, a position he held until his death. I was only twelve, but remember tears of joy running down his face as he told me he would rather be a librarian than the wealthiest Emperor in the world.

He chose to die in his apartment in the *schola cantorum*, the very room, he said many times, that had been mother's. I listened to him say weakly and out of breath as I held his dear hand, "Take the Psalter on the shelf. It belonged to your mother and she put it in my hands when I fled into exile. Never lose it and pass it on to your children. It's all that I have left of her. Now the book is yours." He turned away and smiled. "One more thing, darling, then I'm coming." Looking into my eyes, he whispered, "Your mother and I couldn't be prouder of you, but you must make one last vow."

I bent to hear his failing words.

"Promise that you will love and take a wife and she will bear you a child."

I only nodded, for I could not speak through the tears. Then, serene and smiling, he gave up his soul.

In my youth, I little understood the battle Mother and Father and John Hymonides waged and lost against the nobles for the papacy. Nevertheless, I sadly watched, and my sadness grew to disgust as the noble families used Peter's throne for their own foul purposes, descending from mere corruption into unabated debauchery. Their foul reign became known as *saeculum obscurum*, or the Dark Age.

However, the citizens of Rome sniggered in the taverns and derided the nobles' iron grip on the church as the Rule of Harlots.

As for my dear teacher and friend Ahmad, Father offered him his freedom when Mother died.

"You may not free me," Ahmad said, "for I'm no slave. Cardinal Johanna released me from bondage the day she bought me."

Avraham looked puzzled and scratched his balding pate. "Why did you stay for an existence of humiliation and servitude?"

"I stayed to pay for my great sin, destroying God's word. Allah took my brother's life in payment. It's only right that I give mine also."

"Whose slave will you be?" Avraham asked. "I wish none, and I won't own any."

"I will be a slave to my people. They need me, so I shall return to Ifriqiya to serve them." With those words, Ahmad disappeared into the night.

Father had no word from him for more than a year, until a letter arrived by ship at the port of Ostia. Ahmad did indeed return to serve his people, arriving only weeks before his own uncle's death. Thus did the prince who was made a slave become a prince once again, and then Emir, to rule the kingdom of Ifriqiya with dominion even over North Africa, Malta, Sicily, and the Italian cities of Brindisi and Naples.

He ruled as a kind and benevolent Emir, and historians say Ifriqiya reached its zenith under his wisdom and tolerance. But plague afflicted Ifriqiya, carried by pilgrims, and the people blamed Ahmad for their suffering. Indeed, Ahmad himself believed he'd been cursed. He was deposed by his cousin, who was backed by Berber and Turkish mercenaries. Thus did he return to Rome, arriving at the port of Ostia and making his way in the dead of night to take his place as our slave, although father would not accept his bondage. Instead, he put Ahmad in charge of his finances, and he seemed to make our fortune grow as if by sorcery. He became my playmate and teacher of Aramaic, the law, and the Koran.

Ahmad grew old in Father's service, but in the winter of his life, he delivered his sons one at a time as a sort of internship to assist

Father and me. They, too, were my friends and teachers and students. When they advanced in years, their sons were sent to serve me, and Prince Ahmad's great-grandsons attend me still, although I tell them they owe no obligation. Yet they insist on obeying the will of Allah and their illustrious great-grandfather, who is revered as the holiest of men from their tribe. They protect me and guard the secret books jealously.

So what about me? In my youth, I felt the zeal to transform the world as did Mother and Father. However, lack of wisdom made me ambitious, and I thought the path to change could only be achieved from a position of power. Thus was I prey to the subtle and seductive call. When I served as *primicerius* of the *scrinium*, the scribes believed me to be an uncompromising taskmaster. Once I cuffed the ear of a young novice and he protested, saying, "I simply made a small revision, just a word for clarification."

I lost my temper and told him, "A single change by one lowly scribe, and only to clarify. Multiply it by a hundred scribes or a thousand or ten thousand, day after day for a millennium, and the scriptures no longer resemble our Lord's words. Fie on the forgers, innocent or otherwise. How can we ever know what was truly said or done?" Yet I was the one rebuked by the cardinal and after too many such complaints by my charges, I was relieved of my post. Then I realized that a position of power in the palace that ruled Christendom was not my calling.

So I left Rome to be a simple parish priest in the city of Ostia until the day I was named Bishop. It surely must have been Father's doing for, in truth, I had achieved nothing noteworthy. Nevertheless, I did my best for the Diocese and the priests in my charge and endeavored to be kind and compassionate.

When I reached middle age, I began to write Mother's story and recalled the hundreds of tales told by Father and Rabbi Avraham and Prince Ahmad and Elchanan the tanner and many, many others who knew her. All have I assembled here.

Before father's death, he revealed the location of the crypt under the mausoleum of the Popes beneath Saint Peter's Basilica, where

Mother's precious heresies were concealed. I went there secretly to read and study and try to understand. Upon my death, I instructed Ahmad's grandsons to finish what needs finishing and seal the ancient scrolls and books and Mother's story in the empty tomb beneath the Basilica. I required their solemn vow on the name of their Prophet to guard the hidden place and the secret of her heresies to the end of their days. After the day these things have been done by those who call themselves the *Children of the Book*, I shall count Ahmad's sin, if it were ever such, expiated, wiped clean a thousand times over.

I wrote this history on the finest parchment in the Empire, manufactured by the grandsons of the venerable Elchanan HaKodesh in the Trastevere. If you've discovered it and read these words, then my days are over and you have exhumed Mother's treasures and her own story penned by my hand. I, Johannes Avraham Baraldus Ahmad, for that is the name Father gave me, authored this account so my beloved parents would not be forever forgotten, their memories scattered in the overlooked places of time. My fondest desire is that one day far from now, they will be known for who they were and what they tried to accomplish, yet failed. Moreover, I want you to know how they loved one another.

One last thing, for I am sure you must wonder. Avraham HaKodesh, Rosh Yeshiva of Rome, taught me the hidden writing, invisible lemon juice on parchment and held over a flame to make the words appear. He told me he showed Mother the trickery so she could write Father secretly when he languished in exile. Avraham revealed that the same might be done with ink erased with the foul, smelly concoction. Finally, he said that after she had written many letters in this manner, she had an epiphany: her precious heresies could be hidden in plain sight, underneath the Psalms. Her first experiment was her own Psalter, the one Father bequeathed to me. I carried on her work, cutting ancient scrolls into pages and covering them with the commonest of prayers. In this way, I saved hundreds of scriptures, but not all. The rest are here.

Who can ever be absolutely certain of a thing? Popes and

emperors say they are, and bishops and kings and cardinals, and even the lowliest priests and laymen are confident in their God and their Lord and, most importantly, their salvation. Yet I have lived four score and five years and am at the end of my tired days. If I learned anything in this curiously long life, it's that ardent believers hide within the safety of their absolutes, for much more courage is needed to abandon their cozy security for the questioning of one's own beliefs.

Now, I can't be absolutely certain; nevertheless, I'm quite confident that I am and forever shall be the only man to have had a father and a mother who were both priests and both cardinals and both librarians and both Popes of the Holy and Universal Church.

Johannes Avraham Baraldus Ahmad, Bishop of Ostia

Johanna and Anasthasius' son, Johannes, now a feeble old man, put down his reed pen and got up from his desk. He padded on tired, unsteady legs to fetch the kettle of hot water from the kitchen. He poured the boiling liquid into a plain silver bowl on the table.

Steam rose from the vessel as the Bishop of Ostia seated himself. He leaned forward and peered into the cooling water. The cloud thinned as he gazed at the smooth surface. He strained to look beneath, to the glimmering bottom. Black letters appeared in the bowl, swirling faster and faster like a dark cone, leading his eyes downward to the depth of its inky point. Bishop Johannes cleared his mind and projected his thoughts into the twirling image. *All that can be done has been done. We shall see if it's enough. To you, I entrust Mother's treasures either for yourself or one who will do with them as she would have.*

The Children of the Book

46
The Shrine

I wish you'd stay on," Father Romano said to Pascal in front of the security checkpoint at Rome's Fumicino airport. "You're the best one to translate the Aramaic."

"I hate to leave, but work is piling up at home. Besides, you need Isabelle more than me. The scrolls have to be photographed and digitized and put in her confounded computer. I don't want anything to do with that. Anyway, the Grand Inquisitor agreed to let you send me the photographs so I can translate in the comfort of my dusty den at home."

"I can't believe you got him to give his permission. Still, I'll miss you and I'm sure you meant to say the Defender of the Faith."

"Did I hear my name used in vain?" Cardinal Keller approached the trio, who stared at him, speechless. "You three seem to be joined at the hip. Some sort of conspiracy?"

Pascal eyed the cardinal. "How did you know we were here? Do you have spies in the airport?"

Keller glared at the retired linguist. "I told you before that I have the largest network of spies in the world, you heretic."

Pascal chided back, "Prussian tyrant."

Isabelle was stunned by the exchange. "Do you know each other?"

"Did I neglect to tell you, *chérie*? We're old friends. We were roommates at the university."

"You two were cooped up in a room together, arguing religion?"

Cardinal Keller smiled at his lifelong friend. "Until the wee hours of the morning. It was a spiritual experience."

"You mean to say our ranting at one another kept us out of the bars." Pascal chortled and Keller let out a loud guffaw, making them all laugh. A boarding announcement over the public address system cut short their mirth. "I need to go." Pascal exhaled a long sigh. Isabelle planted pecks on her father's cheeks, and Romano extended his hand. But Pascal pulled the priest close and kissed him as well. "Take care of my little girl."

"I promise." Romano meant it sincerely.

Then Pascal took the Grand Inquisitor by the arm and led him a few steps away so he could whisper in his ear. "I don't know how to thank you. I asked a big favor, and you came through in spades."

"Nonsense, old friend. You were simply part of a grander plan, one foreseen by some of the greatest mystics of the Holy Church. But from now on, you can call me the Super Grand Inquisitor."

The two men stared into each other's eyes for a moment, hugged, and patted one another on the back. Then Pascal disappeared through the door, into the transparent plastic tube conveyer leading to the boarding gates.

The taxi driver maneuvered his car around the streets of Rome as Romano pointed out which turns to take. Isabelle was lost in her private thoughts, then turned to the priest. "How do you think the Psalters got from the tomb under Saint Peter's to the Library and Secret Archives?"

"I've been wondering, too. Popes have been excavating the grotto since the Middle Ages. In the 1940s, a German priest removed relics he found in a tomb down there. Those relics weren't rediscovered until his death in the sixties. I'm convinced that much more was unearthed from the Popes' mausoleum than just ancient bones, and where else would books go than in a Library?"

"Do you think whoever brought them out realized the Psalters were Giovanni's handiwork?"

"Giovanni's Psalters seem to lead lives of their own and have been trying to get out for a very long time."

Isabelle nodded. "It's such a tragedy that the magnificent chapel dome had to be destroyed for them to be found."

"There's an interesting irony, though. Pagan temples and Christian churches which weren't the official version of Christianity were obliterated to build Saint Peter's, and a non-Christian returned the favor. But the basilica will rise again, maybe this time with non-denominational bricks."

They drove on in silence until Romano said, "Did you know, in the Middle Ages, a marble seat called the *sedia stercoraria* was used to crown the Popes?"

Isabelle didn't understand where the priest was going so she answered simply, "No."

"It's an unusual piece of furniture with a hole in the center like a toilet. The Pope sat on it before being confirmed and lifted his robes while cardinals peered from behind and declared, 'He has testicles and they dangle nicely'." Romano blushed.

"You can't be serious."

"The chair is tucked away in the Vatican Museum and accounts of the ceremony are stored in the Archives."

"Do you think the ritual became part of the Pope's confirmation because of Johanna?"

"That's the legend." Glancing out of the taxi's window a few blocks from the Colosseum, Romano told the driver to pull over.

"Why are we stopping?" Isabelle asked.

"I want to show you something."

They got out of the taxi and Romano took Isabelle's hand. He led her down a narrow street, past the ancient church of *San Clemente*, a short block to the unremarkable corner of *via dei Santissimi Quattro* and *via Querceti*. "What am I supposed to be looking at?" Isabelle asked, spotting only a trattoria on one side and the wall surrounding the church of the *Quattro Coronati* on the other.

"Do you see the little shrine with the metal grate?"

"Yes. The plaque says it's dedicated to the Virgin Mary," Isabelle said.

"It does now. This street was once called the *vicus papissa*, the street of the woman pope, until it was razed by Pope Pius V to make the new road. Nothing remains of the original narrow lane except perhaps this small shrine which is over a thousand years old."

"Are you saying this is where Pope Johanna was killed?"

"So goes the tale, and that she's buried at this exact spot. Of course, they're only fables."

"How can you say such a thing after all we've been through?"

"Your own countryman, Napoleon, had an opinion about fables: 'What is history, but a fable agreed upon?'"

They crossed the street and peered into the shrine, trying to make out the ancient, weather-stained fresco. The metal cross-hatch grate had been bent by tourists who wanted a better look at the painting. Michael gazed at the shadowy, faded figure of a woman who just might be Johanna Anglicus.

Isabelle leaned over and spoke softly in Romano's ear. "You don't have to fear us, Michael."

The priest contemplated the painted face of the mother and child and answered without turning his head, "That's what Father Mackey said. He also said something quite unbiblical: *There are more things in heaven and earth than are dreamt of in your philosophy.* I'm beginning to understand." He took Isabelle's hand in his own, lacing his fingers through hers. Isabelle rested her head on his shoulder, closed her eyes, and breathed a satisfied sigh.

The taxi stopped in front of the seventeenth-century apartment building in Paris' Marais district. Pascal retrieved his wallet and pulled out a couple of bills. He handed them to the driver. "Keep the change."

"No, monsieur. You're far too generous."

"I feel like tipping someone, and you're the only one here." Pascal smiled and shut the car door. He rolled his small suitcase through the cold drizzle into the building's entry.

The kettle whistled and he turned off the gas flame on the 1950s burner. But instead of pouring water into the teapot, he walked, kettle in hand, to his study. A little copper bowl rested on a tripod on his desk, and he filled the vessel to the rim. The metal changed colors as the liquid splashed on it. Vapor rose in a thin cloud, drifting and disappearing. The surface was smooth and opaque like a deep, dark, bottomless pool.